THE LAST, BEST LIE

MADISON MCKENNA MYSTERIES

The Last, Best Lie

Kennedy Quinn

FIVE STAR
A part of Gale, Cengage Learning

GALE
CENGAGE Learning®

Farmington Hills, Mich • San Francisco • New York • Waterville, Maine
Meriden, Conn • Mason, Ohio • Chicago

GALE
CENGAGE Learning·

Copyright © 2016 Kennedy Quinn
Five Star™ Publishing, a part of Cengage Learning, Inc.

LIBRARY OF CONGRESS CATALOGING-IN-PUBLICATION DATA

Quinn, Kennedy.
 The last, best lie / Kennedy Quinn.
  pages cm — (Madison McKenna mysteries)
  ISBN 978-1-4328-3162-2 (hardback) — ISBN 1-4328-3162-3 (hardcover) — ISBN 978-1-4328-3161-5 (ebook) — 1-4328-3161-5 (ebook)
  1. Women detectives—Fiction. 2. Murder—Investigation—Fiction. I. Title.
 PS3617.U5785L38 2015
 813'.6—dc23   2015022036

First Edition. First Printing: February 2016
Find us on Facebook– https://www.facebook.com/FiveStarCengage
Visit our website– http://www.gale.cengage.com/fivestar/
Contact Five Star™ Publishing at FiveStar@cengage.com

Printed in the United States of America
1 2 3 4 5 6 7 20 19 18 17 16

To Bob: my best friend, my partner, my hero, my husband.
Love ya, babe.

ACKNOWLEDGMENTS

Writing is an act of creativity. It is joyful and deeply satisfying. Most of the time. Trying to get published, on the other hand, is an act of insanity punctuated by bouts of confusion, doubt, fear, and frustration. Along the way one meets wonderful people willing to roll up their metaphorical sleeves and read your work (and reread it . . . and reread it . . . and reread it . . . and . . . well, you get the picture). They provide thoughtful and valuable critiques that turn shaky prose and awkward dialogue into something worthy of appreciation by more than your mother/husband/bff/paid editorial assistant. They offer encouragement and hope. You also meet snarky people who exercise their apparent need to establish dominance over others via a host of mean-spirited and destructive mechanisms. (To the agent who told my good friend that "paragraphs like this make me lose the will to live," yes, I mean you.)

To the snarks of the world, I say: "Meh. You go your way and I'll go mine."

To the wonderful ones, I say: "You are amazing! Thank you, thank you, thank you!"

Said wonderful ones include, but are not limited to Carin Bigrigg, Keven Spillane, Barbara Warne, and Kristin Scott. You are all utterly and completely awesome!

Chapter One

Perspiration pooled in my cleavage. The low-riding Chicago sun baked the upholstery around me, as sweat glued my jeans to my thighs. I sat on the passenger side of a brown Buick LeSabre that reeked like the dumpster it was on this scorching summer day. And if being sautéed in my own sweat weren't bad enough, my butt itched as if a fire-ants brigade had invaded my panties.

My boss, Jake Thibodaux, ex–New Orleans cop and owner of an intermittently solvent Chicago detective agency, sat beside me, stuffed behind an oversized, leather-wrapped steering wheel. An *American Handgunner* magazine lay propped on the immense globe of his stomach. He flipped to the centerfold: a gleaming forty-five-caliber semi-automatic with a staple through the crescent curve of its trigger. Holding it up, he turned it ninety degrees and whistled short and low. It would appear that one man's means of mayhem is another man's soft-core porn.

Putting the magazine down, Jake grabbed the remainder of his second Double Quarter Pounder with Cheese from the dash and finished it with a staccato bite-and-swallow rhythm—clearly he considered chewing optional—and then tossed the wrapper into the back seat. He let out a long, round burp that filled the car with the stench of pickles, mustard, and under-masticated beef. Cajun drawl and bass voice conveying unhurried imperiousness, he winked at me and said, "Nothing like a good, old-fashioned burger to take the edge off, eh pichouette?"

I screwed up my face in a scowl. "Have I mentioned lately

9

what a pleasure it is to be in your company?"

"Why, no," he said, with a disingenuous grin. "Can't say that you have."

"Feel free to consider the reasons."

He snorted. "Can't you just say 'fuck you' like the rest of us?"

I arched an eyebrow. "Numerous studies have shown that the gratuitous use of obscenities only serves to diminish their effectiveness."

"Wimp."

"Hey, Jake."

"Yeah?"

"Bite me."

"That's a start. There's my girl," he said with an approving nod. Stretching his bulk in the seat, he reached for his magazine before settling once more into reading mode.

I rolled my eyes and turned to look out my window. Six months of working for Jake should have prepared me better for this: steaming in a tin box on stakeout. In fact, we'd spent the last five hours squatting in the August sun across from a South Side alley squeezed between an aged brownstone and a red brick office building, all in hopes of ambushing a cheating husband and his paramour: Big Fun.

I started to lay my arm on the frame of the open window but jerked it back as my flesh hit the scorching metal. Grimacing, I blew on my forearm to cool it. It was all the more refreshing as there was no breeze, just still air, ripe with the smell of melting asphalt, fermenting trash, and someone's liver-and-onions supper. A scruffy mutt trotted by, navigating nose-down to a stop sign. Rotating his backside, he sent a stream of pee high on the post. He was probably hoping to fool the big dogs into believing an even bigger dog had been there. I empathized.

Loping across the street, Bowser launched himself up some

swaybacked steps, then plopped down, his long tongue dripping saliva in puddles as his sides heaved. Large brown eyes came to rest on mine. *Man,* they said, *it's hot out here.*

The prickling butt sensation intensified. I tried to wriggle my backside discreetly on the rough stitching of the seat.

Jake spoke without lifting his head from his reading. "Christ on a crutch, petite, scratch it if it itches."

Fine, then, to hell with discretion. Arching my back, balancing on my toes, I scratched heartily from knees to backside. Grandmother Ivy would not approve, but *God, oh God, it felt so good.* Lowering myself, my jaw wrenching in a huge yawn, I grabbed my warm Big Gulp Diet Pepsi from the console between us. Slurping it loudly through the straw netted me a low-throated growl of warning from Jake. I slid my eyes in his direction, not bothering to hide my grin, and slurped harder.

He flipped a page. "First, it goes out the window, and then you do."

Yeah, that didn't get nearly enough of a rise out of him. "I'm bored," I said.

"Get un-bored."

"Entertain me."

He swiveled his head slowly on his large, thick neck and simply stared at me. Now, let me make this clear. Jake *is* the big, bad wolf. He's six-foot-four, two-hundred-and-a-lot pounds, and, okay, a bit past prime. Most people, nonetheless, would suffer serious bladder control issues facing that stare. Or at least be smart enough to stop flicking the wolf on his ear.

I, on the other hand, shrugged. "Fine, I'll entertain myself." Putting the drink between my legs, I pulled the straw out and bent it, twisting it until it split into two pieces. I tossed the longer piece into the back seat and inserted the smaller one through the *x* in the plastic lid. Then I brought the nearly full drink up and blew hard across the top of the straw. A small geyser of soda erupted out of it, and I rushed to suck the excess off the top. Shaking off the small amount that had landed on my hand, I looked over at him, smiling proudly. "Neat, huh?"

"What the hell was that supposed to be?"

"Differential air pressure. Blowing across the top of the straw creates a situation where the air pressure at the top of the straw is less than that at the bottom. It's like a vacuum, drawing the liquid up and out of the top of the straw. It works best with a short straw."

"Uh-huh, and what are you going to do now that the straw is too short to reach the rest of the drink, Miss Wiseass?"

Ah. Hadn't thought of that. Time to change the subject. I frowned, shoved the drink into its cupholder, and gave him my best long-suffering sigh. "Oh, come on. How much longer do we have to do this? We've been at it every afternoon for three days. I'm dying of boredom here. And I stink almost as bad as you do, which, given your substantially greater surface area, should be impossible unless parts of me have died."

He grinned. "Oh, but you look so pretty."

It was my turn to snort. Okay, with a little work on my part, *pretty* applies. And being twenty-three and healthy buys me a pass, most days, on serious effort. But today, I knew exactly how bad I looked. My blue eyes were bloodshot, my face was bloated from a steady diet of greasy, salt-laden fast food, and my black hair clung in thin, sweaty tendrils to my neck. "You're an evil man."

"So they say."

"Furthermore, I'm convinced that this cheap titanium-dioxide sunscreen you bought is decomposing into its basic elements, which are individually toxic and which, in contact with the porous membranes of my eyes, may well render me blind. And then you'd be sorry."

"How about you swallow it and be rendered mute?"

I crossed my arms over my chest. "You know absolutely nothing about chemistry, do you?"

Jake laid the magazine on the dash. "What I don't know is why I put up with a whiny egghead who can't even follow simple instructions." He pointed to his beloved traveler's mug in the cupholder between us. It was brown and stamped with a large intricate crest around which was scripted, *Cabrini High School, New Orleans.* "Hot coffee. You were supposed to get me hot coffee. Not this iced frappachichi crap you filled my cup with. What's the matter? Your fussy little engineer's brain couldn't handle that?"

I leaned forward, unfolding my arms and counting on my fingers as I spoke. "First, I am not fussy. I'm meticulous, and you're a grump. Second, my brain is not little. I am a physicist, minoring in chemistry. I am not—repeat, *not*—an engineer. I've nearly been kicked out of my family tree for abandoning my studies, as it is, and without adding that slur to my name, thank you very much. Because I am this close," I held my thumb and forefinger a millimeter apart, "to having my Ph.D., I deserve a more dignified characterization than *egghead.* I would be willing to allow you to refer to me as Genius, Savante, or, in a pinch, Mistress Brainiac."

"Mistress Smart-Ass, maybe."

"Third, it's a hundred and ten freaking degrees, Jake. Cows give evaporated milk in heat like this. It's hot, h-o-t, hot! I got you iced coffee because only a lunatic, such as *yourself* apparently, would want hot coffee on a day like this."

"Listen, petite. I don't give a damn how hot it is outside; I don't give a damn how cold it is outside. I drink coffee, and I drink it hot. And I drink regular coffee: dark-roasted, no-frills, no-fuss, no-shit Columbian. Not that fruity, nutty, organic, pussy crap you drink."

"Typical grumpy, old, white guy: intolerant. Just because

something is different—"

His hazel eyes narrowed, as if my comment struck some dark resonance within him. He swung his massive bulk to face me. "That's the problem with you kids—"

"Oh, give me a break. I'm not a twelve-year-old."

He raised his voice as he pointed a finger at me. "The problem with you kids is that you're all about *tolerance this* and *tolerance that* when it comes to what you believe in, but tolerating your elders' opinions is a different story, isn't it? Your generation thinks it invented truth and justice. Everything you do is right and fair and so fucking smart, but God forbid any regular, hard-working Joe, who's spent his life serving his community and tries to live his life by the Good Book, stands his ground on *his* values, because then he's a closed-minded, prejudiced old fogey. Give you a break? You give *me* a break!"

I blinked. Sure, I knew Jake's standard modus—a.k.a. crotchety—was more affectation than nastiness, but this was different. Whatever spot I'd hit was a real sore one, now. Frowning, I said, "Take it easy, Jake. I was just fooling around."

He stared at me for a beat, his eyes still narrow, his expression bleak. Then, as if swatting away a troublesome fly, he waved his hand and shook his head. "Ah, don't mind me. Sometimes you say things . . . you remind me of . . . you remind me of somebody, that's all."

"Is that a bad thing?" I asked carefully.

His gave me a half smile and sighed. "No. It's just . . . hard sometimes. Kids. Always have to be right, don't you?" Then quietly, as if to himself, he added, "No matter who gets hurt."

I cocked my head at him, still puzzled. *Well, that was surreal.* But before I could say anything, he snatched his mug and thrust it toward me. "But when I say I want hot coffee, I damn well mean hot coffee. Now take your geeky little ass down to the 7-11 and get me some real, *hot* coffee."

My jaw dropped. "Are you kidding? You want me to walk five blocks in this heat? There's a reason we haven't seen even gangbangers for hours. They all went home to enjoy their heatstrokes in the comfort of their living rooms. I bet I could collapse on the sidewalk and no one would even come out to steal my iPhone to sell on eBay. I should do this all for a cup of coffee?"

"You're right. We done ate all my Chee Wees," he said, glancing back at the three empty bags of the New Orleans–style cheese curls that constitute a good quarter of his daily food intake. "Get me some barbeque chips. With ridges. The ones in a bag, not the sissy ones in the can."

I reached right over him and snatched the keys from the steering column. "You want hot coffee? Fine."

He bent to look at me as I angled out of the car onto the blistering pavement. "What do you need my keys for?"

I rounded the car and unlocked the trunk. I had two napkins from getting the coffees. Using them to cover my palms against searing, I jerked it open and rummaged through the toolbox. In short order, I had a "D" battery, a small spool of lead-free hobby wire, wire cutters, and every MIT grad's weapon of choice: duct tape.

As I got back into the car, I tossed Jake the keys and laid my booty on the dash. Grabbing the wire, I measured out roughly six inches and snipped it off with the wire cutters in my left hand. Jake rolled his eyes. I'm a leftie, which, for some reason, amuses Jake, but at least he's given up ragging me about it.

"What the hell are you doing?" Jake said.

Laying the wire on my lap, I reached for the duct tape. "Getting you hot coffee."

"Is this another one of your crazy-ass gadgets?"

I smiled. "You know you love them. It's one of the reasons you find me so fascinating."

"Cocky little thing, aren't you?" Yet he peered at the

paraphernalia with curiosity.

"Oh, quit complaining and prepare to be amazed. And give me your pocket knife."

"Only if you promise to cut your tongue out with it."

I gave him my most banal look and wriggled my fingers.

"Jesus, Mary, and Joseph," he grumbled. With a grunt, he dug into his pocket, pushing his shoulder holster with its enormous Colt forty-five to the side as he did. "You're a real pain in the ass. You know that, right?" He handed me his red Swiss Army knife.

I took it and leveraged it open, pulling out the miniature scissors and then using them to cut two small rectangles of duct tape. I closed the knife and dropped it on my lap. Laying an end of the wire on one side of the battery, I taped it down. "This won me five points in the Brain Buster Blow-Out of Milton Street."

He adjusted his shoulder holster into a more comfortable position. "The what?"

"My best friend, Timmy Atwell, and I had summer competitions demonstrating physics principles with whatever was handy."

"Sweet: nerds in love."

I laid the other end of the wire against the other terminal and proceeded to tape it down, effectively shorting the battery. "We weren't in love. We just, you know, hung around."

"Uh-huh. Sure."

"Well, up until the summer Mary Lou Simpson developed breasts." I shrugged. "I didn't see much of Timmy after that."

"Figures."

I looked up at Jake, grinning broadly. "But in the fall, *I* developed breasts, and mine were *much* better than hers."

That netted me a genuine smile. "I'll bet you made that little boy pay, didn't you?"

"You bet I did. That was the year Timothy James Atwell learned that the pressure of his penis on his zipper was directly proportional to the amount of cleavage displayed."

Jake barked a short laugh. "He'd have figured that out without your help."

"Maybe so. But I gave that boy some of the best data points of his life." I held up my device: a "D" battery with a length of wire taped to the terminal ends. "Ta-da," I said, in my best Wall-E imitation. "Touch it."

His heavy brows knit together. He gingerly touched the wire and then quickly let go. "It's hot."

"And it'll get hotter." I took his mug and set it on the dash. Dangling the wire inside the mug, I maneuvered the setup so as to wedge the battery tightly between cup and windshield, holding the contraption firmly in place. "What do you think?"

Jake tipped his head to the side, regarding the device as if it were an exotic insect he didn't know whether to keep or crush. He shrugged. "It might not be the stupidest thing I've ever seen. That'll work, will it?"

I nodded. "The coffee will get hot. I guarantee it." It would, in fact, get hot but not because of the small amount of energy coursing through the wire. Shorting out a single "D" battery wouldn't do much more than make the thin metal hot to the touch. The intense sunlight streaming through the windshield and reflecting off the bare dash would warm his coffee on its own, not to boiling, but enough to shut him up about my going for more. After all, what good is a working knowledge of the laws of the universe if you don't use it to indulge in a little harmless naughtiness now and then? Of course, I was *so* going to rag him about it later. I would wait to find the perfect time to let him know he'd been had, which requires a certain amount of finesse. And a physical distance much greater than arm's length.

As I relaxed into my seat, I noticed black smudges on my fingertips. "What's this?"

"Looks like soot," Jake said.

"Probably from the toolbox."

"Not from my toolbox, I guaran-fucking-tee you that. I keep my tools clean."

"And it's not on the wire, the cutters, or the tape. Look. It's on your mug, on the bottom. Did you set it down on something at work? You've got a little smudge on your sleeve, too."

Jake looked down at his sleeve. He spit on the mark and then rubbed it away with his fingers. "There. All gone. Happy now?"

"Eeeew," I said.

"A little spit solves everything. Here, let me help you." He spit on his hand and reached for my soiled fingers.

I jerked my hands back, hurriedly rubbing the smudges off on my jeans. "No, thank you! God, you are such a pig."

His eyes twinkled. "I thought I was evil."

"You are an evil pig."

He nodded. "I aim to please." He retrieved his magazine and said, "Now, how about my Slim Jims?" Then his cell phone rang. He glanced at the caller ID before answering. "Yeah, Max. What's up, tahyo?"

I *humphed* in aggravation. Maxwell Hunter was Jake's best friend and his partner during their days as Louisiana cops. Hunter now owned the most successful detective agency in Chicago. He was rich, savvy, and built like a pro football player. He was twenty years my senior but still way hot: big, bad wolf's younger, buffer brother. On the other hand, he treated me like an annoying ten-year-old and that mitigated against my attraction. Most of the time.

Jake's eyes lit up at my expression. He mouthed, silently, "Should I send him your love?"

I gave him a simple, one-finger salute.

18

"No, I'm not laughing at you," Jake said into the phone. "The babbette's being a brat." *Pause.* "Yeah, she's still with me. For now." *Pause.* "Ah, she's not that bad." After a moment, he laughed, then looked me up and down. "Uh-huh, she is. I have to give you that. But somebody's got to watch out for her."

I sat up straight. "Yes, I am what? What is he saying about me?"

Jake shook his head, still grinning. "Okay, Max. No sweat. I got the tickets. I'll meet you at Spanky's at four. Beer's on you this time. Catch you later."

I crossed my arms again as he hit the "end" button. "I can't stand that guy," I said.

"If you weren't always such a smart-ass with him—"

"Smart-ass? Me? When am I ever a smart-ass?"

Jake's eyes shot wide open as if I'd tried to deny that cosmic background radiation was two-point-seven-three Kelvin, or something equally irrefutable.

"Well, okay, maybe I am occasionally—"

"Occasionally?!"

"All right, all right. But he starts it! That patronizing way he calls me 'Angel.' And you know what he did? You want me to tell you what he did?"

"Not really. But that won't stop you, will it?"

I threw my arms up. "He told me, point blank, that I'm not qualified for this job."

Jake shrugged. "You aren't." He held up a hand to silence my protest. "Sorry, petite. You may know that science shit, but tech smart ain't street-smart. You still got a lot to learn."

"Hey, I may be starting out, but investigative work is in my veins. My great-great-however-many-times-over-Aunt Kate—"

Groaning, Jake rubbed his hand over his eyes. "Oh, Christ, not the Aunt Kate story—"

I held my head higher. "Kate Warne! This country's first

female detective—"

"Yeah, yeah. I know. I've heard this story a thousand—"

"Hired in 1856 by Allan Pinkerton, forty years before women were allowed to join the police force. Pinkerton, 'The Eye' himself, founder of the Pinkerton National Detective Agency, motto: 'We Never Sleep.' The man who invented private investigation as a profession—"

Jake held a hand up. "I know all this. Do we have to—?"

"Then one day, my great-great-w*hatever*-Aunt Kate walks in to a one-man office in Chicago, just like I did not six months ago, and asked for a job, just like I did—"

"You *demanded* a job."

"And just like I did with you, she won Allan Pinkerton over with her eloquent arguments—"

"More likely she nagged him into submission just like you did to me."

"—and went on to help him form the greatest detective agency the world has ever known!"

Jake rolled his eyes to the ceiling. "Please, God, shut her up."

My heart sped up as I plowed on. "Then, practically single-handedly, she solved the infamous Adams Express robberies. Posing as a convict's wife, she ingratiated herself into the confidence of the dastardly embezzler—"

He barked out a laugh. "Enough! Dastardly? Petite, no more Classic Movies Channel for you. And I *know* the story. Mrs. Naidenheim in the office downstairs knows the story; Mr. Keeper in the office upstairs knows the story; everyone in that drafty, Victorian, code-violation-we-call-an-office building knows the goddamned story. And you can spout that destiny crap all you want. But the truth is, you're an overeducated bab-bette who needed a job, any job, because your mother cut you off for running away from school."

I tried but just couldn't keep the self-indulgent pouting out of my tone. "I didn't *run away*. I'll go back to finish my doctorate, eventually. I just want more out of life right now. I'm fed up with serving as slave labor to tenure-obsessed, bipolar, chronically cheesed-off professors! I need a break. And my mother is being ridiculous."

"She's the fucking chair of the fucking physics department of fucking Yale. I'm betting she doesn't know how to be ridiculous."

"That's not exactly how her business card reads. But, yes, she's . . . accomplished." I felt my jaw tighten and deliberately yawned to loosen it. "In fact, she's brilliant, and cultured, and beautiful. And I'm a poor knockoff. Okay? I've admitted it. I'm a shadow of her *glorious* self!"

"I didn't mean—"

"But that doesn't make her right all the time. And even if it did, I'm not her! And I don't want to be like her, or the rest of my family. With the single exception of my father—God rest his soul—they're all just a bunch of deskbound academics; think first, act never. Never getting out there and . . . well, like you'd say, grabbing life by the balls like Aunt Kate did. Like my dad did." I slammed my left fist into the palm of my right hand.

"Well, I'm not like that! I'm not afraid to grab life's balls no matter how big and hairy and . . . blue and . . . um, uh . . . okay, that's probably as far as I should go with that analogy."

Jake shifted in his seat, seeming both bemused and pained. "Yeah, probably." He exhaled deeply. "Christ Almighty, kid. I'd rather spend ten minutes in the ring with Lennox Lewis than five getting the shit beat out of me by you and your *words*. I swear the way you go on wears a man out."

I squared my shoulders. "From where I come, my manner of speaking is standard. Ergo, if one were to say—"

Jake shot me a sour look.

"I guess if I want to be taken seriously, I should stop saying things like ergo, huh?"

"Fucking A."

"Okay. I can do that. So who's Lennox Lewis?"

Shaking his head, he said, "Never mind." Then his eyes narrowed, and he tipped his head, glancing at the rearview mirror. "Well, what do we have here?"

I twisted toward the back window. One of our targets approached: the cheating husband. To be honest, he looked harmless enough to me: kind of geeky really. He was rail thin and gangly, with pronounced cheekbones and protruding ears, large eyes, and one of the biggest Adam's apples I'd ever seen. He reminded me a little of Alfie, my youngest brother's best friend, who spent most of his visits trotting on my heels, asking if he could "help" with anything. I was always half tempted to throw a stick to see if he'd actually fetch it. *Blast from the past, notwithstanding: finally, some action!*

"Christ in a crunch!" I said.

Jake groaned. "Crutch. It's Christ *on a crutch*. Don't you even *know* how to swear?"

"Apparently, I've yet to master the rudiments of blasphemy. You can teach me later." I grabbed the door handle. "After we get this guy."

Jake reached over me and held the door shut. He nodded toward the front of the car. "Hang on. Let's give her a chance to spice the roux."

A woman approached from the other direction. I'd been expecting full-out Trailer Park Barbie, but she looked more like a young executive, or at least like someone *trying* to be one. She was pretty enough, in a wanting-to-look-fashionable way. Her plum dress fit snugly enough to call attention to her figure but not so tightly as to shout. Her makeup was subtle. But still the dress was a bit too short, and the hair a bit too red. I half turned to face Jake. "Why would they meet in an alley?"

Jake watched the woman intently. "Don't know. Maybe he

likes getting his pecker lubed where he might get caught. Some people are like that."

"I'll have to defer to your expertise on degenerate behavior."

"Hush. Get your game face on." He nodded at the rearview mirror, his eyes solemn and focused. All business.

I leaned forward, adjusting the rearview to reflect our targets. Jake laid a beefy arm across the back of the seat, positioned himself to see the couple through the passenger's side mirror, and leaned in. *Jeez, I wish he hadn't had so many onions on his burger.* I relaxed into the seat, maintaining my line of sight.

My breathing turned shallow and quick. This was it! Here I sat in a stinking, rust-bucket of a car with a weather-beaten ex-cop stalking two human beings. Okay, so we were trying to catch them with pants down and dress up. But, it was life! *Let's see Mom do this.*

"What's going on?" I whispered. "I don't see where he went."

"Shhhh."

"But—"

Jake dug his fingers into my stomach, forcing a burp out of me.

"Pardon me," I said.

We watched for several more moments, and, just when I could almost feel my molecules vibrating, Jake looked down at me. My face flushed with excitement, I said, "Now?"

He smiled, his tone softening. "Got the blood going, eh? Well, don't let it distract you. Listening to the blood rush in your ears will bite you in the ass every time."

"The physiological impossibility of such a mixed metaphor aside, I've got it. But we need to get a picture, and I bet this guy's performance won't push the limits of an egg timer."

Jake grabbed a wrinkled, tan suit jacket from the back seat and shrugged it on over his shoulder holster. "They went into the alley. Get the camera."

I pulled Jake's thin digital Konica out from under my seat. With a surprising fluidity, he exited the car, then strolled across the street. As I got out, I caught his Swiss Army knife—I'd forgotten I'd had it—just before it tumbled to the ground, stuffing it into my jeans. I trotted after him like an over-caffeinated Chihuahua tailing a mastiff.

We rounded the corner, and Jake stopped suddenly. I crashed into him and, leaning around, I looked into the empty alley.

"Where did they go?" My voice bounced off the brick walls.

Jake sliced a hand through the air, his expression wary. I swallowed hard.

The alley in which we stood may have dated back to the twenties and may have sheltered many a mobster among its trash cans, rat droppings, and cigarette butts, but the cans had long since been replaced by city bins. Flyers for local bands on their fifth name change and last hope littered the ground. The purpose of the alley clearly hadn't changed: it *disappeared* people.

Jake's right hand slipped inside his coat. I hung the camera over my shoulder and reached around to pull the nine-millimeter I'd bought just last week from the waistband of my jeans. The gun's stock was hot in my hand and slick with back sweat.

Jake's eyes went wide. In a harsh whisper, he said. "Where the hell did you get that? You can't carry a gun, especially concealed! Are you trying to lose me my license?"

"But—"

"Put it away!" he said through gritted teeth. "Damn it, if that's all the brains you've got, I made a mistake trusting you."

I grimaced, my face flushing with chagrin. "All right! Don't burst a blood vessel." I stuffed the pistol back into my waistband.

Jake's eyes hardened. "Can it. Something's fucked up here."

My shoulder muscles bunched up, and I tried to shake them out. One thing was clear: Jake was worried. *And what chance do you have, Madison, my girl, against something that can spook a man like him?* I chewed my lower lip. "Where do you think they went?"

Jake kept his right hand under his coat. With his left, he pointed to a wooden door a third of the way down the wall. A flyer tacked to its weather-scarred face rustled lightly.

"We checked that entrance days ago," I said. "It's blocked from the inside, remember?"

"Well, either it's been cleared or Scotty beamed them up." With a jerk of his head, Jake motioned me forward. Fighting a burbling urge to run, I scanned his stern face. He smiled faintly, as if to say *it's okay.* But his ramrod stance and hard eyes said it wasn't.

Steeling myself, I walked to the door. An off-white sheet of wide-ruled paper had been folded in half and fixed in place on it. A piece shaped like an isosceles triangle was missing from one corner. As I turned it, the sunlight caught the torn edge, and I detected a faint silvery gleam. "What do you think it is?"

Jake came up beside me. "Read it."

I snatched it from the door. "It says: 'Nice to see you, Big D. Save me a place in hell.' What's that supposed to mean?"

Jake whipped out his gun before I'd finished my question. A sharp crack blasted. Jake jerked and then grimaced. Stumbling forward, he slammed me into the wall. The breath burst from my lungs. I stared, dumbfounded, as his body slid to the pavement, landing with a gut-wrenching thud.

The paper floated from my hand and followed him to the ground. The sight of it kicked my brain into gear. I yanked my gun out of my waistband, throwing myself off balance, falling hard against the door. Searing pain tore through my right shoulder. Cold hit me like a river of ice, needles of pain stabbing me. I dropped to my knees and tasted blood.

The world disappeared.

CHAPTER TWO

Finally, they'd gone—the nurses, doctors, police—leaving Jake and me in his small, darkened ICU room filled by the hum of air conditioning, the rhythmic hiss of oxygen, and the *beep, beep, beep* of his heart monitor.

Inhaling the bitter tang of antiseptic, I stared at him from the end of his bed, gripping the rails at his feet, trying to keep it together. Anguish and anger bubbled up inside me. I tried to shove them down yet again, scrubbing off the tears and wiping my nose with the back of my hand. Pain seared my right shoulder. I reached up to touch the bulge made by the thick bandages beneath my hospital shift. They covered the wound I'd gotten from falling on a nail sticking out of the doorframe in the alley. It had punched through almost three inches of flesh and nicked my clavicle. I suppose I should be grateful it merely hurt like hell and was a long way from life-threatening. But seriously, to have passed out from fear? *How pathetic can you get?*

I shook my head, struggling to wrap my dazed brain around what had happened. My mind wandered back to a day three months ago when Jake had tried to teach me how commonplace were the mindless, cruel acts that so-called civilized humans perpetrate on each other. He and I had been standing outside of the courthouse downtown. He'd just testified in a case against a man who'd been convicted of killing his neighbor over running his lawnmower too early on Saturday mornings. I remember standing there, eating street-vendor peanuts in the cool spring sunlight. "You have to admit," I'd said. "The logical decision would've been to destroy the lawnmower."

Jake dug into the brown bag, coming out with a handful of nuts. Crunching down, he said, "Fucking morons don't make logical decisions. If fucking morons made logical decisions, they wouldn't be fucking morons, would they?"

"Well, I can't argue with that." I stared up at a plane descending toward O'Hare, waiting for the roar of its passing to subside before continuing. "It still surprises me that the killer was absolutely convinced it wasn't his fault, that the other guy *made* him angry so it was *his* fault."

"That's how he saw it. You going to finish those?" he said, looking over my shoulder.

Smiling, I handed him the rest of the peanuts and dusted off my salty fingers on my jeans. "You don't seem agitated or even alarmed by it all."

He shrugged. "Ain't no good in being so. Let me tell you, pichouette, there's folks in this world that, no matter what, will absolutely, goddamned and for sure convince themselves that it's *always* somebody else's fault. Hell, they wouldn't recognize the truth if it walked right up, pinched them on the ass, and called them sweetheart."

I barked out a laugh. Jake paused. Then he looked at me, his eyes boring into mine as if trying to brand his words on my brain. "And I'll tell you this, too. Every cop knows that the best, the most dangerous lie is that last one, the one that lets them pull the trigger, the one that says 'he deserves it.' Delusional fuckers like that, they'll do anything. And you've *got* to know them when you see them. Or I promise you, girl, you'll be dead. You'll be dead fast, and you won't be dead pretty."

"And you won't be dead pretty," Jake's rumbling voice echoed in my brain. And now, here I stood staring at Jake as he lay dying, not fast, not pretty, just dying. And why? Who could have

done this? Was it some pathetic moron who convinced himself of his right to kill over a petty transgression? Or was there some deeper reason for someone to hate Jake this much? I wasn't a fool; Jake was no Sunday school teacher. Yes, he probably had enemies. Any cop—good, bad, or otherwise—would. But for someone to shoot him in the back and think it justified? No. I don't care what the reason; there is no justification, no purported last, best lie that could ever excuse such *cowardice*. I squeezed my eyes against the burning tears. And there could be nothing to excuse my failing him either.

Bunching my hands into fists, I pounded them against the bedrails, wincing as I did. The pain killers were wearing off, and every movement brought hot pain from the stitches lacing my swollen flesh together. The humiliation burned hotter. I was weak, worthless.

Enough! Damn it, Madison, stop being such a prima donna.

I took a deep, calming breath, went to Jake's side, and took his hand. It was cool and fleshy, too large to wrap my fingers around completely. Steadying myself, I said, "Okay, how about this one? Why did the quantum chicken cross the road? Give up? Because it was already on both sides." I squeezed his hand. "Come on, old man. That's funny."

"Madison?"

I turned toward the deep-timbered voice. Chicago Policeman Nestor Lopez stood in the door bathed in the harsh fluorescent lights of the hospital corridor. I knew him. He was the beat cop who worked the area where Jake had his business and one of the most chill cops in the precinct. Jake had introduced us on my first day at work, considering it a priority to be on good terms with the cops, the local uniforms especially. As fate would have it, the place we were staking out was within a mile of the repurposed, turn-of-the-century mansion that's now our office building, well within the beat Nestor covers with his partner. In fact, the two of them had been the first ones to reach Jake and me. And theirs weren't the only familiar faces present. Given that Jake's best friend, Hunter, palled around with members of the force's upper echelons, Jake had come to be known by—and liked by—just about all the local police at all levels. That explained why Captain Vincent Voltaire himself, district chief of the South Side, had set up shop in a conference room down the hall. Yes, familiar faces were everywhere, but that did little to ward off the hollow dread seething in my gut.

Nestor nodded at me. "What are you doing, *Chica*?" he said, an undercurrent of home-spoken Spanish softening his tone.

I wiped the outside of my eyes, affecting composure. "I've been telling him jokes."

Nestor rubbed his thumbs over the black-and-white check-ered band on the wheel cap in his hands. A young cop, brawny with a touch of Latino sharpness in his face, he wore his hair short in what was probably the same cut he'd gotten from the same barber since he was a boy.

He tossed the hat on the metal table behind me and adjusted his utility belt. "Jokes?"

"Yeah. A little quantum mechanics, a little string theory. Funny stuff."

He slanted his eyes. "Uh-huh. Is it working?"

"Not really. He's more the dark energy type." The muscles in my throat seized up, and I gasped, swallowing more tears. Forc-ing a smile, I said, "Now if you were an astronomer, that would be . . . well, actually it would still be lame." I shook my head. "I'm trying, you know. I am. The problem is that I'm not any good at this watching-people-die thing. You'd think, since my dad died last year, I'd have gotten used to it . . . but I don't think I can do this again."

Nestor drew closer. Reaching out, he rubbed my good arm. "It'll be okay."

My head shot up. I glared at him. "No, it won't! My dad was a doctor, so I know what's happening, Nestor. I'm watching a man die. The bullet that took out a chunk of his lung is lodged in an inoperable spot a few centimeters from his heart. He's lost almost a third of his blood supply, he's in a coma, and he's crashed twice since we got him here." I looked back at Jake, swallowing hard. "It's a matter of time."

"*Chica*, you're hurt. Everything seems worse—"

My breath came harder, faster, as words tumbled out of me, spilled over us.

"I'm fine, damn it! Just a stupid nail in my shoulder, and I pass out. I mean, hell, my boss was bleeding to death at my feet, but could I be bothered to save him? No! Why? Because I was too busy being unconscious over a *nail* in my shoulder. Fine, yeah? Hell, I'm *fan-fucking-tastic!*"

Nestor took me firmly by my uninjured shoulder. "Slow down."

I slapped his hand away. "You want to know what's *really* pissing me off?"

His voice steady and calm, he said, "Sure. You tell me."

I pointed out the window, tears burning at the corners of my eyes. "Some bastard, some lowlife son of a bitch, stood in a window and *shot* him. Just shot him! Like he was some rabid dog, like, like, I mean, *God!* How does someone do that? How does a human being just *shoot* someone? I don't, I don't understand—" The words stopped. I couldn't talk, couldn't breathe. My ears roared, and the lights dimmed and flickered.

As if I were detached from my body, I felt Nestor's hands pull me into a chair and his cool palms on my cheeks. My head tipped up, toward the glaring lights in the hall. His voice, gentle but dominant, sounded in front of me. "That's enough. Breathe. Just breathe."

I did, eventually coming back to myself. Nestor squatted

before me, grasping my hands.

"I'm okay," I said. "That was me becoming hysterical. In case you didn't notice, I thought that I'd point that out. It's important to me that you know I'm aware I became hysterical. And I'm possibly on the verge of doing it again. But the talking helps. It holds it in. The words rush out, and the panic stays in. It's when I can't talk that I can't control it. That's odd, don't you think?" Laughter burbled out of me. "And that's laughter, possibly another harbinger of panic." I pulled my hands free of his and put them out before me. "But we're not losing it, again. I mean, I'm not. I can't vouch for you. But you will try to stay calm, won't you?"

"Yeah, I'll do my best." He looked at me squarely. The corner of his eyes crinkled as he gazed intently into my own. "Now you listen, eh? That man over there? Don't you go counting him out. He's not that easy to kill. He's been through a hell of a lot worse than this. And he's brought others through worse too. All the stories they tell about him? They're all true."

I cocked my head, taken aback. "Stories? What stories?" Jake was just an XXL ex-cop with a lousy car, a lousy attitude, and an aspires-to-be-lousy wardrobe; a man whose ambition is limited to finding the best beer and burger combo in town.

Wasn't he?

Nestor nodded, fatalistically it seemed. "Just like him not to tell you."

"Tell me what? What do you know—?"

"It's not my place to say. But there's a lot to know about that man: good—" he paused to glance over to Jake, the set of his mouth going grim, his voice flat, "—and bad." Nestor looked back at me, his dour expression metamorphosing into a smile. It was a brilliant smile, straight white teeth set in a firm jaw, like something out of a 1950s sitcom, reassuring, wholesome: comfort food for the brain. He patted my hand. "You ask him,

31

when he's better."

I stared at him, puzzled: good and bad? That was true about everyone. But the way Nestor had said it seemed ominous and made me wonder what Jake had been keeping from me. Yet, the look on Nestor's face made it clear I wasn't going to get any more information from him. But his smooth and easy confidence had helped, and I felt my panic subside. I licked my lips and smiled faintly at him. "You have a very nice smile. It puts a girl completely off-guard."

Nestor stood, his face falling into shadow. "What reason would I have to do that?"

Surprised at my own comment, I blinked. "I don't know why I said that. I guess I'm not myself. It's been a premium-ticket-ride day. One of those you-must-be-taller-than-the-person-trying-to-kill-you, keep-your-hands-within-the-vehicle-of-death things. Ever have those?"

He moved back into the light, looking a bit bemused. "About every other week. Hang on." Nestor walked over to the door and closed it almost completely. When he came back, he tipped his head, looking down at me intently. "Did you get your pain pill prescription filled?"

I bit my lip. I guessed why he was asking and felt embarrassed. "Kind of."

He narrowed his eyes. "Which means *no*, right? I heard you giving the nurse trouble."

"Look, I don't have health insurance, except for what my mom keeps on me. I've used it thus far because I don't want to stiff the hospital for stitching me up. But I don't want to take advantage. Besides, I don't need pain pills. I've got aspirin at home."

He scoffed. "Oh, do you? Uh-huh. Have you ever had a puncture wound before?"

"I slipped with a pair of pointy tweezers once and got myself

pretty good, right here," I said, pointing to the small scar abov
my right eyebrow.

He tipped his head to one side. "And did it bleed?"

"No, not really." I shifted in my chair. "But pain is good foi
building character, right?"

Nestor dug in to his pocket and pulled out a small brown
bottle. "Pain's good for teaching you not to do stupid things,
and you don't ignore it if you don't have to." He proffered the
container. "Here. There's only a couple left, but you need them.
Take them."

I took the bottle. The label had been scraped off. Inside were
two small white pills. Having worked in my dad's office enough
summers, I recognized them instantly: Percocet. I looked up at
Nestor in shock. "Isn't this—?" Massively illegal, was what I'd
started to say. Only I didn't want to look like some dorky goody
two-shoes in front of the good-looking cop. My vanity never
takes a break. And I needed the pills. "Isn't this, um, pain pills?
Well, actually *aren't these* pain pills? Or, also one could say, isn't
this a pain pill, accompanied by another pain pill, or, um—you
know what? Screw grammar. Where did you get these?"

"I hurt my back in a car chase last year. But I'm about to get
off them. Besides, there's not a cop around who doesn't end up
with a stash of pills, bandages or braces after a few years." He
lowered his voice. "*Mira,* put them in your pocket. You don't
want 'em, flush 'em."

I stuffed the bottle in my jeans, a twinge of discomfort hitting
me. It wasn't that I didn't appreciate what was, frankly, a
somewhat intimate gesture: risking that I wouldn't turn him ii
for giving me a controlled substance. On the contrary,
welcomed the trust. I simply hadn't thought of us being o
those terms yet. The handful of times we'd met—mostly cha
ting on the street or at the police station—were when I'd tagge
along as Jake's designated horse-holder and chief bottle-wash

(whatever the hell that means). So, not a lot of opportunities for deep social interaction there. But maybe getting shot at is an entrée to credibility in "cop world." Go figure.

I said, "I don't mean to offend. I appreciate this. And it might be for the best. I'm prone to vivid dreams when I take painkillers. In fact, I'm prone to hypnagogic imagery in general."

Nestor frowned. "Sorry?"

"It's a type of cognition that occurs when someone enters a dream state. There's anecdotal evidence that people, especially scientists and artists, solve difficult problems in their sleep via hypnagogic imagery. For example, Friedrich Kekulé supposedly came up with the idea that the structure of benzene was hexagonal from a dream he had about a snake grasping its tail in its mouth. On the other hand, my Great-Aunt Ada, who's a Willa B. Casey Endowed Chair for Psychology, thinks that's a crock." I grinned. "That's the scientific term, of course.

"Anyway, she just got a huge research grant from—" I broke off as I noticed that familiar look of horrified bewilderment, that deer-in-the-headlights, what-the-hell-is-she-talking-about look that I see so often on the faces of *normal* people. "Yeah, okay, never mind. The point is, maybe I'll get lucky and dream about the man who shot Jake."

Nestor straightened. "You said you didn't see anyone."

"I said, I don't *remember* seeing anyone. But I know the bullet must have come from the second-story window across the alley. I remember there was this dog that lay down—"

He narrowed his eyes, his demeanor intensifying. "But you didn't actually *see* anyone?"

"No. But if I could just relax, maybe my mind would clear." I reached up with my good arm and massaged the back of my neck, my muscles twisted as tight as a well-wrung dishcloth.

Nestor came around behind me into the shadowed corner. His strong hands came to rest on the back of my neck. "Maybe

this will help." He slid his hand up and down my spine.

They were warm, strong hands: reassuring. I closed my eyes and leaned back into him, muscles releasing, feeling safe. "Hmm. That's nice."

He slipped a hand around to the front of my throat, gently gripping under my chin, lifting it. His other hand came up to the base of my skull.

The door opened and a woman's voice sounded. "Am I interrupting anything?"

Nestor's partner, Lilly Killrain, strode into the room. I smiled, further relieved. Fact is, I'm an outsider in the world of cops and robbers, PIs and perverts. While Hunter would love to send me off the world entirely, Jake was my ticket and shield, and Nestor's support made me cool by association. But, having no-one-says-no-to-Lilly on my side, too, was the surefire trifecta.

She flicked the light switch, and I shielded my eyes with my hand, blinking at the brightness. A tall woman, she was attractive in a solid-but-trim farm-girl kind of way, her long auburn hair pulled into a large bun at the nape of her neck, and a straight, pert nose set between green, slanting eyes. The ten pounds of citizen-suppression equipment dangling from her belt and her tendency to clutch her nightstick by her side were attention-grabbing enough. But it was the self-assured way she carried herself that made her appear all but invulnerable.

Her eyes cut to Nestor and then to me. To my surprise, I saw tension—protectiveness? defensiveness?—in her piercing green eyes. Then it was gone, like a sudden, stiff breeze flicking away the fog, leaving me wondering if the look had been meant for me, for him, or if I'd just imagined it. Before I could sort it out, she dipped her head, running her gaze over me like a she-wolf assessing an injured pup. "Feeling better?"

"A bit. And thanks for the help. It's good to have the 'pit bull' on my side."

Her eyes lit with approval as she smiled at me. Lilly's secondary sobriquet, "Pit Bull Killrain," derived from her reputation for engaging in single-minded pursuit of, well, anything and everything. You name the cause, and Lilly championed it: whether taking point on the department's annual Habitat for Humanity outing, finding homes for the pups that didn't make it in the K-9 corps, or creating the Committee for Gay, Bisexual, Transsexual, and Transgender Policepersons. Lucky me, I seemed to have become her latest cause. She'd been the first one I'd seen when I woke in the alley, and she'd not left my side—kneeling by me on the ground, riding with me in the ambulance, hovering by the trolley as they wheeled me into the emergency room—until Nestor had literally taken her by the elbow and led her away so that the doctors could treat me. Of course, she'd been firing questions at me the whole way: Had I seen the shooter? Where had the shots originated? Had I seen anyone running away? Sure, such intensity can be stifling, and, yes, some people found her "too-high bandwidth" to deal with. But since I shared the tendency to obsess to the point of obnoxiousness when in pursuit of a goal, I *got* her.

Her eyes cut this time to the bed where Jake lay, her brow furrowing. "Anything for a friend of Jake's."

Nestor walked around the chair to stand beside me. I caught the sound of a small sigh coming from him and had the distinct impression her words had annoyed him. I paused, perplexed. Why would that be? What was I missing?

Evenly, he said, "Where did you go?"

"I called Carter Lewis." She looked at me. "He's the head of the local chapter of Retired Police Officers. I thought maybe he'd want to rally the troops to help Jake through this."

Nestor crossed his arms over his chest and looked down at the ground, shaking his head. He was smiling, and while the smile seemed good humored, it also seemed tinged with exasperation. He looked up at her. "Being that Jake's such a good buddy of Captain Voltaire's, I suspect Carter will let him know how thoughtful you were."

Lilly raised an eyebrow, the luminance of her smile dimming a couple of notches. She began tapping her nightstick against her thigh. "He might," she said with a hint of defensiveness.

Nestor looked at Lilly. Lilly looked at Nestor. I looked at them both, and I could almost see the megabytes of data streaming in the photons reflecting their silent conversation between their eyes. But the unspoken intercourse occurring between them was as if via a quantum-encrypted data link to which I had no key. And we all know what that means.

"Um," I said, feeling suddenly like the proverbial third wheel. "I'm going to get a drink. You want?" I said to Nestor. He shook his head, his eyes not breaking gaze with Lilly's. "Lilly?" I ventured, getting the same otherwise-occupied shaking of the head.

I shrugged. "Okay. I'm out of here." But as I walked past Lilly, she raised her nightstick, the dirt-smudged bottom pointing straight at me, stopping me in my tracks. After another fraction of a second staring at Nestor, she broke her gaze free of his, the expression in her eyes clearly strained. "I want you to know that you can come to me. If you remember anything at all, no matter what, no matter how insignificant you think it is, no matter *who* is around"—she flicked her eyes to Nestor on the word "who," and then back to me—"call me. Day or night." Then she looked fully at me, clearly trying for a reassuring smile despite the tight set of her jaw. "I'm here for you." She glanced at the bed. "And I will never give up on Jake, either." She lowered the stick and her voice. "He deserves . . . closure."

Nestor came close, putting a warm hand on my back. I couldn't tell if he meant to comfort me or speed me on my way, but his added refrain of "and me as well" sounded sincere.

As I started forward again, Lilly reached out to touch my arm. "I'm a phone call away."

I nodded and then hurried out. And then—I'm not exactly certain why I did what I did next, curiosity maybe, or paranoia—I paused outside of the room to listen. A nurse with end-of-shift-end-of-patience writ on her face approached at a quick pace. I picked up my left foot and pretended to be looking at something on the bottom of my shoe, giving me an apparent reason to be standing there. When she passed by, I peeked into the empty room next door. Well, the beds were empty at least. A laptop, probably for accessing files and documenting treatments, was partially disassembled on a rolling table. The computer's battery sat to one side, accompanied by a collection of cotton swabs, miniature screwdrivers, and a squeeze bottle of alcohol. Clearly the machine was undergoing maintenance. Good. If someone came in, I could always pretend that I was working on the computer. I might have a hard time pulling off "private detective" but I could channel "compu-gal" well enough to give the most discerning hacker a stiffie.

I ducked into the room and moved the tray table away from the door as silently as possible. Pressing against the wall, hidden in the shadow of a corner, I listened.

"Why shouldn't I go with her?" I heard Lilly say, tightly.

"Why should you?" Nestor said. His tone was one of mild rebuke. "You've already decided she doesn't know anything, or you wouldn't have unglued yourself from her side earlier. Besides, Voltaire doesn't like her, and his good friend, Jake, isn't here to watch you make nice with his protégé. So sucking up to her won't help you, will it?"

I heard what sounded like a strangled attempt to respond from Lilly, but Nestor plowed on. "And what's with calling Carter Lewis? It wasn't your place to do that."

Her response was, understandably, affronted. "My *place*? Who are you to tell me that?"

He sighed. "Okay, I shouldn't have put it that way. But you shouldn't have called Carter. You went over the line. Like grilling Madison, not your job. Gene Rasmen is running this case. He's not going to like you getting all up in his business, *chica.*"

Sharp, swift footsteps came toward me, and I started reflexively as if the wall weren't between us. *Yikes: guilty much?*

Whatever Lilly might have meant to say, Nestor interrupted by saying, "Chill. I'll talk to Gene. We were partners a long time. He'll cut you in as a favor to me. But you have to back off a little. Don't look so desperate. I promise you, *chica,* that kind of thing will backfire on you."

Lilly's response was tight, her words clipped. "So, my trying to see after the welfare of a fellow human being is wrong? Is that what you're telling me?"

He groaned, but when he spoke, his tone was gentler, as if he were talking to a recalcitrant child. "No, it's not wrong."

"Then what's the problem?"

"It's not *what* you do, it's *why* you do it, that's the problem. And everyone can see it. It's all about making grade with you."

"I deserve it! I work hard."

"Yes, you do." *Curious that he didn't agree she deserved it.*

"And so do you," she said. "But do you think we'll catch a break? No, not us. We're not in the inner circle, not one of the privileged few."

"It doesn't work that way."

"The hell it doesn't! How fucking quick did management back you down when you took on Hunter?"

"What's the point in bringing that up?"

"The point is that it's not *fair!*" Then her tone took on a distant quality, like someone who physically hadn't moved but had left mentally. "Don't you see? People like Hunter . . . and like that daddy's girl, they get everything, and they don't deserve it."

Nestor's frustrated sigh sounded clearly through the wall. "There was nothing going on between Madison and me back there."

"What?" Lilly sounded perplexed, like someone waking from a reverie.

"You said *that daddy's girl.*"

"I wasn't talking about her."

"Then who the hell are you talking about?"

That was a very good question. It was clear they were talking past each other, and, unfortunately, the conversational content was passing me by as well.

Lilly groaned, as if in exasperation. "It doesn't matter. Look, I know you, too. And I know what you're really upset about. You're doubting us, aren't you?" That last phrase, so simple on the surface, was delivered with such an intimacy that it rocked me back on my heels.

I couldn't catch Nestor's response clearly, but the harsh hiss of his sotto voce response was unmistakably tense.

Lilly's voice came back. "Who's going to hear us? Jake? He's out of it."

"I . . ." Nestor's voice trailed off, the normally smooth-as-water-on-silk tenor oddly broken and strained.

There were several seconds of silence. I heard Nestor walk away, toward Jake's bed.

After a few more moments, Lilly spoke. "We didn't do anything wrong."

Nestor's snort came through clearly. His tone was as strong as ever, but I could hear the doubt bleeding through his "yeah, right" response.

Her voice firm, Lilly said, "Protecting your family isn't wrong."

"I know that! I don't need you to fucking tell me that!"

"Then why think twice?" Soothing reassurance merging into her tone, she added. "We did our job, and that's what counts. People are safe now."

Okay, what just happened? One moment, Nestor is all big brother, wise and worldly. Then suddenly it's Lilly's turn to drive? Damn it. If I could only see what was happening. Why is there never a terahertz imager around when you need one? Something that can see through walls would come in real handy right now. I pressed against the cool plaster, listening intently.

When Nestor spoke his words were somber . . . and angry. "Too little, too late."

Lilly spoke again. "Yes, but past is past. That's why we have to do this: so that no one will get hurt in the future." More silence and then, "Look, Nestor, it's up to you. We can pull the plug. But then what? We just hope he makes a mistake again, and we're there at the right time?"

Him? Him who? What mistake?

Something clattered on the other side of the wall: it sounded like a table or chair being pushed aside. "*Carajo!* Why did this have to happen now?"

"What?" She sounded genuinely perplexed.

"This!" Nestor said, as if gesturing at something.

"Jake?" Lilly went silent for a heartbeat, and then, in a level voice she said. "This is a coincidence. One has nothing to do with the other, does it?"

Silence.

Lilly spoke again, more pointedly this time. "Nestor? Does it?"

He huffed. "It's just fucking bad timing."

"No shit," Lilly responded, cynically. "But that's all it is. We have to see this through."

"Why?"

41

"Closure," she said simply.

At that moment, I heard a new, low voice that sounded like it was coming from the door to Jake's room. A few seconds later, I saw a uniformed policeman, one I didn't recognize, pass by with Lilly and Nestor on either side of him. They'd moved by quickly and, fortunately for me, they didn't look right to see me lurking guiltily like . . . well, like a guilty lurker.

Swallowing my heart back into my chest, I waited to a count of ten and then poked my head out into the corridor. *All clear.*

With a relieved sigh, I headed in the opposite direction toward a small break room crammed with snack and beverage machines. Going to the latter, I slid in a dollar, selecting the hot chocolate. I leaned on the machine, waiting, but stood back as I noticed a sticky yellowish spot on my arm and wiped it off on the back of my shift. *Don't they ever clean these things?*

As the thin brown stream trickled to a stop, I reflected on what I'd heard. The conversation between Nestor and Lilly had bothered me on several levels. On the one hand, I really do like them both, Nestor especially. Something about him seems genuine and caring. And he seemed serious about wanting to help Lilly. But he could have been a little less patronizing in the way he was doing it. Okay, maybe she was swimming out of her lane, but what was the harm, really? She did a lot of good things for a lot of people. And her dogged dedication not to let bureaucracy and the "good-old-boy network" stop her was admirable. So what if she ruffled some feathers in the process? I scowled. Maybe what was really bothering me was that Nestor had sounded way too much like Hunter for my tastes: making certain the inexperienced girl didn't step out of line. And that was not a comparison I liked making.

Sipping my drink, I grimaced as the hot liquid burned my raw throat. There was more though. Sure, I felt empathy for Lilly, and the similarity, however brief, between Nestor and

Hunter was off-putting. But I was way more disturbed by the second half of their conversation. What was Nestor thinking twice about? If it had nothing to do with Jake—and they both agreed it didn't—then what difference did the timing of him getting shot make? Lilly had mentioned protecting Nestor's family. One thing that was crystal clear from having known Nestor even as short a time as I had: family was everything to him. The man would take a bullet, no, a hail of bullets, to protect his kin. Could he give as well as get?

Still deep in thought, I made my way back to Jake's room. A man in green scrubs was about to go into it as I came around the corner. When he saw me, he did a quick turn and walked into the room next door, the one I'd been hiding in moments earlier. *What's that all about?* Maybe he'd come to check on Jake and didn't want to disturb me.

I went into the room into which he'd ducked. "You don't have to leave on my account—"

The man's arm shot out of the room and yanked me in. Grabbing me by the throat, he slammed me against the wall, throwing the door shut behind us.

My back hit hard. I gasped as pain lashed down my shoulder like lightning. The cup flew out of my hand, splashing his arm with hot chocolate. The man bared his teeth, bringing his thin, pale face closer. Panic surged through me. His lips twisted into a sadistic grin as he pressed harder on my throat. I gulped in air, frantically clawing at his arm, the terrifying claustrophobia of suffocation washing over me.

He brought his lips against my ear. His breath, hot and rancid, reeked of decayed food. His body stunk of manure. "I wish I could let you scream," he said. "I love it when they scream."

Fury blasted through me. *I am not fucking helpless!* My hand shot out to the metal table. The screwdrivers clattered to the

43

floor, but I got hold of the laptop. I yanked at it: a weapon!

Yes! Wait! No! It stuck! *Shit!* It was chained to the table! *Who chains a laptop to a table?!*

His eyes cut to the computer, and with a malicious leer, he slammed my head into the wall, again. A noise like a tidal wave roared in my ears. I felt my knees start to give out.

No!

I hooked the tray with my foot and yanked, ramming it into his back. His grip slackened enough for me to grab the bottle of alcohol. I squirted him in the eye. With a growl, he swatted it away. As it hit the table, the top snapped off and volatile liquid splattered over everything.

I tried to scream, but my traumatized throat only produced a hoarse yelp. I headed for the door, and he blocked me. My eyes fell to the table and inspiration hit.

I grabbed the laptop again. He sneered, brutality disfiguring his face into a caricature of humanity. "You tried that sweetheart. You're not so smart, are you?"

Oh, really?

I slammed the laptop into the lithium-ion battery, driving the free-floating pieces of metal in the fuel cell through the separator to create a catastrophic exothermic reaction. In other words—as I croaked out—"Battery go boom."

The explosion ignited the alcohol into a pool of blue flame.

I shoved the table into the man. He raised his arms to protect his face as the liquid splashed over him and howled as fire raced up his arm. Throwing himself away from the door, he beat at the flames with his hand. I raced past him, yanked open the door, and ran into the hall, plowing into a large Asian man pushing a food cart. "Hey, watch it, will ya?" he said.

The attacker burst out of the room. He glanced toward the man and then at me. Grinning wolfishly, he folded his fingers into the imitation of a gun and pulled the trigger. Then, in a burst of action, he grabbed a knife from the cart and slashed at the man.

The attendant's hand shot up to his chest as blood instantly soaked his scrubs. Stumbling, he fell to the floor, his face twisted in shock. I dropped to my knees and pushed my hands hard against the wound as our assailant ran.

Suddenly, people were yelling and running toward me. I saw the flash of police uniforms go by. Two women came up beside me. One pulled me away and the other piled thick pads on the man's wound. Staggering to my feet, I took off in the direction the police had gone.

I ran down debris-strewn hallways, following shouts and weaving through stunned bystanders. Adrenaline surged through me like a shot of Jack Daniels. My heart pounded, and my breath came in burning gasps. I ran toward the double glass door of the emergency room exit and slid sideways through it just as it closed. From the other side of the parked ambulance in front of me, I heard Lilly shout, "Shoot, damn it!"

I cleared the vehicle in time to see her struggling to rise from the parking lot pavement but toppling forward as soon as she put weight on her right foot. Nestor, his gun drawn, grabbed her arm and pulled her upright. She shoved him hard and limped backward on one foot: "Goddamn it, I had him! Why didn't you shoot?"

Nestor drew back, his breath coming as hard, his face flushed, eyes wide with shock. "What the fuck? Did you see—?" His head jerked up at a sound across the lot. "Look out!"

My brain registered the roaring to my left just as I was yanked backward. A large man slammed me against the ambulance, driving the breath out of me. His body flattened against mine as the car rocketed by within inches of us both. Stunned, I felt my legs fail. I was pulled up by strong arms. Someone shouted close to my ear, and I felt a slap on my cheek.

"Madison? Madison! Are you okay?"

I looked up into the gunmetal-gray eyes of Maxwell Hunter. The sharp planes of his face set hard as his intense stare bore into me.

I braced myself against the hood. "I . . . I think so . . . Oh shit!" I pointed to our right.

The car had done a doughnut and was bearing down on us again. Hunter reached into the open window of the ambulance and grabbed a flashlight from the dash. With inhuman speed and force, he turned, stepped into the vehicle's path, and hurled it at the windshield. The driver spun the wheel hard, but the projectile smashed into the passenger's side, sending spiderweb cracks shooting across the glass. The car plummeted forward, missing Hunter by scarcely a foot.

Pointing at me, he shouted, "Stay!" Then he took off toward his car at a dead run. Out of the corner of my eye, I saw a police car screech to a halt. Before it stopped, Lilly yanked open the passenger door and jumped in. Nestor gripped the wheel hard, and the vehicle lunged forward. Hunter's Lexus peeled out within inches of Nestor's bumper, the squeal drowned out by the sudden blare of the siren as both cars surged onto South Michigan Avenue in pursuit.

I fell back, gripping hard on the ambulance door handle to keep from falling. A redheaded nurse, in white scrubs dotted with rainbows and pink butterflies, jogged up to steady me. I looked up at her. "What the *hell* just happened?"

She looked up at the traffic, now passing by as if nothing had happened, and shrugged. "It's Chicago."

CHAPTER THREE

Half an hour later, I sat huddled in an aged, green plastic recliner in the dark corner of Jake's new room chewing at the raw cuticle of my right thumb. My head pounded and my shoulder burned. Voltaire had arranged for Jake to be moved to a room at the end of the corridor and posted two cops outside the door. Nestor, Lilly, and Hunter had returned ten minutes ago, empty-handed. Their anger, as bitter as it was impotent, spawned an atmosphere of impending disaster. People stood outside the door, rigid and expectant, as if waiting for a tornado to drop out of the sky. There wasn't a damn thing anybody could do but wait.

There was a piece of good news: The orderly who'd been slashed would be fine. I'd been luckier, hadn't ripped a stitch. I didn't feel lucky, though. I felt weak and stupid and helpless.

Footsteps approached. My muscles tightened and my heart fumbled. *Run? Hide? Vomit?*

The door opened, and I sucked in a breath.

Maxwell Hunter entered. Back to me, he walked up to Jake's bed. In his late forties, Hunter stood as tall and broad of shoulder as Jake but was all lean, hard muscles. Dark-haired, he had a Romanesque nose that had taken at least one solid break and large fists, now clenched, which had doubtless broken many others. I bit at my lower lip, trying to stay silent, instinct warning me not to disturb him.

I could see Hunter's reflection in the window. As he looked

down at his ex-partner, lying still and pale in the bed, his eyes narrowed. He swallowed hard. His lips were one thin, grim line, his anguish obvious. I felt my heart go out to him.

Suddenly, his eyes cut left, hardening. "Come to admire your handiwork?" he said in a deep baritone.

I started. *How? Oh, right: Snell's law. If I can see his reflection, he can see mine.* Standing, I moved forward. "What's that supposed to mean?"

He turned, reaching me in two short strides. Pointing at Jake, he said, "You were supposed to watch his back, and he got a bullet in it. That puts blame on you." Hunter had six inches on me and at least sixty pounds. It felt like a brick wall had rerouted itself to within inches from my face. And the wall was pissed.

My thoughts stumbled. This from the man who'd saved my life less than an hour ago? "Are you kidding me?"

"Do I look like I'm kidding, Angel?" Although his bayou accent had been all but polished away by professional coaching, exposure to Jake's long, lean drawl allowed me to discern the subtle cadence that was Cajun. But there was nothing subtle in his meaning.

I grimaced in confusion. "Come on. I tried—"

Hunter put his hands to his hips, thrust out his chest, and pushed back his jacket to reveal a gleaming gray forty-five Magnum tucked in a shoulder holster. "You tried, did you? Well, tell me something. If you tried, why the *fuck* does he have a bullet in his back?"

Blood rushed to my face. "Hey! This wasn't my fault."

"That's right," Hunter said with a sneer. "God forbid daddy's little girl has to take responsibility for her own screw-ups."

"I'm not like that," I said, my jaw pressed so tight I thought my teeth would crack.

"Like hell! I know your type." Hunter turned and paced like a caged leopard looking for a meal—a powerful beast not used to being restrained—and I hated how much he enthralled my attention. It wasn't just his wealth. Yes, while Jake had stayed in the blue-collar world of the hard-working small-business man, Hunter had soared to the stratosphere of society. His gunmetal-gray designer suit probably cost more than I made in six months. And the price of his Italian loafers and silk shirt, the color of a cool, dry Zinfandel, would've paid for my groceries for the year. But it was the potent masculinity of him that made my heart shudder.

Damn it!

Then, suddenly, he was standing before me again, snapping his fingers in front of my face. "Am I boring you here?"

I started, both embarrassed and angry at myself. "Don't be such a jerk."

Hunter scoffed at me. "He couldn't afford you, you know. You were a pity hire: a doe-eyed little girl who needed Daddy to rescue her. God help all men who fall for that one. But let me tell you something, if I'd been there, this wouldn't have happened."

"You don't know that! Look, Hunter, I know you're angry, and it's natural for you to channel it outward. But laying all of this on me—"

Hunter strode up and jabbed a finger into my chest. "Don't you dare psychoanalyze me! I will *not* stand here and let you look down your nose at me."

I swatted his hand away. "Back off! I didn't mean it that way. Why are you so—?"

He snorted. "You listen to me, Angel. That man is my friend. And if he dies, I'm going to put whoever did this into a blender, piece by piece. I'll take out anyone who gets in my way, and that includes you. Now, let's go." He gestured toward the corridor.

My skin prickled with alarm. I wanted to go somewhere alone

with this large, angry man about as much as I wanted to take a long stroll through the savannah with a pack of drooling hyenas. Naked. "Where?" I asked.

"Voltaire wants to see you, again."

Hunter moved forward, herding me out the door and toward the conference room where the chief had set up station. It wasn't a big surprise that, being a friend of Jake's and Hunter's, Voltaire had thrown his weight behind the investigation. That was bad news for the bad guys, as he's known to be ruthlessly impatient at the best of times. And these sure as hell weren't those.

A dozen people milled about as we entered the room, male and female, dressed in uniform and civvies, all hovering around Voltaire like planetoids caught in a gravitational field. The field didn't flutter when I entered. But, as Hunter strode in, all eyes cut to him.

"Here she is, Vince," Hunter said.

Petulance got the best of me. "Here she is, Vince," I murmured.

Unfortunately for me, everyone chose that moment to go silent, and the whole room heard my snide echo. *Ah, wonderful. Just great!*

A voice in the back said, "Looks like somebody missed her nap."

"She needs a time-out," came the reply, followed by a round of low-pitched laughs.

My cheeks burned red. *Way to look like an ass, Madison!*

Hunter leaned down to whisper in my ear. "Good job, Angel. That'll get their respect."

I stared straight ahead. "Blow it out your kazoo."

"Actually, Angel, the big boys usually say: blow it out your ass."

I glanced over my shoulder. Hunter stood so close I could

feel his breath on me: warm and sweet. Shades of midnight blue glinted amidst the slate shade of his eyes. But I was not about to be distracted again. I stared straight into those eyes and whispered. "Why don't you just get some big boys to blow it for you, then?"

He smiled broadly, eyes twinkling. Chuckling as he straightened up, he said, "Not bad, Angel. There might be hope for you yet."

I'd been watching Voltaire out of the corner of my eye. During my and Hunter's exchange, he hadn't looked up once. After all, he wasn't talking so there was nothing worth his attention. Now he turned to look at me, and everyone went silent. The opposite of physically imposing, he was slight, almost anemic-looking, with a sharp nose, gaunt face, and wispy blond hair thinning at the top. But it was his Rasputinesque eyes that got to people: narrow and intense, with almost-black irises that could pin a person in place, like needles through a butterfly. Nor did the butterfly have to be dead. I took a step back toward Hunter, stumbling as I did. The twisting motion pulled at the stitches of my wound, and I grimaced.

Voltaire gave me a look of impatient disdain. I dropped my arm and swallowed to hide the pain of the action. I'd be damned if I showed weakness before any of them.

The police chief stared at me, as if waiting to see if I'd crack. Then he raised an eyebrow and nodded at one of his female cops, who stepped forward and held a photo before me. As Voltaire was not a man to waste time on words, his inner retinue pretty much had to be psychic.

"That the guy you were following?" Voltaire asked, pointing at the picture.

I looked at it. It was the Alfie doppelganger from the alley. "Yes, name is Octaviano Lathos. At approximately 5:10 p.m. we were engaged in a routine surveillance of—"

"Can the Dragnet bit, kid." He looked at Hunter. "You were right about her."

I turned to Hunter. "What does he mean? What did you tell him about me?" Hunter grinned. I faced Voltaire. "What did he tell you about me?"

"Just say what you saw and drop the drama."

I drew a quick breath, ready to snap back, but remembered Jake's admonition that my reputation affected his. I let the breath out. I wouldn't let Jake down. "I didn't see anything."

"You mean you didn't see a face?"

"I mean, I didn't see *anything*. No face, no body, no silhouette, nothing."

"Rasmen!" Voltaire barked, and I flinched.

An unremarkable looking man—balding, brown eyes, tan shirt, tan pants—stepped forward: Gene Rasmen, the detective of record and Nestor's ex-partner. "Yeah, boss."

"The shots came from 400 feet away, yeah?"

Rasmen flipped open a small notebook. "That's about right."

Voltaire turned to me. "Jake was shot in the back. He dropped out of your line of sight, so you had clear view. You did look? Someone shoots at you, and you look?" He held his hands up wide, taking in the whole room with his gaze. "Or is that just me?"

A chuckle rounded the room. I ground my teeth hard. "It happened too quickly. Jake was shot. I tried to catch him. I started to look, but then I fell. I thought I'd been shot too." More snickering. *Tough guys. Like they've never been scared!*

"Seconds?" Voltaire demanded suddenly.

I blinked, confused. "Seconds?"

"Between when he falls and you faint," Rasmen chimed in.

Faint? You—! No, don't give them the satisfaction. The muscles in my neck were stretched tighter than a rubber band on a two-year-old's toy plane. I reached to massage them. Pain shot down my side, and I sucked in a quick breath. Voltaire scowled. I dropped my arm, defiant. "It happened in five, six seconds, maybe."

Voltaire walked toward me, his right hand folded into a parody of a gun. "One-thousand one, one-thousand two . . ." When he got to "one-thousand six," his finger rested on my forehead. "Now, me, with all that time, I'd have looked. Or ducked."

I jerked my head away. "I was surprised. I hesitated. Okay? It's a normal human reaction, and if it doesn't meet with your approval, I'd say that's *your* problem."

The room went still as if all were waiting for the ax to fall, buckets ready to catch my head. I could almost feel Hunter smile behind me. Voltaire stared at me, silent. I held my breath.

His eyes narrowed ever so slightly, and I could have sworn I saw a gleam in them similar to what—in a human anyway—would have been appreciation. Abruptly, he said, "Details." At my puzzled look, he spoke with deliberation, as if talking to a slow-witted child, "Tell me again why the two of you were in the alley."

"Domestic surveillance. Lathos's wife hired us to catch him cheating."

"His wife, eh?" Voltaire raised an eyebrow to Hunter, who nodded in return.

"That's right." I looked at Hunter, but I couldn't catch his eye. I turned back to Voltaire. "What's going on?"

Voltaire crossed his arms and looked down at me, his face grim. "There is no wife."

"No wife? What do you mean? She wasn't at home?"

He unfolded his arms. "Lathos isn't married."

The same spare cop held up a rap sheet before me as if in answer to some clairvoyant command. The "marital status" block was checked off as *single*.

"He's never been married, either," Voltaire said.

I stared at the paper, trying to process the information through a growing fog of fatigue and frustration. "That doesn't make sense. Jake said the wife hired us—"

"Jake said?" Rasmen asked, scribbling in his book. "You never met the wife?"

Sighing, I said, "No. The whole deal was arranged by phone between her and Jake."

"Well, there's no wife," Voltaire said. "And there's no Lathos either, not nearby anyway. It looks like he flew the coop. But we found these at his place." Voltaire nodded and "spare cop" handed me four eight by ten photographs of Jake. One of him getting out of his car in front of a courthouse, one of him leaving a bar, one taken outside the office, and one of him on stakeout in his car. The last was clearly taken from a high window, so I couldn't see Jake's face, only his unmistakably-Jake-side-of-beef-size arm. My gut clutched as I recognized myself standing next to Jake outside the office. Even more disturbing, someone had drawn a "happy face" in bright yellow marker over Jake's head, under which they'd written: "bye, bye Big D."

I shivered, handing the photos back. "This is freaky. So Lathos was following Jake?"

"Looks like it, Angel," Hunter said. "Any idea why?"

"No. We were following him. Or so we thought. Have you found anything in his arrest record? Did Jake ever bring him in? Here, or maybe when you two were cops in New Orleans?"

"Clever little us, we thought of that, Angel. But, no and no. And I looked back through my files. As far as we can tell, their paths never crossed."

"Lathos must be part of the setup, whatever his motivation. Does he have a record?"

"He was a small-time scam artist: telephone and Internet,"

Hunter said. "He'd claim to be the power company and talk harried moms and dads into giving up their credit card numbers, that kind of thing. But still, strictly B-team."

Voltaire looked at me. "Tell me about this file you *say* you put together on the case—"

His tone, laced with sarcasm, put me on edge. "What do you mean the one I *say* I put together? I took Jake's notes from the calls and organized them in a file. That was my job."

Hunter nodded. "Yeah, he was crap at keeping files. I always had to do it."

I turned back to Voltaire. "What about the file?"

Voltaire stared hard at me. "There's no file on the Lathos case in Jake's office."

"That can't be," I said. "I took it out this morning and put it on his desk. Maybe it fell off." I looked at Detective Rasmen. "Did you look around?"

"Oh!" Rasmen said with great exaggeration. "Was I supposed to look around? Nobody told me that." More snickers. "Gee, don't I feel dumb. Du-uh. Here let me make a note of that." He wrote in his book, using the clumsy motion of a child, and then smiled at the group.

I bit my cheek. Clearly, blood—my blood—was in the water, and the sharks were hungry.

"That's enough," Voltaire said. The residual chuckling cut out. "Tell me *exactly* when and where you last saw it."

I searched my memory. "I pulled it out this morning at eight a.m. and laid it on Jake's desk. I put it in the middle of the blotter, smack in the middle, so he couldn't miss it."

"Why did you take it out?" Hunter asked.

"Jake had a phone appointment with Mrs. Lathos—well, with whomever hired him. He was supposed to be at his desk at eleven a.m. She was going to call him for an update."

"And did she?" Voltaire asked.

"I don't know. I wasn't there. I'd gone out to pick up lunch."

Voltaire snorted. "Early lunch. Must be nice to have a boss who pampers you like that."

"It wasn't just for me. See, every Tuesday, like today, the restaurant at the corner makes New England clam chowder, which Mr. Keeper—the guy who runs the watch shop upstairs—loves. I mean, he *really* loves it. And, even though he's like a hundred and something, he'd walk down to get some every week. One day, he almost died of heat stroke. So, Jake made this big deal about how *he* loves chowder and told Mr. Keeper that he bought *me* lunch for picking his up. So, Mr. Keeper shouldn't feel bad about adding one small cup of chowder for me to carry back."

"Jake hated chowder," Hunter said.

"Yes, you know that, and I know that, but Mr. Keeper didn't know that. I'd get Jake the chili instead, and Mr. Keeper never knew the difference."

"Sounds like something Jake would do." Hunter nodded, smiling indulgently.

Voltaire grunted. "So you weren't there when the call came in from this 'Mrs. Lathos'?"

"No. I was where I always am on Tuesday at eleven a.m.: getting lunch."

"And he didn't say anything about it later?"

I shook my head. "No. Jake was gone when I got back. He left a note that he'd gone to buy seed for George. He came back an hour later, and we went on the stakeout."

"George? That's his parrot?"

"Strictly speaking, George is a budgerigar, commonly called a budgie, which is a subset of the parrot species. But, more precisely, he's a para*keet,* referring to any one of a large number of unrelated members of the species, all of whom—" Voltaire glared at me. I nodded. "Yeah. The parrot. Okay, so no file.

What about the note from the alley, the one that referred to Jake as 'Big D.' Did your guys find it?"

Voltaire shook his head.

"Are you sure you saw it?" Rasmen said in a snarky tone. "Maybe you were suffering from some kind of chowder-induced hallucination."

I shot him a disgusted look. "Yes, I saw it."

He arched a brow at me. "Just like you saw the file that no one can find?"

"The note *was there,* and the file *was there,* and if you can't find them—" I shrugged. "Maybe you're just no good at your job."

Rasmen's eyes darkened, and he moved toward me. "You little—"

"Enough!" Voltaire barked. "I don't have time for this shit!" He pointed at Rasmen. "You—find that goddamned note! Take the place apart brick by brick if you have to. Got me?"

Rasmen backed off, ducking his head submissively to his boss but keeping his eyes locked on me. He shut his notebook with a snap and motioned for another of the cops to follow him out. Not surprisingly, he clipped me with his shoulder as he passed by. *How original.*

"This note, are you sure it was meant for Jake?" Voltaire said.

"He reacted as if it did, especially to the phrase: 'Big D.' "

The chief looked over my head at Hunter, who'd moved to stand close behind me. I gritted my teeth, trying to ignore the subtle, spicy scent of his cologne. But, yum, it was nice.

Voltaire asked him, "Did you ever hear anyone call Jake that?"

"Never," Hunter said.

"Okay, you check it out. It has to mean *something*! You knew him the best. Yeah?"

Hunter nodded and pulled out his smartphone.

Voltaire turned to me. "Lathos' playmate: have you remembered her name yet?"

"The wife—or whoever she was—only knew her first name: Tina. What about the man who attacked me an hour ago? Is there any relation between him and her or Octaviano?"

"We haven't been able to match the piss-poor description you gave."

"Oh, come on. I was being strangled to death. I was a bit distracted. And it's not like half the hospital didn't see him too. What about him?" I pointed at Hunter. "He saw him."

Hunter raised an eyebrow. "I was a little busy saving your life, if you remember."

I exhaled and closed my eyes, counting to calm myself down. There was just no way I was going to win here. Everything I said would be twisted to make me look stupid, weak or ungrateful. Instead, I licked my lips and looked off into space.

Voltaire glowered at me. "The only way we're going to find the guy who came to the hospital today is by first finding Lathos or the woman you were following." He put his hands on his hips and stared down at the floor. Everyone stood perfectly still, as if listening for cues—or possibly receiving telepathic commands. Suddenly, he looked up. "Here's how it's going to be." He pointed behind me. Lilly and Nestor had appeared in the doorway. "You two: this happened on your beat, you hit the local snitches. Shake 'em till they shit their pants. Got me?"

Lilly started, whether from pleasure or fear, I couldn't tell.

Nestor nodded, grabbed her by the arm, and led her out. "Got it."

Voltaire turned to the others. "I want answers, people, and I went them fucking now. That's it. Out! Hunter, you stay here. You too, little girl," he said, pointing at me.

I gritted my teeth. One more "little girl" comment, and I was kicking someone in the ankle. After all, as long as you're going to be accused, you might as well be guilty.

The others dispersed. Voltaire looked at me. "Now. What to do with you?"

Hunter stepped forward. "May I make a suggestion, Vince?"

"No," I said, sensing trouble.

Hunter's eyes lit up. "Someone's already tried to kill her once."

"I don't think I was the primary target. He was going into Jake's room, I'm betting to finish the job he'd started earlier. And I interrupted him. I just got in the way."

"You do have that gift for making people want to strangle you, Angel."

"Hunter, you are a complete ass, you know that? And don't call me Angel. I *hate* it."

"Now, now, I'm only thinking of your safety. You want to know what I think, Vince?"

"No, he doesn't!" I shot back, instantly alarmed at the smooth turn of his delivery.

Voltaire tilted his head to one side. "What?"

Hunter reeled him in. "I think maybe you ought to put her in protective custody."

I practically leapt forward. "Jail? Uh-uh. No way! Hunter, I'll get you for this!"

"Good idea. Might be best." Voltaire nodded to one of his officers. "Lock her up."

"Oh, come on! No!"

"Maybe we shouldn't pick on her, Vince. She's probably still upset about losing her gun. Don't worry, Angel, the detectives found it."

"Stop calling me that!" I said.

Grinning, he went on. "Of course, we didn't know it was hers at first, since it isn't registered and she doesn't have a permit. I'm surprised Jake didn't clear it with you, Vince, knowing how much you hate that kind of thing. Must be she never told him she had it."

Voltaire eyes widened. "Were you carrying in *my* city?"

Oh great! Everyone and their dog knew that Voltaire was fanatic about concealed-carry laws. "Thanks a lot," I snarled at Hunter.

"No sweat," he said, his eyes glistening.

My mind raced, and I got an idea. "There's no need to worry. I'm leaving tonight."

"Says who?"

"With your permission, of course!" I added quickly. "My mother is coming to get me. I called her from the hospital." *Yeah, I'm lying. But, hey, I'm fighting for my freedom here.* "She'll be here soon, and I'll disappear into a Connecticut suburb. I'll be safe, out of the way."

Voltaire considered, then shook his head, "No. Might be safer downtown."

Hunter stepped forward. "I tell you what, Vince. I'll take her with me."

I flinched, eyes shooting wide, unable to believe what I'd just heard. "What?"

Hunter kept his attention on Voltaire, smiling smugly. "I've got a safe room at my office. I can keep Angel, here, nice and secure—for Jake's sake. And it'll save the city money."

"Good point. Budget's tight," Voltaire said. "Yeah. Good. You take her."

"Absolutely not! I refuse!"

Voltaire shrugged. "Then you go to jail. No skin off my back."

Groaning, my shoulder muscles so tight I thought they might snap, I considered my options. It was so unfair! *Okay, Madison. Chill. You're not a ten-year-old. Get a grip.* I took two deep breaths and forced my shoulders to relax. "Fine. I'll go with Hunter."

60

Voltaire grunted and walked to a nearby table to retrieve his notepad.

I glared at Hunter. "This doesn't mean you win."

He leaned over me, so close I felt the heat from his body. "Yes, Angel, actually, it does," he whispered. Then he backed up and winked at me.

Voltaire returned. "Give me grief and go to jail, that simple." Nodding at Hunter, he left.

I exhaled a resigned sigh into his wake and looked up at Hunter.

His eyes glittered with triumph and he smiled slightly, a wolf with his paw on the rabbit's throat. Cocking his head to the left, he said, "That way. Parking lot. Move. Now."

"Parking lot. Moving. Now," I echoed.

He growled—he actually, no-kidding, growled. *I mean, who does that in real life?*

Moments later we stood beside Hunter's honey-bronze, gold-trimmed Lexus, vanity plate: THEHNTR. As if the entire world were his prey. *Yeah, right.*

He walked around to the passenger door and opened it. *How gallant.* But as I took my seat, he leaned in and pulled out a pair of handcuffs. That's when I noticed a metal bar under the glove compartment, perfect for securing reluctant guests. *Uh-oh.*

"Listen up, Angel," Hunter said, brandishing the cuffs. "I'm going to watch over you for Jake, but you give me trouble, and I'll drag you to Voltaire on a leash. You don't want that." His gaze shifted to the front of my hospital shift, and in a low, smooth tone, he said, "Or do you?"

I clutched the thin fabric at the hospital tunic's neckline, suddenly very aware of my lack of a bra. Rage bloomed behind my eyes: classic alpha-male crap. But that didn't stop a surge of vulnerability and sexual awareness from washing over me. "Go to hell."

He caressed the cuffs with his thumb and brought them toward me, smiling.

Just then a male voice sounded. "Mr. Hunter! Sir! Just a moment, sir!"

I looked up to see a young uniformed policeman dashing toward us. I exhaled in relief.

The cop held out a cell phone. "Sir, the chief wants to speak with you." Likely Hunter had to turn his own off in the ICU. Shoving the handcuffs into their holster at his back, he straightened, pointed at me as he shut my door, and said, "Stay."

I glared, outraged, at his back. *Stay? Again with the stay! Who does he think he is? That tears it. Whatever it takes, I'm not being pushed around by this guy one second longer!*

Right. Brave words. But what are you going to do? Run? You can't outrun him. Okay, then. Outthink him. That shouldn't be too hard. Should it? I looked around for inspiration. I needed to distract him, or at least to buy time. *But how?*

My eyes raked the console. It was as high tech as they came, a veritable cockpit. Rather than a regular keyhole, there was metal flap fit inside the opening on the steering column. I knew it to be an anti-theft system: the car key had a transistor embedded in it that, when brought into proximity to a chip inside the column, enabled the ignition. No match, no start. The flap was to protect the chip inside from electrical interference when the key was out. *Works great.*

So long as no naughty little girl deliberately bypassed the shielding.

I smiled. All I had to do was prop open the metal cover and introduce a jamming source. Of course, the system was impervious to transmissions from normal ambient emissions, like cell phones, for example. But if I could introduce a source of broadband emissions such as, say, an old-fashioned radio transmitter would put out, it would work. Of course, it would have to have much lower voltage. After all, getting fried would rather defeat the purpose of the whole escape-the-bad-guy plan. Then it hit me. The emissions from some old transmitters come from spark coils. So, all I really need is a spark generator, one strong enough to jam the chip in the column but weak enough to be safe. *Do I have such a thing?* My eyes fell to the well-stocked coin holder built into the center console of Hunter's car. *You betcha I do!*

I pulled out the plastic bottle Nestor had given me and shoved the pills into my pocket. Then I dropped a handful of coins into the bottle and popped the top on. Rummaging through the glove compartment, I came on a small black bag containing breath strips, peppermint gum, mini toothbrush and toothpaste, and a handful of individually wrapped toothpicks. *Perfect!*

I ripped open several toothpicks and slipped them into the keyhole, propping open the flap. Then, holding the bottle up against the hole, I shook it vigorously. Voila! A custom-made, low-voltage spark-generator.

But would the effect be enough? The signal was weak, but I know for a fact that jingling coins will set off LED displays. So, there was a chance it would work.

I shook the crap out of that little bottle!

Anxiously, I stared out the windshield. The policeman stood watching Hunter, clearly wishing to be elsewhere. Hunter nodded as he spoke into the phone. His eyes fell on me. I smiled and waved. Hunter frowned as if disgusted and turned his back. *Fine by me.*

Seconds later—just before my hand fell off—Hunter handed the phone to the cop and walked toward the car. I kept the bottle going as long as I dared, knocking the toothpicks out and stuffing the bottle into my pocket just as Hunter's line of sight crossed the dash.

He got behind the wheel, took out his cell phone, and tossed it on the console between us, then fitted his key in the ignition. I held my breath. He turned it. Nothing happened. He turned it again. *Nothing.* He pulled the key out, glared at it, rammed it back in the hole, and twisted it viciously. *Nothing.* I put my hand to my mouth to hide my smile. *God, I love science!*

"Son of a bitch!" Hunter smacked the steering wheel.

I leaned forward, sliding his cell phone off the console onto my seat. "What's wrong?"

Hunter glared. "Sit back! You're in my way."

I shrugged and leaned back, shoving his phone into the space between the console and my seat. I heard it drop softly to the floor.

Hunter hit the wheel again. "High-tech piece of shit." He heaved an angry sigh and put his hand over the console. That hand froze as a puzzled look crossed his rugged features. "Where the hell's my cell phone?"

"What cell phone?"

"My fucking cell phone. I put it right here."

"I didn't see a phone. Not even a fornicating one." I smiled, totally innocent. *Heh, heh.*

"The hell you didn't." Hunter grabbed my good shoulder and pushed me forward. His hand delved between the cushions of my seat.

"Any excuse to cop a feel, eh, Hunter?"

"You wish." He stuck his hand between the console and my seat where I'd dropped the phone. I held my breath. He pulled his hand out with a jerk: empty. *Whew!* Hunter scrunched up his eyebrows. "I put it right here."

"Having a senior moment?"

If looks could kill, I'd've been dead, buried, and decomposed.

Hunter looked out the windshield, but the cop with the cell

was gone. "Shit. Wait here."

I snapped off a left-handed salute. "Right here," I said.

Hunter huffed in disgust, then angled out of the car and headed for the hospital. I waited until he was out of sight, grinned triumphantly, and then hightailed it, as Jake would say, to the nearest bus stop.

CHAPTER FOUR

By the time I reached my neighborhood—a student ghetto near the University of Chicago—the sun had seared the horizon red. The sky above merged orange, pink, and purple as the buildings turned featureless in the fading light. Though the blistering heat had dissipated, sweat beaded on my upper lip. I wiped it off with the back of my hand and walked even faster.

Mostly renovated brownstones with fenced backyards and large porches, the area had once housed Chicago's Jazz Age elite, its formerly elegant buildings now carved into tiny three-room apartments. Most were rented by students. In a few weeks, the neighborhood would be filled to capacity: school flags hanging as curtains; soiled, sagging couches on every other porch; and chaotic jungles of potted plants on the windowsills. For now, all was blissfully quiet.

I knew better than to go to my apartment; that'd be the first place Hunter would look. Instead, I set out in search of my neighbor, Zach Banks. I knew he'd let me crash with him, no questions asked, *if* I could actually find him. My best bet would be to locate his trailer—an old moving van—and if all else failed, I could simply look for Fido.

At the end of the block, I spotted the van, backed up tight to a tall wooden fence surrounding a large backyard. The place belonged to Mrs. Cape, a nice older lady who was happy to have a polite, God-fearing, young bull-rider about, especially one in tight blue jeans.

Yes, I said bull-rider.

An Illinois-born country boy, Zach rode bulls for a living. And, yes, that made him a "Chicago bull-rider"—he's heard that one a time or two. And Fido? Fido—his temporary moniker—was a yearling descended from a long line of champion bucking bulls. Two weeks earlier, after Zach passed out drunk following a competition in Albuquerque, he woke to find himself the happy, if hungover, owner of a four-hundred-pound prize bull calf worth, potentially, a few hundred grand if he lived up to his breeding. Even if he couldn't remember how he won Fido, when the former owner showed up the next day with a bunch of friends, all shouldering Louisville Sluggers, he knew it was time to get out of town.

Needless to say, a Chicago neighborhood, even with abnormally large backyards and neighbors willing to hide half-wild cattle for kicks, was no place to keep such an animal. But Zach had little choice. Since then, we neighbors had helped Zach keep watch for landlords, dog catchers, and cops, occasionally hastening Fido out of the neighborhood in the nick of time. It turns out that hiding livestock from the law will bring out the inner Jesse James in the most urbane suburbanite—in Chicago anyway. Neighborhood legend would live off this story for generations to come. And sure, our plan wouldn't work forever, but it only had to hold for a few more days while Zach finalized the deal with a buyer he'd found.

Sidling up behind the van, I lifted the lever on the gate and let myself into the backyard. I squinted into the deepening darkness, trying to spot the calf. It shouldn't have been so hard. A Brahma, Fido was already heavily muscled; his hindquarters were solid black and his front half a rich reddish-tan with black spots leading up the thick dappled hump of his powerful shoulders. With a black blaze on his rectangular face, deep black eyes, and small horns budding from his flat forehead, he

67

reminded me a bit of Jake.

Once my eyes adjusted, I saw him. Head down and gently bobbing, he fed from a large bucket. I grimaced. The truth is, I have to fight off a bubbling urge in my colon that says *run* whenever I get near him. Sure, I want to help Zach, and yes, Fido's pretty in his own way—he has incredibly long, feathery lashes and round dark eyes that would melt a bunny's heart—but in a few years he could weigh over two thousand pounds and buck six feet in the air with the torque of a car turning at a hundred miles an hour. So, yeah, he scares the hell out of me.

"Zach?" I whispered.

"Over here, Darlin'," came the response from around the corner.

Keeping my back to the wall and my eye on the bull, I inched toward the voice. Zach sat on concrete steps at the back door, a silhouette in the dimming light. He reached over and flicked the switch on a small electric campfire lamp. I smiled. It was hard not to.

In his early twenties, Zach had a classic cowboy physique: trim with carved musculature. His arms, shoulders, and thighs were especially fine-toned, a by-product of routinely holding onto almost two tons of bull-flesh trying to whiplash him into the ground. His face was narrow with tanned, well-defined features, sunbaked lines radiating from the corners of his eyes, and the stubble of a blond beard lining his jaw. He wore a white t-shirt, jeans, and boots, along with the classic black cowboy hat pulled down over what I knew to be cornflower-blue eyes, a masterpiece right out of the movies. As usual, my first thought was: *Yum!*

Good thing he had a girlfriend. By which I meant, *Damn it, he has a girlfriend!*

Zach grinned and pushed his hat up with an index finger. "Hey, pretty lady," he said. "I like the new look: no bra."

I startled, then glanced down at my lightweight medical shift. As usual, the merest hint of breeze had my nipples at full attention. "Is that the first thing you can think of to say?"

"Momma always said to start a conversation with a compliment," he drawled.

I rubbed the side of my nose with a finger. I guess in "guy world" that made sense.

His grin turned into a frown. "Why are you wearing a hospital thingy?"

Flopping down beside him, my glee at defeating Hunter having worn off, I was nearly lightheaded with fatigue. My shoulder ached deep in the bone and burned on the surface.

Zach put his arm around my waist. "What's going on, Darlin'?"

I leaned against him, comforted by the heat of his body, and told him what had happened. He listened, holding my hand. I broke down at the part where Jake crashed, and the paramedics barely managed to resuscitate him. Sniffling, I apologized for being such a baby, but he just pulled me close and kissed the top of my head.

"Ah, now. Sometimes taking life eight seconds at a time is all a body can do. Don't you waste one of 'em worrying about what people are thinking, or you're going to end up face down on the ground every time." He lifted my chin with a finger and smiled warmly. "And trust me, there's more than dirt on the arena floor."

I scrubbed the tears out of my eyes and tried to smile back. "I'll keep that in mind."

I finished the story, ending with my getaway from Hunter. Zach's eyes crinkled with amusement. "That's showing him. I hope you broke that car good and proper."

"I don't know. Hunter's resourceful. I mean, he worked his way from walking a beat in New Orleans to being one of the most successful and rich businessmen in Chicago. If I didn't dislike him so much, I'd be impressed."

Zach crooked his head and peered at me. "You don't like him, huh?"

"No! And what's that grin supposed to mean?"

He shrugged. "Oh, just somethin' in your look. And you surely bring him up a lot."

I wriggled my butt on the steps. "That doesn't mean anything. I find him competent, that's all. Sure, he takes care of himself. He's got presence, and he's *moderately* clever. And he does keep me on my toes; not a lot of people can do that."

Zach laughed.

"What?" My face flushed.

"And you don't like him?"

"No! Besides, he's mean to me," I said, too petulantly for my own comfort.

"Aw, poor thing," Zach said, but not unkindly.

I elbowed him in the ribs. "Cut it out! I've never done anything to him. But he's determined to make my life miserable. And stop looking so pleased with yourself!" Movement from the corner of the yard caught my eye. I sat up, grimacing at the tug on my wound. "Is that Mrs. Cape's Chihuahua?" My heart leapt. "Oh, my God! Fido will squish him!

Zach pushed himself off the steps in one fluid motion and headed into the yard with long, easy strides. "Don't panic, now. I got it."

So he said. But my heart went into overdrive as Fido, seeing the tiny dog approach, lifted his head and stared intently at it. As Zach neared, Fido snorted, fixated on little Butch. From my optic, that look said: "Lunch!" I jumped to my feet as the bull's restlessness increased. "Zach!"

He didn't look back but gave a little wave. "I said I got it. Don't fuss."

I bit at my thumb. "But—"

Zach whistled. Fido looked over his shoulder, but then swung his head back toward the dog, massive neck muscles rippling. Zach whistled again. "That's enough, you. Let that boy be. He ain't even a mouthful for you." To my astonishment, Zach walked up to the bull and shoved it—*yes, shoved it*— to one side. "Don't make me cross, now."

I sucked in a deep breath and readied myself to call for help.

The calf turned, all four-hundred-plus pounds, and stared at Zach. Fido lowered his head and squared his stance. I yelped, about to jump out of my skin, when Zach suddenly smacked the side of the bull's head. "Don't get uppity with me, boy. You mind your manners."

He didn't hit the calf very hard, but it was apparently enough to do the job. Fido huffed once as if to say "fine, I'm a vegetarian anyway," and then returned to munching on grass.

My shoulders went limp, terror rushing out of me like a balloon deflating. Zach ambled over and picked up the dog, carrying it back in the crook of his arm. I did some deep breaths as Zach walked up to the back door, opened it, and gently let Butch back into his house.

"I'm going to be so glad when you sell that animal," I blurted. "I know you like him, and he's very pretty." Zach grimaced at that. "For a potential killing machine, anyway."

"Oh, his kind's only dangerous when you're bucking 'em." Zach sat back down on the step. "Outside of the arena even the rankest fellas are usually pretty easygoing."

I dropped down at his side. "Easygoing? His father was named Evil Forces. He's cousin to Satan's Revenge and brother of Scene of the Crash. That's hardly a cuddly lineage."

Zach smiled, lifted his hat, and pushed his bangs off his forehead, then settled it back on his head. "We gotta give him a proper name. The boys'll laugh themselves silly at Fido.

Although, I'll admit it was right clever of you to use that on the pet application."

I bit at my hangnail. "I can't help it if the landlord thought a bull-doggie was a new dog breed. Hey, how about Bane of My Existence? That sounds like a bull-riding bull's name."

Zach grunted. "That's a bit high and mighty. And they're called bucking bulls."

"Okay, fine. How about Satan's Snot? Or Lucifer's Lackey? Or Get the Hell Off My Back Before I Snap Your Spine?"

He laughed brightly. "That last one's a might long, but you may be on to something."

I rolled my eyes. "Let the new owner name him. Is he still picking him up on Thursday?"

Zach lowered his head and massaged the bridge of his nose. "Might be a bit longer." He leaned back and looked me in the eye. "So, tell me about that file you say got lost."

Zach's hesitation was unusual for this normally straight-forward man. Narrowing my eyes, I said, "Has something gone wrong with the sale?"

"Maybe those boys were right, and you just misplaced it. The file, that is."

Brought back to my frustration, I said, "Don't *you* start in on me. That file was on the desk. I put it right in the middle. I had just walked by George's cage and—Oh my gosh. George! He's still at the office!"

"Jake's parrot?"

"Strictly speaking, George is a budgerigar, which is a subset of the parrot species—"

Zach raised an eyebrow.

"Yeah, the parrot. Anyway, Jake takes George home every night, so I should go get him in case—" I stopped, biting my lip. I didn't even want to say it: in case Jake dies.

Zach pushed himself off the stoop. "You mean you should

take care of him *until* Jake gets better. And so you should, Dar-lin'. I'll put Fido in the van. Then we'll take my truck."

First- and third-floor lights brightened the old Victorian-manor-now-office building. That meant that our elderly office neigh-bors, Mrs. Naidenheim, the "doll doctor," and Mr. Keeper, the watchmaker, were still there. That wasn't particularly unusual. Mr. Keeper often worked until dawn coaxing some scarred antique timepiece back to life. Mr. Keeper needed to get a life. And her genteel manner notwithstanding, Mrs. Naidenheim would have been happy to help. A fact that was obvious to everyone except Mr. Keeper.

I unlocked the front door, and Zach and I climbed to Jake's office on the second floor. As we stood at the entrance, my heart fluttered. What if Jake never came back? I'd counted on him like I'd counted on my dad. What if I ended up lost and purposeless again? What if—?

Zach put his hand on my back. "You okay, Darlin'?"

I nodded, took a deep breath, and went in. As we entered, George, Jake's parakeet, rose from the bottom of his huge six-foot-high cage, beating his wings and flying about until he landed on his perch. He dipped his snow-white head over his teal body and beat his wings in agitation. I crossed to the cage, picked up a seed-encrusted treat stick from a nearby bowl, and slipped it between the bars. "Easy, sweetie," I said.

" 'Pretty little cajun queen,' " he squawked.

"What'd he say?" Zach asked.

"It's what he calls me. I wish I knew why." George pecked away at the bribe, as I'd seen him do for Jake so many times. The familiar scene—and the fear that I might never see it again—brought a resurgence of dread. Placing the treat in his dish, I clapped my hands together. "Okay, let's find that folder. Look under everything, over everything, on everything." I opened the filing cabinet to my left. "I'll go through these. You take Jake's desk, okay?"

"Will do," Zach said as he rummaged through papers in Jake's inbox. I saw him wipe the back of his hand on his jeans. "Not the neatest of fellas, was he?"

"What's wrong?" I said, looking over my shoulder as I rifled through files.

"There's black stuff everywhere. Dirt, maybe soot."

"Humph," I said as I closed the top drawer and opened the next down. "He's a slob. And God forbid I straighten things up. Why do you think I'm letting you search his desk? When he gets back, someone is going to have to take the blame for messing with his personal things."

"So you're going to throw me under that bus?"

"Under a two-ton bus, under a two-ton bull. I thought you could survive anything."

He went back to searching the desk. "Yeah, but getting run over by a two-ton bull versus Jake Thibodaux? I'd take the bull, thank you."

I laughed. "Me too."

Twenty minutes later, we'd gone through everything and found no file. Zach, however, found something in a former linen closet where Jake kept personal items, including a pile of magazines with a hand towel draped over them that I, to date, had pointedly avoided peeking under. Given the big grin on Zach's face when he lifted the cloth, I knew my instincts had been correct. A moment later, he motioned to me.

"Come take a look at this."

"No, thanks. Pornography doesn't do anything for me." He raised an eyebrow as if he wasn't buying the prudery. "Well, not that kind anyway."

"Those aren't what I'm talking about. It's something else." He was pointing at the dusty middle shelf. It was empty except for a clean rectangular patch, about eight by ten inches, too small for a file or even a notebook. Something had been there for a long time. And based on how spotless the patch was now, whatever had been there had been removed *very* recently.

"Any ideas what was there?" Zach said, as we stood contemplating the empty area.

"Not a clue. I only saw in the closet briefly, when he got the toolbox or tackle out. I never looked inside. It was, um, *private.*"

Zach chuckled. "Yeah, I saw why." He leaned slightly closer. A twinkle in his eye, he said, "So what kind of pornography *does* do it for you?"

I made a "wouldn't you like to know" face and shut the door, a bit too forcefully apparently, causing a startled George to flutter around his cage. "Settle down, cowboy."

Zach leaned back, as if affronted. " 'You talkin' to me? You talkin' to me?' " He turned to me as he walked up to George's cage. "Is this boid talkin' to me?"

I groaned, trying not to laugh. "That's pathetic, the worst DeNiro I've ever heard."

He smiled back. "No good, huh?"

"Horrible. I'll get his transport cage. Do you want to grab the bird for me?"

"Only if you'll return the favor."

"Don't be a smart-aleck," I said, flushing and warming to the banter's sexual undertones. He's got a girlfriend, I reminded myself. And you're not a poacher, not so far. "Get the bird."

He shuddered slightly. "Nunh-uh. Seriously. Birds creep me out."

I gaped at him. "And bitch-slapping quarter-ton bulls doesn't?"

"It's not the same. Birds wriggle in your hands." He lips curled back in distaste. "Yuck."

I shrugged. "Okay, whatever." I went to the closet and pulled out the small cage Jake used to transport George. There was a note sticking out underneath it, which fell to the floor, landing face up and revealing my name in Jake's handwriting. "What's this?" I handed the cage to Zach and ripped it open. It said, "Madison, if you're reading this, something has happened to me. Get the key from George, open the box, and follow the instructions."

Mouth opened, I stared dumbfounded at the paper in my hands.

Zach read it over my shoulder and whistled low. "Well, don't that just beat all?"

"My God, Zach. Jake must have known he was in danger!" I bit my lip. "But why didn't he say anything to me directly?"

Zach shook his head.

"We need to find that key." I turned to George. "Where's the key?" The bird dipped its head to clean its feathers. "George, where's the key?"

"Darlin', it's a bird," Zach whispered in my ear. "It can't carry on conversations."

I shoved him back lightly and clucked my tongue. "I know that. But Jake said to get the key from him. Maybe he's been triggered to say something. Come on, pretty bird," I said, turning to George. "Give mommy the key."

" 'Pretty little cajun queen,' " it squawked.

"Okay, then give pretty little cajun queen the key," Zach said.

I elbowed him in the gut. "That's not helping. Come on, George. Where is the key?"

Zach and I pleaded for several moments. In the end, the bird only fluttered about a bit and then finally lit on his perch and pooped on the cage floor.

"This isn't working," I said, straightening up and clucking my tongue. Okay, I know birds aren't all that smart. I mean there's a reason that it was Lassie, not Tweety, who kept rescuing all those klutzy kids from collapsed mines. But I still felt let down. "We're just going to have to search again. You start in the bathroom and circle counter clockwise."

But Zach was staring at the cage, his eyes crinkled with amusement.

"Pay attention," I said. "I'll start clockwise, in a spiral pattern—"

He cocked his head at the cage.

"Hey, you. Pay attention. We have to find that key."

Zach gently grabbed my good shoulder and turned me toward the cage.

I looked, saw nothing, and threw my hands in the air. "What?"

He grinned and pointed, gesturing at a toy in George's cage: a wooden stick tied with a variety of ribbons, brightly colored bells, and . . . and a key! I groaned. "Now why couldn't Jake just say get the key from the *cage*?"

" '*Pretty little cajun queen!*' "

"Yeah, yeah, tell it to the Navy," I groused.

"Marines," Zach said.

I reached into the large cage, grabbing the key from the toy. "What?"

"The Marines. The expression is: Tell it to the Marines."

"Well, the Marines are a subsidiary of the Navy, aren't they? So, what's the difference?"

He barked out a laugh. "Girl, you better never let one of them boys hear you say that."

I rolled my eyes. "Whatever. Look—there's a note attached to the key. It says: 'Get the lockbox from the middle shelf of the old linen closet.' "

I looked at Zach, and he looked at me. We both looked at the linen closet. I groaned fatalistically. "He meant that missing box, didn't he?"

"I'd bet my boot heels on it."

I sighed. "Crap."

Zach and I had searched every inch of the office, just in case there was another box or the one from the closet had been misplaced. We came up empty, so thirty minutes later we were at the foot of the front porch, him carrying George's cage and me cradling a package of bird food in my good arm. Though the building stood in what had once been an isolated suburb, the city had, over the years, crept ever closer. I paused to look at the forest of skyscrapers silhouetted against the milky-gray night sky. The air thrummed with the sound of traffic, the swift whoosh of cars, the weighty rumble of trucks, and, underneath it all, the rhythm of the "L" as it clunked its way over the tracks. "I really admire the architecture of Chicago," I said. "It's like a forest of delta functions surrounded by a chaotic sea of humanity."

Zach shook his head. "I really like you. But sometimes you are *so* weird."

I puckered my brow. "I thought that was kind of romantic, actually."

Just then Mrs. Naidenheim came out of the door of her little shop and stepped onto the porch. "Ah, there is someone here. Clarisse is always right," she said, a smile on her round, wrinkled and meticulously made-up face.

"Who's Clarisse?" Zach said to me in a sotto voce.

"Um, it's one of her dolls," I whispered. "Edwardian era. It's very pretty, actually—about three feet tall, porcelain, with large blue eyes and curly blond hair. Occasionally, she channels Mrs. Naidenheim's late sister Annabelle in order to warn her of danger."

His eyes went wide. "Sorry, what?"

"To be honest, most of the time what Clarisse hears turns out to be squirrels on the roof or branches scratching the windows. But she did warn of us of a fire in the bushes by the porch once. Mr. Keeper got a little careless with a cigar. And there were the pipes that burst in the basement. Other little things like that. So, it's better to pay attention to her than not."

"Wait. A *doll?*"

"Yes, I know. Just . . . go with it. And pray you never get that lonely." I turned back to the sweet-faced old lady and climbed the stairs to greet her, Zach in tow. "Mrs. Naidenheim, I'd like to introduce my friend Zach Banks."

Zach took his hat off. "Ma'am. Always a treat to meet a lovely lady under starry skies."

I rolled my eyes, but Mrs. Naidenheim's face lit up, her peach blusher turning crimson. "Aren't you the scoundrel? Madison, you should watch out for this young man."

"I'll do that. And how are you tonight, Mrs. Naidenheim?"

"Better now that I know it's you. It's been an odd day. Clarisse heard someone upstairs this morning. It turned out to be no one, but then some police and men in suits came earlier this evening. Is everything all right? Why do you have our little one?" She poked a finger through the cage and petted George on his sea-foam-colored back. "Isn't he going home with Jake?"

I cast an uneasy glance at Zach. "Jake's, um, not feeling well. I'm taking care of George until he's better." I felt bad not saying more, but I couldn't bring myself to relive the day again.

"Oh, dear. Well, you tell him I'll make my lasagna special for him, as soon as he's well."

I gave her my best smile. "That'll speed up his recovery. But shouldn't you be going home? Too much work isn't good for your social life. That's what you're always telling me."

She actually giggled. "Now, you know I don't have a social life. Although," she paused, glancing timidly to the stairs that led to the third floor. "I *did* notice that our Mr. Keeper is still burning the midnight oil. I have cookies that I've just taken out of the microwave. Maybe . . . that is . . . I was thinking . . . I could . . ." She stammered to a stop.

I looked at Zach, who was also suppressing a smile. "You should invite him to join you."

Her hand fluttered to her neckline. "Oh, I . . . I wouldn't want to disturb him."

Zach leaned in, his six-foot-four frame dwarfing her. "Oh, go on. We menfolk love cookies. Especially in the company of a pretty little cookie like you," he added with a wink.

I barely controlled a groan as Mrs. Naidenheim, grinning from ear to ear, said, "Now, you're just terrible. Madison, isn't he just terrible?"

"Yes, ma'am. He definitely is. And, I'm sorry, but we need to be going now."

"Of course. You two children have a nice evening."

Zach and I descended the stairs into the cooling night. The stars were actually out now—what stars could be seen against the washed-out city sky. A pervasive smell of garlic-laden suppers mixed with the aroma of Mrs. Naidenheim's arthritis ointment and some enthusiastic gardener's fertilizer gave character to the night.

"Sweet lady," Zach said.

I looked back and saw Mrs. Naidenheim glancing nervously up toward the third floor. "I hope I still have those urges when I'm that old."

"Amen to that. You and me both!"

I heard a window rise behind us. "Madison, is that you?" a dignified voice called out.

As Zach put the birdcage in the narrow backseat of his red pickup, I turned. A thin, elderly man leaned out the window. He wore a turquoise short-sleeved shirt buttoned to the top, with a red and white polka-dot bow tie. His shirt was tucked into khaki pants pulled halfway up his chest. I didn't know about the cookies, but he could sure use Mrs. Naidenheim to teach him how to dress. He lifted his thick spectacles and peered underneath them. "Is that you?"

I waved. "Good evening, Mr. Keeper. How are you?"

Mrs. Naidenheim rather quickly left the porch to stand on the grass. Peering up at him, she waved. "Hello, Frederick."

He started, banging his head on the window. "Ah, Millie. What a pleasure to see you."

"Yes, yes, very. I, um—" She glanced at me, and I nodded to her. "I was wondering if you might like to join me for some fresh-baked cookies. If you're not too busy, that is."

"Certainly." He cleared his throat. "Very kind. Very kind, indeed."

Zach and I shared a grin as he put the rest of George's things on the seat beside the cage.

"But first," Mr. Keeper said, "I was wondering if our young lady knew anything about that paraphernalia in the bushes on the side of the house."

I looked up at him. "What's that, Mr. Keeper?"

"Right over there," he said, pointing to his right. "On the side of the house, beneath Jake's windows. I noticed it earlier when I was watering my flowers."

"I'll get a flashlight." Zach leaned into the car.

"We'll check it out," I said, walking toward the side yard. As Zach caught up with me, a window rose again. We looked up to see Mr. Keeper leaning out of his side office window.

"It's over there," he said, pointing. "That bush."

Zach and I searched the thick branches—a task difficult enough in broad daylight and just plain annoying in the dark— before finally finding a large manila-colored envelope. I took it, flicking off pieces of greenery from my arm, as something heavy fell to the ground. It was a metal lockbox, rectangular and about eight by ten inches. Zach and I squatted by it. He shone the flashlight over it. "It's dusty," he said, raising an eyebrow meaningfully.

"And the perfect size?" I said, my heart racing.

"Yup, for the empty patch on the shelf."

We both looked up. "Right below Jake's window." I smiled broadly, and he smiled back.

Zach straightened. "Let's go where we can have privacy. I'll put these in the truck."

"Okay." As I walked back into the front yard, the third-floor window slid open again.

"Do you have it?" Mr. Keeper said.

"Yes, sir. We're going to take it with us."

"Oh, and Madison, would you ask Jake if he'd be so kind as to tell the landlord that he needs to be more sparse in his application of fertilizer? The odor of manure has clung to my apartment since mid-morning, and few people say 'no' to our good Mr. Thibodaux."

"Yes, I noticed the smell too, Mr. Keeper. I'll ask Jake."

"Thank you. And I'll be right down, Millie," he called out toward the front porch.

Mrs. Naidenheim's eyes shone. I winked at her. "Good luck. And don't—"

A loud explosion split the air. My body jerked in shock. Knees buckling, I fell to the ground, stunned at the sight of flames shooting from the window where Mr. Keeper had stood!

CHAPTER FIVE

I couldn't move, couldn't breathe. I stared, mouth open, kneeling paralyzed on the ground. Then Zach was there, dragging me to my feet. "You okay?" he shouted.

All I could do was nod dumbly.

"Oh dear. Oh dear, oh dear!" Mrs. Naidenheim stood dazed on the porch, her eyes fixated on the conflagration above her. She stumbled and went down on one knee, her hands trembling wildly. Zach reached her just as she fell. He scooped her up and carried her to me. He laid her on the ground, and I fell to my knees beside her. Zach grabbed my arm, putting it on hers. "Take care of her!" Then he turned and ran back for the house.

"Zach, no! It's too late!" I tried to rise, but Mrs. Naidenheim grabbed my hand.

"Dear, dear. Oh, no. No. No." Her whole body shook in a palsied tremor, and her eyes were wide and wild. "What happened? What happened?"

I grabbed her by both shoulders. "Mrs. Naidenheim, you have to calm down. Millie, look at me!" Her body practically convulsed. She turned to me, no recognition in her eyes, and then her head lolled back, and the color drained from her face. She slumped in my arms, the sudden weight yanking hard at my stitches.

"No! God, no! Millie! Millie! Can you hear me?" I fumbled to free a hand and pressed it to her jugular. No pulse!

"Call 911!" I yelled into the night, my crisis training taking over. I laid her on the ground and began chest compressions. Hot tears flooded my eyes, but I blinked them away and shut out the roaring flames and heat at my back. *Zach's going to be okay. He has to be! He has to!* "Help!" I yelled, my voice breaking. "Call 911!"

A man fell heavily to his knees beside me. I turned. "Hunter! Where did you—?"

"You got this? Do you need me to take it?"

"No, I got it," I croaked. "Zach—my friend—he went back in the building!"

Hunter jumped to his feet and ran toward the house. I didn't look. I wanted to! I wanted to run after him, but if I stopped, Mrs. Naidenheim would die. I swallowed hard, my throat raw from gasping back tears, and kept pushing on her chest. Her body rocked to the rhythm of my compressions, inert as one of her dolls. *Come on! You can do it, Millie! Come back!*

Suddenly, I was being lifted to my feet. I struggled to break away. "I have to help her!"

"It's okay, we got her," a voice said. Strong arms pulled me to one side as a uniformed man went down on one knee beside Mrs. Naidenheim, covering her mouth with an oxygen mask. Another paramedic threw a defibrillator to the ground. I stumbled back, slipping away from the hands that held me. Bright pulsing lights flared in my peripheral vision, and I fought to focus amid the swirl. Orange flames engulfed the upper floor of the building, spiked tendrils—like living barbs—shot high into the night, and black smoke billowed out against the gray night sky.

Zach! Hunter!

I ran for the house, pushing past firemen. Someone clutched at my back. I slapped at the hands and wriggled free of the grip. Then they were both there, in the doorway! I stumbled backward, nearly collapsing from relief. *Thank God! Oh, thank God!*

Hunter had Zach by the arm. They half ran, half staggered out of the building. Zach went down to his knees, and Hunter hauled him up. Throwing the younger man's arm over his shoulder, he pulled Zach off the steps. Two firemen ran forward and took Zach. One put a mask on his face and led him away. Hunter waved off another's help, then coughed hard, wincing and putting a hand to his chest as his whole body convulsed. As he looked up, I caught his gaze.

"Are you okay?" I mouthed.

Nodding, he jerked his head toward Zach, who now sat on the lowered tailgate of his truck, clutching an oxygen mask to his face as a medic took his vitals. I jogged over to him. Zach's face was streaked black. Sweat soaked his clothes and plastered his blond hair to his skull. His eyes met mine, and he shook his head. I understood: Mr. Keeper was dead.

For several seconds, I stood beside him, gently rubbing his arm. He put the mask down and nodded to a space behind me. I turned. Two men pulled a body cart across the lawn, its wheels dancing over the grass, then jumping and shaking against the concrete of the sidewalk. Mrs. Naidenheim lay strapped onto it, her body wrapped in a blanket, a breathing tank strapped beside her. I sighed in relief. *She's alive!*

I caught the eye of one of the men, who shrugged as he and his partner rushed her toward the ambulance. She's alive for now, the look said. They pushed the cart into the rear of the vehicle hard, causing the wheels to fold up with a gut-wrenching clang. The man climbed in beside her as the other ran to the front. The vehicle's lights flared. It jumped into gear and shrieked into the night.

I sat down hard beside Zach. He drew me close. "Eight seconds at a time, Darlin'," he whispered into my hair.

It was almost all I could do to simply nod. "I . . . I need to check on Hunter. Will you be okay?" He smiled but then started coughing again, the hacking coming from deep inside his chest. A paramedic walked by, grabbed Zach's hand that held the mask, pushed the plastic back over his nose and mouth, and kept walking. Zach raised an eyebrow, his chagrin clear even through the translucent covering, and breathed deeply.

I nodded, patting his shoulder. "I'll be back."

By now, a crowd spilled onto the neighboring yards. Along with cops, firefighters, and rescue personnel, I recognized local business owners and a half dozen other passersby. The blaze seemed under control as water streamed into the upper floors from braced fire hoses, but the air was thick with the oppressive stench of soot carried on the flame-stoked breeze. I looked around for Hunter, moving between gawking onlookers, when I noticed Zach's hat on the ground by the porch. I picked it up and rubbed off the dirt. After all, a cowboy needs his hat.

One of the firemen walked by me, calling out to another: "One body, top floor. Not a lot left. Ask the Captain if we can get it now. The floor's too unstable to leave it there."

Mr. Keeper. My throat tightened as despair rushed through me. Lowering my head, I hugged the hat to my chest and stood still, letting the world rush around me, trying to find a still, safe place inside. I heard a familiar voice call out to me. "Lilly?" I said in response.

She jogged up to me. Her muscles were as taut as mummy skin. I could almost feel adrenaline surging through her. She said, "We heard the call on our radio. What happened?"

Wearily, I shrugged. "I don't know. There was no warning. And, Mr. Keeper wasn't even supposed to be here. None of us was." I swallowed hard.

She said nothing, her expression dark and angry as she stared at the building.

That's when I spotted Nestor at the far right of the lawn. He was speaking with a neighbor and listening with the intensity of a man whose life depended on what he was hearing. When the neighbor shook his head and walked away, Nestor looked up at the window where Mr. Keeper had stood. His eyes seemed full of dread, as if he'd heard something he couldn't bear to believe.

"How well did Nestor know Mr. Keeper?" I asked Lilly.

"What?" She glanced over her shoulder at Nestor and then turned back to stare at the house. "I don't know. Ask him." Her attention was clearly fixated on the blaze above. She shook her head. "Timing is everything," she said quietly. Before I could even ask her to explain that cryptic comment, we were distracted by a shout from the doorway. We looked at the same time. Two firefighters came out carrying a body bag between them. My head dropped again. Lilly reached out and laid a reassuring hand on my shoulder. "What are you doing here?" Despite the gentleness of her touch, her voice had a tight edge to it.

"I came to get Jake's pet bird. And, then, I started looking . . . and, well, the important thing is, I think I found something."

She went stock still, not even breathing, as if she were an impala who'd just heard a rustling sound in the grass: Wind? Herd-mate? Predator? Finally, she said, "What?"

"A box. Lilly, I think there's a clue—We should tell Nestor—"

"No!" Her hand on my shoulder tightened painfully. I winced. She stepped closer, lowering her voice, conspiratorially. "Listen to me. I know you trust him, but there are things you don't know and that can get people killed." She glanced around. I followed her gaze and saw Nestor occupied in conversation with a fireman, some twenty meters away. She put her back to him, blocking him from my view. "I know how to end this. You need to come with me."

"I don't know, Lilly. Maybe we should—"

Hunter walked up, his dark eyes glowering. "I'll take it from here," he said.

Lilly stepped between us. "I don't need your help, Hunter. I've got her."

His gaze raked over her. "Oh, aren't you brave? Get out of my way."

She threw back her shoulders and put one hand on his chest, her other going toward her gun. "You don't get to talk to me like that, old man."

Hunter snorted and flicked her hand away. "You'd better be careful, little girl. Everyone knows you're jonesing for that promotion. I know the people who can make it happen, and those who can make sure it *never* happens. Do you really want to cross me?"

Lilly hesitated, doubt creasing her brows. My eyes narrowed, defensive instincts rearing up like a lioness protecting her sister from a pride-male. Sure, I was grateful to Hunter for helping Zach, but that didn't mean I'd let him pick on Lilly when she was only trying to help me.

I stepped toward him. "Can't you act like a human being for one minute?"

"You didn't seem to think I was such a monster when I rescued your boyfriend's ass."

"He's not my boy—Damn it, don't change the subject!"

"How about this for a subject?" He pointed behind me at the blaze. "That wouldn't have happened if you hadn't pulled that harebrained stunt and run away."

Stunned, I stepped back. "Are you insane? Why would you say that?"

"What do you think happened here, Angel? That was a bomb, and I'll bet it was meant for you. If you'd come with me today, this might not have happened. But, no, you're too damn good to play by the rules. Your type always is."

The implication staggered me. "It . . . it could have been an accident. A water heater—"

He snorted. "On the top floor?"

"I, maybe—maybe Mr. Keeper had some kind of equipment, like, a, a propane tank—" I looked back at the flames writhing on the roof. A cold horror settled in my stomach. *Could it be true? Was this meant for me? And that meant—Oh, my God. Mr. Keeper died because of me? And Mrs. Naidenheim? What if she dies? That'll be my fault too!*

Lilly shouldered me aside. "What makes you so sure it was a bomb, Hunter? And while we're at it, how did you get here so fast? Mike over there told me you were already here when the firefighters arrived, but the station is only a block away. Maybe I should look into that."

Hunter glared at her. "Watch your mouth, girl. You think you can start accusing—"

My temper snapped. I whirled on Hunter, slapped him with Zach's hat, and then punched him hard in the chest with my other hand. "You son of a bitch! A man died here! You are not going to blame that on me! Bastard!"

Hunter barely flinched as I struck him again. He grabbed my hand. "Calm down, damn it. I didn't say it's your fault a man died. His death is on the killer's head. But you didn't have to make it easy for him."

My mouth dropped open. I was so appalled by the creeping terror that he might be right that I couldn't formulate a response.

Suddenly, I was being whirled around. Nestor gripped my upper arms hard. His gaze bore down on me, clearly oblivious to Hunter and his partner. "What did he look like?"

"Wh—what? Who?"

"Take it easy," Lilly said, reaching for Nestor's arm.

But he shrugged her off, almost absently, as if he barely registered anyone's presence but mine. "I got a description of a stranger wandering around here this morning. A man. You *have* to tell me what he looked like." Then his eyes roamed my face, as if desperately looking for some affirmation of . . . of what?

"I don't—I wasn't here." I started to say.

Hunter stepped forward, leaning in toward Nestor. "Back off, boy," he commanded as he yanked one of Nestor's hands free of my shoulder. I couldn't tell if he was trying to protect me or just playing alpha and making certain he was seen as the biggest bad around.

I gasped in shock as, with brown eyes blazing, Nestor shoved Hunter with the heel of his hand. "I bloodied you once, old man. I'll do it again!"

Hunter slapped his hand away. "Watch who the fuck you put your hands on, boy!"

Without a word, Nestor swung at him. Hunter dodged, lightning quick, but the blow still caught him on the shoulder, staggering him. He bared his teeth and charged, shoulder first, shoving Nestor backward. Nestor ground his heels in and managed to slam his fist into the bigger man's gut. Hunter took the impact with little more than a grunt. Hunter grabbed Nestor's hands, and they pushed against each other, like wrestlers, each grappling for the upper hand. Other men ran up and tried to drag them apart. Lilly grabbed me by the shoulders, pulling me away, but I twisted out of her grip, locked on the sight.

Lilly yanked my arm, literally pulling me off balance. "Leave them alone. This isn't about you. Maybe they'll finally kill each other and get it over with."

The two were dragged apart, three men on each of them.

"What the hell is the matter with Nestor?" I blurted out, still stunned by my normally uber-chill friend's bizarre turn to violence.

Lilly looked over her shoulder, her look dark. "He's on edge."

"Oh, you *think*? What clued you in, the foaming at the mouth?"

"This isn't the first time those two threw down. Last time, Jake practically had to sit on Nestor to get him off. And Nestor wouldn't talk to Jake for weeks."

"Nestor and Hunter have been at it before? What happened?"

"Who knows why men do anything?" She looked me up and down. "Trust me, they're not fighting over you."

I shook my head, trying to digest the information. True, I'd only known Nestor for a few months, but he'd seemed so easygoing. And why hadn't Jake ever said anything about their quarrel? "I know Hunter has a temper, but it's hard to believe he'd disrespect another cop like that, especially in public. Something else must be going on."

Lilly stopped cold and looked at me. I could almost see the wheels turning in her head. She smiled slightly. "What are you saying? That maybe Hunter had a grudge against Jake?"

Surprise forced a blink. "How could you get that out of what I said?"

"Maybe you're on to something. Maybe we ought to look into Hunter's motivations."

"Whoa, hang on! You can't think for a moment that Hunter would hurt Jake!"

"They're supposed to be best buddies. So why, when Jake came north, didn't they go into business together? Hunter's a big success, so why doesn't he cut his pal in on all that money?"

I shifted my weight from one foot to another. "Well . . . yes, that's bothered me a little. But men are weird. They've got all these stupid contradictory rules. Yes, Hunter came north first and became a big success. Maybe Jake thought working for Hunter would be too much like charity. Or maybe Hunter didn't want to be overshadowed by Jake again."

Her eyes brightened. "You're right. Maybe Hunter was jealous of Jake!"

"That's not what I meant! You're getting carried away. We've got real suspects to worry about. Lathos? And the other guy at the hospital? That's where we should look."

She stared purposefully at me. "I found out that Lathos used to live in New Orleans, and guess who once arrested him for vagrancy?"

"Jake?"

"Unh-uh. Hunter." Her eyes shimmered as if in victory.

"But Hunter told Voltaire there was no connection between Lathos and himself or Jake."

"Uh-huh. When Rasmen asked, Hunter just said he hadn't remembered. And Voltaire won't believe anything bad of him. But I think you're on to something. I can get access to Hunter's files; let's take a look." Lilly herded me backward again. "Besides, we need to get you out of here. This explosion might have nothing to do with you, but we can't take any chances."

I stood my ground. "I don't want to go to a jail cell."

"I'm not taking you there. I'll take you someplace safe."

"No. I can't do anything if I'm locked up somewhere. And I'm not going to sit on my ass, safe and cozy, while everyone else looks for Jake's killer. I can take care of myself."

Her eyes narrowed, and for a moment I thought she might just drag me away anyway. Instead, she took a deep breath. She scanned the crowd still around us and put her hands out in a gesture of surrender. "I know what you've probably heard about me, that I only care about getting promoted. And, yeah, I won't lie, I want it. I deserve it. I do the right things.

"But right now, I'm a lot more concerned about things getting further out of control. You have to believe me. I'm not the bad guy here. People don't understand me. They're always trying to fit me into a box, to make me who they think I should be. No matter what I do, it's never enough. So, sometimes I

rebel a little. But that doesn't make me wrong. You know?"

Visions of my mother, Hunter, and even Jake floated before my mind's eye. How often had I had to defend myself, in much the same way, to each? "Yeah, I do." I tossed Zach's hat in my hand, making up my mind. "Okay, we'll do it your way. Let me give Zach his hat first."

She looked ready to protest but then said, "Hurry. I'll get the car; it's back a block."

I jogged over to Zach, who still sat on the tailgate of his truck washing his face with a hand wipe. He looked almost normal.

He grinned. "Thanks! That's my lucky hat. Used it to distract Murderous Intentions one day. Saved me from getting my head stoved-in." He nodded toward where a cluster of police officers still stood. "What was going on over there? What was that fight about?"

"I'm not really sure but I—"

"You!" Hunter's voice rang out.

Uh-oh.

"Trouble's coming," Zach said.

Hunter strode across the yard. Blood stained his collar, and his determined glower said he'd had enough. "You're coming with me! And I mean now!"

"Yikes!" I ran for the front of the truck. "Let's get out of here."

Zach slid off the tailgate and walked to the driver's side. "I can handle him."

"Maybe so, but he's got Voltaire on his side and that could mean jail for both of us!"

"Fair enough," Zach said as he jammed the truck into gear and it leapt out onto the road.

CHAPTER SIX

We loaded up Fido and drove him to an empty lot behind a friend's convenience store eight blocks away. Once there, we scrubbed up in the store's restrooms, and I ditched the hospital shift for one of Zach's t-shirts. Unfortunately, the best I could do for underwear was a sports bra from the souvenir section. Consequently, "Chicago Rules," stitched in red, stretched from nipple to nipple beneath the thin, white fabric of my shirt.

A half hour later, standing inside the rear of Fido's van, I flipped Zach's cell phone closed. He was securing the last tie of a large black cargo net to a hook on the wall, neatly bisecting the vehicle. Glancing at me over his shoulder, he said, "Was that the landlady again?"

"From the office building, yes. She says Mrs. Naidenheim is doing better. Apparently, there aren't any relatives to call, but she'll stay with her. No one knows what to do about Mr. Keeper; there's no one to call for him, either. Damn it, Zach. I feel so guilty running off."

Zach gave a tug on the net, testing its hold. "You stick your head up too high and you're going to be hauled into a holding cell. Best stay low. How about Jake?"

"He's stable. That's something. The problem is the one nurse who'll talk to me is going off shift soon." I nodded at the net. "Are you *sure* that'll hold?"

"The hooks will hold. They're for strapping in heavy boxes and such."

"I mean will the net hold *him* back?" I jerked my thumb toward Fido, who seemed content munching grass. "I don't want to get stepped on. Maybe we should sleep outside, or in a bed. People have been doing that for centuries now. It's really caught on."

He yanked at the tie again. "It'll be fine. Anyway, bulls can take out most fences; they just don't." Coming up beside me, he put an arm around my waist. "Besides, there's no better bed on earth than soft blankets spread over a thick layer of sweet-smelling hay."

I arched an eyebrow, tempted to ask what his girlfriend, Jolene, might think of the sleeping arrangement. Zach was enough of a straight-shooter that it probably didn't even occur to him it would bother her. And I was kind of a heel for not mentioning it. But I needed his help and was too tired to wrestle with my conscience. Still, I grimaced as I looked down at the bed he'd made us in the forward corner. "It's kind of away-in-a-mangerish, don't you think?"

"If it's good enough for our Lord and Savior, it's good enough for us. And you'll feel a heap better once you get some sleep under your belt. You do look like death warmed over."

"Are you remarking on my state of disarray, or is that another of your favorite bulls?"

He laughed and walked me toward the bed, unhooking the gate to let me through. "I mean you look tired. But that's not a bad name, come to think of it. I wonder if it's taken."

Glancing back over my shoulder, I said, "Any chance his tether will hold him?"

"It's long enough for him to come in and out of the van if he wants."

I knelt on our homemade bed. "That's not what I asked!"

"How about we take a look at that stuff we got from Jake's? That'll occupy your mind."

"But what if he steps on my spleen in the middle of the night?" I bit my lip and stared nervously at the muscle-bound beast. "I like my spleen. I'm attached to my spleen. In fact, I'm attached to all of my internal organs, and I'd like to ensure they remain un-stomped upon."

Zach grabbed Jake's things and sat down beside me, putting the box in my lap. "You're such a girlie-girl. I've been stepped on lots of times." He continued with affected soberness. "It's when they get their horns up under your rib cage and toss you twenty feet in the air and then rear up over your bleeding, broken body with those sharp hooves aiming straight at your—"

I struggled to my knees. "That's it, I'm out of here."

He laughed and pulled me back down beside him. "I'm yanking your chain. Don't worry, he won't come anywhere near us. Besides, he's more afraid of you than you are of him."

"Really?" I said hopefully.

"No. Not really."

I slapped him on the arm. "I hate you. I want you to know that. I really hate you."

"No, you don't. Now, what do you want to bet the key from the cage," he said, nodding at the towel-draped cage in the corner, "fits that box we found under the window?"

I glanced uneasily at Fido but decided to trust Zach's judgment. Okay, I decided to *act* like I trusted Zach's judgment and hope that my brain would buy in to it. It might work. "Fine then, let's look at the envelope first. Although I bet I know what's in it."

"The missing file?"

"Yup. Although what the hell it was doing out in the bushes, I can't imagine." And, indeed, I pulled a file folder out of the envelope. It contained a page and a half of Jake's notes, capturing the two short conversations he'd had with the supposed Mrs. Lathos, and his own observations. "Not much here. It confirms that Jake only talked to the wife, or whoever she was, over the phone. No last name for Lathos's mistress."

"Anything else interesting?"

I scanned the document. "No. Standard stuff. Damn, I was hoping for something more."

"Like what?"

"Maybe a message from Jake saying, 'If anything happens to me, here's the name, address, and a DNA sample of the guilty party.' "

"Yeah. That would've been nice."

I set the file aside, noticing something sticky on my fingers as I did. "What's this?" I rubbed my fingers together and sniffed at them. The material on them was scentless, yellowish, and had a consistency between well-masticated chewing gum and dried petroleum jelly.

Zach held the lamp closer. "Looks kind of like dried-up grease. Strange color, though."

I rubbed it off with hay from the floor. "Jake was always cleaning his guns. Could it be from that?"

Zach grunted. "You put this stuff in your gun, and it ain't never going to fire again."

"You're right. It's inordinately viscous for purposes of lubrication."

"Uh . . . come again?"

"You put this stuff in your gun, and it ain't never going to fire again."

He grinned and slapped me lightly on the back of the head. "Smart-aleck."

I smiled at his playfulness. "On the other hand, Jake was always working on that car of his. He said it was one of the few cars left you didn't have to be a computer geek to fix. And you remember he had that black powder on his desk, too. I wonder if there's a connection."

"Old cars like that have all kinds of parts that get sooted and gummed up. Could be."

I pulled the key out of my pocket. My shoulder throbbed its disapproval. "Ow!"

Zach narrowed his eyes. "Look, you, there's a time to cowboy up and a time not to. You should take those pain pills the cop gave you."

"I'll be all right once I fall asleep."

"Until you roll over on your shoulder."

"Hmm. You have a point."

Zach glared at me until I dug one of the Percocets out of my pocket and swallowed it with a gulp of water from the thermos nearby. "Happy now?"

"Delirious." He kissed the back of my hand.

The tenderness of the gesture warmed my heart but not half as much as the touch of his lips warmed the rest of me. "So, uh, do you think I should be bothered that Nestor gave me those pills? It's not particularly legal. Or am I just being a goody two-shoes?"

"If the two shoes fit . . ."

"Very funny. Let's just see if the key fits."

"Bingo," Zach said as I opened the box. Jake's PI license lay on top of the pile. Beneath that, his office and apartment leases and his concealed carry permit. "Nothing special. Oh, wait! What do we have here?" I picked up a small white envelope addressed to Hunter.

As I started to open it, Zach put his hand on mine. "Hang on. That's personal."

"Look, someone tried to steal this box the same day Jake was shot. But *why*? What's so important about this box?" I tore the envelope open and shook it over my lap. Out fell a single sheet of standard writing paper, folded into thirds, and a small pink receipt. I opened the larger paper to reveal two columns of numbers. The left column was clearly dates, with each corresponding to a thirteen-digit number in the right one. "What do you think?" I said.

"No idea. Anything else on the paper?"

I held it in front of the electric lamp beside us. "Nothing."

Zach clicked his fingers. "Maybe they're bank accounts, and those are the dates Jake opened them. Maybe Jake's secretly a millionaire, or even a billionaire."

"Given what he pays me, if he is, *I'll* kill him. No. They seem more like serial numbers. Clearly they mean something to Hunter, or Jake would have left some kind of explanation."

"What about the receipt?"

I examined the paper. "It's a five-year-old claim check for a suit from the Potomac Cleaners in Sterling, Virginia. I know the area; I have a cousin who's a White House intern. It's a bedroom community outside Washington, D.C." I drew my brows together in thought. "That suit's not likely to be there still."

"My momma puts all her receipts in envelopes. Maybe Jake used this envelope for that, too, and it got stuck there. Heck, I'm always finding them little papers in pockets and drawers."

"Me too, but still . . ." I chewed on my lower lip for a moment before putting the receipt back in the envelope. "Let's see what else is here."

That's when I saw it: a large manila envelope with a note stapled to it: *Madison, If something happens to me, tell Fancy in person. Give her what's in here, and give Hunter the rest. Take good care of George. Jake.*

A trill of adrenaline rushed up my arms. "Zach! Jake did know he was in danger!" A business card was stapled on the note, belonging to "F. Gloria Smith" at a Gorman's Department Store in New Orleans. "Do you think the 'F' stands for Fancy?"

"Must be." Interest lit up Zach's sky-blue eyes.

I tore open the envelope and shook it over the blanket

between us, hurriedly sorting through the contents: Jake's badge, a deed for forty acres in Louisiana, a Christmas Club bank book worth $412.15, and, finally, his will. The will was a fill-in-the-blank document: the executrix was the same "F. Gloria Smith." She got the money and the land. Hunter was to get Jake's guns and any business paraphernalia he wanted. Whatever he didn't want would be sold and the profits given to F. Gloria: Fancy. I got the bird, which, at the moment, seemed rather apt.

My shoulders fell. "This is no help. Is there anything else in the box?"

"Just these." Zach pulled out three small three-by-five-inch photographs.

I took them. The first picture showed a woman—brunette, petite, perhaps thirty years old—proudly displaying a bundled baby to the camera. Muted colors gave the picture a sense of serenity, and, guessing from the style of clothes, the photo seemed to be about twenty years old. The second photo, clearly more recent, showed a woman, eighteen to twenty years old, more robust, smiling at a tiny blue parakeet perched on her finger. Although her face was more angular and her nose longer, the two women were clearly related. And the young girl definitely had Jake's eyes. "They look like mother and daughter."

"Jake's kin, maybe? His wife and daughter?"

"I don't know if he was married. I asked him once but never got a straight answer. Just that stony silence thing he'd do. But this photo of the younger woman is about three years old."

"How do you figure that?"

I pointed to the picture. "Look at the markings on the baby bird. It's George. He's a little over three now." I noted how the young woman gazed affectionately at the bird. "You know that makes sense. If George was Jake's daughter's bird, it would explain why Jake took such great care of him. I mean, Jake's really not a bird person. He's more the floppy-eared hunting dog type."

"So, where's the daughter now? Why does Jake have her bird? And where's Mom?"

"Good questions. If you come up with good answers, let me know." I turned the pictures over. The backs were blank.

Zach took the third photo. "This one doesn't look anything like the others."

Taken maybe five years ago, the picture featured a blond, maybe in her late twenties, thin, pretty, with model-perfect makeup. She wore short shorts and a skimpy halter top, *very* skimpy. Her eyes, the kind of blue that would make a Montana sky envious, stared out of the picture like a dare. And as much as I hated to say it, this woman was clearly from a lower socioeconomic class than the others.

I turned the photo over. In Jake's hand were the words, "Fan-Glorious!"—exclamation point and all. Below, in different script, were the words, "Miss you, Big D." It was signed, "Fancy."

I sat bolt upright. " 'Big D' was the name on the note in the alley!"

"And if she called Jake, 'Big D'—"

"Then maybe we actually have a suspect." I stared at her picture. She had a strong, direct gaze. Was she a woman capable of violence? Absolutely. But murder? "On the other hand . . . I don't know, Zach. Call it gut instinct, but I think if this woman wanted to shoot someone she wouldn't do it as an ambush. She'd want to look him in the eye. Besides, why kill Jake when she's the only heir to his vast Christmas Club fortune?"

"But doesn't it make you wonder why his wife and daughter aren't in the will? Where are they? And who is this Fancy lady? A second wife, maybe?"

"Maybe the two women in the other photos aren't his wife

and daughter."

"Then who are they?"

"I don't know." I flipped Fancy's picture toward him. "But maybe she does. And you know what? I'm going to go and find out."

"What do you mean, fly to New Orleans?"

"Why not? Jake obviously knew he was in trouble, but he was still willing to send me to see her. Clearly he trusts her. Maybe we should too."

Zach rubbed his jaw. "Well . . . I would like to see you leave town. I reckon you'd be a might safer. But how do you know she's still there?"

I snatched Jake's handwritten note. "This only has the department store number."

"New Orleans is in our time zone. And big stores stay open late."

"That's true." I borrowed Zach's cell phone and dialed the store. After two rings, a woman answered. "Gorman's Department Store. How may I direct your call?"

"Is Ms. Smith there, please?"

"We have several, ma'am. Do you have a first name?"

"F. Gloria. Oh! Or maybe Fancy. She goes by both."

"Just a moment, please." I looked at Zach and crossed my fingers. Seconds later, the woman said, "I'm sorry, but Ms. Smith has just gone for the day. May I direct you to someone else in her department?"

"Which department would that be?"

"That would be the Quetile Cosmetic line in our Beauty Department." The woman's voice took on a suspicious tone. "And who did you say you were, ma'am?"

"A friend."

"And you don't know the department she works in?"

"Um. She changes jobs a lot."

"Not in the last ten years, according to my records."

"I don't suppose you could give me her home phone?"

"No ma'am, most definitely not. May I have your name, please?"

"Oops, sorry. Bad connection, I'm going through a tunnel." I punched the off button.

Zach said, "What was that all about?"

"I think she suspected I was some kind of stalker or something."

"You handled it smoothly, though. Nobody suspects that going through the tunnel thing."

I screwed up my face at him, then felt fuzzy-headed with the effort. "Whoa. I think that Percocet is starting to take effect. Anyway, at least we know that Ms. Fancy Smith still works there, and she's been there all day. So she wasn't here taking shots at Jake or planting bombs. Tomorrow I can fly down and—" I stopped, immediately realizing why that wouldn't work. I clucked my tongue in frustration. "Wait. I can't. I'm broke! Come to think of it, who knows if I'll even have a job in the future? Crap!"

"I'll loan you the money."

"I couldn't—"

"My money not good enough for you? I'm doing all right. I won a nice little purse in Omaha. Besides, that way you're beholden to me. And think of what I can do with that." He waggled his eyebrows like some silent movie villain.

I laughed. "You are the best! But I'd still feel bad."

"Darlin', it ain't safe for you here. Now, I'd prefer to watch after you myself, but I got a competition in two days, and who knows how long this'll go on."

I opened my mouth in protest.

He held up one hand, palm first. "Yeah, I know. You're a big, brave, independent woman who don't need no man to look after her. But if I'm out *there* worrying about you alone *here*, I'm likely to get throwed and get my skull split open like a melon. And it'll be all your fault. So, you're getting on a plane tomorrow." He pulled his phone from the holster on his belt and dialed his travel agent cousin. In no time, I had a flight to New Orleans for ten a.m. the next day.

"You're such a great friend, I—" A yawn overtook me. My weary body and woozy head joined forces. "I'm just so tired." I yawned again, so hard that it almost knocked me over.

"I'm amazed you've stayed going this long. Here, give me this," he said, taking the box from my lap. "And you lay down now."

I kicked off my boots and scooted down flat on the giant sleeping bag atop the hay. Zach grabbed the blankets and lay down beside me, covering us both. I rolled against him, letting him put his arm around me as my body convulsed with another yawn. "This really is nice."

"I think so," he said into my hair.

A sense of indescribable contentment blanketed me. The bed was soft and giving beneath me. It smelled sweet and earthy, and Zach's chest was warm against my cheek. "I wish I knew why someone threw the box out the window. If they were trying to steal it, why leave it? Do they want the numbers in Hunter's envelope? Or maybe there's something in the will I'm missing."

"Maybe it wasn't stolen. Maybe Jake threw the box out the window."

"Why?"

He hugged me. "I don't know. Shush now. Go to sleep."

"Hmm. This is comfy." Typical me, I start dropping off, and all the events of the day come rushing in, as if for one final parade review. "You know I was just thinking about Hunter."

"Great. You lie down with me and start thinking about another man. That's flattering."

"No, silly. I don't mean that way. In fact, I was thinking about Jake, too."

"This just gets better and better."

My head felt so light I thought it might float away, but I was so warm, so comfortable. "It's, um, where was I going? Oh, yeah. Why ask me to talk to Fancy? Why not ask Hunter? And why don't they work together anymore?"

His chin brushed against my head as he looked down at me. "What do you mean?"

"At first, I thought Lilly's suspicions were ridiculous, but I'm not so sure we should throw away that data point prematurely. I mean, they were partners, yes? But Hunter's a wealthy man, and Jake's just scraping by. You'd think Hunter would want to help his old friend."

"Maybe they had a falling-out."

"They get along fine as far as I can tell."

"I don't know, Darlin'. But you can't strike oil if you don't dig for it."

I tried to lift my head, but it wouldn't budge. "What's that, a wise old country saying?"

"I mean you need to dig deeper to find out what was really going on between those two. Now how about you stop talking about other men when you're lying down with me?"

"Oh, I'm sorry." I smiled, feeling like I was about to purr. I knew it was a side effect of the pills, but you know, I just didn't give a damn. I tilted my head back, and my nose brushed against the soft bristles of his chin. "That tickles. And you smell good."

"It's all those lemony hand wipes we used to wash up with."

"It's nice. I like it." I kissed the underside of his chin.

He shifted slightly, and his voice sounded strained. "Maybe you ought not do that."

"You're right," I said, although my hand slid slowly up and down his chest. "Jolene would have every right to be angry."

He rolled my body closer to him. "I meant to tell you. Me and Jolene broke up."

Yay! "Oh, I'm sorry." My damned hand started massaging his arm. "Are you sad?"

He swallowed hard and looked down at me. "Not at the moment."

"But I feel so sorry for you. It makes me want to—" I wrapped my fingers in his hair and drew his head down, bringing his lips to mine. He hesitated, but then his arms tightened around me. Our lips moved against each other, soft and yielding, then increasingly insistent. My shoulder ached, though it didn't compare with the ache lower down. I pulled him closer.

Zach broke off, gently pulling away. "I don't believe I'm about to say this, but maybe we ought not. It ain't right to take advantage of you when you're in this state—"

I gripped his hair tighter and pulled his face back to mine. "Shut up, cowboy." As my mouth met his, I ran the tip of my tongue over his lips. He shuddered and drew me hard to him.

Just then the floor shook. I broke off. "What was that? Did Fido come in the van?"

Zach nuzzled my neck. "Don't worry about him."

My toes curled, and I groaned. "But what if he comes over here?"

He feathered my throat with kisses. "He does, and he's Sunday dinner, I swear to God."

His mouth covered mine again, and I pulled him on top of me. *Oh, this is heaven!*

Then it happened: The most tremendous stink I'd ever smelled in my life filled the air.

I pushed Zach away. "What is that *smell*?! Oh my *God*!"

Zach's eyes were glazed. "What? It's nothing. Don't worry about it. Let's just—"

The stench nearly gagged me. I pushed Zach away, rising to

my elbows. Fido stood on the other side of the net, his tail high in the air. "That animal just *shit* all over the floor!"

Face screwed up in helpless frustration, Zach said, "Well, it's what they do. You can't house-break cattle, Darlin'." He put his hand on the back of my neck, massaging it as he lowered himself close to me. "Just give it a second. You'll get used to it. Now, why don't we—"

I straight-armed him. Logy head or not, my nose was sharp. "Clean. It. Up. *Now!*"

Zach dropped his head to his chest and groaned. "All right." He threw the blanket off and walked toward the bull. "Probably best anyway." He shouldered Fido toward the van door, none too gently. "You couldn't give me five more minutes? Just five lousy minutes. Gosh-danged, cussed, ornery creature. Walking bag of fertilizer."

Grogginess rushed over me, pushing my body back down on the bed. My mind slipped sideways, and I heard myself say, "Explosive stuff: fertilizer. It goes off like—"

. . . I stood in a field of snow.

Startled, I looked around. A thick forest of evergreens covered the horizon. The ground stretched flat, subsumed in drifts of deep, white snow. I stood alone.

What the hell? Zach? I heard scribbling and turned toward it. *Ah. I'm dreaming.*

I knew this because *she* was there: The Evil Dream Pixie. Well, I say pixie, but I don't actually know what she is because her face is always in shadow, even when she's standing in the middle of bloody nowhere under full light. She just *seems* pixie-like. And I hate her. I mean, I really hate her. For as long as I can remember, she's appeared in my dreams, usually before a big test or major paper was due. And she's always, *always* writing on that damned pad of hers. She never says a word, just watches me, taking notes. What's really frustrating is that I *know*

107

the answer I need to any question is written on that pad. She won't let me see it, but if I ever get close enough, I'm going to rip it out of her smart-ass little hands and beat her with it.

Evil Dream Pixie looked up. I knew she was staring at me, even though I couldn't see her face. "What the hell do you want?" I snarled.

She pointed her pencil at my feet. I looked down to find myself standing in a steaming pile of cow crap. I danced to one side, shaking bits of shit off my boot. "You did that on purpose! You irritating, arrogant, know-it-all—"

"Now you know how I feel," Hunter said, walking in front of me.

My annoyance swelled. "What are *you* doing here?"

He put his hands in his pockets and shrugged. He wore my favorite of his suits: silk, navy and fitted perfectly over his muscular physique. "Hell if I know. It's your dream."

"I like that suit on you. And since you're not actually here, I can admit that I've thought you were hot from the moment we met. Until you opened your mouth and ruined everything."

"I thought the same thing about you. But maybe you ought to be paying attention to that." He nodded to something behind me.

When I turned, I realized that I stood on the edge of the forest. A tree branch hovered above me, something fluttering in its branches. "What is it?"

"Again: your dream."

As I squinted up at the thing, it floated into my hand, and I realized what it was. "The note from the alley. But—" I paused thoughtfully. "It's completely silver. Why would that be?" A breeze blew the glittering paper out of my hands and carried it into the sky. As it went higher, it got larger until it actually became the sky. Then the snow turned into glistening silver flakes. On a whim, I closed my eyes and caught one on my tongue. It tasted like metal. When I opened my eyes, I watched the snow change from silver to black when it hit the ground, covering everything in a fine, ebony powder that rose in wisps as the wind blew over it. "That's odd," I said to Hunter. "Shouldn't the drifts be silver too?"

He walked up behind me. "You think that's odd, look over there."

I looked at the pile of cow dung, now half buried. Black snow slid down in a tiny avalanche, setting off puffs of flame, like little soundless explosions.

"Well, that's just bizarre."

"Fertilizer is unstable," Hunter said.

"I know. The chemistry is such that—uh, Hunter what are you doing?"

His hands encircled my waist, and he put his lips on my neck, slowly, softly kissing the length of it. "What part of 'this is *your* dream' are you not getting?" he said as he nuzzled me.

I shivered under his warm touch. "I, um—oh. That's nice. I quite like that."

His hands traveled up my abdomen and cupped my breasts. "That's probably why you have me doing it," he murmured into my hair.

"Makes sense." I moaned and closed my eyes, pressing my back into his chest as his thumbs caressed my nipples. "I mean, I really, really like that."

"So it appears," a harsh voice said.

My eyes snapped open. I was still lying on the bed in the van. My arms were stretched over my head, my back arched. Hunter crouched beside me. "Looky what I got." He dangled a pair of handcuffs above me. "Just for you. And this time, you're not getting away from me."

CHAPTER SEVEN

I jerked into a sitting position. My head swam, and a searing pain rushed down my back. "Ow," I growled.

"Stop whining. I'll see you get aspirin back at the safehouse. Come on. Up you go." He slipped the handcuffs into their holster and scooped me up, depositing me on my feet. "I've had all the trouble I'm taking from you. Let's go."

I swayed and looked around the van, willing my head to clear.

Hunter grabbed my boots and thrust them at me. "You can come along on your own or cuffed to the bar in my car. Your choice."

I glowered at him and snatched my boots. Leaning against the wall, I struggled to pull them on, dancing in place to keep my balance. "Where's Zach?"

"Your boyfriend's down the street at a coffee shop."

He held my elbow as we walked down the ramp of the van, although I wasn't sure if he was steadying me or making sure I didn't make a break for it. Nodding at Fido, who lay on the ground, tethered and apparently fine with my being kidnapped, he said, "Good-looking animal. Your man looking to sell it?" He marched me to a nearby car. "I've always wanted to try my hand at raising bulls."

I shook my head hard enough to break through the cobwebs. "What?"

Hunter opened the passenger door and blocked me between him and it. "You're not a morning person, are you? Is that the

110

best a genius like you can do first thing?" His gaze slid over me. "Or did your boyfriend wear the smarts right out of you last night?"

Indignation snapped me awake. "He's not my boyfriend." *Yet.*

"Just a one-night stand, then? Needed to get your pipes cleaned?"

"You are so out of line, mister."

He shrugged a bit too nonchalantly to be convincing. "Not like I care. Look, we can wait around until your not-boyfriend comes back. I'll be happy to start my morning with a throwdown. But I thought it might be easier to wait until he was out of the way. On the other hand, if watching a fight gets you all hot and bothered, fine by me."

I scanned the street. The sun was barely up, peeking under bands of gray clouds. Distant traffic sounded, but nothing moved nearby. No sign of Zach. "I can't leave Fido here alone."

"Fido?" Hunter snorted out a laugh. "You call it Fido?"

"For now. We were considering Satan's Snot."

He shook his head. "You are the weirdest damn female. Get in the car."

"But the calf—"

"First of all, that's a yearling, not a calf. And second, Mick will watch it." He pointed to a black car parked across the street.

"How long has he been there?"

"All night. In fact, he's been following you since you pulled that little piece of sabotage on my car. And by the way, you're paying for that." He leaned in, forcing my back against the door frame. "One way or another."

"So, that's how you found me at Jake's. But Zach and I were sure we weren't followed."

"Any of my guys get made on a tail, they don't finish out the day. I only hire the best. Jake, sadly, tended to pity every stray that came along. And you can see where it got him."

111

I sucked in a breath, my mind instantly awake and alert. "Is Jake okay? Is he . . . ?"

"Alive? Yeah. He's one tough tahyo," he said, his well-disguised Cajun accent making a rare appearance on the last word. "I should've known no little bullet would take him out."

"What does that mean?"

"It means I shouldn't have worried." He looked down at me, his eyes hardening again. "You're my biggest problem now. But I'm going to take care of that. Get in."

I sighed and did as I was told. We drove in silence, drawing ever closer to Chicago proper. Hunter had his offices in the Hancock Building in the middle of the city, and I assumed that's where we were going.

Great. The little girl being sent to her room. How humiliating! I huffed and looked away.

"Stop being a baby," Hunter said, not taking his eyes off the road.

"Bite me."

He smiled and shook his head. "Such a lady."

The skyline loomed closer and defeat gouged deeper. *No. I'm not going down without a fight.* The vision of the alley where Jake was shot came to me. That would be a good place to divert him to, and maybe get away from him. "Can we stop at the alley?"

"Hell, no. I'm getting you out of the picture as quickly as possible."

"But I remembered something." I wasn't lying exactly. My dream pointed to something about the note. The police couldn't find it, but they missed the file too. Maybe I'd get lucky.

Hunter whipped around, gripping the wheel so hard I thought it'd crack. "What?"

That simple, but powerful, act reminded me how much stronger he was than I, making me think that I'd better tread carefully. Nibbling at the stubborn hangnail on my thumb, I said, "I think I know where the note went." *As good a lie as any.*

"You *think* you know? What does that mean?"

"I can picture it falling out of my hands. I think I know where it might have landed."

He shook his head as in doubt. "The cops practically pulled that place down. If the note were there, they'd've found it. But tell me where you think it is, and I'll have them check it out."

"Oh come on, Hunter, have a heart. I'm already on Voltaire's bad side. If I can find the note, I might have a chance of recovering a little dignity."

"And what have I ever done to make you think I'd care?"

"Okay," I said, "then think of it this way. Jake always says that my reputation affects his reputation. So, you're really helping your buddy out, not me."

"Nice try, Angel. No way. I've got a cozy saferoom with your name on the door and a chain hooked to the bed just long enough for you to reach the bathroom. You'll love it."

My eyes shot wide. "You're not serious!"

Hunter grinned and kept driving.

That's when I knew I had to use the one weapon in my arsenal guaranteed to work. "Okay, you've forced my hand. I'll give you one more chance to take me to the alley."

"Or you'll do what? Stamp your feet and pout? Hold your breath? I'm so scared."

"You should be, mister, because I have a foolproof device to get what I want." I puffed my chest out. "I will talk to you."

He snorted. "That's it? You're going to talk? I'll admit that's annoying but—"

"You don't understand. You think you've heard me before but wait until I really get started. Believe me, I learned from the best. My mother could talk a dead man into tears and freeze the balls off a sailor at fifty feet with the tone of her voice alone. Trust me, Hunter. I will do more than simply talk. I will reason.

I will lecture. I will question. I will soliloquize, sermonize, and rationalize."

"Look, I'm not going to be—"

"I will be loquacious and largiloquent, flippant and fluent, garrulous and glib, magniloquent and multiloquent. And, trust me, I will be most aeolistic. And it gets worse."

He groaned and rolled his eyes. "Don't be such a child."

"You see the real problem, Hunter—for you, anyway—is that I'm willing to talk about *anything*. I'm a liberal, feminist American female, and I have no fear of any subject whatsoever. Feelings, for example—let's talk about yours."

His jaw ratcheted tight, and he clenched the steering wheel. "I'm serious. Cut it out."

"No? Not your feelings? How about your mother then? I mean, do you really regard her as a human being? Do you see her as a vivacious, exciting, and caring person capable of the same passion, the same strong sexual urges—"

His glare singed my cheek. "Hey! I will pull this car over—"

"And I will just keep talking. You can't exactly pull over and employ physical force on a busy city street, can you? Oh and look, there's a red light." The tires screeched as we rocked to a halt. Early-morning commuters rushed out in front of us, like horses from the starting gate.

"Son-of-a—" Hunter shook his jammed thumb in the air.

"The way I figure, it'll be a good fifteen, twenty minutes before you can actually get us out of sight of witnesses. By which time, I guarantee, your ears will be bleeding. In the meantime, why don't we try an exercise that I went through at the Emotional Cleansing Retreat my Aunt Victoria runs? The idea is to get in touch with your gestation process, from conception to birth. Let's start with impregnation. When your mother and father were having sex—"

He gaped at me in horror. "What?"

I could barely keep a straight face. "No, really, give it a try. It'll help you relate to your parents as full, sexual beings. Knowing your parents as you do, do you think the moment of your conception was tender? Vigorous? Passionate? Perhaps a touch of domination and submission, which is, of course, a completely normal expression of sexual need, and quite harmless if not carried to excess. And think about the sounds. Would you envision loving sighs or more guttural groaning and moist smacking sounds of—?"

"All right!" he thundered.

I sat back in the seat, smiling. Hunter, on the other hand, breathed as if he'd just survived a battering. "Ten minutes," he said. "I'll give you *ten minutes.* If you don't find anything, we leave. And you don't say a word, *not one damn word,* until we get there. Got it?"

I nodded and made the classic zipper-my-mouth-and-throw-away-the-key move.

A horn honked behind us. Growling, he slammed the car into gear, and we rocketed forward. I grinned out the window at the many passersby hurrying by. *Men are so easy.*

Half an hour later, Hunter and I stood in the alley. Not twenty-four hours earlier, I'd stood there with a man I respected more than any, save my father. And now that man was hooked up to machines, fighting for his life; another good man was dead; and a lovely, old woman lay alone and maybe dying. I sighed, trying to will away the anger churning in my gut. Morning traffic roared by as the neighborhood kicked into gear. Down the street, a school bus glided to a halt, the noise of the squealing children drowned out by the heavy rumble of a store owner raising a corrugated steel shutter from in front of his door. Raising my head, I squinted against the bright sun clearing the building across the street. I shielded my eyes against the glare and stared up at the window from which Jake had been shot. My jaw clenched so tight I feared I'd crack a tooth.

"Stupid Pixie," I murmured.

Hunter walked over from the far side of the alley where he'd been searching. He'd been right; the note was nowhere to be found. "What are you muttering about?"

My gaze wouldn't leave the building. "Why dream of the note if there isn't something here? And what's the point of silver snow and coal-covered bull dung? Annoying, evil bitch."

"Are you out of your damn mind?"

"Huh?" I turned to Hunter. Though still morning, the slight shadow of a beard outlined his strong chin, and, in the bright light, his eyes seemed more blue than gray. I cocked my head, studying his face. Not a bad face; actually it was really nice. Too bad it belonged to a jerk.

He glowered at me. "What are you lookin' at?"

"You."

"Well don't." He seemed disconcerted by my staring at him. *Isn't that interesting?*

I shrugged. "Okay. How about I look over there?" I pointed at the window. "That's the room where the sniper was, right? Let's take a peek."

"Forget it. You had your chance, and we—" *Bee-dee-bee-dee* went Hunter's cell. He pulled it out and glanced at the screen. "Damn it, this wild goose chase is making me miss an appointment." He touched the Bluetooth receiver perched on his right ear and began to speak a moment later. "Get me Liz," he said without opening pleasantries, "I need her to take the Hennessey meeting." Hunter cocked his head at me, signaling me to get into the car.

I pointed my thumb behind me to the alley and said, "I want to take one more look."

He snarled and, I'm guessing, was about to refuse, when his

attention was drawn to his cell. "Yeah, it's me. You need to start without me. Get the file, and let's go over it now."

I started to turn away, and he snapped his fingers at me, pointing again to the car. I mouthed something deliberately incoherent, as if not wanting to interrupt his call. But in fact, I knew that forcing his brain to multitask between carrying on a phone conversation and working out the silent communication would have a deleterious effect on his ability to focus—with luck specifically on his ability to focus on booting my ass into the car. A rudimentary knowledge of neuropsychology has its uses.

But I'd need a bigger distraction to get away from him and into that apartment. I fast-scanned the end of the alley, chewing my lower lip anxiously; I had precious little time. *Aha!* A broken table-tennis paddle jutting out of a trash can caught my eye. *Hmm. I wonder . . .*

I went to the can and two-finger picked my way through the top layer of trash. Sure enough, I found what I'd hoped for: ping-pong balls.

Here's the great thing about ping-pong balls: they're made of celluloid, which smokes like crazy—if one knows how to light them.

And guess who does?

But I needed some foil and a heat source. I smiled. I knew where to find them, too.

I palmed the balls and jogged over to the car, mouthing more nonsense and making exaggerated chewing motions while pointing at the car. Hunter, as desired, scowled in confusion, verbally stumbling over his phone call.

I angled into the car and opened the glove box. I sat with the door open, one leg on the sidewalk as I knew I would have to move quickly when my plan took off. He was standing well behind the car, but I canted the side mirror to see him and saw him peering at me intently. I took some gum from the black bag that I'd stolen the toothpicks from earlier. Turning my head to him, I held a piece up, asking with my eyes for permission to take it. He scowled and turned his back on me. Grinning, I unwrapped the gum and popped three pieces in my mouth. Then I laid the aluminum foil on the seat beside me, overlapping them to form a three-by-five-inch sheet. My heart was racing hard now from a combination of being hurried and that tingly adrenaline rush that came with pulling one over on a bully. Revenge, however nerdy, is *so sweet*.

I pulled Jake's knife out of my pocket; lucky I'd kept it! Leveraging open the scissors, I quickly cut the balls into shreds over the foil. That done, I carefully, but swiftly, wrapped the aluminum wrappers around the shreds, wonton-style, and twisted the ends into a small handle. I'd pushed in the cigarette lighter on the dash as I worked, and it popped out. Now for the tough—and dangerous—part: lighting my smoke bomb. Ping-pong balls are hard to light, but once they catch, they do so *immediately*. And the resultant smoke is thick and toxic. I had to be in position!

Glancing over my shoulder at Hunter, I saw he was still distracted with his call. That boy's going to learn not to take phone calls around me. *Heh, heh, heh.*

Shielding my actions with my body, I held the aluminum foil outside the door and pushed it into the glowing cigarette lighter. I bit my lip, waiting. Normally, it's best to do this with an open flame; the lighter might not get quite hot enough or be concentrated enough to catch the wrapper on fire. I cut my eyes to the rear again, nervously checking on Hunter. *Sigh. What broad shoulders the Big Bad has. Honestly, does he have to be so—*

HOT! Ack! The foil caught as dense, gray smoke roiled off it. Fortunately, my instinctive panic reaction helped, and I flung it hard into the back of the alley. "Fire!" I yelled, pointing.

Hunter whirled, saw the smoke, and sprang into action. Okay, I wasn't exactly certain what that action entailed because once he ran toward the smoke, I ducked around the front of the car and dashed across the street. I jogged inside the building without a backward glance. Yeah, I was going to get it when he caught up with me, but that would be then, and this was now.

Taking the stairs two at a time, I flew up three flights, exiting onto a long hallway. I paused to catch my breath, hands on my burning sides. I rolled my aching shoulder and looked around. Torn carpeting crowded one side of the hall. Paint fumes nearly overwhelmed me; I wrinkled my nose. I spotted yellow police tape across a doorframe down the hall and started toward it, then suddenly skipped to the side to avoid a still-tacky paint tray. Black dots, like soot, scattered the surface of the drying layer. Had some idiot actually had a fire around paint?

A door slammed on the floor below. *Hunter!*

I dashed to the exit at the other end of the hall. Slamming against the silver release bar, I leapt onto the landing and pelted down the stairs. At the last moment, I veered off at the second floor, hoping Hunter would think I'd run for the exit.

Footsteps pounded above me. My heart pounded just as furiously, and I could barely keep from gasping aloud. I pulled the door closed seconds before the footfalls hit the landing. I held my breath as Hunter ran past me. Moments later, the exit door banged open two floors below.

Fantastic! It'll take a while for him to search the alley between this block of houses and the next. Enough time to get away!

I ran to the open staircase leading to the front of the building. Just as I cleared the doorway, an arm shot out and pushed me, sending me flying face-first down the stairs. I flailed about, grabbing wildly for purchase. I skidded on my stomach, my chest slamming each step, smashing the air out of my lungs, until I finally crashed, shoulder first, on the floor below.

Someone ran down the stairs toward me. I started to roll over, clutching my wounded arm in agony, when something long and dark rushed toward my head. Everything went black.

Rolling. The world rolled beneath me. A deep, aching pain split the back of my head. *Where—?* I opened my eyes, temporarily blinded. *Sunlight? I'm outside? No, I'm lying down. Focus! Damn it, Madison, focus!*

In an instant, my brain processed the scene. I lay in the rotting back seat of a sunbaked car. It bucked, as if hitting a rut, and then rolled forward. I rose onto my elbows, watching in horror as the hood of the car hit the water.

It started to sink.

CHAPTER EIGHT

My heart slammed into my rib cage, blood surging with pure terror. *Can't panic. Get out! Have to get out!* I yanked on the door handle, but it wouldn't open. *What the hell?* In seconds the water would be too high! I twisted, propelling myself against the other door. *Damn! No good! For Christ's sake! Who the hell puts child locks in sinking cars?*

A hand shot out from the floor. I screamed and pulled away as a man sat up. *Lathos!*

He struggled to rise. Dried blood, caked black, covered the right side of his face. His matted hair stuck out like porcupine quills over his large, protruding ears. His gangly arms flailed, thin fingers clutching at the seat, and his eyes, stretching wide, were tiny black beads in a circle of white. Panic rose from him like stink.

"Tina!" he cried out, grabbing at air.

I clutched him by the shirt and hauled him up to the seat beside me. "I'm not her! She's not here!" Whether dazed or too panicked to understand, Lathos clutched my shirt, his fingernails digging red welts into my flesh. Terror surged, and I fought to beat it back.

Seizing his wrists, I pushed down and broke his grip. "Let go! Look, it'll be all right! Once the car sinks below the surface, the pressure will equalize, and we can open the doors! You have to let me go! I have to get into the front seat—"

I reached over the seat, determined to show him, but my

121

fingers slammed hard into a barrier. *What the*— We were in an old taxicab with a scarred, yellowed plastic wall between the seats. There was no way up front, no way to open the doors!

I looked down at the sound of sloshing. Mucky water filled the footwell, rising relentlessly. Lathos snatched at my shirt, mewing in fear. I slapped his hands away. "Stop it! You'll get us both killed!"

I threw myself on my back and kicked at the side windows, knowing it would take serious power to break through the tempered glass. Cold water crept over my hands. I flinched but held tight to the seat to brace myself. *No good!* Tears welled in my eyes, and I started to hyperventilate. *There's no way out!*

Behind me, I heard Lathos claw at the frayed door panel and then pound at the back window. "Stop it!" I screamed. He fell back and began to cry. Disgust, pity, and self-reproach hit me. I gritted my teeth and patted him on the shoulder. "I'll get us out. Stay calm."

But how? Icy water sloshed around my midsection, stinging my exposed skin. I only had seconds. *I had to shatter the window! If only I had something sharp—wait! Jake's pocket knife!* I yanked the knife out, splashing my face, and gave thanks for the corkscrew set in the cover. Hands shaking as much from fear as from cold, I levered the screw open and wrapped my fingers around the knife body so the steel jutted out between my middle and ring fingers.

Water chilled my shoulder. Lathos pounded on the barrier and gulped for air, his head pressed against the roof. I got onto my knees, cursing my sluggishness. "Take a deep breath!"

Lifting my arm out of the water, now neck high, I aimed up, right, and to the rear—the weakest point of the thinnest window. I filled my lungs and, with all my might, hammered the corkscrew into the glass. It shattered in one piece, and bone-chilling, muddy water rushed in.

Unbalanced, my body thudded into the plastic barrier. *Out! Out! Get out!* I kicked against the front seat and propelled myself out the window. Every instinct screamed at me to go, but I reached out to Lathos. Out of the green-gray water, his hand snatched mine, pulling me back into the car. Full-out panic twisted his face. Clawing at me, he dragged me downward.

I raked my nails over his hands. But he wouldn't let go. Desperate, I clawed at his eyes.

And that's how I killed him.

He gasped, water filling his lungs. His eyes rolled back in his head. He let go.

Horror rushed through me. I jerked, fighting contradictory urges: save him, save me.

Freed from his weight, it felt like I was flying. The car slipped into the murk below. I couldn't help it; my lungs were bursting. My body took over. I had to leave him!

Frantic for air, I kicked hard and split the surface of the water just as my breath gave out. I gasped, then took in water, gagging and coughing. Shouts exploded in front of me.

Automatically, I swam toward the sound, my strokes awkward, fueled by the pure need to make one more pull, one more kick, one more . . . Somehow I flopped onto hands and knees in the muck. Someone took hold of me, pulling me forward. Everything swirled gray and black around me, formless shapes. The stench of waterlogged weeds and stagnant mud choked me. I tried to stand, but my legs wouldn't hold me. I gave up and let myself be dragged.

When my body hit dry ground, I pulled loose, hunched over, and retched. I tried to gesture to the water behind me, but dizziness swept up and over, made me concentrate just to stay conscious. Between heaves, I finally croaked, "Someone . . . still trapped. Inside the car—" Exhausted, I fell forward and curled up in the grass.

I have no idea how long I lay there. People moved around me. One came closer. Hands rolled me on my back. Something soft fell over my torso, and warm fingers tucked me in.

A shaft of sunlight fell over me. I closed my eyes and covered my face, vaguely aware that someone prodded me, as if looking for something lost. Sirens blared closer, and I felt myself being lifted in someone's arms. We rushed into the night. I landed, seated, on something hard, then tumbled against a warm, solid chest. Hands moved up and down my arms, warming me.

"Chica?" a deep voice said into my ear. "Come back to me. You're going to be okay."

Nestor! I collapsed into him, burying my head in his chest. The shouting increased, and I looked up to see a fire truck bounce onto the grass in front of the water—one of the canals off the river—followed by an ambulance. Several men stood by the water. One slogged into it up to his knees and snatched a man's jacket that had floated to the surface. He trudged out, and I grimaced as he dropped the fabric to the ground with a wet smack.

"I killed him," I heard myself say. My stomach, still tight with the strain of vomiting, roiled. My head pounded so hard I felt my flesh pulse. My brain knew it was Octaviano Lathos who'd died, but my memory conjured up images of the overeager face of my brother's friend, Alfie, which made my cowardice seem all the more personal and utterly despicable.

A large, pale man, a medic with bulging arms and a shaved head, knelt before me. "Let's take a look." His voice was calm, and his hands were warm as he touched the side of my face.

Panic, fury, guilt, pain, it all burst out of me as overwhelming rage. I lunged at the man, slapping and screaming. "Don't touch me!"

Nestor pinned my arms to my side and dragged me back. My screams spewed on and on, emptied me, and stole my strength.

124

I sank to my knees.

The paramedic's dark eyes blazed at me. Nestor hugged me to him and put up a hand to stop the man. "It's all right. I've checked her out. No broken bones, she just—"

"She's fucking crazy," the paramedic said. "Fine. You got her." He stalked away.

Nestor turned me to face him. He wore jeans and a black shirt, no uniform. "*Dios, chica.* That's enough," he said. "You need to get control—"

My body trembled. "You don't understand." I flopped down on the concrete bench.

Nestor wrapped me in a coat. Sitting close, he pulled me to him, again rubbing my arms and back. He looked out at the water. "Who was in the car?" he said in a strained voice. Alerted, I picked my head up, and the tense look on his face brought me up short. Rather than the typical calm, even bemused expression he usually wore, his pupils were wide, the large, black circles almost subsuming the chocolate brown of his irises. His flesh gleamed with sweat, and his gaze darted about, scanning the landscape. Then, as if sensing my concern, he dropped his eyes to mine and gave me a forced smile. "It's okay. You're safe. Tell me who was in the car."

For a second, it felt like I had awakened from a drugged nightmare; I couldn't make my thoughts come together. Then, mercilessly, they coalesced. "It was Lathos."

The breath rushed out of him, but I couldn't tell if in relief or distress. He nodded and rubbed my arms so vigorously it almost burned. "It'll be okay," he said without conviction.

"No. I tried to pull him out, but he wouldn't let go. He was like a child begging for help. But I hit him. I killed him!" My throat closed up and despair overwhelmed me.

As if suddenly waking himself, he pulled his attention back to me. His arms gripped mine. "No! I'm not going to have this, do you hear me? Hey!" He captured my face between his hands. "You listen to me. You didn't kill him." He licked his lips, and his face was set with determination. "Whoever put him in that car is the guilty one."

I scoured the tears off my face with the back of my hand. "So many innocent people: Lathos, Mr. Keeper, Mrs. Naidenheim, Jake. Why is this happening?"

Nestor scratched at his chin as he looked toward the canal. The man who had strode into the water walked by, his wet jeans slapping against his legs. "Divers are on the way," he said, nodding to Nestor in passing. He was some kind of off-duty cop or fireman, I supposed.

Nestor nodded back and then muttered. "This is getting out of hand."

"He didn't deserve to die. None of them do. They're innocent—"

He shook his head. "No such thing . . . innocent."

I yanked my hand free of his. "Are you saying these people deserved to die?"

He turned toward me, lips tight. "Calm down. I'm not saying that. But it's time to face facts. Lathos climbed out of the cradle and headed straight into jail. He was hardly an innocent. And, like it or not, Jake is no angel." His gaze bore down on mine. "No one is innocent here."

I shot to my feet, anger warming my chilled flesh, his coat dropping off my shoulders onto the cold cement bench. "You're blaming Jake?" I glared at him, angry and betrayed by his callousness. How could I have been so wrong about him?

Nestor looked at me as if confused by what I was saying. Then he took a deep breath. He reached out, a pained look on his face. "*Chica,* I'm sorry. I'm out of line, I know. But think about it: the attempt on Jake's life? That ambush was deliberate and well planned. When somebody wants someone dead that bad, there's a reason."

Gritting my teeth, I tried to fight the emotions swirling in my head, tried to deny what he was saying. "Who do you think did this? Tina? The man from the hospital? The bomber—"

His body went rigid. "What do you mean?"

"Uh, what do you mean, what do I mean?"

"You said the man from the hospital was the bomber."

I blinked. "No, no I didn't. It was just two sentences close together."

"Why do you think they're the same person?"

"Nestor, I, I don't—"

"Did you see him? Was he at Jake's office?"

"What? Who?"

"A guy who runs the business across the street gave a description of a man who matched the one at the hospital. Madison, look at me. This is important. Have you ever seen the man in the hospital before?"

I shook my head. "No."

"Are you sure? Are you *absolutely* sure?"

"Well, I mean I suppose I *might* have seen him in passing. I guess that's possible. But, I have to think that if I'd ever seen someone that sick and evil, it would have registered. Could Lathos have been conspiring somehow with the guy from the hospital?"

Nestor looked out at the water and took a step closer. "It could be a coincidence."

"I'm not following you," I said, but he didn't seem to hear me. I raised my voice. "Hunter thinks the office bomb might have been meant for me."

That got his attention. He looked back at me and snorted. "Hunter's an ass. Don't listen to anything he says. Hunter's not the point. The point is that you got lucky—"

"Lucky! I almost died! And Lathos did."

"Which makes you lucky and him not." Nestor stroked my arm as if in sympathy, but I tensed under the touch. He sighed and dropped his hand. "Listen, serious shit is happening. But do you take the warning? No. You go back to the scene of the ambush—"

"How did you know where I went?" A prickling wariness flowed up my spine. Come to think of it, how had Nestor known I was in that car?

He hesitated. "What?"

"How did you know I went to the alley? And how did you end up here?"

He gritted his teeth. "Is that important now?"

"I want to know."

"I was following you, okay? I was worried about you." A grimace creased his features. "I know I shouldn't . . . get involved, but, well, you're really kind of an idiot."

My eyebrows climbed high on my forehead in surprise. I didn't get that very often. Smart-aleck, know-it-all, yes. But idiot?

He put out a hand as if in appeasement. "Not idiot in the traditional sense. You're just . . . naive. You've spent too much time in your ivory tower, and you don't know how to watch your back. But you're not a bad kid."

Again with the diminutives!

"Actually, I was following Hunter, following you." He smiled crookedly. "I've got a mole in his office. It bothered me that he was shadowing you, again."

"He said he was just—" I stopped as my brain registered what he'd said. "Wait a minute, what do you mean, *again*?"

"He watches you. A lot."

I jerked, the standard mule-kick-to-the-heart reaction to being stalked. "He does what?"

"He's always *looking* at you when your back's turned. Do you remember two weeks ago Tuesday, when you were with Jake at the courthouse?"

I nodded, my attention riveted to Nestor's every word. "Yes, Jake took me with him routinely, ostensibly for training, but I think it was so he had someone to fetch coffee and donuts. He was staying behind to wait for Hunter. They were supposed to meet for lunch, I think."

Leaning in, he said, "I was there. I saw you go to the bus stop. I didn't see Jake, but I saw Hunter follow you out. He stood in the shadows staring at you until the bus came, just staring."

A stiff breeze wrapped my hair around my face, and I shivered, but not from the cold. The fear is primal in women, the fear of being man's prey. It often comes too young to a girl, a brute blow to the mind, a brutal clubbing of the consciousness, when first she realizes that *some* daddies and uncles, brothers and cousins, friends and strangers *want*, and what they want, they'll take, and if it hurts, that's how it is, and if she screams, that's better.

Nestor's words seemed distant. "—this look on his face like—"

I glanced at him sharply. "Like what?"

"Like he couldn't figure out what he wanted to do to you."

I stumbled back a step, edgy and angry at that familiar twitching need to watch for shapes in the shadows. "What am I supposed to do with a statement like that?"

Nestor shrugged. "Maybe he likes you."

"Sure, except that he doesn't."

"Maybe it's nothing," Nestor said. "But I don't want you getting into a car alone with him again. You hear me?"

I nodded. Why was he telling me this? Was he really worried? Or did he just want to make as much trouble for Hunter as he could? What makes him, Nestor, the one to trust? I peered up at him, watched him frown and flex his big hands before him, as if trying to work out an ache. The fresh scrapes on his knuckles— red, raw reminders of his battle the day before—caught my attention. Without thinking, I said, "Do you hate Hunter?" I said.

Nestor's lips curled in disdain. "What? No. He's not that important to me."

"Lilly seems to think you're still carrying a grudge from some past incident."

"It was nothing. Hunter threw down with some guy in a bar once, something to do with a case he was on. Rasmen and I got called in to break it up."

"And?"

"I felt I had to arrest him, and he felt he had to resist." He paused. "Only Jake called in some favors and got him released almost before we finished booking him." He shook his head. His eyes narrowed, and he looked down at his sneakers. "Jake shouldn't have done that."

I couldn't help but feel suspicious at that, even though I knew it might only be my paranoia prowling about, looking for something to snack on. "Did that make you angry?"

"Not angry, disappointed. But Jake was always saving Hunter's ass from a proper whipping when they were partners."

"Is this one of those stories you mentioned at the hospital?"

Nestor nodded. "Among others. Rumor has it some real serious shit happened when Hunter and Jake were both cops. There's a reason that they both ended up in Chicago."

"The reason is?"

"I don't know," he laughed once, humorlessly. "I was hoping you did. I'm surprised you never heard more about what went down between them."

"Jake didn't tell me, and Hunter won't talk to me, except to insult me."

"Well, you can't rescue everybody, *chica*. I've found that out

130

the hard way."

"What do you mean?"

He flexed his hands again, staring at the ripped flesh. "I tell you what—we can have a nice, long talk about me someday over a cold beer." His cell phone chirped. "Yeah?" He paused. "No, she's fine. How'd you hear?" *Pause.* "Lathos was in the car. He's dead." He lowered his voice and paced a few steps away from me. "I will." More darkly, he added. "I *said* I would. Chill. I gotta go." He thumbed the off button.

"That sounded tense."

"Lilly. And it was. But you can't really blame her, what with people ending up dead everywhere. But we've got bigger issues now. Lathos wasn't in this alone because he sure as hell didn't put himself in that car."

Grimacing, I tried to ignore the flashes of memory. "Tina," I said thoughtfully.

"What?"

"Tina. He called out her name. I got the impression he thought I was her at first."

"Or maybe he was telling you she put him there."

"What if she's a co-conspirator? Will the killer go after her next?"

"Damn good question, *chica.* Everyone's looking for her. We were hoping to get a lead from someone in the neighborhood. We came up empty. And Lilly really wants to crack this. She thinks it's her last chance at promotion. She's more pissed than ever, especially at you."

Wonderful. Another shadow to jump at. "What did I do to her?"

"She thinks you disrespected her, sneaking off with your cowboy friend when she was trying to help you."

Irritated, I said, "That's not what happened. She's being ridiculous."

"Welcome to my world," he said with tired derision.

"Why is she not here?"

Nestor pointed to his clothes. "We're off duty, but she volunteered for another shift."

I nodded. "That's Lilly, always volunteering."

"That's a fact."

"Something wrong?" I asked, raising an eyebrow to his distinctly snarky tone.

His face softened, and he looked chagrined. "She's a good enough sort. It's not what she does, it's why she does it that upsets me."

I nodded. "So you've said."

He cocked his head, as if perplexed. "I've never said that to you before."

Oops. No, not to me. To her. While I was eavesdropping from the next room. But maybe best not to admit to that. "It could have been Jake who said it." *It wasn't, but, hey, it could have been.* "But what did you mean by it?"

"She volunteers to *lead* a lot of things and sure as hell makes certain the bosses know about it. But she pushes the actual work on to other people. And sometimes . . . well, let's just say she almost always benefits in some way or another. She'll put together a charity event, all right, but it'll end up at the ritziest hotel in town, and damned if she doesn't *have* to stay over-night—at taxpayer expense, mind you—so that she can *oversee* preparations. And rumor has it she's spent a lot of those nights with one committee chair or another."

"Rumor?"

He sighed and rubbed the back of his neck with his hand. "More than rumor, I guess. Hell, I've tried to tell her how that kind of thing looks, but she just makes excuses. She's convinced that as long as the powerful committee types are singing her praises that's all that should matter." He dropped his arm to his side. "She's smart but doesn't get that people see right through her and that's why she's not getting traction with the bosses.

"Aw hell, it's not up to me to judge, and a lot of people are better off because of all her crusades. But I get sick of hearing her whine about how she's not getting her due." He rubbed his hands over his eyes for a few seconds. I noticed he was looking unusually flushed, and his face seemed years older. "I've got other things to worry about. And it's not like I have to put up with it outside of work. She's not family."

"Family can be as big a source of misery."

He stopped and stared hard at me, disapproval carving creases around his mouth. "Family is what's important. They are truly God's gift. No matter how fucked up they are." He looked into the distance again. "Family is what you live for. What you die for. What you . . ."

I cocked my head, taking the next logical step in the conversation. "Kill for?"

His head whipped around, and his fierce gaze impaled me. "No! You don't kill. That's wrong. That's why I became a cop—to stop the bad guys, the killers and conmen and just plain assholes." He rubbed his hands together, hard and fast. "That's why I became a cop, but . . ."

I looked at him, saddened by the look of what seemed like pained resignation on his face. After a few moments of silence, I said, "But?"

"But I'm helpless," he sighed, holding his hands, palm up, before him.

"You?"

He nodded at the water. "I'm helpless to stop crap like this from happening. I'm just cleanup, *chica*. I pick up the pieces after it all goes to shit. But I don't stop it. She's right—why is it so much nobler to pick up the bodies than to stop the bullets?"

"Who's right? Nestor, I'm not following you."

He stopped, and we both looked up as a rescue truck, boat in tow, pulled up to the curb. Two well-muscled men jumped out and proceeded to pull out diving equipment from the rear.

I stood. "Nestor, I don't understand—" But as he stood to join me, he grimaced. Twitching, he put his hand to his back. "Are you okay?" I said.

He groaned and gritted his teeth. "It's my back, again." He pulled a small tin out of his pocket and shook two Percocets into his hand. He swallowed them, using only saliva to wash them down. "I'll be fine." As he rubbed his eyes, fatigue evident in the spidery-red shooting through the whites, I saw his hands were shaking.

"Are you okay? How many of those are you taking a day?"

One of the rescue workers called his name, and he looked over at the man, frowning. Reaching back to massage his neck, he grimaced again. "Be right back."

I put my hand on his arm as he started to leave. "May I borrow your phone?"

He tossed it my way and walked off, rigid with tension. Something was mightily wrong with my favorite cop, and it was eating away at his normally unflappable demeanor. Maybe it was just as he said: his helplessness at preventing all these deaths. Or the chronic back pain. Or maybe it was Lilly. Or maybe his family, because I'd sure as hell flicked a sore spot there. But stable, he currently was not.

Deciding to put that aside for the moment, I called Zach, not telling him any details but asking him to pick me up. The distress in his voice pained me. Apparently, he'd been driving around looking for me for hours. I heard the car roar into gear as we hung up.

Wind gusted behind me, and thunder grumbled in the distance, as if impatient at holding back, irritated by the slow, forward plod of rain-pregnant clouds. I counted slowly to myself, a trick I often employ to distract my attention from fear or migraines—or from the admittedly uncharitable desire to pull words out of the mouths of people who speak very, very slowly.

Just then Zach arrived. Speeding up as he saw me, his car then came to a bouncing stop, one tire rolling up and over the edge of the sidewalk. Even before the car finished rocking, he was out the door, running across the lawn. "Sweet Jesus, you're soaking wet." He looked over my shoulder. The truck with the boat was backing up to the canal edge. "What happened?"

I told him as calmly as I could, trying to focus on the case, on Jake, on Hunter, on anything but the sight of Lathos's face as he died. Still, by the end, my throat had gone tight and raw again. Zach's expression grew more alarmed, his eyes first wide and then narrow.

"That's it!" He snatched my hand and pulled me toward his car. "We're getting you gone, and we're getting you gone, now!"

He turned and ran headlong into Nestor. In one fluid motion, Zach dropped my hand and pulled back a fist. In the same second, Nestor yanked out his gun.

I jumped between them. "Stop! Nestor, Zach, no!"

Nestor pulled up, eyes blazing. "*¡Chingao!* I could've shot you!"

Zach gripped me by the upper arms and moved me behind him. He balled up his fists and squared his stance, clearly ready for a fight. Nestor tensed and raised his gun. I slipped between them a second time, one hand on Zach's chest and the other atop Nestor's gun. "That's enough! Nestor, what's *wrong* with you?"

Nestor glared. "I don't let people raise their fists at me."

"If you don't sneak up on people, you don't get pulled on," Zach shot back. Whether he was giving in to an overstimulated sense of protectiveness or old-fashioned testosterone poisoning, I didn't know. But this was not the time for this crap.

Resisting the urge to grab them both by the short hairs, I said as calmly as I could, "Guys, c'mon. Just say hello, okay? For me?"

Zach's jaw ratcheted tight, but he unclenched his fist. "Howdy."

Nestor's lips twisted in a snarl. "Howdy? What cow town are you from, Jethro?"

Zach's eyes flashed; he stepped up. "You got a problem with the way I talk, city boy?"

Nestor matched his movement. "Nothing I can't handle with ease."

"Maybe I ought to show you—"

"You threaten an officer of the law again, and your ass will be behind bars so fast—"

I slammed a fist into both of their chests. "I said, enough! For God's sake! We've got snipers and bombers and crazy killers trying to drown me, and the two of you decide to play *cave man*?" They both spared me a sidelong glance but neither relaxed much. I groaned. "Can we just focus on what's happening here? Nestor, what did the cops want?"

After the space of a few heartbeats, Nestor turned to me, slowly dropping his gun into the holster on his side. Zach stepped back and wrapped his arm protectively around my waist.

"One of the guys, working in that warehouse down the street, says he saw three people in the area about the same time the car must have hit the water: an old black guy who walks the neighborhood all the time; an SUV with a man in it, no good description; and a woman in a beat-up Chevy with shoulder-length red hair. Are you sure you didn't see who hit you in the building? Could you at least tell if the person was male, female, black, white, Latino?"

I looked down, trying to cast my thoughts back to that split second. But there was nothing. Shaking my head, I looked up again. "I'm sorry."

Zach tightened his arm around my waist. "That's enough. Let's go."

Nestor put his hand out. "This is not a game. Someone's trying to kill her."

A car pulled onto the street. Déjà vu quickened my pulse, and I groaned. "Hunter! What does it take to shake that man? I've got to get out of here. Nestor, you know the pull he has with Voltaire! Even if you take me in, he'll have me in some dungeon of his in a heartbeat."

"I can take care of you. I'll take you somewhere—"

"Back the hell off," Zach growled. "You ain't taking her nowhere."

"Cut it out, you two!" I glanced over my shoulder. Hunter couldn't see me yet, but he'd find me soon. "Nestor, please, I've already made arrangements to fly home to New . . . uh, Haven. To my mom; my family, they'll protect me. It's what families do." He brought his head up sharply and swallowed hard, nodding. I went on. "I just have time to catch the plane if I leave now." My own fib startled me, and I grimaced to myself, guiltily. I knew I shouldn't be asking this. I was the only witness to what had just happened, and Nestor could get in trouble for letting me go before I gave an official statement. I grimaced to myself guiltily, knowing I was taking advantage of his befuddled state. But, honestly, Nestor was really freaking me out, and right now I didn't want to be alone with him, either.

Zach smiled perversely, clearly happy to help me lie. "We got her a ticket this morning."

A door slammed, and I ducked behind Zach. I looked back at Nestor. "Please? If you really want me to be safe . . . And it's what cops do, keep people safe."

He worked his jaw, staring at Hunter, who approached a group of police officers by the tow truck. Body language telegraphed a tense conversation. Finally, Nestor heaved a sigh and then nodded tersely. I stretched up on my toes and kissed him on his cheek, ignoring Zach's bristling. Then I grasped Zach's hand and pulled him in a full run to his truck.

It took four-plus hours to get from Chicago to New Orleans, including a thirty-minute delay on the tarmac as a summer storm raged by. Fortunately for me, Zach had thrown my duffle bag in his truck, including not only Jake's lockbox but a change of clothes from my apartment, which he picked up between getting me coffee and finding me gone. His offer to take care of George while I was gone both saved time and put my mind at ease. And I'd had just enough time before taking off to buy a small container of baby powder and some powdered chocolate at a food stand. I'd taken both into the handicapped stall in the bathroom, along with several handfuls of soaped-up paper towels and a few dry ones.

Peeling off my clothes, I washed myself. I felt incredibly vulnerable at being naked in an airport bathroom stall, not to mention freezing my ta-ta's off. I doused myself thoroughly in baby powder, until the woman in the next stall and I both sneezed. Taking the paper cup I'd gotten from the food stand, I filled it with baby powder and a touch of cocoa and dumped it on my head, working it into the roots. The powder soaked up the oil from my scalp, and the dark cocoa over my dark hair saved me from looking like a refugee from a sixteenth-century wig shop. Okay, not perfect, but at least I didn't smell like rancid canal water anymore.

Exhausted, I slept most of the way. Or as best I could, considering I sat by a heavy-set man who kept sniffing me. I couldn't tell if his interest was epicurean or sexual. Or both.

Plus, the kid behind me kept trying to eat my hair.

Once we landed, I took a cab to Gorman's, an upscale department store in an impeccable highrise. Unfortunately, the answer to my inquiry was, "Yes, Ms. Smith is here today, but, no, she is not in at the moment." At four p.m. Ms. Smith would be in. Who shall they say called? I left my name and promised to come back. I had fifty minutes to kill, so I went for a walk.

The highrise containing Gorman's sat on the border of modern New Orleans and the French Quarter. On one side, glass, steel, and concrete; on the other, cobblestones, shingled roofs, and wrought-iron balconies. Anxious to see the latter, I jogged across the street. Like many Yankees, I was both awed by and envious of the Old South and, for me, New Orleans had always been an idea as much as a place. I'd pictured slim tendrils of fragrant vines snaking over baroque ironwork balconies. Delicate southern belles, bedecked in yellow flounce and broad-brimmed hats, sipping iced tea on a sweltering summer day, beads of condensation gathered into rivulets, tracing lazy, winding trails down the sides of the tall glasses. The barest hint of times past filled the air, full-bodied, with a touch of sadness but still strong and vigorous, like a fine French brandy. At least that's what I'd always imagined.

Boy, had I been wrong.

Humidity swaddled me like a wet blanket. The scent of decaying fish, so strong I could taste it, wafted up from the water on a hot breeze. I walked on, wiping at lipline sweat, while the brown water made nasty, little lapping sounds against the dock. To add to my grief, after the hours of inactivity, even hoisting my duffle bag on my good shoulder made me grimace in pain.

I struggled on, passing emaciated houses with narrow windows and thin doors. Their second-floor porches, rimmed with iron banisters, clung parasitically to unsteady buildings, warped with age. Tropical greenery lined the balconies, overgrowing in pots of all sizes; tiny jungles gone mad. What, at first glance, appeared to be ice cream parlors turned out to be shops selling giant plastic cups of a high-octane drink called a Hurricane. Along the narrow streets, large-breasted women, braless, in tight, strategically tattered t-shirts, cooed at customers outside of "gentlemen's clubs": women selling women. Nope, not the New Orleans of my fantasies.

I found myself in front of a three-spire white church. Each spire held a cross, high above a verdant lawn. In front was a park, skirted by a wrought-iron fence, a somber barrier that would have differentiated where men of stature could walk from where those without it should stay.

As I sat wearily on a bench, my pocket buzzed. Startled, I pulled out the phone. "Hello?"

There was a pause and then: "Who the hell is this?"

I ground my jaw, annoyed at the unwarranted aggression. "Who the hell wants to know?"

"Madison? What are you doing with Nestor's phone? Is he with you?"

"Oh, it's you, Lilly," I said, relieved to hear a familiar voice. "Nestor's not here. I borrowed his phone and forgot to give it back. Any word about Jake? How's he doing?"

"He's the same. Are you sure Nestor's not with you?"

"What kind of question is that? I'm not even in Chicago anymore."

"So I heard. Hunter told Voltaire you skipped, and they're both pissed! You're in big trouble."

Oh, crap. Hunter knows I'm gone? "You don't have to sound so happy about it."

"Well, I don't like being disrespected. You ran out on me."

I groaned. "Come on, Lilly. Don't take it like that. I wasn't running away from you. I was running away from Hunter. I'm not your enemy here."

"Yeah, right!" Her voice was more helpless than angry. I'd really hurt her feelings.

Guilt washed over me. I softened my own voice. "Look, Lilly. I'm sorry. Really. I didn't mean to disrespect you. And, honestly, I'm not after Nestor." Mostly honestly, anyway.

A long silence filled the phone line. I could almost hear her thinking. "Just stay away from him," she said finally. "You don't know him as well as you think you do."

"I'm beginning to realize that. He's so fisty lately."

"He's what?" she said, rightfully perplexed.

"You know, fisty," I said, pantomiming throwing a fist with my free hand, a gesture she, of course, could not see. "Lately he's been given to bouts of fisticuffs: fisty."

"Is that a real word?"

"Oh, sure, let's say it is. My point is that he's so on edge. What's going on with him?"

"Family issues. Nothing you need to be concerned with. Where are you?"

"Well, uh," I paused, stalling. It's not that I didn't trust Lilly, per se. But Nestor had raised just enough doubts in my mind that I was worried she'd relay my location to Voltaire. And I had no doubt that the man's reach could easily extend to the very bench on which I sat.

On the other hand, Nestor had been acting so oddly lately. Come to think of it, the only negative things I'd ever heard about Lilly had come from him. So why believe him over her? Then I remembered something. Lilly had told me at the scene of the fire that there were "things I didn't know, that can get people killed." She said that she "knew how to end this" while being very careful not to let Nestor see us. Did she know that he was involved with all the killing? Was she merely being loyal, too loyal, to her partner, trying to handle things on her own without exposing him while simultaneously trying to protect me by spiriting me away?

Sure, Nestor was behaving abnormally, and, okay, it was a

little hard to believe that a mere "family issue" would ruffle Officer Smooth's feathers so fully. But I'd seen the fervor in his eyes when he mentioned family. Exterior calm aside, Nestor was clearly a man of strong convictions. If something was going wrong with his relatives, then I could believe he'd go a little nuts. Indeed—even with all the problems between my mother and me at the moment—I'd probably do the same. *Rats.* My gut instinct told me to trust him. But was it gut instinct? Or did I simply want to trust him because I wanted a square-jawed hero cop in my life? *Whoa. Where did that come from? No more late-night "women's channel" romances for you, Madison, my girl.*

I said, "I, uh, I have an appointment now. I'll call you back—"

"Wait! No!" The desperation in her voice was almost palpable. "I, I've been working on this Hunter angle you suggested. I have something."

My pulse picked up its pace. "I didn't suggest—oh, never mind. What did you find?"

"I don't want to say over the phone. But it's big. Tell me where you are, and I'll fax it."

"I'm not near a fax machine." Even if I were, the New Orleans area code would give away my location. I felt bad holding out on her, but I just couldn't risk her telling Voltaire where I was. "I need you to trust me, Lilly. I know how badly you want to get this right. And I'm trying to help. Look, email it to me. I'll hit a cyber café and pull it off."

"We need to move on this." I heard doubt and anxiety in her voice.

"Then tell me what you have now."

Her voice dropped. "I can't. I'm in the precinct waiting for Nestor to finish some paperwork. He'll be back any second. People keep walking by. I don't want to be overheard."

"Then email it to me. I'll get back to you as soon as I can. I promise."

"I'd feel better if I knew where you were."

"It's better for you if you don't. Trust me." I gave her my email address and hung up.

Trust me? Hah! And whom do I trust? I chewed at my lower lip. I couldn't help but be disturbed by the strength of Lilly's conviction. Could Hunter really be guilty? He doesn't like me, so why stalk me? On the other hand, I had only Nestor's word for that. Yet, Lilly suspects Hunter, too. Was he the one who ran out the back door of the apartment building, or was he the one who hit me? On the other, other hand, both he and Nestor also had enough time to put me in the car and double back. Lilly, in contrast, had been working. Unless, of course, Nestor had lied about that. So who knocked me out? I groaned out loud and rubbed my hands across my eyes. Who to trust? Lilly? Hunter? Nestor? All of them? None of them? My stomach twisted.

And what about Tina? Lathos had called out for her. What if he was telling me it was she who put us in the car? Maybe she and Lathos *had* set Jake up but then they had a falling-out. Or maybe she was working with someone else. Maybe she'd joined forces with Jake's attacker from the hospital. Maybe the two of them are in cahoots and they'd put Lathos and me in the car. *Wait!* I sat forward, brain tingling as I remembered what Nestor said hours earlier. The witness who saw a woman by the canal said she had shoulder-length red hair. Tina was a redhead! I gasped. *Another connection! But, damn it, what's it all mean?*

The timer on my watch went off. Enough with the mental Sudoku. These clues weren't adding up. Someone was lying. Or maybe they all were.

I slung my duffle bag over my shoulder and left the bench. The best person to help me figure out how Tina knew Fancy's nickname for Jake was Fancy herself. Time to talk to her.

On the way, I came upon an open-air market. Under the canopy, a man sat on a wooden crate. His deep black skin glistened. He wore a purple beret set at a jaunty angle over close-shorn silver hair. On his lap lay a gleaming saxophone. A cigar box at his feet contained a few bills and change. I stopped, and he winked at me. He brought the instrument to his lips, closed his eyes, and played a deep, haunting melody with long, slow notes as rich as old bourbon. A smiling young couple strolled by, sharing a doughy beignet.

Okay, so New Orleans is not as simple as my fantasies would have it. It's tougher, but somehow still courtly; vile and lecherous, but smooth and savvy. A town that knows exactly what it is and doesn't much give a damn what either the priggish or the profane think of it. I could see Jake here, walking these streets, talking with these people, laughing with them, guarding them, or, if need be, calling them out. A deep longing to see that in the flesh came over me. I wanted him to live. But more, I didn't want the evil son of a bitch who shot him to kill again.

And I wanted revenge.

The music stopped. The man smiled at me. I dropped a dollar in the box and walked away.

CHAPTER NINE

I entered the cosmetics department and sneezed. I love perfume as much as the next female, but the invisible layer of spices, citruses, and florals that permeates such enclaves can be a bit much. Pulling Jake's lockbox from my duffle bag, I tucked it under my good arm and scanned the mirrored aisles. I didn't go unnoticed long.

A middle-aged woman, mink-brown hair impeccably coiffed in a languishing swirl atop her head, dressed in a white lab coat with pink trim, strode purposefully toward me. As she got closer, I could see from the way her lipstick feathered into the lines of her mouth that I could easily have been her granddaughter. She was armed with a bottle of perfume and scent cards.

"And how can I help you today, ma'am? Our latest Calvin has just arrived."

Calvin, as in Klein. How nice they're on a first-name basis. I returned her smile with equal insincerity. "I'm looking for Ms. Smith. I was told she'd be back by now."

The sides of her wide mouth fell slightly, seeming to realize that she wasn't going to get a percentage out of me. "Ms. Smith works the Quetile line. Next counter down and to the left."

"Thank you." I started past her.

She flicked me a perfumed card with a smoothness that would have impressed Wyatt Earp. "Oh, but you must try this. It's *the* scent of the moment, and my *personal* favorite."

I blinked, not sure if she was pressuring me or coming on to me. Smiling neutrally, I took it and walked toward the dramatic black sign with the Quetile logo, the name scrawled graffiti-like in racecar-red and with a lipstick trailing the last letter. I waved the card as I walked. *Hmm, very nice.* I rubbed the card on each wrist. *You know, Hunter would probably like—*

Whoa! No! Do not think of that man in any kind of sensual context. I forbid it!

Having shouted my libido down, I found my target. F. Gloria was a blond, a real blond from the way the fluorescent lights caught hints of gray in the long silken ponytail draped over her left shoulder. She had a complexion that some women would have bathed in virgin blood for. Her makeup glowed with an adroit artistry that made me wonder what was paint and what was real. But light lines radiated from the corners of her eyes and an uncompromising straightness in the butter-blond brows hardened her blue eyes, making me think of iced-over lakes. She wore a red-on-black name tag reading F. Gloria over the right pocket of her black smock. Correction: her smock wouldn't be called black; it would probably be called *Midnight Romance Ebony* or some such. As I drew closer, I noticed a thin metal something sticking up out of her right breast pocket. It looked like a caliper with an eyebrow brush attached. Gee, didn't that look scientific?

Smiling serenely, F. Gloria helped a young woman sporting a faded perm of dull, brown hair and the small, round eyes of a starving gerbil. The woman gazed at her with the kind of faith usually seen only at tent revivals. I couldn't hear their words, but I knew F. Gloria was delivering the standard promise that desperate gerbil-eyed women fell for. This cream will do it, the promise went, this blusher, this shadow. Buy this, and you'll be irresistible. Don't buy it, and you'll be lonely and unfulfilled for the rest of your life. Buy now, while you still have your youth, while we still offer a special giveaway package with any purchase over twenty dollars.

Gerbil-eyes nodded and offered up her credit card. I stared down at the muted rainbow of eye shadows in the display counter before me, ran a finger over the greasy residue of hands well lotioned. Attention split between studying the cosmetics displays and watching F. Gloria ring up the sale, I waited until Gerbil-eyes was on her way, clutching the black and lipstick-red bag as she scurried by, then smiled purposefully at F. Gloria.

She walked over to me, the same distant but pleasant smile on her face. "How may I help you? A gold eye shadow would accentuate those lovely blue eyes of yours." Her accent rang true: bayou to the last muted vowel but modified for the urban consumer.

"On my budget, I couldn't even afford silver."

Her practiced smile stayed put, but annoyed boredom flicked across her eyes. "Yes, ma'am," she said. "Have you seen our new Double-Matte, Moisturizing, Kissable-Color, Day-Long Wear Lipstick line? It's guaranteed to stay in place through the most rigorous activities."

Rigorous activities? That sounds interesting. "Actually, I'm investigating—"

All pretense of pleasantry disappeared. "There's an information booth by the elevators," she said abruptly and walked away.

"Hey, wait a minute." I trotted around the corner after her. "I only want to—"

She turned so quickly I was brought up short. The polished saleswoman persona disappeared. "You got a badge, missy?"

"Pardon me?"

The woman's eyes darkened to the color of thunderclouds, the kind that suckle tornadoes. "You don't got a badge, you don't got my time."

I reached under my arm for Jake's box and from it pulled out Jake's badge. In an instant, she snatched it out of my hands, scoffing at it. She tossed it back at me, and it bounced off my chest. I grabbed for it and fumbled it back into the box.

F. Gloria leaned forward, her face inches from mine. "Where'd you get that trick, sugar? Late-night reruns of *The Rockford Files*? If you're going to try such a tired routine, at least get a recent badge. Ours were redesigned two years ago." Again, she strode away.

Desperation made my stomach feel suddenly weightless. "Why did he call you Fan-Glorious?" I called out.

She stopped, and I gulped. Pivoting, she walked slowly toward me. I'd seen such an expression before, when my oldest brother was in his women-in-prison-movie phase and made me watch them when he babysat. I shifted my weight to my back leg, ready to run. She reached up and fondled the caliper/eyebrow brush in her pocket. I still had no idea of its purpose but had no doubt it could leave a scar. Then she dropped her hands onto the counter between us. "Only one person calls me that. You're about to tell me you're a good friend of Jake's, ain't you?" Her glare intensified. "That would be the safest thing to say."

Jeez, are the words "threaten me, please" tattooed on my forehead or something? I pulled Jake's note out of the lockbox and held it up. Her eyes narrowed at the signature, and she reached for it, but I pulled it back. "You want to talk now?"

"Where'd you get that?"

I realized that I hadn't decided how to tell her what happened. I flushed and bit at my lower lip. "I, I work with Jake. He was shot yesterday. Oh, he's alive!" I added quickly. "But he's in . . . bad shape."

Her perfect skin paled. The hard set in her eyes melted away. "How bad?"

"Very. He's hanging in there, but—"

She swallowed hard. "Is he going to die?"

My heart fell as the reality hit home again. "It's very bad. We don't know."

Her eyes blazed, and she thrust a finger at me. "Don't you go counting him out, you hear me? That man's a rock. He's a bull. He isn't going to go down so easy. So don't you go helping Satan along with all your doubts!"

Both impressed and intimidated, I could only stammer, "I, I'm sorry. I don't mean to."

"Yeah, well don't. You hear me? Don't you—" She blinked as the corners of her eyes filled with tears. Her breathing quickened. "Oh, fuck," she said softly. Her hand went up to the side of her mouth, and she brushed at her lipstick as if it suddenly annoyed her.

I heard dainty steps behind me.

"What are you lookin' at?" F. Gloria barked. Heels clicked quickly into the distance. "Come on," she said, walking toward the opening in the counter.

I followed along on my side of the display case. F. Gloria paused to murmur something to another Quetile saleswoman whose robe sported an extra row of scarlet piping along the collar, probably the chief scientist. The woman frowned her disapproval. That caused F. Gloria to say something quick, sharp, and low. Ms. Chief Scientist paled and backed off in a hurry.

With me in tow, F. Gloria crossed the gleaming floors to the back of the store. She pushed her way through a set of green swinging doors. I ducked in before they swung closed.

Stacks of boxes lined the walls, and a plastic table, surrounded by matching chairs, sat near a kitchen-type counter. Notices and schedules were tacked to a corkboard above a scarred white microwave. A McDonald's fish sandwich wrapper and a half-empty drink lay in the middle of the table. F. Gloria tossed the cup into the sink and brushed the wrapper onto the floor, then motioned for me to sit. I did, putting the lockbox on the table before me. F. Gloria fetched an unopened pack of Marlboros from a side pocket, took off her smock, and tossed it over the back of her chair. She sank wearily into the seat opposite me.

Beneath the lab coat was a different woman. Her simple dress, peach and sleeveless, hung on her sharp shoulders. Braless, the dress draped over nipples on the leeward side of youth.

She held the Marlboros in hands that looked older, then crinkled the cellophane and dropped it to the floor on top of the sandwich wrapper. She stuck the cigarette between her lips, staining the white paper with lipstick that now seemed orange and garish. Images flashed through my mind. I saw homecoming queens who had once reigned supreme in small towns all over the South, flounced prom dresses their regalia. I saw their male minions, the jocks, their hard-ons straining to get free from their jeans. Their court, the bed of a pickup parked beneath a blooming magnolia. But F. Gloria's reign had ended long ago, the last tailgate flipped up on a final autumn night, leaving her to find her own way home.

Fancy struck a match and the sharp scent made my nose twitch. Cigarette lit, she rested an elbow on the table and blew smoke into the air above her. For several long moments, she stared quietly at the ceiling. I studied her now-fragile face as she watched the smoke eddy up and around from every new puff.

When she had herself under control, she took another deep drag and let out a long, shaky breath. Her eyes turned to me, her expression calm and unwavering. "What happened?"

"We were ambushed. I'm trying to find out who did it."

"Here, in N'Awlins? I thought he was up Chicago way."

"It happened in Chicago."

She stared with a detached, menacing intensity that knotted

150

my stomach. I swallowed hard. She knocked the ashes off with a deft flick of her thumb. "Y'ain't no cop and y'ain't his type. So what's it to you?"

"I worked for him. I was there when it happened."

"You were there? And you didn't see anyone?"

I shook my head forlornly. "I wish I had."

Her eyes softened. "Did he know he was shot, before he went down?"

"Yes."

She laughed a short, two-pulse laugh. "I'll bet he was pissed. That'd be just like him. To get shot and be all pissed about it. That's my man for you."

Conflicting emotions, sadness and joy, merged in me, like two mismatched chemicals swirling together, producing vapors at once disorienting and invigorating. Her intensity, the rawness of her manner, stung like cold water, both harsh and bracing. But in her eyes, her love for Jake was palpable, and I wondered what it would be like to be loved that deeply.

The door creaked open, and a man walked in. Physically nondescript, he was a standard watered-down white boy, the kind who didn't get why he'd never been given the keys to the executive washroom. His pale brown eyes widened. "Gloria baby, you okay?"

F. Gloria blew smoke at him. "Go whack yourself off somewhere else, Chester. Me and my girlfriend here are having a conversation."

Chester peeked at me, as if hoping I hadn't noticed the verbal emasculation. I averted my eyes, and he backed out of the room. I turned to watch F. Gloria form a perfect smoke ring three inches above eye level. "Dick-wad," she said, nodding at the door. " 'Gloria baby,' my ass. Give a guy one blow job, and he thinks he can be your weekly lollipop."

My eyes went wide, and I actually gasped.

She grinned. "What's the matter, sugar, you didn't ever go down on a guy?"

"Um. Not in the last ten minutes." *Well, what the hell else was I going to say?*

She took another drag. "Got me off Dead Tuesday shifts."

I couldn't help but smile. I was beginning to see why Jake called her Fan-Glorious.

"Jake wasn't anything like that walking dildo," she said. "He never assumed, just because he had it once, he could have it again. Jake always asked. I liked that about him."

My smile froze. I blinked. "You mean you and Jake were . . . um . . . ?"

"Yeah, we were 'um.' We used to 'um' two, three times a day on a good day. That man had stamina, I'll tell you."

I shook my head in disbelief. "Jake Thibodaux? Big, redneck ex-cop, can belch out 'God Bless America' on a single beer? We're talking about the same guy?"

She turned a smile on me; it was brazen and genuine. "He didn't always look like he does now. Oh, you should have seen him ten years ago. God, he was something. Built like a bull elephant, solid, hard everywhere. And I do mean everywhere. And all the time too."

The scene of Jake in the car that last night popped into my head. *She's got to be kidding.*

She let the cigarette dangle from her mouth. "You don't believe me."

"Well, uh . . ."

"It started with him and me a long time ago. We were both a lot prettier. He didn't let himself go until he left here. Small wonder why."

The smoke seeped into my lungs, but I didn't want to cough in front of her. "How old were you?"

"Like the song says, 'old enough to know better, young

enough not to care.' Back then I was just plain old Fancy Smith from Bocatelle." She spread her stick-thin arms open wide to encompass the stockroom, cigarette dancing as she spoke. "But look at all I have now."

"Fancy? That is what the 'F' is for then?"

She tapped ashes off on the edge of the table, watching them fall. "Fancy Gloriana Scarlet Emilina Smith."

I stared.

"Mama read too many romance novels," she said.

Staring still seemed to be my best option.

"She named my brother Chastain Beauregard Emery Sinclair Smith. I swear to God that must have been what they fought over the night he was killed."

Not being able to come up with anything else, I said, "Tell me about you and Jake."

Her expression darkened. "You writing his memoirs or something?"

"Whoever tried to kill him has killed at least two people, maybe three if a very nice lady doesn't recover. Not to mention trying to kill me." I shook my head. "I thought I knew him."

F. Gloria stared pensively at the cigarette in her hand. "Jake brought Mama home one night about, oh, eleven years ago. I was a hair under eighteen."

My God, she's only twenty-nine? Out in the showroom lights, I could believe that. There in the back room, under the neon lights, I'd've put her in her forties.

"Mama had been shoplifting." Fancy leaned forward, her eyes intense, "Now, you got to understand Mama didn't realize that's what she was doing. She was a good Christian woman."

I nodded.

She sat back and took another drag. "Mama kind of lost track of reality once Papa left and all." F. Gloria breathed out a long cloud of smoke. "To her, those high-priced showrooms

were like her front parlor. The way she saw it, she was just moving her things from one room to another—from the showrooms to our house—to make things pretty for visitors." The woman's thickly lacquered lips curled up in an affectionate grin. "Mama wasn't all there."

"But I'll bet she was quite the lady."

A start of emotion—surprise? gratitude?—shone in her eyes. She flicked at her cigarette. "It happens that way to Southern women sometimes, the craziness. Especially to the ones who are poor white trash on the outside but the belle of the ball on the inside. It started happening to Mama after I was born. It had something to do with Papa leaving, or getting dumped in the swamp, or whatever the hell happened to him. All I know is that one day he was gone. And no one would talk about him. But you don't want to know about that. You want to know about Jake."

"You tell me whatever you want to tell me. I'll listen."

Her cheeks reddened. I waited. She brought out a fresh cigarette, lit it with the dying ember of the last, and tossed the still-glowing butt on the floor. "It was late fall, right after Halloween, when Jake brought Mama home. My brother wasn't due onshore for months, so it was just me watching her. But I never could keep track of her proper. Anyhow, Jake brought Mama home in the squad car. She carried a little bag from Dillard's with some lacy place settings in it, or some kind of crap like that. He could have arrested her. But he'd paid for the stuff himself and brought her home."

F. Gloria looked up at the ceiling, smiling at a memory. "Oh, did I let into him. I was all like, 'Who the fuck do you think you are?' I told him we weren't a charity case for some do-gooder cop to make Sunday school points on."

"Wait. You yelled at him for *not* putting your mother in jail?"

"Yeah. It was stupid, I know."

I nodded. I also struck out at people when I was embarrassed. Or scared. Or hurt. Or pretty much for any reason lately.

"I tell you, though, there was something about him that looked *so* good. And that pissed me off even more. Like I said, he was a bull of a man back then. Or maybe he looked too much like I always dreamed Papa did. I don't know. Anyway, there I was shouting at him: fuck this, fuck that, fuck you. Mama tittering around trying to decide where to put what she took. Jake, he just stood there and watched me, all calm-like. I yelled myself blue in the face. When I finished . . ." Her voice trailed off.

"When you finished?"

"He pulled out a Marlboro and lit one up. Then he offered it to me."

"You're kidding."

"Nope. Just like in the movies. He held it out and I took it. I'd run out of cigs that morning. Don't know how he knew I was dying for one, but he did." She showed me the cigarette that she was smoking as if it was a legacy. "Then he lit one for himself. He never said a word."

"And then?"

"And then he left."

"That's it?"

"Oh, he came back, from time to time. He even brought me and Mama a turkey one Thanksgiving. He got it from one of those charities that the rich folks put out so they can buy their way into heaven. Mama was so happy. She pulled out our best plates and went to cooking. So I took him in the back room and give *him* something to be thankful for. At least that's how he put it. And God help me, but that man knew how to put it." She chuckled, clearly enjoying the stupefied look on my face. "After that, he'd come by two or three times a week. He'd bring pretty trinkets for Mama and then do me in the back room

155

while she fell asleep in the rocker."

I thought back to that last night, that fat guy belching out the scent of mustard, meat, and onions. What had happened to bring about such a change? "And you were only seventeen?"

"Near enough to eighteen." She shrugged. "Hey, I started it."

I didn't know whether to be disgusted or charmed. *But hell, what did I know about being poor and lonely? Okay, what did I know about being poor?* I shook my head, then pointed to her cigarette. "Can I have one of those?"

She flicked her wrist and a Marlboro slid halfway out of the package. I took it and leaned forward as she lit it with a match from the Boot Scoots Bar.

"You don't smoke," she said.

"I tried it once." I took a careful drag, remembering my brother's warning not to swallow the smoke. I let it swirl around in my mouth and exhaled, but it still didn't feel right. "My mother wouldn't keep ashtrays in the house, so I didn't have any place to put the ashes."

F. Gloria smiled halfway, not buying my bravado. She knocked her ashes to the floor with a flick of her thumb. I tried to do the same, nearly dropping the cigarette in the process.

I perched the cigarette on the edge of the table and reached into Jake's lockbox. "I wonder if you could help me with something. There were a few pictures among Jake's things. Do you know who the woman in this picture is?"

She took the photos, expression neutral. "This one's Jake's wife, Corrine. She died of breast cancer about six years ago." She handed the picture back to me.

"Six years?" That meant Corrine had been alive during Fancy and Jake's affair.

"That's right," she said, her gaze unwavering.

"So, what, then? Jake was unhappy at home?"

She shrugged. "He was happy enough."

"I mean, like his wife didn't understand him or something?"

"Sugar, let me tell you something. Most men who screw around do it because they can. More often than not it doesn't have anything to do with their wives, or jobs, or any of that crap. They just fucking do it. Yeah, some guys invent excuses when they get caught, mostly because they don't have the balls to 'fess up. Maybe Jake told his wife, maybe not. All I know is that he was nice to me, and I was nice to him. We were friends. Sex was a bonus, and it didn't need to be more than that for either one of us. Even when his wife died, things didn't change between us."

"He never talked about his family then?" Disappointment welled up in me. Interesting as it was, nothing in Jake and Fancy's love life seemed relevant to who had tried to kill him.

"He talked about his daughter. She was a couple of years younger than me. He didn't go into detail, just bragging on how beautiful she was, how smart she was. God, he doted on her."

I handed her the picture of the young woman holding George. "Is this her?"

F. Gloria took it and nodded. "Uh-huh, that's Adalida. What else you got there?"

I handed the third picture across the table. She flushed, taking it as if it were some fragile artifact. "He kept my picture with theirs? He really did that? With his wife and kid? No shit?" Tears played at the corner of her eyes, but she wiped them away with a thumb. She brushed the burned-out cigarette that she'd propped on the edge of the table onto the floor and slowly went through the ritual of lighting another.

I waited for her to take a few puffs, watching as background light scattered off the smoke particles, tinting the cigarette smoke blue. I considered telling her the effect was caused by Rayleigh scattering, then decided the explanation would cost me whatever "cool points" I might have gained. "Do you know where I can find Adalida?" I wondered again why Jake hadn't left this box to her and why Hunter hadn't mentioned her either.

Fancy drew her brows together, scowling as if confronting a memory she'd run off once and had no patience to do so again. "Not going to happen. She killed herself three years ago."

I stared. *Man, I really need to work on my comeback repertoire.*

"Things between me and Jake had slowed a bit by then. I still saw him once a month or so. But with me trying to go back to community college, I got real busy."

It was my turn to take a drag. "Fuck," I said.

F. Gloria nodded appreciatively. "There you go."

"Why did she kill herself?"

"Don't know. Jake wouldn't talk about it. And I didn't know anyone else in his life, so I couldn't ask. Jake went north soon after. He didn't come back for any funeral. I don't even think there was one. He wrote to me on and off, but he wouldn't talk about it."

"But there were rumors?"

She considered me carefully. Finally, she said, "They say it was because of Adalida's beau. Jake didn't like the boy."

"Why not?"

"Don't know that either. Jake wouldn't talk about it. But I tell you one thing: it was more than him thinking no one was good enough for his little girl. From the look in Jake's eyes the few times the subject came up . . . Whew! Jake was really pissed! I figured there was something bad wrong with the kid, like he was married. Or a Yankee."

So Jake—a married man having an affair with a teenager— got upset about his daughter possibly having an affair with a married man? That's pretty hypocritical in my book, but I remembered the old saying that everything a cat does makes sense to the cat, and reflected yet again on how that seems to apply so well to men. "How did Adalida feel about her father?"

"She worshiped him to death from what little I knew. Rumor was she couldn't live without her beau, but she couldn't bear to disappoint her Daddy neither. So she did herself in."

"Adalida actually killed herself for that?"

Fancy picked a piece of tobacco from the corner of her mouth. "Worked for Juliet."

"That's true." We smoked while I thought. *So there's an irate boyfriend out there. Someone irate enough to want to kill Jake?* I thought about the letter tacked on the door in the alley. "Tell me something, Ms. Smith—"

"Call me Fancy, Sugar."

I realized I'd never introduced myself. "Madison McKenna."

She raised an eyebrow, smirking. "Madison? Like the avenue in Monopoly?"

"It's a family name," I said, raising an eyebrow defensively.

"Yankees got strange names."

Smiling pointedly, I said. "Tell me something, *Fancy,* on the back of your picture, you called Jake 'Big D.' Did everyone call him that?"

"No, only me and Adalida, as far as I know. It means Big Daddy. I got it off a note she left him, used it before I knew what it meant to him. It surprised me that he didn't mind. I don't think anyone else could've gotten away with it. Why?"

"A note at the ambush addressed Jake as 'Big D,' so his would-be killer knows his nickname. I have to wonder how many people he could have gotten that from."

Fancy shrugged.

"Did you ever hear of a man called Octaviano Lathos? Or a woman named Tina?"

She thought for a moment. "His name doesn't ring a bell. I guess I might have met a Tina sometime in my life, but I can't think of anyone now. You got a last name?"

Exhaling in frustration, I said, "I wish I did. But can you

159

think of *anyone* who might have known Adalida's nickname for Jake?"

"Jake had a partner—a real badass."

I grimaced. "Yeah, Maxwell Hunter. I know him."

"Lucky you."

"Tell me about it."

She ground her cigarette out on the plastic top of the table. I followed suit. "There's got to be someone. How about an old girlfriend of Adalida's or a confidante?"

"A what?"

"Someone she would have told everything to."

"A girl tells everything to her mama."

I scoffed mentally. "Not in my house. But never mind that. Anyone else?"

She considered a moment. "There's Miss Livy."

"Who's that?

"Adalida's old piano teacher. I heard they were close."

"Do you know where she lives?"

"I think she lives up toward Slidell, off the Lake."

"The Lake?"

"Lake Pontchartrain. You can look her up in the white pages under L. Brouchard."

"Or in the Yellow Pages under piano instructors."

"Hah! A lady like Miss Livy don't advertise in no Yellow Pages. She don't need to; she's teaching second and third generations now." Fancy looked down at her simple shift and pulled the neckline closer together over her braless chest. "The likes of me don't go to the houses of the likes of her. Classy out on the sales floor is one thing, but that don't erase who I am."

So that's still how things were down here: "The Likes of Me" and "The Likes of Her"? It burned me to think that Fancy didn't feel she could go anyplace she wanted to. But as I looked at her, I realized that my grandmother wouldn't have been comfortable inviting Fancy into her home. And, I realized to my embarrassment, up to a few moments ago, I probably wouldn't have either. Suddenly, the likes of me didn't seem good enough to be talking to the likes of her. I stood. "Thanks for the help."

She stood too. "I want to go see him."

"Of course." I ripped a piece off the fish wrapper and wrote down the name of Jake's hospital and room number, as well as my own address and Nestor's cell phone number. "If you think of anything that could help, call me. Or if there is anything you need, ever, just ask."

"I always wanted to see Chicago."

"I hope you visit us. Oh, don't be surprised if the cops show up asking questions."

"About Jake or about you?"

"Probably both. But if they ask, I'd appreciate it if you never saw me before."

Her smile radiated innocence. "Never laid eyes on you in my life."

I smiled back. "Thanks."

Her brows furrowed—the dangerous look returned. "But if you find out who hurt Jake, you'll let me know?"

"I promise."

"A couple of my brother's old buddies still work the heavy booms. They'd be happy to help that son of a bitch find Jesus. We might even let you watch."

I felt a rush in my stomach: a tumbling combination of hoping to see said sight and guilty realization that doing so should bother me but wouldn't. "You have a deal."

Fancy followed me to the door. I cracked it open and my breath caught in my throat. Maxwell Hunter trailed another powder-perfect saleswoman, not twenty yards away! I ducked back into the room. "Damn!"

Fancy came up beside me. "What's the matter?"

I jerked my head toward the door. "See that guy?"

She peered out the portal. "The dick in the Armani suit?"

"How did you know he was a private detective?"

"He is?"

"Don't you recognize him? That's Hunter."

"I never met him."

My diaphragm muscle tightened, my fists clenched, and my jaw set hard with the visceral desire to fight or flee; the decision, swiftly made, pegged my "flee meter" to the wall. "Well, I don't want him to find me. He's tried to get me thrown in jail once. I have a feeling he'd succeed this time around. Is there a back way out?"

She jerked her thumb right. I headed in that direction. "It's blocked off," she called out.

I stopped and stared.

"Inventory just arrived," she said calmly.

This was no time to be calm! "That's a fire-safety violation!"

She raised an eyebrow. "Yeah, I'll bring that up at the next meeting."

I glanced around in desperation.

Fancy pointed to boxes stacked several feet tall. "Hide there, and wait for my signal. Then slip out."

Hunter would hit the door at any second. I ducked behind the boxes. "What signal?"

"You'll know." Her tone made me wish I could see her face.

The door opened, and I slipped further between the boxes and the wall, banging my bad shoulder. I stifled a yell. I heard Hunter's voice, muffled by the stack between us, and squeezed myself tighter into the narrow opening. I stuck my head out as far as I dared. Fancy led Hunter past the stack and kept his back to me.

They spoke, their voices low. I settled in against the wall and thought about my next step: finding Miss Livy. If Fancy was any indication of Jake's associates, the meeting should be interesting at least. The slow, deliberate sound of a zipper interrupted my musings.

Wide-eyed, I leaned forward and took a look.

Hunter's back still faced me. Fancy stood in front of him. He had both hands on her upper arms, but I couldn't tell if he was holding her off or keeping her in place. One way or the other, I figured I'd received my signal. I slipped out, silent as guilt.

Nearly to the escalator, as I lagged behind a woman balancing three toddlers and sporting a look that spelled doom for her husband, a scream of "Rape!" rang out through the store.

I burst into laughter and ran the rest of the way down.

Jake sure knew how to pick them. Fan-Glorious indeed!

CHAPTER TEN

I called Miss Livy on Nestor's cell. She spoke with the balanced sweetness of a grand Crú Chardonnay and called me "my dear" as if she meant it. And she agreed to see me despite my vague explanation.

I rented the cheapest car I could: a baby-puke-green subcompact, the size and frailty of which made me wonder if it would grow up into a real car someday. Fortunately, I only needed to coax the Matchbox lookalike as far as the eastern bank of Lake Pontchartrain. This was good, considering the last person who'd rented the car apparently had penchants for cheap cigars and fishing. Worse, though, the radio buzzed. I took this as long as I could before pulling over.

You see, I have this *thing* about static. It dates from childhood, when I decided I heard a pattern in the snap, crackle, and pop from my Rice Krispies. Mom tried to set me straight by explaining the difference between structured and nonstructured noise, which, of course, I didn't appreciate. But, hey, I was seven; I wasn't quite mature enough for the white noise discussion. Plus, my oldest brother kept flicking soggy Cheerios at me every time Mom turned around to draw on the kitchen white board. Thus, I ended up feeling both overwhelmed and soggy.

So, the static problem *had* to be fixed. After a little trouble-shooting, I tracked the problem to the speakers. In the process, I found a wad of gum under the driver's seat. *I can use that.* But when I picked up the gum with a paper napkin, I felt the hairs on the back of my neck prickle. Something about the gum, or at least the texture of it, was disturbingly familiar. I searched my memory but nothing came to me, so I removed the panel, re-seated the wires leading from the amplifier onto the hook-up jacks, and got back on the road. I'd fixed it in ten minutes, but I was unable to shake the feeling that I'd just missed something important.

Following Miss Livy's instructions, I went east on I-10 toward Slidell, a drive that carried me over the vast stretch of Lake Pontchartrain. The water, an unremarkable gray, reflected a quiescent sky as a light wind pushed low, lazy crests across the surface. I found my exit and wound my way through the narrow streets of a well-groomed suburb. Miss Livy's was a modest, one-story plank house painted butter cream with porticos the color of vanilla icing. The door was a crisp green, inlaid with cut-glass, and the lawn as squarely kept as Great Uncle Sammy's crew cut. A weed-free flagstone path led from the porch to a freshly painted picket fence.

I exited the car, closing the door carefully so as not to shatter it. As I reached the bottom step of her porch, a woman the size of a tall child opened the door, her face both aged and ageless. Though heavily wrinkled, her skin glowed with health, and her deep brown eyes sparkled with the kind of self-awareness that comes of having seen enough to know that one can never see enough. Her white hair, angora-soft and plaited into a long braid, draped over the shoulder of her pink sheath dress. Thin arms ended in hands that, though peppered with age-spots, still displayed sinewy strength and long-fingered grace. Her fingertips had a pronounced spade shape, the nails short and shiny, the quintessential mistress of the piano.

I mounted the porch hoping that an hour marinating in cigar smoke and fish stink wouldn't be too obvious. "Ms. Brouchard?"

With a warm smile and delicate drawl that spoke of small

talk outside the Piggly-Wiggly, chit-chat by a raffle-ticket booth at the State Fair, and firm but gentle admonitions to rambunctious six-year-olds on the porch at church, she said, "Now, my dear, if you don't call me Miss Livy, I won't know to whom you are speaking."

I smiled, instantly charmed. "Yes, ma'am, I will. I hate to bother you. I'm wondering if I could ask you about a former student of yours, Adalida Thibodaux."

Her brows drew together, and her eyes softened. "My heavens, that's a name I haven't heard in many a day. But I'm afraid she passed on, oh, three years ago now."

"Actually, it's as much about her father."

"I see. Mr. Thibodaux's been hurt, hasn't he?"

I blinked. "How could you possibly know that?"

"My dear, I've seen so much tragedy and death, I can recognize it in a person's eyes. It has followed you to my porch this day." I turned, half-expecting to see the Angel of Death, scythe and all. She chuckled. "I was speaking metaphorically, child."

"Oh. Of course. Sorry."

"Don't you worry. Mr. Boogedy's not behind you. My, but you spook easily. Yankee?"

"Yes, ma'am, I'm afraid so."

"Don't fret. We all have our crosses to bear," she said, a teasing twinkle in her eyes.

I broke into a wide smile, which she returned with a gentler version. Stepping back, she gestured me in. "You come in, now. I am a little old lady, so, of course, there is tea inside. And I have found the most wonderful recipe for cinnamon rolls for my bread machine. I made some this morning. We can pop them into the microwave and heat them right up."

I stepped in, and the rich scent of fresh baked rolls wafted over me. I could almost taste the icing drizzling over each spicy crevice. The décor of the small, neat home was equally inviting, shades of vanilla and blueberry predominating, the light of crystal lamps mutely reflected in the surface of well-polished furniture. As we cleared the door, I spotted her piano, a grand of immensity and grace. Its surface gleamed like an ebony mirror. Even more impressive was the sight above it. My mouth formed a silent *oh* as I gaped at dozens of small portraits suspended from the ceiling on colored ribbons.

At least half the pictures were in black and white and most were school portraits. Every face smiled. I approached, mesmerized. "Who are all these people?"

"Students. The old and the new."

Unable to resist, I reached up toward the display. My hand grazed a black-and-white in a simple silver frame that hung from a faded red ribbon. A girl gazed at me from under a soft bob of dark hair curved around pudgy cheeks. Cat-eye glasses surrounded her large eyes, and a small choker of pearls rested above her Peter-Pan collar.

"That's Patty-Jean Turnbout. She married Jimmy Stanslin. He owns a local hardware franchise." Miss Livy touched a newer, silver-framed color portrait of a young man with the same pudgy face and large eyes. "Jimmy Junior when he was a boy. He's just started his first year at Georgia State."

"You must have been doing this for a very, very long time."

She nodded somberly. "Since God was a corporal."

"Oh! I'm sorry. I didn't mean to imply that you were—"

She chuckled, her eyes aflame with amusement. "Older than dirt? That's all right, my dear. I'm just teasing you. Look at this one." She pointed to a washed-out color photo of a boy kneeling beside a golden retriever. "This rapscallion is Stevie Knox. He might be our senator next year. What a fine young man. He never practiced, but he never lied about it. Of course, the way things are in politics, his honesty might mean a short career."

She chuckled again.

Her smile faded as she caressed a more recent picture of a woman. "Carol Simmons, forty-year-old mother of four. She started taking lessons two years ago. She was so looking forward to learning to make music. She would not let her age deter her. She was determined to show her little girls that a woman can accomplish anything if she puts her mind to it." Her brows drew together, wrinkles carving soft furrows on her face, the light in her eyes dimming, like a bulb being draped with fine linen, the diminished glow forcing an observer to peer that much deeper, to mentally venture out of narcissistic self-awareness and focus, for one moment, on the suffering of someone other than oneself. "She died in a car accident last year. Her nephew came to the porch one day and told me. He had the same look you have now."

Unable to think of an appropriate reply, I looked into the forest of photographs until I found the one I sought. It was of a much younger Adalida than in the picture in Jake's lockbox. But the nose, the eyes—Jake's eyes—were unmistakable. I brushed away a curlicue end of the ribbon that hung in front of those joy-filled eyes.

"Yes, that's our Adalida," Miss Livy said. "But that sweet child's been gone for some time now. And her mother left us well before. I knew her better than her husband, as it was mostly she who retrieved Adalida from her lessons." She smiled as if picturing some poignant memory. "Although, I remember many years ago, when Adalida was nine, or perhaps ten, her mother had gone to Savannah to tend a sick aunt. A terrible storm broke out in the late afternoon, and only Mr. Thibodaux could pick up Adalida. She was my last of the day. He called to say the entire police force had been called out to duty. I assured him I would be happy to care for his little girl until he arrived."

"She must have been so frightened."

"She was. But Adalida was not an anxious child by nature. She asked me to turn the chair, that one in front of the window, so that she could watch the road. And there she sat, her hands folded, patiently waiting. She knew how dangerous it was out there and that her daddy was in the middle of it. But she did not fuss. The only contrary thing she did was refuse to go to bed until he came for her. So I drifted off on the couch, and she slept in the chair."

"What happened?"

"He came in about three a.m., and he was a sight: bone-tired, muddy, soaked to the skin. Oh, but when his little girl rushed to him, he picked her up and held her like she was his only salvation." Tears filled the corners of her eyes, and she dabbed at them. "He hated sitting on my couch as dirty as he was, but I made him do so and brought him sandwiches and coffee. And when I came in from the kitchen, Adalida sat there next to him, patting his hand. Like this." Miss Livy reached over and stroked my hand gently. "He was a strong man but so tired, close to collapsing. And his little girl comforted her daddy like she was the grown-up. I will never forget that." She smiled at me. "Dear me, now I've got you doing it."

I wiped the corner of my eye, the scene reminding me of my own father. In his calm way, my dad had been a real man of action. With his death, my strained relationship with my mother deteriorated even further. I sniffed back the tears, pushing aside the guilt that accompanied my every thought of her these days. "Ma'am, I heard that Jake and Adalida were very close but that they fought over her boyfriend."

A white eyebrow rose. "Did you now?"

I went on gently. "And that Adalida committed suicide as a result."

Miss Livy's eyes flashed. "She did not! I don't know what truly happened, but that child would *not* have done that."

"People have killed themselves over irreconcilable relationships before."

Her small chin went up. "No. Not her. Not that child. Absolutely not."

"Did Jake feel that way too?"

"My word, yes. He quit his job and investigated to the exclusion of all else, but nothing was found to indicate foul play. Mind you, the details of the incident were hushed, as is appropriate. She was a policeman's daughter—a well-respected policeman. Happily, at least *some* news people have the good manners to mind their *p*'s and *q*'s in such a situation."

In my family, the latter would be considered censorship, but imagining this delicate, well-mannered pianist, who could undoubtedly reverberate the walls to the ardent rhythms of the third movement of Beethoven's "Appassionata," squaring off with my Great Aunt Gertrude, an endowed chair of Feminist Jurisprudence at Cornell Law School who could rev up from "free speech" to "fascist manipulation of the media" in 6.7 seconds—and not being willing to bet as to whom might win such a contest—I decided not to pursue the subject. "I see. Do you know anything about Adalida's boyfriend?"

"She was no longer my student by then. I don't like to gossip, but . . ."

"Please, Miss Livy. It could be important."

She folded and refolded her hands on her lap, as if reluctant to proceed. "Well . . . to be honest, my dear, I suspect that Adalida's beau might have been a married man or some such."

"Why do you say that?" Curious. Fancy suspected the same.

"There was something, how would one say, *forbidden* about the affair."

"Forbidden?"

"Perhaps that isn't the right word. It's rather difficult to say since it all occurred the summer Adalida went to Chicago, three years ago."

"Chicago?" I said with a start. "What was Adalida doing in Chicago?"

"She followed young Christopher."

"Christopher? Wait, hold on. Who's Christopher?"

"He was one of her best friends since childhood, although he mostly went by Chris." Miss Livy touched a candid snapshot of a young boy, a baseball cap shading his phenomenally light blue eyes beneath which escaped short tendrils of jet-black hair. I cocked my head, staring intently at the youthful face. I couldn't put my finger on it, but there was something familiar about him. A second ribbon looped around the back of the picture and I brought it forward, revealing a lock of hair tied in a bow at the end. "What's this?"

"That lock of hair is his. It's an old southern tradition dating back to before the War of Northern Aggression. Ladies made trinkets from their hair, jewelry and cords for necklaces. They gave locks to friends, and, of course, to their husbands to carry into battle. People even wore rings made from the hair of a dead loved one."

Yuck. "Um, how romantic," I said.

"Christopher gave me strands of his in exchange for some of mine." Miss Livy stroked the white braid that lay across her shoulder. "Oh, my hair was much darker then." She laughed, a twinge of girlish self-consciousness echoing in the lightness of the sound. "It made me feel absolutely foolish. But there was something about that young man. He had a way about him."

I smiled, enchanted. "How do you mean?"

"He had a genuineness about him. It was as if he could hold up a magic mirror to a person that reflected the best in them, make them believe in themselves. And he was one of those rare few who could see the good in everyone." She grinned at me, "I can see you don't understand."

I tried to affect an accepting smile. "No, no, he sounds very nice."

"True, young Christopher had to be seen to be believed. I'll show you."

She led us to the sofa before the large bay window. I took a seat on cushions of blue and cream flowers. As she sat beside me, she touched the screen of a tablet computer that sat propped on the coffee table before us. With a series of quick flicks across its face, she pulled up a video. It started in the middle of a young woman's squeal of laughter, which abruptly ended with a high-pitched giggle and "No, stop, stop, stop, stop! I can't hold it still." The validity of that statement was born out by the shaky visual, initially focused on short withering grass but then swooping up to pan about a dozen sneakered shuffling feet, before finally settling on a clearly over-stimulated gaggle of teenagers. They jostled for position, mugging for the camera: boys flexing their muscles and shouldering each other out of the way as the girls struck diva poses that would make Ru Paul proud. There was nothing glamorous about any of them, however. They were dressed in torn, dusty jeans and t-shirts. Their skin, ranging from Nordic pale to almost ebony black, gleamed with sweat; faces, bodies, and clothes were streaked with dirt and paint. Despite the signs of hard labor, the energy they exuded was like a tsunami of adrenaline washing over me.

From the background a familiar voice boomed out. My heart leapt with surprise and joy but then sunk with dismay as the memory of the current state of its owner rolled over me.

Jake strode into view, and I gasped. I recognized the voice as he said, "Hey, pichouette, give it to Papa." The body, however— holy crap! Was that really Jake? F. Gloria had been so right. He *had* changed. For one, I wouldn't have believed Jake could ever have been more intimidating than he is now. But this younger version of my boss would have made a Special Forces drill sergeant step back: tall, lean, and square-shouldered as Captain America.

What in God's name had happened to him?

Before I could evaluate further, the camera was passed off to him, and another figure came into view: Adalida. With another high-pitched laugh, she bounded in front of the camera before turning to face it. Alight with guileless joy, she blew kisses like the queen of a county fair. She wore a faded red "Cabrini High School" t-shirt and was caked with dirt and sweat. But that didn't tamp her verve one iota. Indeed, Adalida Thibodaux was life incarnate. She had a country-girl figure, feminine and round but still firm; muscles that could lift a bale of hay but overlaid with maybe one too many beignets. Robust was the word for her—and vibrant, energetic, alive.

And now she was dead.

I licked my lips in thought. My Aunt Marina, an anthropologist, had studied "ghost concepts" and found a common theme among even the most widely disparate cultures. Many saw ghosts as lingering snippets of a person's soul, forever trapped into repeating some action of profound importance to him or her: walking a turret in anxious lookout for a loved one who never returned; contentedly kneading bread for a family long since passed; or joyously leaping into a lake from which they had never emerged.

As I watched images of Jake's dead daughter play to the camera, face bright with heat and life, I smiled. If someday my "ghost" were immortalized as a stream of zeroes and ones stored on the cloud, swapped between servers to be recalled, at will, by the swipe of a finger, I hoped I'd be forever trapped in joy as Adalida now was.

I rubbed the back of my neck and stole a smile at Miss Livy, who smiled back knowingly, as if having read my mind.

I returned to the video. I couldn't tell whether the kisses Adalida blew were meant for the camera or her father, but they elicited a low chuckle from him. "Okay, you monkeys," he said, addressing the swirling, bouncing group of adolescents. His grumpy delivery didn't hide the pride and affection in his voice when he said, "Settle down! It's been a hard day's work, and we've got a long drive home. So let's get this done. Up on the steps. Let's go! *Move it!*"

The camera panned as the whooping teens leapt onto the porch of a modest house that still gleamed of drying paint. They arranged themselves into two ragged rows.

"Boys in front!" Jake shouted. "Down on one knee. Girls in the back row." To the groans of male protest and the taunting laughter of females, Jake added, "Quit your complaining, fellas. I promise you, life will be a whole hell of a lot better for you if you learn to give a lady her due."

A tall black girl slipped her hip to one side and said, "Oh, hell yes!" And then blushed and lowered her eyes, adding, "Sorry, Mr. Thibodaux. I know you don't like swearing."

What?! Wow, has he changed!

"You're fine, Alyssa," he said in a tolerant tone. "Okay, who's got the sign?"

"I do, sir!" said a male voice, quickly followed by the appearance of its owner: Chris.

All eyes turned as a young man strode into the picture. At first glance he was a typical American teenager in the prime of his youth. He had the build of a baseball player, muscular shoulders and legs but without the bulk of a quarterback or the rangy height of a basketball player. His black hair was short, the front gelled like an ebony fence, and he was covered in paint and glistening with perspiration. But when the camera caught his face, I caught my breath. The picture had not done him justice! His eyes! I'd never seen such color before; a pale hue so distinctive they reminded me of Hera, Queen of the Greek Gods, whose peacock blue eyes could capture a mortal's soul and hold it in eternal bliss. He may not have had the classic chiseled handsomeness of a Zach Efron, but with those eyes, Chris would have stolen the show from him easily. Yet, as he ran up the stairs, I could see what Miss Livy meant about his ability to put people at ease: the kids smiled like they'd just eaten some truly special brownies. Chris was definitely BMOC but without the cocksure bravado that would have sent nerds like I was in high school sulking resentfully into the background. I found myself really wanting to meet him.

On reaching the top stair, he handed one edge of a white, plastic-coated sign to a short Asian boy, saying, "Evan, dude, help me out, my man."

Evan leapt up from his down-on-one-knee pose. Face alight with the honor of being singled out by Chris, he took one end of the sign and together they unrolled it to reveal a huge black font on a pale green background that read "Cross the Line, Build the Future." The teens lined up behind it as Chris and Evan anchored either side.

"Cross the line?" I said to Miss Livy.

She tapped the "pause" icon on the screen. "It's a local youth organization sponsored by our police. It refers to crossing the lines that divide us: race, gender, religion, social status. Mr. Thibodaux even added a 'crossing the Mason Dixon line' element by getting a friend of his from Chicago, a chief of police I believe, to arrange for children from a high school there to form a similar group. This video is of a project they did jointly with Habitat for Humanity to build new homes in a predominantly Hispanic neighborhood in that city."

I nodded, and she hit the "play" icon.

"Mr. and Mrs. Rodriguez?" Jake said, off screen.

A middle-aged man and a heavily pregnant woman, accompanied by a toddler of perhaps four years old with deep brown eyes and cascading tendrils of brown hair, solemnly walked up the stairs. They were met with friendly hoots and a chorus of "Hey, Mrs. R.! Hola, Mr. R.! Hi, Maria, did you see your new bedroom?"

As they took their place standing beside the kneeling Christopher, Adalida, who had been standing behind him, draped her arms around his neck and kissed the top of his head. Her face radiated contentment and love. He looked up at her, beaming. She bent, brushed his cheek with her lips, and then stood, resting her hands on his shoulders as all eyes turned to the small family.

From behind the camera, Jake said, "Juan, Emma, and Maria, on behalf of Habitat for Humanity and members of the New Orleans and Chicago chapters of "Cross the Line," welcome to your new home."

"Yeah!" Chris shouted. He turned his head. "On three, guys! One, two, three—"

"Cross the line! Build the future!" The teens shouted in raucous unison, flashing hand signals and pumping arms in the air. This followed by choruses of "Yeah! All right! Woohoo!"

Mr. Rodriguez cleared his throat, his eyes swimming with tears he was clearly trying to hold back. His wife made no such attempt. She glowed with pride and anticipation, large tears rolling unabashedly down her face. "It's so beautiful," she said with heavily accented English. "*Gracias,* everyone. You cannot know what this means to us. We can raise our family with pride in this house. Family is everything. And you are all now our family, too. Maria?" she said, hugging the little girl to her legs. "Will you say thank you?"

Maria swayed, smiled shyly, and clutched the hem of her dress. "Mommy, I got to pee."

Laughter erupted. "Me too!" A boy shouted.

"Oh my God, so do I! Me first!" Alyssa squealed and then merrily jostled with the boy to get through the door of the house before him.

Jake's voice rang out as the video picture swayed and dipped back to the ground. "Everyone hit the head. I'm not stopping a hundred times on the drive home. Where the heck's the off—" The screen went blank.

We both took a deep breath. I felt the weight of despair starting to sink in my stomach. They'd been so happy, Jake and Adalida. And now she was dead and he . . . was he next?

I straightened my shoulders. *No. Not now.* Now I need to move forward, to find what kind of monster would do such terrible things to this once-happy man and so many others. And to me, if he could. *No. Mope later. Act now.*

Moving us back on track, I said. "Um. You know, Miss Livy, from what I saw there, I'd say Chris and Adalida had something going. Are you sure Chris wasn't her boyfriend?"

Miss Livy lifted an eyebrow. A subtle flush bloomed on her cheeks. "There was a time when I thought that they *were* a couple. We could all see the affection. I hate to say it, but . . . I heard that Christopher had, upon occasion, been seen in the company of . . . well, *others.*"

"Other women?"

"Not exactly."

"Not exactly other women?"

"Correct."

"I don't get it."

"Well, my dear, if one is not a woman then one is . . ." She motioned with her hand as if expecting me to complete the sentence.

I shrugged. "A girl?"

She raised an eyebrow. "No, dear. A man."

177

"Ohhh. Chris was gay. Was that a problem?" I said, immediately on the defensive that, in this day and age, people could still carry such ridiculous prejudices.

She waved a long-fingered hand in the air. "There were *rumors*. And, for some people, yes, my dear, that is still an issue."

I sighed, not really wanting to pry as to whether she was one of those people. Never ask a question if you don't want to hear the answer.

She went on. "Still, Adalida and Christopher were always close. They were both artists: he a painter, and she an interior designer. I believe her pursuit of art brought them both to Chicago the summer she died. As I recall, Christopher was accepted by a rather prestigious summer arts program, one he became aware of during their stay in Chicago for the project you just saw. After high school, Adalida applied for an internship at a Chicago school of design and was accepted. Her father would not let her go to such a place alone, of course. So, Mr. Thibodaux arranged to join her for two months. I don't really know what happened after that. But I do know that Adalida came back angry enough to spit fire at young Christopher and equally furious with her father." She shifted her stance, her physical fidgeting displaying the mental discomfort her voice intimated. "When Christopher came home a few weeks later, they made up, as I heard it, yet things remained horribly awry between Adalida and her father. I'd like to believe that, given time, a father and daughter's love would have seen them through the anger." Miss Livy looked away, the shadow of regret on her face.

I rubbed my hands together, touched with sadness for the man I knew and cared about. "But before that happened, she killed herself." Miss Livy opened her mouth to protest. I quickly added, "Or was said to have done so."

Miss Livy inclined her head. "That seems the case."

"I wonder if she met that boyfriend in Chicago when she went to visit Chris?"

"I honestly don't know, my dear."

Hmm. Hunter would have been in Chicago by then. If Adalida's beau had been a married man or otherwise "forbidden" as Miss Livy said, maybe Jake had talked to Hunter about . . . whoa! Could Adalida have had a fling with Hunter? Maybe she went to Chicago not to study art with her childhood friend, but to be with Hunter! Oh, Jake would have been furious!

Wait. Madison, get real. Jake and Hunter couldn't possibly have remained friends if that's what happened. Unless Adalida had been the aggressor. I put my finger to my lips in thought and then went on. "Okay, so I can see her being mad at her father for not accepting her boyfriend. But why was she angry at Chris?"

"I couldn't say."

"It sounds like I should talk to Christopher." I stared at his portrait, perplexed. Where *had* I seen him before? "Do you know where he lives, Miss Livy?"

Her easy smile turned downward. "I'm afraid he disappeared soon after Adalida died. He may have gone back to live with his sister who'd moved to Chicago to be with him."

"Chris had a sister in Chicago?" There was a pricking at the back of my neck, as if my body knew I was on to something and was poking at my mind to *catch up already.*

"An older sister," Miss Livy added. "She went to the city to become someone, as they say today. Although she, eventually, moved again to join family in Canada. Québec, I believe."

"You wouldn't know how to get in touch with her, would you?"

She nodded. "I'll print the address for you." With a few more finger flicks, she'd called up an address book on the tablet, selected the information, and sent it to a printer that I heard whir to life in the room next door. She left the room to retrieve the document.

I stood and went back to study Chris's picture as I waited for Miss Livy's return. He seemed so very familiar, but I couldn't place him. It was infuriating!

My stomach rumbled as delectable aromas wafted from the kitchen to taunt me. Miss Livy came back, scented like a cinnamon roll, and handed me a paper. "It's the address of Chris's cousin, Melissa DuChampes. Even if Christopher is not there, his sister, Tina, may be."

My knees almost buckled in surprise. "Tina! Did you say *Tina?*"

"Why yes, my dear. Christopher's sister's name was Christina. But she went by Tina."

The woman from the alley was Chris's sister! I grabbed Chris's picture, covering those distracting and magnificent eyes with one hand. Light bulbs went off in my head like popcorn as the similarity of the shape of the cheeks and jaw became immediately obvious. "*That's* why Chris looked so familiar! This explains everything!"

"It does?" Miss Livy asked, seeming alarmed by my intensity.

"Um. Well, maybe not everything." I paused, scratching my ear. "Actually, it doesn't explain much of anything. But it must mean something. It can't be a coincidence."

I paced, my heartbeat quickening. Tina was the sister of Adalida's best friend, Chris, who may or may not have been her boyfriend because he may or may not have been gay. Three years ago, Adalida may or may not have committed suicide. After which Chris disappeared. Or did he kill Adalida, making it look like a suicide, then run away? But why? And why, after three years, did Chris's sister want to kill Jake? And if Chris wasn't Adalida's boyfriend, who was? Hunter? Could he stoop that low? No. Jake would never have forgiven him for that. Yet what if Hunter had wanted revenge for being denied Adalida? But after three years? What was the trigger?

Wait! Jake taught George a trigger to warn me because he knew he was in danger. Something must have happened *recently*. What? Maybe Tina killed Adalida, and Jake just found out. But why would Tina want Adalida dead in the first place?

I shook my head, trying to break free the haphazard strands of my thoughts. "Miss Livy, I need to find Tina."

"Then let's try to call her." She led me back to the couch and to a cordless phone sitting on the glass and mahogany end table. Taking the paper, she dialed the number for Melissa Du-Champes and handed me the phone.

Melissa answered on the first ring. I asked for Chris, but she cut me short and told me my question wasn't funny. I sputtered, and Miss Livy motioned for me to hand her the phone. Within moments of congenial, but firm, conversation, Miss Livy hung up.

"She wouldn't let you talk to him, either?"

"She was very circumspect, but she's obliged to protect her family, after all. However, I think if you went there, you might get to see Tina, at least."

"Go there?" I rubbed at my stiffening shoulder and rotated my neck. I'd have to ask for help now. I couldn't afford to let Tina get away. "Hunter," I grumbled absently.

"My dear?"

"I was thinking about Maxwell Hunter, Jake's ex-partner. I'll need his help."

"Not a pleasant thought." Miss Livy raised an eyebrow.

"You know him?"

"Not personally. If you will pardon my un-Christian attitude, I should not like to. I have heard he is quite difficult, especially since his wife died."

181

"Wife?" I said, irritated with myself for the jealousy the word enflamed.

"As I heard it, his wife was the calming influence in his life. He'd always been hot-tempered, but after she passed on, some ten years back, he became as the devil himself. Mr. Thibodaux truly had his hands full keeping that man out of jail. In fact, Mr. Hunter was, how do they say, *allowed* to retire following some sort of trip to our nation's capital five years ago."

"Really?" I remembered the dry cleaning ticket from Jake's lockbox. Perhaps there was some connection. "I'd bet that put Hunter in bad with his precinct."

"Indeed. Heaven help him if he ever gives them reason to cast him in jail, I can tell you."

The devil tapped me on the shoulder. "Is that so?"

Miss Livy narrowed her eyes. "You look like the cat that just got the birdcage open."

"I think I just did. Do you mind if I make another quick call? This one's local."

"Not at all, my dear. Go right ahead."

I called F. Gloria to see what had happened to Hunter. He was in jail, as I suspected. She told me it had taken several of the store's security personnel to do it, but they'd taken Hunter down and held him for the local police. Hanging up, I told Ms. Livy about the incarceration. I didn't say why Hunter was in jail; it felt too indelicate to mention the circumstances to such a lady. Happily, she didn't press for details. I said, "If I can get in to see him, I think I can convince him to fund a trip to see Tina."

"That would be uncharacteristically kind of him," she said doubtfully.

Not really, because I'm going to blackmail him. "Well, we, um, have a relationship."

Her eyes widened.

"Oh, no!" I said quickly. "Nothing like that! It's more that we're both indebted to Jake and want to help him. But I doubt the local police will just let me stroll in to say hello."

Miss Livy smiled, her eyes dancing. "Do you know that I attend church with the mothers of many of the policemen at the eighth district where Mr. Hunter is currently being detained?"

That brought a wide grin to my face.

"Hand me the phone, my dear."

CHAPTER ELEVEN

Less than an hour later, I was following a young New Orleans policeman to Hunter's cell.

My escort had a boxer's heavy, square frame and a buzz-cut sharp as porcupine quills. But he also had the sweetest eyes: long, black lashes surrounding the kind of chocolate brown that melted in my mind.

"So, tell me," I said as we walked, "did you know Hunter or Jake?"

"No, ma'am. They were before my time. But I heard of them, all right."

"What did you hear?"

He shrugged. "That they knew how to get the job done. And they did it the right way—Jake anyway. But after his missus passed on, Hunter was nothing but trouble. He kept pissing people off—pardon my French—left, right, and center. A lot of people are getting a kick out of seeing him behind bars."

That should have made me happy. So why was I suddenly feeling sorry for Hunter? So what if he lost his wife; he's a rat. Why should I care how he feels? I exhaled forcefully, as if trying to push the thoughts out with my breath. "But Jake, he had a good rep?"

"Yes, ma'am. I heard you're working with him. That puts you in good around here."

"Where did you hear that?"

"Miss Livy called. That's how come the boss let you back here."

"Just like that?"

"It was Miss Livy," he said, as if that clearly explained enough.

"Tell me more about Jake."

We paused at a door. My companion tapped a keypad on the wall to the right, and I heard a heavy bolt slide back. We walked through it into another, darker, decidedly warmer and more humid corridor. "I heard he was a straight-shooter. Took care of the good guys, whipped up on the bad. People put up with Hunter on account of him, mostly. Jake kept his ass—pardon my French again—from being grass more than once. I heard, though, that Hunter finally did something so bad Jake had to get him out of town or arrest him himself. In the end, he convinced the bosses to let Hunter walk without charges."

Doubt, whether from instinct or wishful thinking, nagged at me. I couldn't see Jake putting up with a crooked partner, although no one's actually accused Hunter of dishonesty, so far, just bullying. "I don't suppose you know the details?"

The officer shook his head. "Nope. I heard Jake kept the evidence though."

"But if that were true, wouldn't Hunter hate Jake?"

"Who says he didn't?"

Just then, two policemen turned into the corridor from a side hall. Older men, one blond and one a redhead, both wore uniforms stretched against age-widened bellies. They laughed in a nasty way, like high school dweebs who just vandalized some bully's locker.

As he passed, the blond brought his hand to a nonexistent hat. "Ma'am," he said, but as he looked me full in the face, his eyes went wide. "Holy moly! Sara?" The man's broad mouth split into a grin and his eyes went wide and bright, glee shining out from them. He glanced back down the hallway. "Hunter's gonna shit a brick!"

The man's partner narrowed his eyes and shook his head. "No," he said, peering at me like a specimen on a lab slide. "That's not her." He grabbed his buddy by the arm and pulled him away. "Sorry, miss, our mistake."

Sweet-Eyes and I watched the two men stride away.

The blond sputtered. "But doesn't she remind you of—?"

"Let it go," the redhead said. "It's nothing to laugh about. People died, remember?"

I looked up at my escort. "What was that all about?"

The man shrugged, seeming equally perplexed. "Don't rightly know. I could ask—"

"No," I said, an uneasiness settling over me, like I was missing out on a clue I couldn't afford not to get. "Let's get this over with."

He pointed to the hallway from which the men emerged. "Yes, ma'am. This way."

We turned the corner and proceeded another fifty feet. Most of the jail was modern: hardly luxurious but relatively clean and in working order. But here, the fluorescent lights weakened and sputtered intermittently. A swamp-like humidity pressed in around me. I'd bet someone "accidentally" turned off the air conditioning back here.

Hunter sat in a cell at the end, perched on a cot so frail it looked like it might collapse from exhaustion. In the diffuse lighting, I glimpsed a toilet, skewed to one side, and a sink hanging on the wall. The faucet dripped an annoying *drip, drip, drop, drip, drip, drop*. Hunter looked a bit battered, but otherwise relatively at ease, as if he'd just ordered a crème brûleé and was more bored than angry with the waiting.

If he was surprised to see me, he didn't show it. Instead, he focused lazily on my escort. "Phones still out, boy?"

Sweet-Eyes rested his weight against the bars. Grinning, he

said, "Damnedest thing. They worked fine this morning. Then you go to make a call to your lawyer, and every phone in the building up and dies." He smiled. "Don't you fret, though. We all know how important you are. I'm sure everyone's just a'scramblin' to set it straight."

Hunter smirked. "Don't be a fool, boy. Your sorry-ass bosses are shooting their wads trying to get back at me. But they're shooting blanks."

"Looks to me like the sorry ass is sitting in this jail cell." He shot me a smile.

Hunter stood and stalked toward the bars until he and Sweet-Eyes stood toe-to-toe. The young man straightened but didn't back off.

"You know, boy, I hope you're not going to be too disappointed."

"In what, old man?"

"Well, I'm going to be so busy screwing over your bosses that it'll take time to get around to a little pissant like you." The cop started to speak, but Hunter raised a hand. "Now, don't get me wrong, boy. I admire your tough act in front of *the female*. But she won't let you do her; you're not her type. Is he, Angel?" Hunter reached through the bars and traced my jawline with one finger. "You don't want this poser, do you?"

I jerked my head away, angry at his arrogance, but even more so at the way my body warmed to his soft touch.

The cop's youthful face turned bright red. He shot me the same look Chester gave Fancy, then turned and glowered at Hunter. "You got me quaking in my boots." He threw his shoulders back. "Want me to stay, ma'am?"

"No, thanks. I can handle this." Or so my mouth said.

Hunter smiled. "That's right, boy. Walk on. Me and my girl want to be alone."

I smiled, hopefully with more conviction than I really felt.

"I'm okay, really."

Sweet-Eyes nodded and, with a final glare for Hunter, left us alone.

The cop's footsteps faded into the distance. I turned my attention to Hunter. His expensive Italian shoes were dirty, and the knees of his trousers smudged. The torn right shoulder of his silk suit flopped to one side, and his pearl-white shirt—stretched taut over the arms anchored over my head on the bars—gapped several buttons' worth, revealing dark chest hair. I swallowed and forced my eyes upward.

Near black in this light, the hair on his head was swept back into his usual Euro-vogue style. Yet one strand had fallen loose, arching gracefully over his forehead, a sudden reminder of boys I grew up with. I could see them, dressed in their Sunday best, scuffed at the edges, poised to run loose the moment the service finished, leaving me to stare longingly at their escape.

He licked his lips and smiled. "Like what you're seeing, do you?"

My attention rocketed back to the moment. I shrugged, trying to appear nonchalant, despite the intensity of my body's reaction to being so near him. *I mean, seriously, hormones—who needs the damn things? Especially when they're going to activate over exactly the wrong man!* "I'm just admiring the cops' handiwork. Or did the store detectives take you down?"

"It took four of them; only one was worth his salt. I've hired him."

"You hired a man who arrested you?"

"He was just doing his job, and he held his own despite having Larry, Moe, and Curly underfoot. I appreciate competence, and I reward what I appreciate. Does that surprise you?"

"A little."

Hunter reached between the bars and captured my hand, rubbing the back of it with his thumb, his light touch sending shivers through me. "I can do a lot that might surprise you."

I yanked my hand away, wiping it against my jeans to quell the tingling. "Don't start."

He chuckled, low in his throat. It was a low reverberation that resonated down my backbone. I raised my chin, staring directly at him, hoping my eyes reflected defiance and not the warm flush of sexual awareness traveling, like a teasing caress, over my flesh. "You don't seem surprised to see me."

"I'm not. In fact, I'm impressed. You and that woman set me up real good. You know, every now and then, you do seem *almost* capable."

"Hey, you walked into it. Why would you get caught so easily, knowing who she was?"

He shrugged. "We'd never met. If I had known, I wouldn't have let my guard down."

"Or your zipper?" I smiled at his questioning frown. "I was hiding behind the boxes in the store room, slipped out right under your nose." I glanced down at his crotch. "So to speak."

He nodded, his smile seemingly approving. "Not bad, Angel, sneaky and underhanded."

"I'm glad you're pleased. And I have news that will make you even happier. But first I want to know how you found me."

"You're supposed to be Polly P.I., you figure it out."

"I suppose with an organization as large as yours it wouldn't have been too hard to keep an eye on all the train and aircraft manifests."

"Especially with a bizarre name like yours."

"You know what? My mom picked that name. If you're not careful—"

He grinned. "What? You'll tell your mommy on me?"

"Laugh it up, but my mother is a formidable woman. She can handle the likes of you."

"I guess that makes you a real watered-down copy."

I glared at him, the truth of his observation stinging like a swift slap. "Bite me."

He hummed low and leaned in. "Come a little closer."

I simmered in silence, unable to get over those old feelings of inferiority.

Finally, Hunter backed off, smiling as if triumphant at shutting me down. "I called someone and had him follow you from the airport."

My head jerked up, my gut clenching again at the fear of being stalked, my ego furiously trying to deny the vulnerability that my mind couldn't.

He grinned. "You didn't know, did you? Someone followed your every step." His voice took the tone of amused, yet intimate, threat. "He was right behind you, Angel. So close, he could have touched you, grabbed you. Could have just—" He thrust a hand through the bars.

I squealed and jumped back.

Hunter laughed. "There's the big, bad detective for you, squeaking like a mouse."

"Shut up, jerk!"

"Gee, I guess that puts me in my place."

I tapped on the bars. "I'd say you're in your place."

A smirk bloomed on his lips. "Voltaire's got a nice cell just like this waiting for *you.*"

I felt my hands clench, feeling trapped, options slamming closed around me like heavy steel doors. "I'll bet that makes you so happy."

"Don't blame me. If you would do what you're told—"

I slammed my hand into the bars, anger rising. "Where the hell do you get off—"

His brows creased, and he pointed a determined finger. "Listen, Missy. I'm a part of an official investigation. Where the hell do *you* get off thinking you deserve special treatment?"

"I'm a part of this too."

"What you are is a spoiled brat! A pushy, arrogant—"

"I'm arrogant? *I'm* arrogant?" I said, my voice shrill with frustration.

"Pitch it a little higher, Angel. I don't think you broke *every* glass in the place."

I clamped my jaw shut and breathed hard through my nose, trying to regain control. "Why do you have it in for me?"

His eyes held mine for several seconds, the message unreadable. He relaxed against the bars. "Don't flatter yourself. You're nothing special." His taunting smile returned. "You said you have something. Surprise me. Show me you do."

My eyes narrowed and I smiled, confident my knowledge would put me back in control. "Fancy called Jake 'Big D.' Adalida did too. Obviously, Adalida couldn't have killed him."

Hunter raised a brow as if impressed. "You found out about Adalida? Well, well. How can you be so sure Fancy is innocent?"

"She was at work all day yesterday."

"You know that for certain?"

"There were witnesses."

"Friends of hers?"

"Colleagues. People with no reason to lie and good reasons to tell the truth."

Hunter nodded. "Hunh. Passable. Not brilliant, but passable."

"Downplay it all you want. But I found the 'Big D' connection before you did."

Seemingly unimpressed, he cocked his lips in a snarky smile. "Angel, all you did was eliminate two potential suspects, one of whom has been dead three years. Good job. Any other deceased people you think we can eliminate?"

"You know, Hunter, if you said one genuinely nice thing to me, I'd pass out cold."

"You have beautiful eyes," he murmured.

And there it was again, the flush of awareness, like lowering my body into warm water. I bit my lower lip, awkwardly shifting my weight from one foot to another.

He stroked my hair. "And beautiful hair. Soft, cool to the touch. A shiny black curtain."

My cheeks burned hotter. His eyes met mine with unguarded sincerity. I blinked and tried to hold brave under his gaze. His gaze shifted to my chest. "Nice rack, too."

As much disgusted as angry with the break of mood, I crossed my arms. "Must you always go one step too far? Okay, so you had me followed, but how did you get here so fast?"

"I have friends." He grinned. "One of them gave me a ride on her jet."

"Sheesh, that's some friend."

"I give her rides; she returns the favor. She practically begs for my version."

Jealousy swatted me upside the back of my mind. "Just because you've got some rich, pathetic old woman—"

"Nothing old or pathetic about her. She makes you look second rate."

"Hey, I got your ass tossed in jail. How second rate is that?"

Hunter's amused expression didn't waver.

"Hunter, do you really think women can't resist you?"

"You can't deny the evidence." He looked me up and down, his eyes moving languidly, taking in each curve of my body. He purred. "Hmm. You clean up real good. I like what I see."

I stepped back from the bars, my face so hot I must have glowed. "You aren't so delusional as to think I'm attracted to you?"

"I know the way a woman holds herself when she's interested: the flushed skin, the shallow breathing." He reached through the bars and slid his hand slowly up and down my arm.

I flinched. "I don't want you to touch me."

"Yes, you do. But you want me to ask first. Or, so you tell yourself." He grabbed my arm firmly and captured the small of my back with his other hand. His voice dropped as he caressed me through my clothes. "You think I don't know you, but I do."

My heartbeat quickened. "I . . . I don't know what you're talking about."

"Angel, I know the places your soul wants to go to."

A penetrating intimacy filled his eyes, as if he could see into some corner of my mind where even I didn't dare venture. Exhilaration trickled down my spine. "We're not going to do this," I whispered.

"Yes, we are." He released my arm and reached up to tap me on the forehead. "You think you only live here." He dropped the hand to my abdomen. "But this is where you want to live." The hand on the small of my back dropped lower, and he pulled my hips forward, pinning me against the thick, hard jail cell bars. "And here." His voice turned gravely. "You like the blood rushing in your ears, too loud to let you think, to hesitate. That's what you want. Isn't it?"

"I . . . I don't . . ."

His eyes glistened. "Those thin-blooded, brainy types, they don't do it for you, do they? They're not men enough to get the juices flowing."

Desire resonated in my mind, like a lion's roar, at once anticipating and commanding the fulfillment of appetites too visceral, too primal to even want to deny. "You're wrong," I said, my voice thin and strained.

He wet his lips, cupping my chin in his hand, stroking my lip with his thumb. My knees almost buckled as he said, low and hoarse, "Did you know I've been watching you? Do you want to know what I've seen?"

My gaze darted about his face as my blood trilled in my

veins. I could barely breathe. *What had he seen?*

He stroked my hair again, then leaned in close. "How does this feel? Do you like it?" His baritone reverberated in my head.

I looked into his eyes, reveled in the deep blue marbling the steel. My lips parted.

But then something else swirled in those enigmatic eyes: triumph. Triumph over me! Anger flared in my gut. *Bastard!* I tensed, just as a plan flashed through my brain. Taking a calming breath, I relaxed into the bars between us and stroked his bicep. "You really think you have me pegged, do you?" I said.

He stroked my back. "It's why you're here."

"Is it?" I matched his sultry tone and shot him a look of daring. I leaned forward, pulling my shoulders back, my breasts rising. "Maybe I just like seeing the big bad wolf behind bars."

Chuckling, his confidence palpable, he said, "You're not stupid. You know they won't hold me here long. If you really wanted to get away, Angel, you'd be gone already."

His other hand stroked my neck. I leaned into the caress. "Mmm. You're right. I admit it, I do want something."

He brought a lock of my hair to his lips. His eyes glistened through narrow slits as he stared hungrily at me. "What's that, Angel?"

I ran my tongue over my lips. "I want a ride."

He pulled my hips firmly into the bars; his voice dipped. "I want it too. You must have known that."

"From your girlfriend."

His hands halted; confusion twisted his rugged features. "What?"

Staring into his eyes, I said. "I want you to talk your girlfriend into giving me a ride."

He stood back. His expression clearly broadcast his indecision. Was I asking for a three-way, or had he misjudged my sexual orientation?

I allowed a grin. *Excellent. The ball was back in my court. And not a minute too soon; a few more seconds and I'd have been doing a pole dance on the jail bars.* I folded my arms over my chest. "Your girlfriend with the jet is going to take us to Canada."

Brows knit, he narrowed his eyes at me. "What the hell are you talking about?"

"I found her. Tina, the woman from the alley." His disorientation filled me with delight.

All play and seduction disappeared from his demeanor as his body tensed. He raised his head, and he looked down at me. "How did you find her?"

"All you need to know is that I've picked up her trail."

"Where is she?"

"Quebec. I'll tell you precisely where when we get there."

"You'll tell me now, damn it." His voice recovered its hard, cold edge.

"You're not in a position to demand anything, Maxie."

"Don't be stupid," he said, putting his hands on his hips and squaring his stance like a quarterback daring someone to make a charge. "Those idiots out there know I can sue their asses so bad their grandkids will be born in debt. When I get out—"

The baleful gleam in his eyes began to eat away at my confidence, but I took a deep breath and tried to tough it out. "When you get out, you and I are going to find this woman. I don't care whether you convince your friend to take us there, or you pay for our tickets, but—"

"Or *I* pay? You've got some nerve, Angel."

"Do you want to catch this killer or not?"

"I won't be blackmailed."

"This isn't blackmail. I'm . . . bargaining. I'm trading my valuable services as a private investigator." I ignored his derisive snort. "I have an important lead, and my fee is nothing more or less than the cost of the trip, plus expenses. That's more than fair."

"That's withholding evidence."

"Only if you were a cop."

"I will *not* be dictated to by some wannabe—"

I grabbed the bars, sick and tired of being spoken down to. "Get off your high horse! All I have to do is call Voltaire and—"

"Hah! And he'll have you extradited for obstruction." Hunter pointed at me, a triumphant gleam in his eye. "Then he'll get the information out of you from a jail cell."

That brought me up short. I stepped back. Voltaire was not to be toyed with.

Hunter leaned forward, closing the space between us as if to seize it as his own. "I'll make you a deal, which is more than you deserve. You give me the information, and I'll get Voltaire to drop the charges against you. Or he'll drag your ass in on concealed carry, and you won't see the light of day for a very, very long time."

I slammed my hand into the bars. "Don't think I don't have leverage. Voltaire won't want the media to get wind of the fact that one of his closest friends got thrown in jail for rape."

"The charges won't stick. And all you'll do is make him angry by starting trouble."

"Oh yeah?" My mind raced for a counter. "What about what happened in D.C.? What do you think he'll say when he finds out about that?"

A silence fell so cold that I almost felt ice crystals in the air between us. Hunter's eyes narrowed. A very real, very deadly anger emanated from him. He stood tall and stiff, like a cobra poised to strike. "What the fuck do you know about D.C.?"

Uh-oh. Now I'd gone that step too far. I wrapped my hands around my arms, trying to warm myself against the chills racing down them, knowing suddenly what the mouse feels like just before the flash of fangs. "I know that Jake saved your ass, yet again."

His simmering response let me know I'd chosen the right track. Speaking carefully to keep the trembling out of my voice, I said, "Jake left me a souvenir of the adventure."

Hunter flinched. Old suspicions resurfaced. What if Hunter thought Jake had betrayed him? Would he have killed Jake? Could the look I thought I saw in Hunter's eyes at the hospital have been guilt rather than loss? I realized I was holding my breath, like that same little mouse just wanting it to be over. I let it out slowly.

Hunter's gaze held steady, studying me as if looking for a weak spot, a breach to blow open. "You have proof?"

"That's right."

A slow, humorless smile curved his lips. "You're lying."

His confidence shook me. The guy was either the most omniscient man on Earth or the world's best poker player. *But you're not bluffing, Madison. Something did happen in D.C., something Hunter doesn't want known. Don't blink, don't let him rattle you.* "Jake left me a box full of interesting items. How do you think I tracked down Fancy?"

Doubt flickered in his eyes.

I gripped my arms harder. "What do you think of that, Maxie?"

Hunter glanced behind me. Foolishly, I turned. He grabbed my hair and pulled me toward him. "Don't you threaten me!" he hissed. "I won't be made a fool of by the likes of you again!"

"Let go of me!" I grabbed his belt-less pants and yanked hard. Iron bars did wonders to break a man's grip. Not to mention his balls.

We let go simultaneously. Hunter reeled back and fell so hard that the springs on his cot shook. I tumbled into the wall, then rubbed my head, grateful not to feel blood. "Bastard!"

He sat on the bed, holding his crotch. Unmitigated fury radiated from his eyes. I had the terrifying notion that he'd have skinned me with a potato peeler if he could have gotten his hands on me. After long moments of mutual glaring, he said breathlessly, "What do you want?"

My shoulder pulsed with a dull, rhythmic ache. I rubbed it gently. "I told you. I found Tina. And I know how to get to her. You sponsor me financially and you back me politically. No more crap like trying to get me tossed into jail. In return, I get Fancy to drop the charges, and I take you to Tina. I won't tell anyone that you were in jail." I gripped the bars again, staring intently at him. "I'll even let you bring Tina to Voltaire and get all the brownie points.

"Come on, Hunter. We get the killer, you get the credit, and I'll get out of your life. How brilliant is that? You know that's what you really want."

He considered briefly and then stood. "What I want is what you have on the D.C. trip."

"No way."

"Then forget it. If you can find this woman, so can I."

I glared defiantly at him. "Maybe. But can you find her before someone else dies?"

His gaze faltered for a moment. He looked away as if thinking. When he looked back, his eyes were set hard again. "You'll show me the box?"

I nodded. "Then I'll send it home to a friend. And we head out together. That's it. Take it, or I cut you out." I thought he was going to explode—literally. "Do we have a deal?"

He drew a deep breath, his smug mask settling back in place. "Why not? Watching you make a fool out of yourself is good for laughs. I suppose I can tolerate you a little longer."

"You are such a charmer."

He pointed at me. "But you listen to me, and you listen well,

Angel. If you think you can make a fool out of me and get away with it, then you've got another thing coming. You watch your back, woman, from here on out. Got me?"

I forced a grin despite the shiver his words sent down my arm. "Whatever."

"Get on with it then. Get me out of here."

I headed down the hall, and my mood lifted. I'd bearded the lion and still had flesh on my bones. Okay, it might get flayed off in the future, but, for now, I was finally getting somewhere.

My smile stiffened. Damn. I'd forgotten to ask Hunter about Sara. Jake had always hinted of a resemblance to someone, and the association didn't seem to be a good one. The cops in the corridor indicated the same. And Hunter blurted that he wouldn't be made a fool of by the "likes of you again." Had he meant Sara? And why did I remind him of her?

But now was not the time to press that. I turned on my heel, yet again, and headed toward the front desk. From there, I called Fancy, who then spoke to the precinct commander with whom she was apparently on excellent terms. The Commander deemed the whole incident an innocent mistake, though, more likely, the thrill of a metaphorical swirly to a bully wore off and the cold reality of false arrest sank in.

Sweet-Eyes agreed to overnight Jake's lockbox to Zach with a message of reassurance. But not before we did a show-and-tell for Hunter, close enough to confirm the authenticity of the contents but far enough to deny physical contact. I gloated, Hunter growled. Life was good.

Hunter took me to a jet crewed by a male flight attendant yummy enough to be a pool boy. My attention, however, quickly detoured to the owner of the jet. Hunter was right; nothing pathetic about her. She was, in fact, Tribeca Thomson, the wealthiest socialite in Chicago.

Tribeca—Tri-Tri to her friends, a position I ran ten million dollars short of qualifying for—had supposedly been named after the lower-Manhattan neighborhood. The official story boasted that her father made his fortune on the rebirth of an area known as Triangle Below Canal, bordered in part by Canal Street and the Hudson River, now one of the most trendy (read: pretentious) locales in New York. The *unofficial* story whispered that the name derived from her mother, an ex-beauty queen and part-time porn star, for whom "Triangle Below Canal" referred to a specialty involving two men and her ability to do a headstand for extended periods of time.

And Tri-Tri had certainly inherited her mother's looks: flawless skin; high, rounded curves; legs up to here and hair down to there. When we arrived at the hanger, she strode out to greet Hunter in an emerald, hand-embroidered Prada mini-dress with lime-green Roberto Cavalli strappy sandals, all of which likely cost more than my entire wardrobe.

Leaving me near the steps of the plane, Hunter met her halfway. She melted into his arms and kissed him so thoroughly that, if kissing alone could make a baby, she'd have conceived twins. Waiting out of earshot, I tried to ignore the surge of blood to certain parts of my body, trying to convince them that my mind was in charge of my sexual responses, their incessant throbbing making it quite clear which parts really were in charge, and if my mind didn't like it, it could take a hike. I hate it when my body gets pissy.

Tri-Tri listened as he spoke, casually twirling sunglasses worth two months' rent. Moments later, she glanced over Hunter's shoulder and gave me a look most people saved for the bottom of their shoes after a walk in a cow pasture. Then she pouted; heiresses must pout at least daily, after all. After that came the eye-fluttering and then, finally, the coup-de-grace giggle, complete with cleavage press, and a peck on the cheek.

Seemed like high school all over again: the cool kids covertly feeling each other up in the hall as they whisper in my direction, and me on the sidelines longing to re-sequence their DNA. *Hey, a girl could dream.*

Finally, we boarded. Tri-Tri breezed by without a glance, and Hunter herded me up the stairs like a troublesome pet. I guess I was lucky I hadn't been consigned to the cargo hold.

The pilot disappeared into the cockpit and did his "tower this and tower that" routine. Decorated in shades of peach and beige, the small plane sported four leather seats to one side of the plane and a triple-long couch on the other. The rear end, which included a galley and bathroom, could be partitioned off by a folding door. Presumably, this spared the mistress of the plane the sight of others working for a living.

I took the front seat to the left; the attendant took the one behind me. Hunter and Tri-Tri sat on the couch, her long legs tucked underneath her and her breasts never more than two inches from his arm. I caught a few snippets of their conversation above the whine of preflight procedures, mostly simpering about how he was "too generous" and being "taken advantage of" with a final comment about a "hanger-on." Gee, I wonder who she meant by that?

Fine, whatever. As long as I get what I want, he can tell the evil Bitch Queen anything he likes. It doesn't bother me at all. Well, not much, anyway.

We took off without a safety briefing. Apparently, nobody cared if I'd locked my tray table, probably because I didn't have one. Or, I concluded after long moments of fumbling with the armrests, the little bugger was extremely well hidden. I abandoned my search and retrieved a *Time* magazine from the side pocket. As we leveled off, "pool boy" offered me a snack.

Behind me, Tri-Tri turned up the drama, cooing and whispering louder than ever. I rolled my eyes and searched some more but still couldn't find the damn tray. I did, however, find a set of Bose earpods and an MP3 player strapped to the armrest. Toggling through the menu, I delightedly called up one of my favorite Sarah McLachlan albums and settled back into the seat. The attendant returned, carrying a silver tray. He'd fixed the mistress of the plane some kind of pale, peachy martini drink and poured Hunter a tall, dark beer. Coming over to me, he flicked a button on the front of the armrest and released a tray from near my elbow. *Jeez. How did he find that thing?* With a friendly smile, he deposited an effervescing glass of soda and a basket of gourmet cookies and smoked nuts. I saw him glance at Tri-Tri, who gave him a dismissive finger wave, after which he took his seat and buried his head in a paperback.

As I watched the interchange, I caught Tri-Tri's gaze. She cuddled so close to Hunter that she was practically on his lap. Her arm snaked between his arm and chest, boobs squashed against his bicep. Cocking a professionally shaped eyebrow my way, she raised her martini glass to her fashionably mauve lips, a slight, thoroughly conceited smile playing on them. Eyes locked on mine, she wrapped her arm around Hunter's neck and whispered in his ear. The look she shot me was unmistakable: mine and you can't have any, with a definite *nyah, nyah, nyah* subtext.

I dragged my attention to my snack basket and ripped open a package of Chessmen cookies. Desperate to find something else, *anything else,* to focus on, I checked out my surroundings. A loose side panel, attached to a small video screen, caught my eye. Instinctively, I started to pry it open in search of the wiring. A memory, like a flat-handed slap to the mind, stopped me. The last time I'd been curious about what was behind a panel on an airplane, I was ten years old. Fortunately, Mom had the foresight to check on me in the bathroom. Even more fortunately, she had reconnected the arcing wires and slammed the panel closed before the stewardess came back to find out why the "Bathroom Occupied" light blinked in Morse code. I wasn't allowed to go to the bathroom alone after that.

Irritated by that familiar sensation of the geeky inadequacy of my youth, made even more poignant by the soft-porn play going on behind me, I pulled my hands back and dove into more snacks. I'd almost managed to shut out the wriggling behind me when Hunter and Tri-Tri went to the back of the plane. I glanced back and saw her pull him by his tie into the partitioned section. She closed the door behind them, grinning broadly.

I blinked. They had to be kidding. There was no way—I glanced at the attendant. He arched an eyebrow, then stood and went into the cockpit, leaving me alone.

My jaw fell open. *Oh, come on! I mean, I'm sitting right, freaking, here! There's nothing but a crummy, thin door between me and them, and they're going to—they wouldn't.* I took a deep breath and squared my shoulders. *Ignore them. She's just looking for attention.* I liberated two cookie squares, sat back, and cranked up the volume. For the next several moments, I luxuriated in the crumbly ecstasy of shortbread and the dulcet tones of Sarah M. I tapped my feet and stared out the window. *La, la, la.*

A thump shook the partition.

Ah, crap.

I dropped my head to my chest. *This cannot be happening.* I shifted uncomfortably at the sudden vision of Hunter's muscular chest; his ripped abs; a broad swath of dark hair descending in a tapering triangle over his hard, flat stomach into a slender black line snaking downward to—*No! Stop it! Madison McKenna, you will NOT have that vision. You will NOT think of . . . of . . . of what you ARE thinking of.*

Man, I so need a boyfriend.

I took deep breaths through my nose and breathed out through my mouth, yoga style, for several long moments. Once

I got my heart rate out of the danger zone, I raised my head and stared straight ahead. *I'm not paying attention. I don't care what they do; it has nothing to do with me. I'm going sit here and read my magazine. That's what I'm going to do. Read my magazine and not pay the slightest bit of attention.* I flipped the magazine open only to note with annoyance that I'd already finished this one. *Well, heck, now what?*

Thump. Thump, thump.

I glanced back at the door. The magazine rack was mounted on the wall beside it. I chewed my lower lip. *I really do want another magazine. I could just walk back there, find what I want, and walk back to my seat like the mature, unconcerned adult that I am. I have absolutely no ulterior motives in mind.* I stood. *Here I go. One mature, unconcerned adult walking over to a magazine rack . . . arriving at a magazine rack . . . taking a magazine . . . nothing to it.* I glanced at the door. *I should look through the magazine, to make certain I'd like it. No sense in—*

THUMP! The partition fell open.

My body jerked like a jackrabbit flushed from cover. Panicked, I dropped the magazine and grabbed the handle, catching it before it opened fully. The sounds of rhythmic moaning flowed over me. *Oh, man!* I froze, eyes closed, awaiting the impending disaster. After several seconds, when no affronted screaming manifested, I opened one eye and then the other. I sighed and meant to pull the door closed. Honestly. But restraint and curiosity launched into battle in my psyche, and, unfortunately for restraint, curiosity had an army of horny minions on its side.

I peeked.

Hunter had Tri-Tri bent over the counter before them, his back to me. His trousers, shirt, and boxers lay on the floor beside her clothes, leaving him wearing only black socks and a white, sleeveless t-shirt. His chiseled muscles bulged as he pulled her hips back and forth against him. She gripped the surface, white-knuckled, and lifted her smooth, tight buttocks high to meet him, her whole body rocking to the rhythm of his thrusts. And I'd have to say that the guttural groans were pretty damn indicative of her mood.

Far better, however, was the sight of Hunter's own firm ass. So taut, so—*oh, my God! He has a tattoo! Halfway up his right cheek, is that . . . ? Yes, it is! It's Taz, the Warner Brother's cartoon, Tasmanian Devil! That's so cool! No, it isn't. Yes, it is. Grow up!* I nibbled on my ring finger, watching little tattoo Taz watch me, watch him. *I can't believe I'm doing this. Mmm, but I do love the sight of a man's butt, especially when it's at work. Those smooth, deep hollows that form when his muscles tighten and . . . no! No, you are not doing this, Madison. You are NOT that hard up. Speaking of hard—no! Enough!*

I yanked the door, slowing at the last second to click it soundlessly closed. Grabbing the magazine from the floor, I ran on tiptoe back to my seat. Once there, I ripped open a package of cashews and tossed them down like a kid mainlining Skittles. I gulped the remainder of my soda so quickly a burp erupted before I finished.

Okay, Madison. Get a grip. You're an adult . . . and he's an adult . . . and we could do adult things . . . No! None of that. Hunter's a mean, self-righteous—yeah, but the way he moves those rock-hard muscles. Older men aren't supposed to look that good! I mean he's way too old for me. Right? But, that utterly bite-worthy ass and that cute tattoo—I moaned, squirming in my seat. Then, in that cruel way the mind has, I remembered the last time I'd been so uncomfortable in a seat. In the car with Jake. The thought chilled like ice water in my lap.

A sigh escaped as my inner slut slunk back into her dark corner. I picked up the new magazine. Still, I thought, as I buried myself in the desensitizing sputter of irresponsibly inflammatory political rhetoric, it's a good thing Hunter and I hate each other. I glanced at the closed partition. *As long as we hate each other, things can't get complicated.*

CHAPTER TWELVE

Hunter and Tri-Tri returned ten minutes later. He dropped into a seat as if nothing had happened and fell asleep almost instantly. From the triumphant look on Tri-Tri's face, I knew she knew that I knew, and that I was meant to know. She probably left the door unlatched on purpose. I should have felt sorry for her—that kind of exhibitionism indicates deep self-esteem problems—but I was too preoccupied with the thought of flushing her head in the toilet.

A few moments later, the attendant returned. He didn't even blink when I joined him in the galley and took a mini-bottle of amaretto. In fact, he palmed me two more. I sensed pity, but I ended up with booze and cookies, so what the hell.

We all settled down to the post-coital rumbling of Hunter's snores. Even Tri-Tri slept, her breathing gentle and feminine. *I'll bet she does that on purpose.*

High above vast forests of the Northeast, my mind finally relaxed and allowed the low-throated engine drone to lull me into a soporific stupor. Upon landing, we were hustled through customs and led to a limousine. It was nearly one a.m. as we cruised through the tree-lined streets and into the walled city of Vieux Quebec. We passed under stone bridges flanked with Arthurian watchtowers and past Continental shops, neatly aligned along narrow avenues.

Our destination was the Chateau Frontenac, a castle overlooking the Saint Lawrence River in old Quebec City. Like some medieval fortress, complete with spires, the center building stood taller than wide and more than a dozen stories high with wings flanked to either side. Lights illuminated the castle, bestowing the verdigris of its copper-sheeted roof with an ethereal glow that hovered like a mystical turquoise cloud. *Guinevere would have totally dug the place.*

We passed under stone archways to an inner courtyard where the limousine glided to a stop before the front steps. A doorman, sporting a uniform the same forest green as the four-posted canopy above, greeted us in a local French dialect. Tri-Tri replied in impeccable continental French, emerging from the limo as light and fresh as spring. I, on the other hand, contemplated faking a faint just to get someone to carry me in.

Mr. Doorman escorted us through gold-trimmed, mahogany-bolstered rotating doors into a cavern of burnished metal, cool marble, and warm hardwood. Tasseled chandeliers of vaguely Egyptian design lit the room. Deep rich tones intermingled with subtle watercolor hues as murals of fruits and flowers lined the upper walls.

The desk staff attended to us in a professional manner, alert and bright-eyed despite the hour. Then a bellboy whisked Hunter and Tri-Tri off to a distant tower room, no doubt with private gargoyles to guard against evil spirits. *Sure, but who'll protect the spirits from them?*

I ended up in a tidy room on the sixth floor with a stunning view of the river and the lower city that lay at the bottom of the steep cliffs. Better yet, a luxuriously appointed canopied bed, big enough for serious acrobatics, waited for me. I worked to ignore the images of the gymnastics in which Hunter and Tri-Tri were, doubtless, engaged. Instead, I scrubbed my face, stripped, and wrapped myself in the plush hotel robe. I spotted a computer and, with the best intentions, logged on to my e-mail account. I saw a post from Lilly but couldn't bring myself to deal with it. I clicked on an icon and walked away as the printer whirred to life. Bone-deep weariness washed over me, and I threw off my robe and crawled into bed.

As a rule, I sleep naked; nightclothes make me feel claustrophobic. I'd only been able to sleep in my clothes the previous night because of my incredible exhaustion. Of course, if not for that damn bull, I might have ended up naked after all.

"And that would've been a bad thing?" said the voice behind me.

I turned. "Zach! What are you doing here? Oh, I'm dreaming again, aren't I?"

"Girl, I hope so. This is too weird for me otherwise."

I looked around. We were on Tri-Tri's plane. But now there was a set of jail bars segmenting me from the back of the plane. On the other side was a giant canopy bed upon which Hunter and Tri-Tri romped, in the midst of full-out, dynamic sex. The whole damn bed thumped.

"Oh, that's just rude!" I ground my teeth and gripped the bars.

George, the parakeet, landed on my shoulder. " *'Pretty little cajun queen.' Awk.*"

"Hello, little one. Aren't you pretty? Hey, you never did the *'awk'* thing before."

In a high-pitched tone, he replied, "It is part of the standard bird repertoire, after all. To be sure, I never would have demeaned myself to utter such a cliché in reality. But it appears you see no harm in including it in this dream sequence cum analytic foray." He cocked his white head to one side, round black eyes reproachful. "It's really rather speciesist of you, don't you think?"

I blinked. "Oh. I'm, um, sorry?" I looked from the bird to Zach.

Shrugging, my bull-riding buddy said, "As long as you don't

have Fido saying *moo.*"

George clicked his tongue, although I'm not sure how. "That would be silly." He shook his feathered head and turned back to me. "Humans. Anyway, back to my part." Wriggling his shoulders, he brought himself to full height and squawked out in proper bird voice, " *'Pretty little cajun queen.'* " He stared at me intently, adding, "But then you always had a bad memory for lyrics, didn't you?" Shaking his teal wings, he flew out the open door into the stark blue sky.

"Wait!" I reached out for him.

A male voice said, "It's too late. She flew away three years ago."

I turned, expecting to find Zach, but Chris stood there instead. His exotically beautiful eyes transfixed me; their gaze lay as gently on my face as a caress. Dream rendering of a years-old video or not, I felt the reassuring charisma of his presence. He smiled, and I felt compelled to smile back.

"George's a male bird," I said, without thinking. "You said *she* flew away."

Putting a hand on my shoulder, he nodded at the door and said, "I've missed her." Then he stepped out the door into the sky and disappeared.

I gasped, inexplicably dismayed by the departure of a person I'd never even met.

Zach came up behind me again, putting his arms on my shoulder and kissing the top of my head. "You have to wonder where he went."

"Out the door, after the bird," I said absently.

"Silly girl," he chuckled into my ear. "I meant, where's he been since she died?"

"Why is he coming into the picture now?" I added thoughtfully. "And why am I so sad?"

"Maybe this will help cheer you up." Zach wrapped his arms

around me from behind and ran them over the top of the hospital shift I'd once again donned. He nuzzled my neck.

The warmth of him soaked through the thin cloth, a comforting feeling that quickly gave way to more. "Um, yeah, that, um, that," I said, leaning back into him. "I like that."

"She thought you would." He freed a hand and pointed to the figure by Hunter's bed.

Damn it! The Evil Dream Pixie! That bitch! There she stood, face in the shadow, scribbling on her stupid notepad. All the answers there, and she wasn't sharing a one of them.

"Can't I catch a break? You get out of there!" I yelled between the bars.

Zach pulled my hips against his. His hardness pushed against me. *Okay, maybe she's not my first priority right now.* I closed my eyes and leaned back into him.

" 'Candygram for Mongo,' " a familiar voice said.

I opened my eyes. *What the heck?*

" 'Candygram for Mongo.' "

Zach had worked his hands under my shift and made slow circles over my breasts.

"Who the hell was that?" I said.

"Cleavon Little." Zach murmured. He traced the tendons of my neck with his tongue.

"The guy from *Blazing Saddles?*"

Zach pulled back and began to strip off his shirt. "Uh-huh, from the scene where he's trying to deliver a bomb to the bad guy. Only he's not that bad a guy. Just misunderstood. Should I take off my pants first or should you?"

I blinked, both perplexed and fixated on his tanned chiseled six-pack. "Um. Uh. What's Cleavon Little doing in my dream?"

" 'Candygram for Mongo,' " the voice said again.

"Yeah, I got that," I said to the air. "You can stop now. It's starting to annoy me."

211

Zach wrapped his arms around me and parted my legs with one of his own. His hands dropped down to the small of my back, and he pressed me closer. Over his shoulder, I spotted Fido munching on a huge pile of hay from on top of the instrument panel.

"Does he know how to fly this?" I said as I unbuckled Zach's belt.

"Yes, but he doesn't have a license; he couldn't pass the test." He kissed my collarbone.

"Well, that's just ridiculous."

"You try holding a pencil with nothing but hooves." He feathered kisses up my neck. I groaned as my muscles started to twinge.

Yeah, those muscles.

"Pencils are very important," Zach said into my hair. "You thought about them at the jail today because the bars looked like pencil lead. She noticed them too," he said, nodding at the Pixie, still scribbling on her stupid pad, as Tri-Tri got to her knees and turned to Hunter, doggy style. He rose up and grabbed her hips from behind. The Tasmanian Devil on his ass applauded.

"Oh, hi Jolene," Zach said as a woman walked up to the bed. I wriggled around to face them as he waved to her.

She waved back and crawled onto the canopy bed. Hunter let go of Tri-Tri and took Jolene into his arms. Tri-Tri turned onto her back and smiled, clearly enjoying the addition.

"But that's your girlfriend!"

"Ex," Zach answered. He drew me back into his embrace and kissed me, his tongue softly probing my lips. My body quivered. When he pulled back, my knees almost buckled.

"But that's not important," he said. "It's what's in the pencil that's important."

"Huh? What?" I swayed, and he pulled me closer. *Oh God,*

this feels so good!

" 'Candygram for Mongo,' " Cleavon said.

"Shut up already!" I yelled over my shoulder, then turned back to watch Zach step out of his jeans. "You mean graphite?" I said, admiring the bulge beneath his red silk boxers.

Zach scowled, pointing to the boxers. "I wouldn't be caught dead in these girly things."

I grabbed his upper arms and pulled him to me, arching my back to press my chest against his. "Yeah, well, this is my dream. Deal with it. What about the graphite?"

He grabbed my hair and pulled my head back, kissing my throat. "It's a form of carbon."

"Mmm. I know that, but how did you? Oh, that's so nice!"

He stood back and pointed to his own chest. "I'm Dream Zach, remember? It's not really me. You know it, so I know it." Gripping my arms, he kissed me passionately.

I moaned with delight; I was feeling really neat spasms by the time we broke away from the kiss. "And sometimes they're made of charcoal, too."

He ripped open my shirt and kissed my bare breast. "Now you're thinking." He caught my face in his hands and made me look at him. "And what was on the floor of the car today?"

"Gum?" I said and tried to pull him closer.

He pressed my cheeks to hold me still. "What did it remind you of?"

I struggled to think. "I don't know. It was sticky, thick, and yellowed. Like, like resin?"

"You got it on your hands when you handled the file folder."

"Gum?"

He stared hard into my eyes. "No, the resin. And why is it important?"

I searched my memory. Resin and charcoal. Charcoal soot. *Why is that familiar?*

Zach looked over my head. "Oh, look. Here's Fancy."

I turned. Fancy had a smiling Hunter on his back. Tri-Tri and Jolene laughed.

Frustration and envy forced out a groan of exasperation. "That's it! I've had enough of everyone but me having sex with that man. Stop it, or I will turn this plane around, right now!"

" 'Candygram for Mongo.' "

"Shut the hell up!"

Zach grabbed me hard by the arms again. "Madison, listen to me! The Candygram is important, the bomb is important. Timing is everything! Remember, soot and resin. And shining, silvery snow. Remember the smell at the office."

I shifted my weight, my hormones raging, my thoughts racing, stuck between my body's urge to break free and run my tongue down the front of his chest, and my mind's incessant, annoying, stentorian commands to pay some goddamn attention to what's being said. I couldn't keep the whining out of my voice as I said, "What are you talking about? What smell?"

Something pounded in the distance. " 'Candygram for Mongo,' " the voice said above the growing sound. " 'Candygram for Mongo.' "

"Enough!" I slammed my hand into the jail bars, and they fell into a pile of soot. The pounding grew closer and more violent. I looked around; I was alone. The plane shook with the pounding. Louder and louder, closer and closer. I put my hands over my ears and fell to my knees like a child trying to block out the shuddering closet door, knowing there was nothing to stop the raging monster inside from getting me now, hearing the door slam open and then—

The plane disintegrated around me, dissolving into silver snow. And I was falling.

My eyes snapped open. My hotel room door shook. Jumping out of bed, I stumbled toward the pounding, managing to wrestle my nakedness into the robe just before I opened the door. Hunter pushed past me. I yanked the belt of my robe into a knot and tried to steady my adrenaline-wracked body. "What the hell?"

"What's wrong, Angel? Did I scare you?"

"Um, no. I was dreaming."

He smiled. "And what'd you dream about? Me?"

I pulled my robe to my throat, instantly awake. "Not everything's about you!" I stalked away from him. *Am I that obvious?*

He looked me up and down. "You look like crap."

To be fair, I felt like crap. Of course, he looked wonderful: fresh, pressed, and thoroughly composed. He wore a meticulously tailored blue suit that enhanced the lines of his physique. His shirt, a buttery silk, complimented the slim yellow diagonals across his navy satin tie. *God, I wish I had his tailor. And that he wasn't such a jerk. But he's a good-looking, great-smelling, broadshouldered jerk and—no! You are not going there!*

I grabbed my duffle bag off the dresser. "What time is it?" I snatched at my clothing and pulled out a pair of lavender lace panties, then shoved them back inside as he saw them.

Hunter gave a half-smile and sat on the bed. "Six o'clock."

"In the morning? Are you nuts? I just got to sleep! Who the hell gets up at six o'clock?"

"I didn't get any sleep, if you know what I mean."

I glared at him. I knew exactly what he meant. "And where's the Princess Tribeca?"

"Sleeping. You can't blame her, really."

"More likely it's constitutionally impossible for her to get up before noon."

"Keep talking, Angel. Jealousy becomes you."

"Puh-leese. Look, just order me something to eat while I change, okay?"

"Order it yourself."

"Come on. It can be here by the time I finish my shower."

"Eat later, move now. I've got better things to do than be with you."

"Ditto, Max. Trust me, I'll move at lightning speed."

I started toward the shower, then noticed the papers still sitting in the printer: Lilly's e-mail. My pulse sped up, fearing I'd be caught spying on him, not something he'd take well. So as Hunter fussed with the TV remote, I grabbed the papers and stuffed them in my bag and then hefted the duffle onto my bad shoulder. The pain prodded hard, clearly not through with me yet.

"Still whining about your little boo-boo?" Hunter said as he clicked on the tube.

"Sod off, old man." I slammed the bathroom door. As the sound of the television drifted through, I showered and brushed my teeth vigorously, trying to convince myself that I was simply anxious to get on with the chase. But the truth was that Hunter being so close while I was naked excited me, and I really didn't want to deal with that right now.

I toweled off, smoothed on some of the lavender-scented body lotion from the hotel gift basket, and pulled on my underwear and jeans. After finger-drying my hair, I spread out the printout of Lilly's e-mail on the counter

"Hey!" Hunter yelled through the door.

I jumped and actually squeaked. "What?"

"Let's go! I promised Tri we'd get out of here as soon as possible."

My heart plopped back into my chest. "All right, all right." I cracked the door so Hunter could hear me. "How's Jake? I keep calling, but the hospital won't talk to me because I'm not a cop or a relative. But I'm sure you managed to get around that."

The TV clicked off. "No change," Hunter's voice echoed

somberly. My eyes flew over the three-page printout. The first was a copy of a rental agreement for an apartment in Chicago. Not in the best neighborhood but far from the worst. My pulse stalled. The tenant was listed as Adalida Thibodaux—co-signed by Maxwell Hunter!

I scanned the lease: the rental dates corresponded to the summer that Adalida had been in Chicago. There were other papers too: photocopies of five checks made out to Adalida from Hunter. Most for a few thousand each, but the last was for fifty thousand. *Holy crap! Hunter had gotten Adalida an apartment and had been giving her money, a lot of money. And gee wilikers, Batman, why would a wealthy older man be paying the bills of a pretty young girl?*

I felt a surge of outrage on Jake's behalf and at the same time the thrill that I might have found something significant. Tapping my fingers against the marble countertop, I thought it over, trying to get some emotional distance and think clearly. What if Jake had just found out? Maybe he threatened to ruin Hunter's business. But in today's world, a rich older man with a young girlfriend was practically expected. Besides, Jake really was more the type to beat the shit out of someone than blackmail him.

I huffed out a breath. *Now what?* I slipped a light coat of pink gloss over my lips, then stuck the tube in my pocket. My tummy rumbled, and I shushed at it. Grabbing my cami from the hook on the door, I called out, "I may have a lot to learn, but I beat you to Fancy, didn't I? And I found Tina before you did."

"Beginner's luck." He stepped toward the door, and I darted behind it, pulling the cami on over my bra. Apparently oblivious, he went on. "Angel, you've got too much to learn, too little patience, and nobody to show you the way." The resonance of his voice slipped through the crack in the door. My heart pounded with competing emotions: anger, embarrassment, and that special thrill borne of being partially unclothed in the vicinity of another. Especially if one has recently seen a tattoo of a cartoon Tasmanian Devil on the gorgeous, tight ass of the other.

"Face it," Hunter said, as I fumbled my arms into my pink oxford. "You haven't got a chance in hell. And the sooner you admit that, the better off we'll all be." I stepped out of the bathroom and into the warmth of Hunter's appreciative glance. "Better," he said. "Now I won't be embarrassed to be seen with you." The warmth disappeared.

He rolled the barrel of a thirty-eight snub-nose revolver in his hand, checking the bullets.

I nodded at the gun. "Isn't that a little petite for you?"

He shot me a "don't be a smart ass" look and shoved the gun into a shoulder holster. "This was all I could get on short notice. I couldn't carry mine legally across the border."

"And that stopped you?"

"Look, if I choose to break the law, I'm willing to take the heat. But if I transport on Tri's plane, it implicates her." He cocked his head to one side. "Oh, I'm sorry. You look disappointed. Does my taking responsibility for my own actions disturb you?"

I scowled self-consciously. Actually it did. Unremitting jerks didn't act responsibly, damn it. I grabbed Nestor's cell phone, turned it on, and clipped it to the waistband of my jeans, then threw my dirty clothes and toiletries in the knapsack. "You know what I find odd? Voltaire's letting you in so intimately on this case. You might have been a cop at one time, but you're a civilian now. Why shouldn't I find that suspicious?"

He took my bag out of my hand and strode out the door to the elevator. "Why should you? Budgets are tight all around. He can't afford the extra people, and I'm not charging."

I hurried after him and snatched my bag back. "Why not? I figure you're the kind who thinks money is everything."

He whirled on me. "Jake is my friend. I would do *anything*

for him. Do you hear me?"

Okay, went one step too far again, I guess. "I'm sorry, I didn't mean—"

He turned away and punched the call button, then stared straight ahead, tight-jawed. I ground my teeth. No matter what I said, he took it the wrong way. *Fine, then. Let's just get this done. The sooner I got away from this man, the better.*

Outside the hotel, a sterling-gray Mercedes waited for us. Our chauffeur, an older man with neatly trimmed gray hair peeking out from beneath his emerald cap, held open the back door. He blinked as Hunter brushed past me, angling into the car and pointedly claiming the whole seat. Snapping open a paper he'd picked up in the lobby, he said, "The help sits up front."

I clucked my tongue and headed for the other side of the car. "Whatever!"

The driver shot Hunter a discreet but clearly disapproving look, then strode swiftly before me and opened the front passenger door.

"*Bonjour, monsieur. Comment sont vous, aujourd'hui?*" I said, wishing him a good morning and hoping my high school French would be understandable and possibly even accurate. "*Pardonnez, s'il vous plaît, mon pauvre accent. Je n'utilise pas votre jolie langue très souvent.*"

My sad, doubtless laughable, effort brought a smile in return. "Your accent is charming, Miss." Nodding at Hunter, he whispered, "*Parle-t-il le français?*"

I grinned, as much because I love the softened accents of Canadian French, as because of Hunter's knack for offending people. The driver wanted to know if Hunter spoke French, and I guessed that if Hunter didn't speak French, the driver would suddenly forget how to speak English. But the likelihood was that, being from New Orleans, Hunter would have picked up at least a little Cajun French, enough to get us both in trouble if we tried to talk around him. I made a sympathetic face. *"Il comprend probablement un petit français. Il est de Nouvelle-Orléans."*

The driver nodded fatalistically. As he took his seat, I handed him the address that Miss Livy had given me. "Would you take us here, please?"

As we rolled out smoothly onto the roadway, I pulled out an apple I'd taken from the basket of fruit in the hotel lobby and bit in with gusto, glancing at Hunter in the rearview mirror. Without looking up from his paper, he said, "How long is this going to take?"

Of course, he asked while I was in mid-bite. I swiped at the juice that dribbled on my chin. The driver handed me his handkerchief, which I used and returned with a smile, then hurriedly swallowed. "We're heading toward Charlevoix, up the mouth of the St. Lawrence. Wait until you see it. It's one of the most beautiful areas on Earth—majestic mountains, rolling vales, steep cliffs overlooking cold, sparkling waters—"

"What are you, a freaking travel guide? I asked a simple question: how long?"

"The address is between here and Charlevoix; I'd say about 80 kilometers."

Hunter glared at me over his paper.

"That's about fifty miles. Once we clear the city, we'll make good time, although we have to veer off and take coastal roads near the address. Maybe an hour and a quarter?" I said, looking at the driver, who nodded his confirmation.

Hunter grunted and went back to his reading. I settled into my seat, folded my arms over my chest and dropped my head back against the headrest, closing my eyes.

The next thing I knew, I heard a hissing sound and a warm hand gently shook me. Groggily, I struggled into a sitting position. "What? Huh? What's happening?"

The driver, his hand on my arm, said, "*Réveillez-vous, Mademoiselle.* Wake up, Miss."

I realized the car was stopped. "Wh . . . what? Sorry, I didn't get much sleep last night. I must have totally passed out. Thank God I didn't dream again; I needed the rest." I turned to face the back seat. "Hunter, I guess—" But Hunter was gone. Confused, I looked over at the driver.

The driver hissed again and motioned out the windshield. We were parked on the shoulder of a dirt road next to a thick forest of pine trees. To the right, the trees ended abruptly at the edge of a construction site, a few scraggly weeds dotting the uprooted landscape, trying to regain a foothold in the bare, brown dirt. Several hundred feet away, in the middle of the barren plain, sat a white wooden building in the center of a group of smaller, similar buildings.

The driver frowned apologetically. "The man, he told me not to wake you. But I think he is a horse's ass, *mais oui?*"

I shook myself awake and reached for the door. "*Mais oui.* A bucketful of *mais oui.* Thanks." The driver smiled. I got out and strode out after Hunter. "Jerk," I muttered. "Big, frigging, poop-head jerk." *Yeah, way to go, Madison. That's telling him.*

I surveyed the area as I got out, forgetting my irritation in the face of its beauty. We walked on a large, flat plain edged with trees on one side. On the other was a high, vertical cliff that fell to the ever-frigid St. Lawrence River. Ahead of me stood a cluster of buildings, some kind of resort-in-the-making, complete with picturebook cottages. I could tell, though, that this had once been an old homestead, as a half-collapsed brick house sat off to the side of the new construction, all alone, as if awaiting the final indignity of its razing. Not fifty feet beyond the cutoff of the woods was a large white sign. It proclaimed this area to be the future home of the Northern Glory Resort and promised luxury accommodations and five-star dining amidst the breathtaking panorama of unspoiled nature—once they replanted it, that is.

When I was on the verge of breaking the cover of the trees, I heard the angry rising of male voices. My gut tightening in wariness, I skittered close to a nearby tree and peered out between the branches. To my surprise, Hunter stood amidst a half-dozen sweat-streaked construction workers, each displaying various states of annoyance. The one nearest Hunter, a square-shouldered, heavily muscled man whose skin shone almost blue-black in the sun, seemed the most irritated. My surprise, though, was due entirely to Hunter's appearance, since I hadn't recognized him for a split second. Shirt sleeves rolled up unevenly, tie askew, he stood hunched over, looking several inches shorter, his brawny physique shrunken under the weight of his subdued demeanor. Black, thick-rimmed glasses perched on his nose, his hair a disheveled mess, he tapped on papers on a clipboard he held with one hand in the incessant manner of a sci-fi fanatic trying to make the vital point that Scotty had his drink in one hand before the fight with the Klingons but in his other the next scene.

"Here! Right here!" he said, his voice having taken on an immensely annoying nasal quality. The glasses slid down his nose and he pushed them back, sniffing wetly and wiping his nose with the back of his hand before rubbing it off on his pants.

The man beside him, the foreman I guessed, shot Hunter a disgusted look, rolling his eyes at the man closest to him. He reached for the clipboard. "If you'll let me look at the damn—"

Hunter tucked the board under his arm. "I've already told you: paragraph 15, subparagraph 6, section 2a, clearly states that all new construction, being heretofore approved by appropriate local council, notwithstanding concomitant approvals by federal and/or indigenous governing bodies, must nonetheless, when under clear statutory regulation as administered by said federal and/or indigenous governing bodies, and in consideration of duly registered complaint, whether from private personage or wholly incorporated—"

A burly, blond, sunburned worker took off his hat and rubbed the sweat off his brow. "What the fuck is he talking about?"

Hunter pointed at the man, like a grandmother reprimanding young hoodlums. "There is no need for that kind of language."

My jaw dropped. I couldn't believe what I was seeing. Could this possibly be the same man? I knew it had to be, but frankly, he looked like someone had modulated his genetic makeup, clearly removing those genes governing the production of testosterone.

The foreman waved a hand at the blond, his forehead shimmering with sweat, probably as much from the exertion of resisting punching Hunter out as from any physical labor. "Just tell me what you want me to do about this."

"Well, clearly, I need to see your exigency forms."

The man put his hands on his hips, practically boiling over with impatience. "My what?"

Hunter snorted and wiped his nose noisily again. "As this is formerly, yet duly registered indigenous lands, granted by treaty dating on or before eighteen—"

"Don't start that shit again." the man said, holding up a hand. "Just tell me where to find these fucking forms."

Hunter looked down at his clipboard, rifling through the papers. "There is no need for such rudeness. The forms should have been attached to the permits obtained from local council."

"Come on, man! All our paperwork is back at the trailer! It'll take us more than an hour to get it and get back. It'll be lunch time by then. Give us a break, huh? Can we do this later?"

Pushing his glasses high up on his nose, Hunter, the consummate image of the self-important bureaucrat, said, "I'm only doing my job. It's not my fault your people haven't done theirs.

You can proceed once I have ascertained appropriate documentation is in hand."

I tensed as I watched the foreman ball up his fist, certain he was about to take a swing at Hunter. Instead, he took a deep breath and flexed his fingers. "Fine! We'll get you the *fucking* paperwork. Well boys, it looks like we just got an early lunch."

Several of the men high-fived each other; all shouted their approval. The group walked to a battered white pickup truck parked close by, all but one vaulting into the truck bed, while the foreman and another climbed into the cab. "You coming?" the leader called to Hunter.

Hunter tucked the clipboard under his arm once more, then pointed at the main house. "I need to further ascertain the state of all construction edifices pertaining to—"

The man waved him off. "Yeah, yeah, whatever."

The driver started the truck, loudly revving the engine, yelling above the noise. "Hey, bud, I tell you what. There's a great view from that real steep cliff over by the big house. Why don't you go check it out? And *don't* watch your step. Asshole!" With that he jammed the truck in gear and rocketed forward, dirt and rocks spewing out behind, the men in the back clutching their sides and laughing loudly. As the truck whipped around onto the road, the driver flipped Hunter off.

Caught in a cloud of dust, Hunter shouted, "There is no need for that kind of behavior!"

I ducked behind a tree as the truck roared past me. Hunter stood glowering after the vehicle, waiting as the growl of the engine faded into the distance. Then, with a confident cock of his eyebrow, he raised himself to full height, going from geek to gladiator before my eyes. Sweeping his hair back, he rolled one sleeve even with the other and strode purposefully toward me, pausing to pick up a pile of clothes laying strewn over a water cooler nearby.

Stepping out of the trees, I crossed my arms before my chest. "What was *that*?"

Hunter didn't break stride but walked straight past me to the limo. "Finally woke up, did you? Anyone ever tell you that you snore like a sawmill with asthma?"

"That doesn't even make any sense," I said, embarrassed. We approached the car and the driver got out, taking the clipboard Hunter handed to him. "And I don't snore."

Hunter slid a side-glance at me. "Like hell you don't. You flushed a couple of moose back there, and they're probably still running." He nodded at the driver. "Tell her."

The driver smiled apologetically. "Perhaps a little." He hurried back into his seat.

Snorting, Hunter said, "At least it kept you out of my way. Now that those jamokes are taken care of, we can get to the main house. I saw two women: one upstairs who matches the general description of the woman from the alley, and another downstairs, blond, heavy-set, and a lot older. I'll go in the front and you—"

I put a hand on his arm. "Hang on. Why did you do that back there?"

He sighed and scratched his nose. "Did you expect that we could question a potential murder suspect, maybe take her into custody, with a half-dozen construction workers around? I had to get rid of them. Nothing will make real men scatter quicker than whiny little bureaucrats."

Still struck with amazement, I said, "Weren't you afraid that they'd call their office?"

"We passed the office on the way up here; it was empty. I took a calculated risk. Besides, I could've fought my way out if I had to, and I had a getaway car nearby."

"I can still barely believe you pulled it off. How did you learn to do that?"

"Look Angel, Jake and I spent nearly as many years being cops as you've been alive. Out on the streets with crooks and con artists, one thing you learn is that most people don't *really* look at what's right in front of their faces. And *no one* thinks they can be taken for a ride, which is what makes it so easy to do just that. A change of posture, a prop, and even a half-convincing lie will get you into a lot of places you couldn't power through with a bulldozer. You get them to look here," he said, waving his left hand before me, fingers splayed, "while the action goes on here." I flinched as he pulled a painter's ball cap over my head, cramming it down hard.

"Hey," I said, reaching up to loosen it. "What's this for?"

"Keep it on." He snapped open a soiled, paint-stained jacket. "And put this on too."

Perplexed, I struggled into it even as Hunter bent down and picked up a handful of dirt. "Hey! What are you doing?" I said as he smeared dirt over my cheeks. "Cut it out!"

"We can't risk the suspect recognizing you. You need to look like a worker."

"I suppose. But—" He grabbed another handful of dirt and rubbed it over my breasts. I swatted his hands away. "Are you enjoying yourself?"

He grinned, his eyes sparkling. "Just trying to be thorough."

I glared at him. "Can we just get on with this? What's the plan?"

Pointing at the house, a tenth of a mile down the road, he said, "I go in front, do the inspector bit again. You sneak around back. Keep your head down, cap on tight. Act like you know what you're doing. And God help us on that one."

I glowered at him but said nothing.

He went on, "When you're in position, signal me. I'll find a way to get the suspect by a window. We need to know she's the right woman first. Then—"

"Hang on. How do I signal you? Oh, wait, this is a construction site. There's probably some kind of flammable material. I could make a controlled fire, maybe use some chemical to create a subtle change to the smoke, differentiating it sufficiently from the background to—"

He grabbed the cell phone from my belt, holding it before my face. "Just call me! I'll put my phone on vibrate, so it won't attract a lot of attention."

"Sure, that'll work."

"Egghead and still a moron," Hunter said as he keyed his number into Nestor's cell.

I snatched the phone and put it back on my belt. "Lighten up! I'm trying to help."

"Then do what you're told. This is a simple operation. We don't need any fancy science crap. Go to the back door and signal me when you get there. Leave the rest to me. Understood?"

"Sir, yes, sir!" I said.

He glared at me, "If you're not going to take this seriously—"

"I am! Let's just go." I glowered at him, amazed at how quickly things had gone from my admiring him to my wanting to boot him over that cliff the men had talked about.

Hunter regarded me a few more moments, then pounded his palm on the hood of the car and said to the driver, "We'll be back soon. Keep an eye out for anyone coming up the road. Come get us if you see anything. And come in a hurry."

The driver nodded. He caught my eye, and I saw worry there. I smiled reassuringly at him and turned to follow Hunter, who was already several yards away.

I split from Hunter, keeping my head down, my hands shoved in my pockets. I walked in a diagonal away from the house, swiftly turning to circle it once I was out of sight of the front. As I came around behind, I heard voices. Hunter and a woman were talking on the front porch.

"*Oui,* I am the owner: Melissa Duchampes. And you are, *Monsieur?*" the female said.

Hunter launched into his nasal-voiced bureaucrat routine, spouting the same gibberish he'd so masterfully used to con the construction workers. I spotted a narrow set of stairs, with a rail to either side, just outside a screen door. I crept up the stairs and gingerly opened the screen, resting my ear against the wooden back door. The voices were more muffled but still audible.

Taking my phone off my belt, I toggled in Hunter's number, signaling I was in place.

I had just put my ear back to the door when it flew open, sending me tumbling over the rail, the air pushed out of my lungs in one mighty rush. Stunned, I lay on my back, vaguely aware that someone was running away. I shook my head and scrambled to my knees, gingerly touching my nose, now burning with pain.

Suddenly, the door flew open again, and Hunter launched himself out and onto the porch. A heavy-set blond woman ran up behind him, grabbing him by the arm. "No!" the woman cried out. "Leave her alone. She hasn't done anything!"

Hunter shook her off. "Are you all right?" he said, genuine worry on his face.

I looked up, still dazed. "I hurb by dose." I touched it gently, sniffed and returned to my normal voice. "I mean I hurt my nose. It's okay, though. It's not broken."

He rolled his eyes. "Were you standing *behind* the door?!"

I exhaled, too humiliated to answer, and pointed behind him. "She's getting away!"

Hunter turned, growled, and vaulted the railing, hitting the ground at a run. He was well behind the woman but running like a tailback. I could tell instantly the sprinter was Tina. Hauling myself to my feet, I fought off an initial wave of dizziness and then ran after them.

Tina didn't have a chance. By the time she'd crossed the remaining distance to the half-demolished nearby building, she'd slowed considerably. Hunter never lagged for a moment. Tina glanced back, then ran faster, shooting through the open gate of a chain-link fence.

My heart pounded, and not only with the exertion of running after them. Tina ran dangerously close to the edge of the cliff, barely slowing as she swerved around short, thick bushes dotting the edge. I yelled a warning. Hunter threw on a heroic burst of speed and caught up. Grabbing her by the shoulder, he spun her around.

"Come here, you idiot!" he yelled. "You're too close to the edge!"

But Tina struggled harder. She drew up her knee, aiming at his groin. With a reflex no man could forestall, he stepped back, tripping over a bush. She shoved him and he fell, one hand landing only inches from the cliff edge.

Still running at top speed to catch up, I yelled again. The soft ground near the cliff edge started to crumble beneath his weight. He threw out a hand and grabbed one of the short, sturdy bushes. I gasped and ran harder. Tina staggered backward toward the edge of the drop.

"Son of a bitch!" Hunter released the branch and lunged for her.

She screamed as they toppled over the edge together.

CHAPTER THIRTEEN

My cry of terror melded with hers. Within seconds, I reached the cliff. I dropped to my knees, crawling as quickly as I dared toward the crumbling edge. "Hunter! My God! Hunter!"

"Get a rope!" he called, his voice strained.

I nearly fainted in relief. Scrambling closer, I peered over the side. Though the cliff face miraculously sloped enough to stop their fall, it plunged into a vertical drop a few feet lower.

Pressed hard against the side of the cliff, Hunter kept one arm around Tina. He dug his fingers into a boundary between the sedimentary layers, shoving his feet hard into the slope to reinforce his stand. Tina clung to him and twisted.

"Hold still!" he growled.

As if finally catching on to the danger, she did. He glanced up at me as he stamped hard into the ground to get hold.

I reached out, but he was a good eight feet beneath me. Clods of earth broke off beneath my hand and tumbled over the edge. Hunter shook the dirt off his head. "You can't reach us!"

I pushed myself to my feet, legs trembling and fear cramping up my insides. "Okay, okay," I chanted. "Rope. I need to get a rope."

The heavy-set blond woman ran toward me. She screamed something, but I couldn't have cared less what. "Get help!" I yelled as I ran toward the construction site. I prayed for good debris: a rope, some sheets or cloth, anything!

She stopped in her tracks. "I don't—I don't—what?"

If my arms had been long enough, I would have slapped the shit out of her. "Go get the driver! They can't hold on! *Run!*"

She ran. I lunged through a doorway. Nothing but leaves and bits of roof littered the floor. *No good!* I turned back to the cliff. *What do I do?* My throat constricted, but I fought off the rising panic. *You can do this. You have to find*—my gaze lit on a partially fallen segment of chain-link fence. It was at least ten feet long! I ran to it and started to drag it toward the cliff. It pulled free, then caught hard, sending me stumbling to the ground. I yanked, but it wouldn't give. Furious, I jumped up and tugged again, then realized it was still attached to the steel fence post by one remaining metal tie. *Shit! Shit! Shit!*

I dropped the fence and ran to the post. I grabbed the tie, twisting and pulling until my hands stung. Although weakened with rust, it wouldn't break. Shouting in frustration, I tried to wrestle the post out of the ground, heaving with all my might. It wouldn't budge either.

"What the hell are you doing?" Hunter yelled.

Helplessness tore at my heart. "There's no rope!" I ran to the cliff edge, this time not bothering to kneel. Tina buried her face in Hunter's chest and cried. Hunter fought to reposition his bloodied fingers into the cliff. His feet slipped a few more centimeters under their combined weight. He looked up at me.

In his eyes, I saw the mirror of my own realization. If he let her go, he could hold on. But the river lapped against rocks below at a drop equal to a ten-story fall. He'd live, but she'd die.

My eyes widened; his narrowed in determination. He tightened his grip. "Hurry up!"

Swallowing hard, I ran for the house. I knew there would be something there, but the distance seemed insurmountable. My breath burned in my chest. I ran harder.

A makeshift alcove haphazardly filled with half-assembled

vending machines beckoned to my left. Did I dare waste life-saving moments to search it? Did I dare pass it up?

Desperation roaring in my ears, I knew I had no choice. I veered into it.

A soda machine stood against the back of the three-walled building and near it was a large, silver commercial ice-maker. A squat, yellow canister took up the space between them, a charging-hose and release valve attached. As I pushed and pulled at the machines, I bumped my shin on the canister and stooped to look at it. The label warned of a Freon-type refrigerant: an extremely cold liquid used in ice-makers that vaporized at normal temperature.

Then it hit me. I could almost certainly fracture the worn metal tie on the fence with liquid nitrogen. Now, commercial refrigerants couldn't bring things down to the seventy-seven-degree Kelvin temperature that nitrogen could, but it might just shatter a thin, time-stressed metal wire. I looked up at the house, swallowing hard. It seemed so far away. *But I have to try!*

Suddenly, the driver ran from the house, followed by the blond. I shouted for him to get a rope. With that as my backup plan, I grabbed the carry-bar on the twenty-pound canister, hose and all, and sprinted back to the fence, skidding to a stop beside it. The dangling mesh vibrated as I dropped the container to the ground with a thud. Arms trembling, lungs burning, I took the open end of the hose and broke off the stem designed to prevent the refrigerant from shooting out when the valve opened. "Hunter, I'm here!"

There was no sound.

Fear flew in icy waves up my arms. "Hunter! Hunter!"

"Hurry the fuck up!" came his strained reply.

A sigh of relief was all I wasted energy on. I ripped off my shirt and wrapped it around the now-mutilated end of the hose. Then I pulled off my camisole and wrapped it around my hand.

If liquid refrigerant touched my bare skin, it would mean instant frostbite and the possible loss of my fingers or even my hand. I pushed the hose against the metal wire and stepped back as far as my reach would let me, making certain to put the wind to my back. If there was blowback onto my torso, protected now by only a lacy pink bra . . . no, I couldn't think about that.

Gritting my teeth, I twisted open the valve on the top of the canister. I winced, nearly dropping the hose as it jerked to life. A fine mist of gas shot out onto the wire. It took only seconds—precious, endless seconds—but finally the hissing stopped. I threw the sputtering hose to the ground. Frost lay like white icing over the wire, but it didn't look any different.

Screaming in fury, terrified that I'd cost Hunter his life, I grabbed a heavy rock from the ground and smashed it into the wire again and again, harder and harder each time. After three tremendous blows and a bloody, bruised hand, the wire finally split. An animal-like cry escaped me as I threw the rock aside and yanked the ten-foot mesh segment free.

"I'm coming!" I ran to the edge of the cliff, dragging the fence behind me.

I knelt and pushed the mesh over the edge. Hunter still held Tina, but a trench had formed beneath his feet, marking how far he'd slid. With his free hand, he fought for purchase on the cliff wall. I saw his strength ebbing as sweat traced a wavy course through the dirt on his face.

"I'm here, I'm here," I said stupidly, sitting down on the fence to anchor it.

As the mesh reached them, Hunter shoved Tina onto it. "Grab it!" he yelled as she hesitated. "I swear I'll drop your bony ass if you don't climb up that fence right, fucking, now!"

Tina wrapped sweat-soaked fingers around the interlocking wires and started to hoist herself up. As she did, the fence slid toward the cliff edge. She screamed and let go. In a flurry of movement, Hunter pushed her back up against the cliff, and I scrambled to the end of the fence. I grabbed it, dug my heels into the ground, and pulled back. "It's all right," I said, not at all certain that it was. "I've got it now. Come on up."

The fence vibrated again. By the time Tina made to the top, my arms shook with fatigue. She rolled to the ground, gasping and spent. But I knew I couldn't anchor the fence against Hunter's weight alone. "Help me!" I said, tightening my grip. "You have to help me hold it."

She turned to me, her eyes glazed. Then, focusing, she crawled over and grabbed the fence, digging her own heels in. "We've got it, Hunter! Climb up."

The fence lunged forward. We both gasped and pulled. My hands stung as metal dug into them. Suddenly, dirt flew up beside me as the driver fell to his knees and wrapped his fingers through the mesh. Within a second, the blond dropped beside him, all of us anchoring the fence as it quivered and jerked with Hunter's every movement. Finally, he heaved himself over the edge and fell, exhausted, onto the ground beside me.

I collapsed onto my back, breath heaving out of my lungs. My fingers landed on a rough tangle of fiber, and I couldn't help but smile at the rope, lying where the driver dropped it. "Oh, sure, now you show up," I said to it.

Hunter lay two feet away, on his stomach, eyes closed. Long deep breaths eased his overworked lungs. Without his traditional grimace to mar his features, I could appreciate the strong set of his jaw, broad brow, and rugged angularity of his cheeks. I reached out and brushed a sweat-soaked strand from his forehead. "You okay?" I said softly.

His eyes opened and, for a moment, a light, weary smile tugged at the corner of his mouth. Then, as if jarred by some memory, his face morphed back into its mask of disdain. He brushed my hand aside and pushed off with his arms, rising to his knees. "Took you long enough. What the hell were you doing, taking a tea break?"

Tina stirred and made a movement as if to crawl away. Hunter grabbed one of her ankles. "Try it, and I'll toss your ass back over the edge."

I chuckled. "Such a gentleman."

He made a grumbling noise and stood, then pulled Tina to her feet, making a point *not* to let go of her arm. He sneered my way. "Are you going to lie there all day?"

"You're welcome," I replied.

"For what?"

"For saving your life, you jerk."

He started to lead Tina away. "Get over it," he called over his shoulder. "I have."

"Hey, Hunter!" I said, still flat on my back.

He turned. "What?"

I flipped him the finger.

"There is simply no need for such rudeness," he said and walked away.

A shadow fell over me. *"Mademoiselle? Miss?"* The driver's uniform was filthy and sweat dripped from his nose. His eyes held a mix of relief and amusement. "You are well?"

I let him help me to my feet. "Yes, I are well. About as well as I can be around that man." We watched Hunter stride away, a captured Tina trotting beside him, Melissa in their wake. From the confident set of his shoulders and the steadiness of his gait, you couldn't have guessed he'd just cheated death. "He is a horse's ass. But, you must admit, he's a brave horse's ass."

The driver scooped up his hat and held out his arm. I took it, and we set off for the house. *"Mais oui,"* he said. "A bucketful of *mais oui.*"

★ ★ ★ ★ ★

By the time we returned to the main house, Tina had wisely, if dejectedly, abandoned the idea of trying to flee. Hunter's unrelenting grip on her elbow doubtless helped with that decision. She nixed Melissa's offer to fetch the men from the construction site and sent her off.

With a curt command from Hunter and a reassuring smile from me, the driver left us as well, but not before offering me his suit coat, inasmuch as my shirt and camisole were freshly frosted with Freon somewhere out by the fence. In contrast, Hunter's idea of cover was to keep watch on my cleavage. Though my breasts don't have that porn-star, silicon-balloon look guys seem to go for, the twins fill a C-cup quite respectfully, if I do say so myself. And in a pink, lacy bra specifically designed to push the kids together, I didn't feel I had anything to apologize for. Nor did it bother me when the driver's coat left a nice view of the valley from which Hunter had to repeatedly drag his attention. With the oversized sleeves pushed high up my arm, I thought I completely pulled off the "Annie Hall Does Dallas" look.

Tina led us to her bedroom in the partially completed second floor of the house.

She had taken what would eventually be one of the better suites in the resort: a large two-room, single-bath affair, high-domed windows dominating a small sitting room, its walls painted pearlescent white. An overstuffed chair claimed the corner, bisected by slanted rays of morning light. Tina sat in the chair, clasping her hands tightly on her lap. She'd traded her plum dress for a crimson sweatshirt, jeans, and sneakers, all now dirt-caked from her nearly fatal fall. Her hair hung loose at her shoulders, the red having been bleached to light brown, like sandy soil left fallow over the winter. Her eyes, though still bright green, stretched wide with anxiety.

"End of the line, Tina," I said. "You'd better come clean. Why did you try to kill Jake?"

"Who?"

Hunter stepped forward. "I'm not playing this game, girlie. You tried to kill him, and you offed your boyfriend too. Not to mention some harmless old man."

Her gaze darted between us. She seemed genuinely perplexed. "What are you talking about? Has something happened to Tav?"

"Like you don't know," Hunter snarled. "Your little playmate drowned, and you tried to kill our girl here. I don't much like that. You talk now, and I might be able to help you out. But you keep playing this dumb-sister routine—"

She jumped to her feet, and Hunter pushed her back down. Tears welled in her eyes. "Tav's dead? Oh my God. Oh my God! No! No!" She put her head in her hands.

I turned to Hunter. "I think she's serious. She didn't know."

"Angel, I've seen this a thousand times. Men who've gutted their grandmothers, moms who've drowned their kids, all sobbing their hearts out. But not because they didn't do it; because they got caught." Hands on hips, he glowered down at Tina. "Keep it up. I like the show."

Aghast, I said, "For God's sake, Hunter, don't be such a jerk."

Tina peered up at him. "I swear I don't know what you're talking about. I only left because Tav told me to. He was afraid, said he'd made some deal that went bad. But he never said with who or what the deal was." She grabbed my arm, clearly desperate.

I pulled back almost without thinking, unwilling to be drawn into her emotional well.

"I didn't do anything." She looked at Hunter, "You've got to believe me!"

I expected a nasty retort from Hunter, but instead, with

complete calm, he said, "I do."

Tina blinked and stared into his eyes. Her shoulders relaxed. "Thank you," she said.

I turned my head, peering intently at him, just as nonplussed as she seemed to be by his sudden change. "You do?" I said to him.

"Sure." He looked at her. "Tell me more." He half turned my way. "Pay attention, Angel, I'm trying to teach something," he murmured sotto voce.

I sat back, realizing I was watching a master class in manipulation. First, he intimidated her into begging for acceptance. And then he gave it to her, or at least made her think he would, if she kept talking. *It's one layer after another with this man.* I began to understand why he was so successful. He knew how to get what he wanted out of people, including, to be honest, me.

Tina seemed to shrink in on herself, casting her gaze about the room as if looking for shelter. "I don't know what to do." She looked at me. Her eyes brimmed with tears. "I lost my brother last month. Now I've lost Tav." The words deteriorated into sobs.

Chris is dead? I froze as a deep, anomalous sadness filled me up. *But, wait, why should I care? He was nothing more than an image on a screen. Some random kid laughing, playing, and teasing with his crew, like a million others. Yes, there'd been those amazing eyes, surreal and compelling. But, it wasn't only that. He'd been so full of life, both he and Adalida. And they had been loved, by people I loved. Now they were both dead. Why? Had it been suicide? Or murder?* I felt my jaw tighten and eyes harden. Video ghosts or not, Chris had mattered. And Adalida had mattered. And I'd see to it that whoever was doing all this was damn sure going to know that.

Hunter walked away, gesturing to me to comfort her. I

frowned at him but sat down beside her, putting my arm around her shoulder. She turned into me. Unfortunately, she chose my still-sore shoulder to weep upon. I gritted my teeth and patted her back. "It's going to be okay." When her sobs subsided, I ventured a new question. "Tina, part of the reason we came was to see your brother. Are you saying he's dead?"

She dabbed her nose with the ratty ball of tissues, nodding mutely.

Hunter reappeared with more tissue. "What brother? Have you been holding out on me?"

"No. Well, yes. But only so you wouldn't dump me before we got here." Before he could retort, I held up a hand. "Give me a second." I turned back to Tina. "How did Chris die?"

Sadness filled her eyes. "Really, it was just a matter of time. He tried to commit suicide with his girlfriend. But he didn't take as much poison, so he ended up in a coma. He's been hanging on for years, a vegetable."

Hunter's expression shifted from perplexed to comprehension. "Wait a minute. Are you talking about Chris Crowel? Is she—" Hunter turned on Tina. "Are you Christina Crowel?"

"It's DuChampes now. I married my second cousin, George, but he ran out on me."

Hunter threw his arms in the air. "Nobody gives a fuck who you married!" He whirled on me, his eyes blazing. "You knew she was Chris Crowel's sister, and you didn't tell me?"

"If I'd told you earlier, you would have ditched me. Look, I didn't know she existed until I went to New Orleans. And, yes, maybe I should have told you sooner about the connection between the woman we were following and a friend of Adalida's—"

Hunter snorted. "Friend! That's a good one!"

Tina's brow furrowed. "Adalida Thibodaux? What does she have to do with all this?"

"Her father was the one shot in the alley," I said. "Didn't you know?"

At first, she looked genuinely shocked. But then her face contorted with undisguised fury. "Jake Thibodaux? He's the man who was shot? Well, you can count me out! I won't help you find the shooter unless I get to give him a trophy!"

I pulled back from her, my mouth gaping open, trying to process the shock. Finally, I shook my head, stammering, "Whoa, hang on. What—?"

She jumped to her feet. "He deserved to die! That bastard murdered my brother!"

"That's bullshit!" Hunter advanced on her. I stepped between them, stopped him with a hand to his chest. "Jake was no murderer!" he said, tone full of bile. "He wouldn't kill anyone without a reason, not even that shithead brother of yours!"

"Bastard!" Tina shouted.

I put my other hand out toward Tina, trying to calm her down while still maintaining a steady pressure on Hunter's chest. "Don't do this. What's going on?"

His breathing was labored against my palm. His eyes focused like daggers on her; her own shone bright with defiance. "I know the little puke finally kicked off," he said. "And about time, too. It was taking all of Jake's money to keep him alive."

Tina screamed, "I hate you!"

"Oh, sister, you're breaking my heart!"

"Enough, both of you!" I turned to Hunter. "Just tell me, okay?"

At first he said nothing, just breathed through his nose like an enraged bull. But then he stepped back. "The fag was Adalida's boyfriend."

"Don't you call Chris that!" Tina yelled, stamping her feet on the ground

"That's right," he said, his tone mocking. "Technically, he

was AC/DC."

Affronted, I put my hands on my hips. "What did you say?"

"He liked it both ways. Drilled any hole he could get into."

"I know what it means! For God's sake, have a heart. He was her brother."

"And Jake is my *friend*! And that bitch," he said, raising to full height and pointing down at her as if he could loose lightning bolts from his fingertips, "that bitch wants him dead? Well, fuck her! Fuck her feelings! And fuck you! I don't give a shit how she feels! She wants Jake dead? Well I'm glad her *faggot* brother is dead!"

Tina bellowed and rushed him. Hunter grabbed her by her arms. I slammed into Hunter with all of my weight. The pain caused me to yelp like a wounded puppy, but my momentum did the job. Hunter lost his grip, and he and I tumbled to the floor. He got tangled in the legs of a small plant table as he fell, which kept him down momentarily. Seizing the opportunity, I jumped to my feet, grabbed Tina and practically flung her into the chair. "Sit!"

Tina glared at Hunter. He stood slowly, small table in hand. The deadly look in his eyes made my gut clench. I stepped between them, swallowing hard. "So, what part of the lesson is this? Tell me how this helps get the job done? Huh? You're the teacher. What do I do now?"

His furious gaze shot to me, and my body jerked instinctively. After what seemed like a second short of an eternity, his anger seemed to subside, a little anyway. He put the table down.

Taking a shuddering breath, I went to him and touched his arm. "I know you're hurting."

His arm flew out, tossing my hand to my side. "Don't you dare try to get into my head! I won't make that mistake again."

"Oh, for crying out loud. You don't want to let me in? Fine. But we still have a job to do. Just help me understand, okay?" I shook my head, grinding my teeth together. "I care about Jake too, you know. And I care about those people who died." Crossing my arms over my chest, I said, "And I damn sure care about who's trying to kill me. So, will you please get off your high horse and tell me what you know about Chris's death?"

"What's to know? The kid was sick, he died. End of story."

"And Jake did nothing about it," Tina said, her voice laced with impending sobs.

"It was his money keeping the kid alive!" Hunter bellowed.

Tina turned to me. "Jake was there the night Chris stopped breathing. The nurse said he might have lived if Jake had gotten help right away. But he didn't. That's as good as murder!"

"Bull!" Hunter said. "Jake told me that the kid died while he was asleep in a chair. He never had a chance to call anyone."

"Do you expect me to believe that?" Tina said, her lips curling in disgust.

"I don't care what you believe! Jake wouldn't have killed the kid. Hell, he bankrupted himself to pay for hospice. He sold his house, his car, and most of the land that had been in his family for generations, all to take care of that cheating brat. He ended up with nothing, driving that piece-of-shit car. And he hired *you*," Hunter said, nodding at me, "which he couldn't afford to do. If he's guilty of anything, it's caring about worthless people."

"Don't start that again." I turned to Tina. "I knew Jake for six months, and he never told me about Chris, or that he was taking care of him."

"It was none of your damn business." Hunter radiated resentment. "What happened between Chris and Adalida shamed him. And, unlike women, men don't go blubbering out their problems every time the moon rises. Or, maybe Jake didn't trust you. Maybe you weren't as goddamned important to him as you seem to think."

His words hit me hard. He was right, though. However much

I trusted Jake, he clearly didn't trust me the same. I'd been such a stupid child, thinking a savvy, street-tested man like Jake could take a geek like me seriously. My blood burned with resentment toward Hunter. "Oh, yeah? Well, he left behind the goods on you, didn't he? What does that say?"

What I saw next made my heart fall heavily into my chest. In Hunter's face, in the flush of his cheeks and the flinch of his gaze, I saw the same doubts in him as I had in myself. After all, Jake was Hunter's best friend. And, yet, Hunter had played the same role with Jake as I had: an extra set of hands, a distraction, and a sounding board. Comic relief. Had he, too, tried so hard to gain as much trust as he gave, only to fall short and, despite his riches and success, still and always lost in Jake's shadow? I peered intently at him, thinking that I could see, in the firm set of his jaw and sad downcast of his eyes, pain and uncertainty. Jake had left something behind that could hurt him, and I wondered, yet again, could such anguish manifest in murder?

I looked away, unable to give a name to the swirl of feelings in my head. "It looks like neither one of us had the monopoly on Jake's trust, doesn't it?" I braced my back and turned to Tina, trying to trade emotional disorientation for cool analysis. "Hunter has a point. After sacrificing so much, why would Jake let Chris die?"

"You've never been around someone who's dying a slow death before, have you?"

"No."

"Well, you don't want to be. It's hard, watching the life drain out of someone you love. Watching them shrivel up into something that doesn't even look like the person you knew. And every day it gets harder. Even for someone like Jake, who didn't give a shit about my brother's suffering, it would've been hard. After a while, you pray for them to die. You just pray for it."

Hunter stared at the floor. Was he thinking about his wife and of her long, painful death? I thought back to the video I saw at Miss Livy's, remembering the genuine affection in Jake's voice when he talked to the kids. "I'm sorry you went through that," I said. "But if you think that Jake would just watch someone die, you're wrong. I know in my heart that he wouldn't."

Tina shrugged. "That's your opinion."

Hunter sighed. "This is going nowhere. She's admitted to a motive, and she had opportunity. I'd say we got ourselves a prime suspect."

Tina leapt to her feet. "I didn't do anything! You said you believed me!"

"I lied!" he snarled.

I stepped toward him. "Hunter, come on. You saw how surprised she was when she found out that it was Jake who was shot. I know you don't think she did it."

"You don't know anything."

"Maybe not, but I'll tell you what I suspect."

"This should be entertaining."

"I think Chris's death was a tipping point, something that drove someone over the edge after three years of waiting. Tina, do you know of anyone who might have been so upset over Chris's death that they might want to kill Jake for revenge?"

She threw her hands up in frustration. "No, I don't know."

"Maybe someone in your family?"

"We didn't have much family left, only Lissa and her husband. I mean, Lissa's husband . . . he had . . . *issues* with Chris's lifestyle, too. But, no, neither of them would go that far."

"Maybe one of Chris's friends, girlfriends or, um, well, boy-friends?"

She looked at Hunter and then at me. I got the impression

that she wanted to say something but wouldn't in front of him. She shook her head.

I inched close and nudged Hunter. "Why don't you let us have a few moments alone?"

He scowled.

"Trust me," I murmured. "She's got something she wants to say but not in front of you."

He pulled his cell phone from his suit jacket. "You've got ten minutes. I'll call Voltaire and have him send people to the sanitarium where the kid was kept. We'll find out what really happened. And I fucking guarantee you that we'll find that Jake's no murderer."

"Come on," I said to Tina. "Let's get you packed."

Tina and I went into the bedroom. A well-worn black leather piece of luggage sat on the bed. I watched her gather toiletries from the bedroom and dump them into the bag.

Could she really have hated Jake enough to kill him? She clearly didn't have the most stable of temperaments. She'd nearly run off a cliff, almost gotten herself killed by her own panic, and then attacked the man who'd saved her life. But was she clever enough to have lured Jake into a trap? Could she have calmly shot a man from across a city street? Detonate a bomb and kill innocent strangers? And did she kill her lover to keep him quiet? Or was her grief real?

And what, if anything, did this all have to do with Chris and Adalida? I exhaled in exasperation. In a mere forty-eight hours, I'd been shot at, almost blown up, and nearly drowned, and I'd killed a man—I took a deep breath and willed away that sight. Not to mention strong-arming one very powerful man into bankrolling me. But with all of that, I felt like I was still in the alley, scared and helpless, staring down at Jake's body, wondering what the hell to do next.

Tina went to the closet and pulled an old shoebox off a shelf above the hangers. She sat on the bed, put the box on her lap, and then looked up at me. "This is all I have left of him."

I sat down next to her. "Of Chris?"

She sniffed. "Yeah," she said, becoming again the grieving sister.

I fought the urge to rip the box out of her hands. "May I see it?"

"Sure, I guess."

She handed me the box that had once housed a pair of men's Nike court shoes, size 11. As nonchalantly as I could, I sorted through the contents. Inside were old pictures: a few of Chris and Tina; one of him and Adalida; and one of an older couple, probably parents from the resemblance. Several locks of hair, tied up in ribbons, littered the box. One bunch of strands, woven together in a tight, neat braid, looked to be Adalida's color.

Tina reached for the slim braid. "It's so delicate, isn't it? When Chris first told me about making hair jewelry, I thought it was gross."

"But his work is certainly beautiful." I reached down into the box, fingering the half-a-dozen locks of bound hair. "All of these were from people who meant something to him?"

She held up a mule-brown lock. "This one's mine. Yuck, huh? That's why I keep dying it. I thought about going natural again, but stores don't carry mud brown."

"It's not that bad."

"Easy for you to say. Yours is beautiful. Did you get it from your mom?"

"Mom's makes mine look like a cheap wig. Whose is this?" I picked up a graying specimen.

"That's my mom's, before she died." She grinned and added. "Obviously, before."

I grinned back, even as a slimy feeling crept up my spine. Truth was, I didn't like Tina. Yet here I sat, acting as if I cared.

To do Jake's job, I'd have to smile at people I didn't like, feign sympathy, use them, and possibly even betray them. Did a good cause make it all right?

I fingered a long, red braid intricately tied into a necklace, then put the box down. "Do you know anything about friends Chris met that summer?"

"You mean the guy he shacked up with?"

"It was a guy then, a man?"

She grimaced. "When I say guy, I mean man or woman. I don't want to talk about it."

I touched her on the arm and she looked back at me. "Please. I need your help."

After a moment's hesitation, she said, "He had a fling. It didn't last long, and it was over when I moved in with him. He was upset about it, although, honestly, mostly because Adalida was. Whatever that ass in there thinks, Chris loved her. It's just that he, well, he loved everyone. At least once," she added sardonically. Then she looked, pleadingly, at me. "He had this knack for making people feel good about themselves. Unfortunately, he didn't have any *borders,* so he palled around with all types, good and bad. But he never intentionally hurt anyone."

I took in what she said, mentally comparing it against the guileless, high school boy I'd seen on the video whose mere presence had lit up faces, male and female. So maybe he meant no harm with all his dalliances. But meaning no harm and doing no harm are not the same thing. "Tina, don't let Hunter get to you. It's how he was raised. It's no excuse, but that's how it is."

"It's not that. It's that . . . Chris was, well, he was what he was. And I hate to say it, but it did bother me. I didn't want it to." Her eyes shone with anguish. "The way we were raised . . . you don't *do* that kind of thing. But he was my baby brother, and I loved him!"

"So concentrate on that." I felt a growing impatience but fought it off, trying to remember I had to gain her confidence. Taking a breath, I said, "Tina, I need to find this ex-lover."

She shrugged. "I don't know who it was; I didn't want to. I liked Adalida and wanted them to be together. In fact, nobody knows this, but . . ." She glanced over her shoulder. I met her eyes as she looked back. "They were going to get married after that summer."

I took a breath. "Married?" Miss Livy's first instincts were right. And that's why Adalida was so upset when she left Chicago. She'd gone all the way to the city to be with her fiancé, only to find out that he'd been cheating on her. "But you never knew this other person?"

Tina shrugged. "I found out accidentally when I saw his phone bill. I jumped on him over how big it was, and he let it slip that they were *hers.* So I knew he hadn't been alone."

"Wait a minute! He was with a *woman* then?"

"I don't know! He called his lovers 'she' for my sake; I called them guys for his."

I clucked my tongue, frustrated. "I see. Go on."

"When I found out he'd been shacking up that last time, I lit into him big. Adalida was such a great girl. Makes you wonder how her father could have been such an asshole."

I clenched my jaw and said nothing.

Sadness covered Tina's face. "My brother never meant any harm to anyone. He couldn't imagine someone wanting to hurt him. So, sometimes he ended up with dangerous people."

"How did Adalida find out about Chris's affair?"

"Her father. At first, Adalida wouldn't even see Chris to let him explain."

"Well, if I found out my boyfriend had been cheating . . ." I gave her a look that said Chris had largely brought this on himself.

She met my eyes and nodded reluctantly. "I know, but . . . Yes, you're right."

"And you and Jake never spoke when he moved Chris to Chicago? Didn't you have to give your permission to get Chris into the hospice?"

"I signed some papers. But I couldn't stand the sight of him— Jake. It was because of him they did what they did. I couldn't afford to take care of Chris myself, and he owed Chris!"

"I really believe Jake felt the same way."

She shifted on the bed, clearly unwilling to cede the point. "Chris and I loved Chicago. And I thought it would be great once I met Tav. He was good to me. We had fun."

"Is that what sneaking into the alley was about?"

She nodded, almost shyly. "We'd slip in the back door at work, so we could do it on my boss's couch. The guy was such an ass and a real prude. We were just, you know, messing around." Her face fell. "But now everything's ruined."

I put a hand on her shoulder. "I know it's hard to believe, but it'll work out."

"I hope so." She reached for the shoe box. "But not if that jerk out there is involved."

"He's not really that bad."

"Don't tell me you like him!"

"Not even! But he is . . . complicated. And he knows things I don't. For me, that's an aphrodisiac." Tina gave me a "what kind of geek are you?" look. "Sure, he frustrates and confuses me, but he intrigues me, too. He's a challenge. But, yeah, I think he *might* be a decent person deep inside. Deep inside. Really, really, deep inside. Possibly at the subatomic level."

Hunter appeared in the doorway. "You. Out here. Now."

I wasn't happy about being so peremptorily summoned, but I told Tina to finish packing and joined Hunter. He closed the door and led me to the far side of the room. Putting his hands to his waist, he pushed back his coat jacket, giving me a glimpse of the black revolver in his shoulder holster. "Okay, what'd you get?"

His expectation pleased me, until I realized I didn't have that much to say. "Um, well . . . she . . . she told me that Chris had both girlfriends and boyfriends."

"Christ. Keep up, Angel. *I* told you that."

"Yes. Okay . . . that's true."

"Names. Did you get names? You were supposed to get names."

"I . . . um—"

"You didn't get anything, did you?"

"I wouldn't say I didn't get *anything,* just not much."

He shook his head. "This is what I get for giving you a break, for letting you in."

"Letting me in? You call this letting me in? Mister, you have a bizarre notion of—"

"Shit! I let you waste our time playing PI and what do you get? I'll tell you what: squat, nada, nothing, bupkis. You're useless."

"Well, she didn't know any names! You can't blame me because she didn't know any names. I can't get information out of her that she doesn't have."

"A good investigator can."

"That doesn't make any sense! It's not my fault if—"

"Wah, wah, wah. Not my fault, not my fault. You're pathetic."

My cheeks flushed. "Jesus, Hunter. What is wrong with you? You give me these impossible tests. It's as if you're trying to prove that I can't—"

He shook his head and muttered to himself, "I knew better than to trust again."

"Trust me? When the hell have you ever trusted me? Or are you talking about *her*—about this Sara character those cops at the precinct confused me with?"

His eyes shot wide. "How did you find out about—" Then his teeth snapped together. "You do *not* mention her to me! You do *not* have that right! I'm telling you, and now—"

"You tell me this, and you tell me that, but in the end you say nothing but to shut up—"

"And do you listen? Look, I gave you your chance. You've got no one to blame but yourself that you didn't get jack shit."

I could feel the vein pulsing in my forehead. "Oh, really? I don't have jack shit, do I? Well, I have the goods on you, Mr. Holier-Than-Thou."

"What are you bleating about?"

I crossed my arms and tipped my chin up toward his. "I know about you and Adalida."

He blinked. "You know what about me and Adalida?"

"I know that you were having an affair with her."

His mouth literally dropped open. "Wha—are you out of your fucking *mind*?"

"Give it up, Hunter. I have the proof. You paid her rent. You gave her money. I've seen the lease and the cancelled checks."

Gaping at me, he stepped back. "I do *not* believe this! Are you accusing me of screwing my best friend's little—?"

"Oh, get off it! How good of a friend could he be if he got you kicked off the force?"

"That's not what happened!"

"And God knows you can't keep it in your pants. Fancy had no problem proving that. And neither did your rich-bitch slut! So, you and pretty little Adalida start playing house—"

"That's enough!" Anger flared in his eyes. "God! Do you really think I'm that low?"

"Yes, I do!" Actually, I kind of didn't, but I was far too incensed to be reasonable.

Hunter stared at me. "Fuck this," he said finally, turning his back on me.

I grabbed the back of his jacket. "Damn you, I want answers. How do you explain those receipts? Maybe we should talk about your motives."

He turned his head slightly, enough to look at me over his shoulder. "Do you, now?" he said with deadly calm.

"That's right!"

"You're saying I have a motive?"

"I . . . yes . . . more or less." I stammered. I knew I was being ridiculous, saying things I didn't mean, but I was too angry, too full of indignation to care.

"You think I had the opportunity? And means?" His voice was low, like a lion's purr.

"That's . . . certainly possible."

"You've got proof?

I nodded defiantly.

"And you think I'm capable of murder?"

"Well, maybe—you know what? *Yes!* Yes, in fact, I *do*!"

He stood silent for several long seconds. I shifted from foot to foot, unnerved by his complete stillness.

"So," he said, voice devoid of emotion. "You're accusing me, then?"

"Maybe I am. What do you think about that, Mr. Mighty Maxwell Hunter?"

"I think this about it." He whirled, pinned me against the wall, and put a gun to my head.

CHAPTER FOURTEEN

A gasp convulsed my lungs. I struggled, but Hunter pressed an arm against my chest, his full body weight behind it. Somehow, he'd pinned my hands, palms inward so I couldn't scratch him. He covered my mouth and pushed the gun barrel to my temple.

"Shut up!" he growled. "For once in your spoiled brat life, do what you're told, and shut the fuck up!"

A disorienting buzz, like panicking wasps, sounded in my ears. I tried to stay calm, to think, but shook uncontrollably, my limbs jerking about, stupidly trying to break free.

He leaned down, face inches from mine, his gray eyes stony with the intensity of his glare. His lips drew back in a white-toothed snarl, and hot, sweet breath rushed my face.

"You think you're so goddamned smart, do you? Little Miss P.I., you've got your proof, eh? Well, I've got this!" He pushed the gun again. "Not so smart-mouthed, now, are we? No? I didn't think so. Well, you listen to me, Angel, because I'm going to teach you a lesson. I'm going to teach you real good."

I kicked out, but he shoved forward with his hips, trapping me against the wall. His groin pressed at my belly, and, as I struggled, I felt him grow hard against me. "A lesson you'll never forget as long as you live," he said. He put his cheek to mine. "Though you may not have that much time to remember it."

Again I tried to shout, but his hand muffled my cries. He laughed low and thrust his chest into me. "You just don't know

253

when to keep quiet, do you? I keep telling you to shut up, but still you push, and you push, and you fucking push!" His eyes blazed with fire and menace.

Tears flooded my eyes. I'd been so stupid! I'd let my desire blind me. So stupid!

He smiled, sending chills over every inch of my skin. "This is the lesson, Angel. You don't threaten a murderer when you've got no escape."

My eyes cut to the bedroom.

"Her?" Hunter jerked his head toward the door. "She sticks her head out, and I blow her away. Then I claim that she admitted to the murders. I say she shot you with this gun, which, conveniently, isn't registered. I had to wrestle the gun away and had no choice but to shoot her."

I tried to shake my head.

As if reading my mind, he said. "But by admitting I shot her in self-defense, I have a reason to have my fingerprints on the gun and residue on my hands. Then when she's dead, I put the gun in her hand and shoot the wall next to you and simply say she missed the first time."

My glance flitted to the doorway of the suite. That got another headshake from him.

"The cousin? Poor thing catches another wild bullet from crazy Tina's gun." He paused and dipped his head to my neck, inhaling. "Nice. Lavender? I like it. Did you wear that for me?"

Fury replaced fear. I struggled against him and felt him get stiffer against my stomach.

He lifted his head. His breathing grew more labored, and his eyes blazed with desire. "You're doing that on purpose, aren't you? Squirming around, trying to get me hot. You think I won't kill you if you make me want to fuck you? Oh, sweetheart." He kissed my neck. "You don't have to be alive for that."

My eyes shot wide. I pushed and squirmed, but he didn't

budge. He raised himself to his full height, lifting me onto my toes with the weight of his body. I felt his voice reverberate in his chest. "You really don't get it, do you, Angel? I'm doing you a favor. I'm teaching you a very important lesson, and you're trying to skip out of class early? What would your mother say?"

Mom? Oh, God, I'm going to die, and it'll destroy her. Mom, Mom, I'm so sorry.

"Now, now, what's this? Tears?" Hunter kissed my wet cheek. "We can't have that."

I jerked my head away from his lips.

"Well, then," he said. "We'd better finish the lesson. It goes like this." He pushed my chin up, forcing me to look at him. "You think you find proof that someone's a murderer and, like an idiot, you accuse him. Only you've got no backup. And so the murderer immobilizes you. Like this." He glanced down at my cleavage, traced the globes of my breasts with his gaze and licked his lips. "Then he does this." He pressed the gun hard into my temple. "And then."

My ears roared and my stomach lurched. I couldn't breathe!

Hunter put his finger on the trigger. "And then . . ." He leaned over and whispered into my ear. "Bang, you're dead." Then he stepped back, releasing me. "Thus ends the lesson. Think you can remember that one?"

My knees nearly snapped. I slumped against the wall, unable to think, fear convulsing my stomach like poison begging to be vomited out. My chest heaved and tears streamed down my face. I looked up at him through the wetness. He stood before me, gun hanging harmlessly at his side, his face impassive.

I screamed and lunged at him, punching him hard in the chest. He barely recoiled as I struck. *"You dumb fuck!* You goddamned, stupid, son of a bitch! You fucking *asshole!"*

"That's telling me."

"I HATE YOU!"

"Maybe, but you're not going to do anything that stupid again, are you?"

"Who the *fuck* are you to tell me—"

He grabbed my shoulders and pulled me to him, my chest once more inches from his. His eyes blazed. "God damn it, Madison! This is not a game! You can't go around accusing killers when you've got no backup, no weapons, no escape. There are men out there that will do what I threatened and *worse*! When they're finished with your body, your mother won't recognize it! I've seen that happen to women. I don't want that to happen to *you*!"

Mutually dumbfounded, we stared into each other's eyes.

What the hell just happened?

He released me. Straightening his tie, he cleared his throat. "You do something that stupid again, and it just might. I owe it to Jake to keep you from getting hurt."

I leaned against the wall, trying to detangle the knot of my thoughts and emotions. "Well . . . well, I . . . I don't want me to get hurt either . . ."

"Then don't be stupid."

Anger fell out of the tangle, and my cheeks flushed. "All right, already! I got it!"

"I'm just telling you—"

"I heard you!"

"Good!"

"Fine!"

"All right!"

Tina peeked through the doorway. "Is everything okay?"

"YES!" We shouted together.

Hunter pointed at her. "Get back in there and finish packing!"

She looked at me. "Do you need—"

"It's okay," I said, rubbing my cheek. I felt weak, but my

trembling had lessened. "We were just . . . talking."

She gazed at us, clearly doubtful, but ducked back into the room.

I glared at Hunter. "You're a jerk, you know that? A complete, utter, fucking jerk. Complicated? Layered? You're *damaged.* I don't know what this woman, Sara, did to you, but she fucked you up bad. And any other woman would have to be insane to want you."

He grimaced, his cheeks going red. Then he shrugged as if he didn't care, but it was an unconvincing gesture. "Quit whining. You were never in any danger."

"Never in any—? You put a loaded gun to my head!"

He shoved his hand in his pocket and pulled out six small projectiles. "I took the bullets out." With a flick of his wrist, he swung out the cylinder and thumbed them into the holes.

I stared at the gun, blinking, relieved but far from pacified. "So, what? You think that makes it all right? Are you so mentally twisted you think that was in *any* way appropriate?"

His face hardened with arrogance. "Listen, Angel. This business is dangerous enough without you setting yourself up to get killed. If I scared you . . ." He shrugged again, closed the cylinder, and shoved the gun firmly into its holster. "Fear's a part of the game. Deal with it."

I stared hard at him. "Jake would never have done anything that low."

He flinched, looking away.

"But, then," I said, "you never could measure up to him, could you?"

He looked back at me. Pain and doubt flickered in his eyes. *Good!*

I set my jaw. "I'm sick of playing your game. You're going to answer my questions, damn it. You owe me, you son of a bitch. And if you've finished getting a hard on pushing me around, tell me: if you weren't messing around with Adalida, why did you pay her rent?"

His condescending smile flitted back. "What makes you think I did?"

"I have a copy of the lease agreement."

"Where'd you get—"

"I got it, that's all you need to worry about. Now, talk!"

"Humph. You need learn to get your facts straight if you want to do this job. Sure, I signed a lease. Jake took an apartment that summer for them both. She came up first, but he got delayed for a couple of days. The management company of the apartment wouldn't let her sign the lease alone because she had no credit history. So I co-signed, as a favor to Jake."

"That . . . that's it? That's all?" I grimaced.

"That's it, Sherlock. A dickhead manager who wouldn't wait, nothing more."

"But . . . no! Wait. There were checks! Some were big—tens of thousands of dollars."

Smiling derisively, he said, "Sorry to keep disappointing you, Angel, but you're way off base there too. I let Adalida redecorate my lake house. Sure, I could have hired a company, but she had good taste, and she cost less. I let her buy what she wanted and even helped her get a credit card to pay for it. I'd give her a check to cover the purchases and her commission, and she'd pay her card off every month. Neat, huh? That was my idea; it helped her establish good credit, not easy for a kid her age. I may be a big, bad bully, but I've got good business sense."

Defeat forced a sigh. "That's all there was to it?"

"You know, you may have it together when it comes to all of that technocrap. But you got shit-for-brains when it comes to street work. Go back to mommy. You'll be a lot better off." He added in a murmur. "We all will."

But when he looked back at me, I sensed something beneath

his derision, as if he fought some internal battle. Did he actually care what I thought? *Crap. Maybe, in his own ultra-macho, uber-asshole way, he was actually trying to teach me something with that stunt.* I clenched my jaw. *But he sucks as a teacher. And there's no damn way I'm going to let him get away with it.*

He made a move to leave.

I stepped in his way. "I'm not finished with you yet."

"Is that so?"

"Yes, that's so. You tell me what happened in Chicago. All of it."

"Why should I?"

"You promised we'd work together. Or does your word mean nothing?"

He rolled his eyes. "Fine. What do you want to know?"

"I know Chris and Adalida fought because he cheated. Jake told Adalida to break it off, but she wouldn't. And, supposedly, she and Chris tried to kill themselves rather than be parted."

"That's about right," he said.

"I want to know what part you played in all of this."

"I got the proof on Chris cheating, for one. At least one of the many times, anyway. He'd hooked up with some small-time crook he met in a gay bar, claimed they were just friends. Also I pulled strings to get him in some summer study, art thing he'd applied for in Chicago."

"Why would you do that?"

"Jake wanted to put distance between his daughter and the little boy-banger." He stopped and scoffed at me. "What? Am I not politically correct enough for you?"

Exasperated with his haughtiness, I said, "It's not a matter of being politically correct. It's a matter of being wrong. You have no right to judge—"

"Whoa! Before you get your socialist ideals in an uproar, Missy, his sick-ass lifestyle aside, that's not why I had problems with the kid." He put his hands on his hips and looked hard at me. "He betrayed someone who loved him. Straight or queer, in my book that's wrong."

"I'm not trying to defend that."

"What then? Because he lived some freaking *alternate lifestyle,* I'm not allowed to say he fucked up? I'm supposed to pretend his kind are perfect? People are people, Angel, some good, some bad. I don't actually give a shit whether the kid did it with men, women, or ducks. He cheated. That's wrong. You're with someone, you're loyal to them. Period. End of story."

I cocked my head, peering intently at him. Something in his tone said there was more behind his passionate outburst than met the eye. "You feel strongly about fidelity, don't you?" I almost asked if that had to do with his animosity toward this Sara, and, by extension, to me.

He shrugged and glanced away. "What I feel is none of your business."

Irritated to feel that emotional door clang shut in my face again, I shook my head. "Whatever. How about we stick to what happened three years ago?"

"Fine by me." He crossed his arms over his chest. "Unfortunately, Adalida convinced Jake to let her take an internship in Chicago, too. He never had the heart to refuse her anything. Not two weeks after she'd arrived, Chris got caught again."

"What did Jake do?"

"What do you think? He went to Chris's place and read him the riot act, practically standing on the kid's toes all the while. He got the boy to admit to screwing the crook, even got him to admit he'd been shacking up with someone before Adalida got to town."

"And then?"

"And then Jake did what any good father would do." He

spread his hands out before him. "He told his daughter the truth."

"To break them up?" I said angrily.

"Hey. It's not like Jake had to lie. The little shit had his johnson out every time the wind blew. What happened to him was his own fault."

"My God, you are so judgmental!"

"I have morals."

"So do I!"

He pointed at me. "No, you've got this naive, romantic concept that there is no right or wrong. Typical bleeding-heart, liberal crap. But, hey, if no one's right and no one's wrong, and there is no God, then you can do whatever the hell you want, can't you?"

I reared back. "How did God get into this?"

"Exactly!" He was breathing hard, staring at me.

Putting my hands out in front of me, exasperation overwhelming me, I said, "You make me crazy! I don't understand what you're saying half the time. And the rest of the time when I'm talking to you, it's like you're hearing someone else. Listen, I don't know who you're confusing me with—maybe this Sara person. But I'm not her. I'm not your enemy! And while you are, without a doubt, an absolute *ass,* I think you're not mine, either. So, will you *please,*"—I put my hands together as if in prayer—"will you *please* just stay in the moment and *talk* to me?"

He looked me up and down. "What are you getting so emotional about?"

I groaned. "You are such a *man.*"

"Thank you," he said, as if surprised at my admission.

"That was not a compliment. Let's just stay focused, okay? I need to understand what happened. Adalida and Chris fought, but clearly they made up. Is that right?"

"Yeah, I don't know how. Jake couldn't believe it."

"So he forbade her to be with him, and she killed herself?"

"Christ, I don't know," he said, seemingly exasperated. "Jake sure as hell didn't think so. But we never found evidence of foul play. And we looked. God, we looked."

"What about the poison they took?"

"Methanol in their iced tea. Chris didn't take as much, and it left him brain-damaged. Nobody thought he'd live, but Jake wouldn't give up on him." Hunter shook his head, frustration creasing his rugged features. "He quit the force. I did what I could. I helped get the kid into a good hospice in Chicago. Jake couldn't stay in New Orleans. He didn't want pity, and he couldn't take the memories."

"He moved north, with no income, but he still intended to care for Chris?"

"I'd have *given* him half my business for as often as he saved my ass."

I moved a step closer, sensing Hunter letting his guard down as he talked about his friend. "And yet he started up his own business in competition with yours."

Hunter snorted. "He was no competition. He was his own man. It cost him a lot to let me help him as much as I did. I'm not saying it was a bad idea to keep an eye on Chris. Who knows, maybe the kid would have come out of it, and Jake could have gotten the truth."

"You don't honestly think Jake only wanted to keep Chris alive in hopes that he might one day reveal what really happened?"

"It would have been the smart thing to do."

"Maybe it would be the thing you would do, but Jake wouldn't have used him like that. He did it for the same reason he took care of George: because of what they meant to Adalida."

"You're such a female."

"Thank you," I said, with deliberate sarcasm.

A smile played briefly at the corner of his mouth. "That wasn't a compliment. So, are we done? I gave you your story. That's all there is to it."

"But where does that put us, Hunter?"

"It puts us back on a plane to Chicago. You've had your run, Angel. I've got serious work to do now. We're out of here." He walked over to the bedroom door and rapped on it, motioning Tina out when she opened it.

I watched them go and then ran down the stairs after them. At the bottom, I grabbed Hunter by the back of his coat. "Hold on."

Hunter had Tina by the arm. "What *now*?"

"You went way over the line back there. You ever do it again and I'll—"

He let go of Tina and put his hands on his hips, towering over me. "You'll what?"

Body on a mission, I grabbed his lapels and pushed him against the wall. I kissed him, slow then deeper, entangling my fingers in his hair. He flinched at first, gripped my arms as if to push me away, then he moved them around my back, pulling me into him. Leaning down, he bent me backward with the force of his kiss. Just when I felt his body give in to the passion, I pushed him away. Holding him at arm's length, both of us breathing hard, I stared him in the eyes. "You remember this, mister. You ever try another idiotic stunt like you did back there, and you'll never taste me again. Understood?"

He nodded mutely, his shell shock gloriously obvious.

Grinning triumphantly, I took Tina by the arm and marched her away, not looking back.

Her eyes wide, even a bit horrified, she said, "What was that all about?"

"I'm not sure, but it was very empowering. And don't you

ever tell my mother!"

She flashed a bemused smile and looked over her shoulder as we reached the open door.

"Is he coming?" I said.

"Well, he's following us, if that's what you're asking," she said, chuckling.

I grinned. "Yes, that's what I—"

The shot rang out, and something wet splattered my face. Tina sank to her knees, smearing blood against the white door as she fell against it.

Hands grabbed me from behind and thrust me into the cover of the wall behind the door. Hunter shielded me with his body, his gun drawn. Eyes narrow and focused, he pushed me back farther, scanning the horizon from our safe place. "Get down!" he whispered harshly.

As we knelt, I reached for Tina, her body caught half in and half out of the doorway. Hunter pushed my hand back and shook his head. That's when I noticed the top of her head was blown open and fragments of bone and gray matter were splayed in a cone behind the body.

I fell onto my hands and knees and held my stomach in, trying desperately to keep from vomiting. Hunter's hands were soft on my shoulder. "Keep it together," he said quietly. "We're exposed here, too many windows, too many doors. We have to get upstairs. Can you manage it?"

I nodded.

"That's my girl." He grabbed my hand. "Let's go."

Crouched low, we ran up to Tina's bedroom. Hunter went to the window and frowned.

I sank to a seat on the floor in the corner. "What is it?"

He shook his head. "I'm not sure. I thought I saw—never mind."

My nausea returned. All the blood rushed out of my head,

and my body shook. I put my head between my legs, praying to God I could just calm down. I heard Hunter sit down beside me. He put one arm around me, his other hand holding the gun and pointed at the door. He pulled me closer. "It's going to be okay," he said into my hair. "I won't let anything happen to you."

I nodded as tears stung my eyes. "And who's going to protect you?"

He scanned the room, visually securing all entrances. "I guess you'll have to."

"Deal," I said.

"That's my girl," he said again.

We sat still. I struggled to stay calm, but he was a rock. His eyes never left the door, his focus as sharp as a surgeon's scalpel. After another few minutes, when it became clear no further danger would manifest, he pulled out his phone, gun still held high, and dialed 911. Then he called Voltaire, who said he'd smooth things out with the locals—cop to cop—and get the next flight out. He'd be with us in a few hours. Hunter didn't let loose of me until we heard sirens.

A contingency of Sûreté du Québec police officers took us to safety, surrounding us on our way to their cars. We passed the limo, and I spotted a blanket-covered body slumped in the front seat, an emerald green cap flipped upside down near the wheel. Hunter pulled me closer, trying to spare me the sight. But I'd had enough—enough fear, enough anger, enough bodies. I felt dullness, an emotional emptiness sweep through me. Why was this happening? Revenge? It couldn't be just that; this wasn't a single act of vengeance but a blood-thirsty spree. Nestor had as much as said it: No innocent person brings on this much hatred. What had Jake done that could cause all this? "Nestor was right," I murmured as the patrol car pulled away.

Hunter leaned closer, pulling me up against him. "What did you say?"

My jaws ached with exhaustion. "I was remembering something Nestor said."

"You saw him too?"

I looked up at him. "Saw who?"

"Nestor. I thought I saw him out the window back there. He was in the distance, but—"

A scream of fury erupted out of me. I kicked the back of the front seat. "That son of a bitch! She warned me! I was so fucking stupid!"

The two policemen in the front whirled around, the one in the passenger seat drawing his gun. "What the hell—" he said.

Hunter pulled me back, pinning my arms to my sides. "She's all right. I've got her. Madison, calm down. Come on, Angel." He turned me into his body, freeing one hand to caress my hair, rocking me and making "shhh" sounds.

I struggled against him as my mind shrieked in rage. "They didn't have to die! Don't you see?" Then the fight drained out of me as suddenly as it had erupted. Tears came, and I groaned, burying my face in his chest.

Hunter cupped my chin. "Madison, look at me. You have to get control. You're supposed to be protecting me, remember?"

"I could have stopped this. Lilly warned me he was danger-ous. I didn't want to listen."

Locking eyes with me, Hunter scrubbed away my tears with his thumbs. "Lilly knew that Nestor tried to kill Jake?"

"No." My head pounded and my throat, raw with emotion, burned. "But she warned me that he had a grudge against Jake. And that I didn't really know him. Why didn't I listen?"

Hunter looked off into the distance. "We'll sort through this. We'll get him." He looked down at me. "And I won't let him hurt you."

"It doesn't matter about me! Don't you get it? If I'd gone with you from the beginning, no one else would've died." I could barely speak now for the pain. I just wanted to crawl away, to hide. "But I had to be so fucking smart. It's my fault."

"Stop it!" he barked. "It's not your fault. You didn't pull any triggers, you didn't plant any bombs. Nestor did. It's his fault. And we're going to stop him. Do you hear me?"

I fell into his arms. "I don't care anymore! I want to go home. You were right. I can't do this. I can't! Please, I want to go home!"

He sighed and held me tight. "It'll be okay. It'll be okay."

I lay curled up on my side on a cot in the back room of the local police station. For the last two hours, I'd been a zombie. Emotionally and physically exhausted, I'd tried to answer questions, the police bearing down hard, pushing for clarity that I just couldn't muster. Hunter put an end to it, surging forward like a lion, his baleful glares and tensed muscles getting me the time-out I needed. Thus, I'd been allowed a half-hour rest, while in the rooms outside Hunter liaised between Voltaire on the phone and the local police in person.

As I lay there, Jake's earlier warning echoed in my ear, *"The best, the most dangerous lie is that last one, the one that lets them pull the trigger, the one that says 'he deserves it.' Delusional fuckers like that, they'll do anything. And you've got to know them when you see them. Or I promise you, girl, you'll be dead."* That last phrase resonated in my mind: *you'll be dead.* But it wasn't me who'd ended up dead. Others had. So many people had died in the last two days, all because I didn't know a delusional liar when I saw him.

I curled up tighter. There was now a full-out hunt on for Nestor. Voltaire had confirmed that no one could find him in Chicago. He seemed to have disappeared into the air.

But he hadn't. The man I'd once trusted lurked somewhere nearby. He'd tried to kill Jake and had killed Mr. Keeper and the chauffeur. He'd killed Lathos and Tina, and, all the while, he'd been trying to kill me.

That bone-deep despondence, born of the sure knowledge of betrayal and of the anger and shame it evoked, shook me to the core. And what if I'd gone with him at the canal? I closed my eyes. I'd be dead. But Tina would be alive. And the chauffer, I didn't even know his name. Did he have a family? Kids? Grandkids? Who else would Nestor kill to get to me?

I closed my eyes. Despair sapped my will and my strength, leaving my limbs too heavy to move and my mind trapped in a loop of guilt and anguish.

A thought crept its way through the blackness: If I let him kill me, would he stop? Is that so unreasonable a thing for the universe to ask of me? *Oh, make it stop. Please, make it stop.*

The door creaked open. I lifted my head.

"Lilly," I said hoarsely. "Has Voltaire arrived, then?"

Despite civilian clothes—jeans and a red plaid shirt over a gray t-shirt—she looked stiff and authoritative, from her polished boots to the small bun knotted at the nape of her neck. Her somber expression said everything. There seemed no fight left in her either, no fire. She was just as exhausted as I was, and I could tell that she, too, wanted it all to be over.

Lilly closed the door quietly behind her, as if any loud noise would make me crumble into pieces. I couldn't blame her; my eyes felt swollen to golf-ball size, and I could barely talk for the pain in my throat. One of the police had given me a white cotton uniform shirt, but I still felt cold. I sat up and rubbed my arms.

I said, "Are you here to help them find Nestor? Or try to talk him in?"

She shook her head, her face etched with disappointment. "It's beyond repair now. We just have to do what we have to do." She stared at me for a moment and then rubbed her hands together briskly. "You need to come with me. I'm supposed to get you safely to the airport."

"Aren't I special?" I said apathetically. "This is my fault, you know? I led him up here."

"What do you mean?"

"I have Nestor's phone. It has a GPS locator service. That's how he found me."

She shrugged. "Any cop can find a way to do that. Don't feel bad about it."

"But I led him to Tina." I struggled against the overwhelming weight of my guilt.

Lily crossed the room and knelt at my feet, resting her hand on my own. She sighed, as if she couldn't figure out what to say to comfort me. "We have to go. He's still out there."

My head shot up. "They found him?"

"I meant he's probably close. He's followed you this far and won't stop until it's over."

I hugged myself, shivering. "He's not going to stop until either he's dead or I am, is he?"

She stared at me, lips pursed. "We're taking multiple cars. Voltaire's already at the airport, and there are Canadian cops waiting in ambush in case Nestor follows us. There will be cars around us at a distance. Hunter's already started out. We have to go."

I shook my head. Behind these four walls was safety. "I'm not leaving."

She took me by the elbow. "You have to."

I shook her off. "No!"

Anger flared in her eyes. She turned away, and when she turned back her expression seemed set with resolve. "I'm sorry. I didn't want to be the one to tell you. You've been through enough. But I have to make you understand that no one's safe until he's caught. He'll get to anyone to get to you. He already has."

Like a lit match, the urge to fight flared in me. But I spit on it. *Enough! Damn it, Madison, don't lie to yourself anymore. You're a spoiled, elitist child, just like Hunter says. How many people have died because of you? Will you lead Nestor to more?* "I won't go."

She stared into my eyes, her mouth set in grim determination. "Jake's dead."

My ears roared. My knees buckled. I sat down hard on the concrete. My mouth moved but nothing came out. *No!* I felt my chest constrict and my mouth went dry. I groaned and pulled my knees up to my chest, rocking myself, my eyes shut tight. *Please, God. No. Please, please!*

Lilly strode over and hauled me into a sitting position. "Nestor told the guy guarding Jake that he was there to relieve him. It looks like he smothered Jake as soon as the guard left. You need to realize that nothing is going to stop Nestor. Our best chance is to get you out of this country and into a place where we have control! We have to go *now!*"

I shook my head. "I don't know what to do! If I leave, everyone with me will be in danger. Mr. Keeper, Tina, the chauffeur—they were killed because they were near me."

"So, you're just going sit here and let him go after your friends to flush you out? Who do you think he'll go after next? Hunter? Zach? Your mother?"

I stared at her, incredulous, terrified. *She's right. Until Nestor's caught, everyone around me is in danger.* And yet, the sickening truth was that as much as I feared for the people I loved, I was even more terrified to expose myself. I closed my eyes, trying to think of a way out. But I knew I had no choice. I swallowed hard, scrubbing away the tears. "All right. I'll go."

Lilly helped me stand, then led me to the door. Rather than turning toward the front of the station, we turned left. "This way, out to the parking lot in the back," she said.

When we got to the rear door, she motioned me back, peering out ahead of us. "Keep your head down and follow close. Got it?"

"Yes." That sickening sensation of mortal fear tumbled in my stomach again.

She ran, and I took off after her. In seconds, we were in a gray Nissan Versa, rocketing away from the police station. As it was a small outpost in a tiny village, we hit the open road in no time at all. The St. Lawrence River was to our left, open lands to our right, and a large forest loomed into view. I looked around us. "I don't see any other cars."

Lilly gripped the wheel. "If you can, so can he. Don't worry. They're out there."

I closed my eyes and dropped my head back, wincing. The exertion and lack of sleep were taking a toll. My temples throbbed. "In the hospital—" I said, my mind prodding at me.

"What?"

"Before you came into Jake's room, Nestor had his hands on my neck. I thought he was trying to soothe my pains. And the pills—just one knocked me out. Was I that tired, or were they something other than Percocet? What if I'd taken both?" I turned to her. "Would I be dead now?"

She cut her eyes to me. "Don't think about it."

I sat back, trying to find calm as we barreled down the road. Cool breeze flowed over my arm resting on the open window. I breathed in the heady scent of pine and listened to bird calls over the drone of the engine and the whoosh of air as the car split the atmosphere before us.

I closed my eyes and forced myself to breathe steadily. *Jake's dead.* My mind repeated it again and again. *Don't let him down,* a voice whispered in my thoughts. *Don't give up. Think. It's your only weapon. Something doesn't fit. Timing is everything. Think!*

"Why would he do this?" I said, as much to myself as to Lilly.

She glanced over. "Who? Nestor?"

"He can't have been so angry with Jake over his intervention for Hunter. That's too petty. But what other reason would there be? Maybe it had something to do with Chris dying. Think of the timing: it happened a few days ago. But what relationship could Nestor have had with Chris?" I scowled, staring into the trees on either side of the steep embankment as we entered the forest.

Lilly chewed at her lower lip. As she shifted, I caught a glimpse of her holster. Apparently being part of an official party meant she could carry her gun into a foreign country. "Chris?"

"Chris Crowel. He was Jake's daughter's boyfriend, except he also had his fair share of boyfriends and girlfriends. And that caused a lot of trouble, especially the extra boyfriends. Wait!" A thought circled around in my brain. "It's so obvious! Lilly! Nestor was Chris's lover!"

"What!" She whirled to face me, the wheel turning with her. The car skidded into the shoulder, bumping and sliding as the tires dug into the dirt. She gripped the steering wheel hard, twisting it, and slammed the gas pedal down, propelling us back onto the road. "Are you crazy?"

The jolt had thrown me into the side of the car, right onto my bad shoulder. Grimacing, I reached up to massage it. "Think about it! In the note, Nestor called Jake 'Big D.' Chris must have told him Adalida's nickname for her father. And that's how he knew about Tina and her affair with Lathos. He would've realized their regular rendezvous provided the perfect opportunity for setting Jake up. Maybe Lathos was involved, or maybe not, but even if not, he could have easily gotten someone to play Lathos's so-called wife." I struck the ceiling with a fist. "It all fits. Nestor said he'd been following Hunter and me, that's why he was close when the call on the submerged car came in. Hell, maybe he was waiting there to make sure I died!" Anger churned in my gut. "The bastard! He knew you were working a double shift, so he could follow us without drawing suspicion. He attacked me while Hunter went out the back door of the apartment." *Timing is everything*, a voice in my head said. "That's a fact," I murmured.

"What is?"

"It's just something that I keep thinking: timing is everything. I even dream about it—stupid dreams about silver snow and piles of soot. Not to mention 'Candygram for Mongo,' " I said in my best Cleavon Little imitation.

"What the *hell* are you talking about?"

"You know: 'Candygram for Mongo.' From *Blazing Saddles*. When the sheriff tricked the bad guy into taking a bomb. The Zach in my dreams kept going on about the Candygram and how timing is everything and—wait! That must be what the Evil Little Dream Pixie has been trying to get me to focus on." I held a finger up. "I kept seeing the ingredients of the bomb. The silver snow and disintegrating airplane were aluminum powder. The snow and the jail bars turned into soot: powdered charcoal. The piles of bull manure, like fertilizer, contain explosive chemicals. And Semi-Naked Dream Zach reminding me of resin was a clue too."

Suddenly, I was slammed hard into the door as we were struck from the side. Airbags slammed Lilly and me backward. I screamed and clutched the dash as the car whiplashed left and veered across the road. We hit the gravel shoulder and went skidding before, just as suddenly, we rocked to a stop.

Disoriented and dizzy, I pulled myself up and looked at Lilly. Her body was limp, and her head lay on the steering wheel, blood dripping over the deflated airbag and onto her lap. As I reached for her, the door fell away behind me, and a hand gripped my arm with manic strength.

I was being dragged away from the car, desperately backpedaling to keep on my feet. A large, rough hand grabbed mine, spinning me around so that I was running in tow down the steep, wooded embankment.

"Nestor!" I yanked, breaking loose from his grip. He reached out again and gripped both my arms so hard I thought my bones would crack. I yelped in pain.

To my surprise, he let go and stepped back. But when I got a good look at his face, I nearly fell to my knees with shock. His eyes were bloodshot and rimmed with red, swollen tear ducts. His unshaven face was streaked with sweat, and his unwashed hair was plastered against his head. Yet it was the look of desperation and despair that staggered me.

"Oh God, Nestor," I said, in barely a whisper. "Why? How could you do this?"

He looked up the hill, toward the car, and then back to me, his eyes roving my face as if looking for salvation itself. I shifted my footing, readying to run, hopeless as that would be.

Nestor stumbled backward. For a moment, he looked like he might fall. I almost reached out for him as pity flooded through me.

He licked his parched lips. "I'm sorry."

I stared at him, momentarily incredulous. Pity melted like butter under a blowtorch from the sheer inadequacy of that statement. "You're, you're sorry? That's all you have to say?" My blood rose, pounding in my ears. "You're *sorry*? You traitorous bastard! I fucking trusted you!"

He flinched, eyes darting away as he rubbed the thick, short bristles of his beard. "I didn't mean for it to go so far. It was for my sister. I was trying to save her. That son of a bitch was destroying everything. I had to stop him. But we couldn't catch him. We tried. God, you have to believe me. Madison, please!"

He took lurching steps toward me. As I flinched, he stopped. His hands dropped to his sides, and he swayed, eyes closed. When he opened them again, tears streaked his filthy face. In a coarse whisper he said again, "I'm sorry. Please. I'm sorry."

I shook my head, resisting the urge to care as I watched a man whom I'd admired and even longed for crumble before me. "Now what? You'll kill me? Like you did the others?"

He nodded, his red, brimming eyes betraying utter and complete wretchedness. His voice was a hollow echo of his former humanity. "I'm a murderer."

"Yes, you are, you bastard. And none of them deserved it."

He broke down, sobbing. Rubbing his hands over his eyes, he nodded. "He didn't. He didn't. To die like that, in flames. Did he suffer? *Dios, Dios.* Forgive me. You were there. Did he suffer? You have to tell me." He fell to his knees, his hands raised to me in supplication. "For my family, my sister. I was trying to save her. I swear to God. You have to believe me!"

"Fuck you," I spat at him. "You're a monster. I don't believe anything you say."

He sank down on his haunches. "I don't," he said, still sobbing. "I didn't know—at the office, when the bomb went off—until I heard his description. I only suspected. But he was at the hospital." He swallowed hard. "It couldn't be a coincidence. And now they found his body."

"Whom did they find? Sweet Jesus, Nestor, did you kill someone else?"

He shook his head and dragged a sleeve across his running nose. "On his body . . . receipts . . . in my name. The powders, the fertilizer, in my name. I don't know what happened." His shoulders slumped. "It's my fault."

I studied him. He was distracted, off guard. Carefully, I edged away. "It'll be all right."

He laughed a short, hopeless laugh. "No," he said, his voice

275

almost too weak to carry.

"Sure it will. We can go back. You can make amends. No more killing."

From behind his back, he pulled out a huge forty-five-caliber handgun.

I jerked to a halt. Ice ran down my spine as I watched death pointed at me. "Please," I said, my voice quiet and trembling. "Please, you don't have to do this. I don't want to die."

He was still on his knees, his body shaking, but the gun held steady enough. His eyes were full of pleading. "I came for you, because you saw."

I nodded, my eyes flooding with tears of frustration, my throat too swollen to speak.

"You saw. Did he suffer? Please, I'm begging you. Tell me."

My mind swirled, buffeted by both rage and terror. "Who? Which of your victims do you want to know about? Do any of them matter? Why would you care?"

"The old man," Nestor said in barely a whisper. "Did he suffer?"

Swallowing hard, I blinked in confusion. "Mr. Keeper?"

He nodded.

I hesitated, not knowing whether a lie or the truth would save me, or kill me. Finally, I said, "No, I don't think so. The blast was too big. I think he died instantaneously."

Relief washed over him like a baptismal rain. He groaned and smiled, lifting his face to the sky. "*Gracias, Dios.* God is merciful."

"Not from where I stand," I said sullenly.

Tears continued to stream down his face. "He is. He forgives all. I know I have to pay: an eye for an eye. But I had to know if he suffered. And now I can put my soul in His hand." He sniffed back his tears, wetly wiping his nose again. I saw a shadow of his former calm strength return to his features. He gestured toward me with the gun. "Now, you have to go."

"Go?" Salty tears flowed over my lips, and I scrubbed them away. "You mean die?" I stepped backward, glancing up the hill. "You think God will forgive you for that?"

"I've done what I could, up there, for you." He nodded to the road. "Now, turn around."

"Why, so you can shoot me in the back? Fuck you!"

"Will *you* forgive me?"

"No! Never! I hope you rot in hell for eternity, you fucking traitor! You bastard!"

He smiled. Yes, he smiled. It was serene, relieved. "You're safe. And God will judge me as He should." Then he raised the gun to his chin. My eyes shot wide. He closed his eyes and whispered something low. His finger contracted on the trigger.

I stepped forward, reaching out to him. "Nestor, no!"

The blast ricocheted through the surrounding forest, startling the birds into flight. A red fountain exploded from the top of his head. He fell forward.

CHAPTER FIFTEEN

Stumbling backward, I tripped over a root and landed on my ass. I sat there, dumbly watching Nestor's blood seep into the dirt and then form a puddle when the earth could drink no more of it. Nearby a squirrel skittered over dried pine needles, and the wind ruffled leaves above me. The scent of sunbaked earth mixed with the iron tang of blood and my own sour sweat.

And I just sat there, staring.

Finally, I struggled to my feet and then used the bottom of my shirt to scrub away the tears and snot, sniffing wetly. I looked around, my numbed brain trying to remember the way back to the car. I chose a direction and, out of sheer luck, found myself climbing the rise to the road. My head pounded and my stomach churned, harbingers of a migraine. *Fuck!*

Lilly's car came into view. It was half off the blacktop, tires sunk into the soft dirt, the chassis perched at a precarious angle on the steep embankment. The left rear panel was caved in. Yellow paint from Nestor's car—battle-scarred and thirty feet away—was streaked across it.

Seeing Lilly still slumped over the wheel brought me back like a slap to the face. I ran to the car, hauling myself up the last steps by grabbing on to the listing bumper.

I wrenched open the door. Breathless with exertion, light-headed with pain, I touched the face of the woman who had tried to save me from her own partner. Had it cost her life?

As she stirred beneath my touch, I sighed with relief.

Gingerly, I felt for broken bones where her clavicle had impacted the wheel. No breaks. My hand brushed against her shifted shoulder holster, which I gently settled back into place. Damn it! I could have used that gun to stop Nestor. The thought filled me with regret. But why should it? He deserved what happened. A murderer was dead and any of his future victims were now safe.

So why was my heart breaking?

Lilly groaned and tried to push herself up. I put my hand to her back and carefully eased her into a sitting position. "Shh. Shh. It's okay," I said. "I have you. You're safe now."

"What—"

I lowered myself, sitting on my heels, beside her. "It was Nestor. He's dead now."

She blinked and took several deep breaths. Blearily, she said, "Tell me."

I related everything as exactly as I could, empathizing with her every grimace.

Finally turning to me, her expression resolute, she said, "Take me to him."

"Lilly, there's nothing you can do. You're hurt. Our first priority is to get you help—"

Pushing me aside, she rose to her feet. She swayed a step but brushed aside my offered hand. After a few steadying breaths, she started down the incline through the tall pines.

I blew out a breath and stood. "That way," I said, gesturing left, noticing as I did sticky yellow paint from the bumper on my palm. I brushed it off on my jeans. In so doing, my hand impacted Nestor's cell phone, still clipped to my belt. Oh for God's sake, how could I have forgotten about it? I could have called for rescue a dozen times already! *I'm such an idiot!*

As we trekked down the hill, Lilly's stride becoming steadier, I trudged wearily in tow, brooding on Nestor's obsession with

Mr. Keeper. Why had he been so fixated on only one of his victims? Surely the old man was just an innocent bystander. Jake, Octaviano, and Tina all seemed to be part of the same story; probably Chris and Adalida were too. But Mr. Keeper? How did he fit? The office building was his only link to Jake, a place that had been bombed in an attempt on Jake's life. Nestor had admitted to being involved. He'd even rattled off the ingredients—

Wait!

I stopped dead as the reality hit me like a 30GeV electron beam. Rocked with the insight, I weaved as I looked down at the paint I'd just wiped off on my jeans. It wasn't the same color as Nestor's rented car. And dried paint isn't sticky. I'd seen this gummy material before.

And I knew.

Nestor wasn't the *only* killer in these woods.

Like Dorothy—flinching as the screens crashed to the floor, fabric ripping, the discordant cacophony of clanging pipes, nuts and bolts skittering across polished marble, echoing through the cavernous hall as the illusion fell apart, revealing the fussing, inept Wizard—I got it!

Timing *is* everything, Dream Zach had said. But who had *first* said that to me? At the scene of the fire, while Mr. Keeper's body was being hauled away, who had uttered the comment that had started my dreaming? Those surreal forays had cryptically taunted me, berated me to focus on the bomb. The timing of it, yes, but, even more on when I *first saw* the ingredients.

I glanced at the woman tramping purposefully through the brittle forest undergrowth and caught clear sight of the yellow resin streaked across the butt of her gun that I'd touched moments before. And who had I touched at the hospital only to come away with the same gummy resin, thinking at the time it had come from the coffee machine? On whose nightstick had I seen what I thought was dirt, but I now knew had to be charcoal dust?

Lilly!

My mind soared with that dizzying joy of discovery, like the first leap from an airplane, parachute strapped to your back, that *yahoo* feeling of doing something wildly alive and daring—followed immediately by the deafening roar of wind in your ears, the sight of solid, unyielding ground rocketing at you at bone-pulverizing velocity, and the bowel-evacuating terror screeching *now what the hell are you going to do* in your ear.

Reacting to my reflexive mew of distress, Lilly glanced over her shoulder. "What is it?"

You're an evil bitch, that's what it is! I wanted to scream. But the last time I thought it a good idea to confront a murderer with no rescue at hand had netted me a gun to the temple.

Oh! Wait. I know what to do.

Surreptitiously, I felt for Nestor's cell. Fatigue was taking its toll and my hand shook, but I still managed to thumb it on. I hit the "talk" button twice, calling the last number I'd dialed. Palming the speaker, I coughed to hide the muted ring and pickup.

Lilly stopped fully and turned, narrowing her eyes. "What's wrong?"

"I was just thinking how close I came to being Nestor's latest victim," my voice was thin and thready. I rubbed the bridge of my nose as the thumping behind my eyes intensified.

I told you the handsome, square-jawed cop was a good guy, a pixie-like voice in my head said. *Shut up,* my dominant inner voice replied. *We can fight it out later. If we survive!*

I went on. "It's terrible that Nestor's dead. But Lilly, you're right about backup."

She blinked. "I didn't say anything about backup."

I swallowed as the urge to throw up surged. "You're right. It was someone else who recently told me never to confront trouble without backup. But you don't have to put a gun to my head to teach me that lesson. Nope, no gun to the head needed."

"What's with you?" She glanced at me sideways, and then shot a look toward the road.

"It was a lovely drive out here, wasn't it? It's the same road that Hunter and I took to find Tina. We're, what, five miles down the road? To think we made it this far, only to have Nestor ambush us and kill himself. And then leave us alone in the woods." I rearranged the phone covertly, aiming the microphone toward us. *Hunter, I hope you're getting this! You've got to know by now that I'm missing and that Lilly isn't supposed to be here. Come on! Figure it out!*

She cocked her head, studying me, and then looked around. Was she thinking that we were isolated enough? Her hand moved toward her side. My blood pounded in my ears so hard I could barely think. My stomach churned with bile. And any second now I could die! *Helpless!*

Then an invisible hand smacked me upside of my mind, which is a bad thing when one has a headache and is fighting back nausea. Inside my head, I heard Jake say, "You will *not* let this bitch decide when and where you die. Distract her; buy time. *Do* something!"

So I threw up on her shoes.

"Jesus!" she said, dancing back. "What the hell!"

"I'm sorry!" I wiped my mouth with the back of my hand. "It's been a rough day."

"Damn it!" She growled in irritation as her eyes went hard.

"Oh, man," I said, belching. My gaze fell on a large branch at my feet. "I'm going to throw up again." Bending low and acting like I was on the verge of vomiting, I grabbed the thick stick and clenched it tightly, shielding the action with my body.

"On the other hand," she said, with deadly calm, coming to

within a couple of feet. "I guess this is as good a place as any."

Out of the corner of my eye, I saw her reach for her gun. I put my right hand out. "Like the man said, get them to look here." She frowned, glancing at my hand. "But the action is *here!*" With a yell, I tightened my grip with my left hand, straightened, and swung for her head.

And I missed.

Completely.

I stumbled onto my knees and we both stared, dumbfounded, at the branch in my hand.

I mean who misses in a situation like this? *Seriously!*

Lilly barked out a laugh and pointed the gun at me. "You are such a—"

I grabbed a handful of dirt and threw it in her face. Her hand flew up to her eyes, and she stumbled back with a screech. I launched myself at her, tackled her mid-abdomen, and we fell into the thick forest peat, a tangle of limbs. Spying the gun lying in a bed of pine needles two feet away, I scrambled, crab-like, over her body. I grabbed it and whirled, still on my knees, holding it out before me with both hands.

Back on her feet, Lilly towered over me. She smiled. "You don't have the guts—"

The gun went off, my wrists jerking as the recoil slammed my arms backward, the echoing crack buffeting my eardrums like a punch to the head.

Lilly's hand flew to her arm. The sleeve of her shirt was torn, but the blood barely trickled. She looked over at me, her eyes wide with incredulity.

"That was a warning!" I shouted. *Actually it's a fucking miracle! A total accident. But I'm okay with that.* I got to my feet, revolver straight-armed before me. "Sit down!"

Rebellious fury blazed in her eyes.

"Sit down or I'll shoot you where you stand!" My words rang

with power, but my knees wobbled. I was reaching my limit. If she didn't sit down soon, I was going to fall down.

I nearly did—with relief anyway—as Lilly slowly sank to her knees.

"I said, sit!" I barked.

She did.

Yes, God. You are so my favorite entity right now! Thank you, thank you!

I stepped forward, mostly to unlock my knees. "Put your hands on your head."

The hate in her gaze was palpable. Glaring, she laced her fingers on top of her head.

I sneered at her. "You cut your hair, Lilly. I don't think Chris would have approved."

She gaped at me, shock slackening her features.

"I noticed in the car that your hair is shorter than a few days ago. It would be shoulder length now if you let it down, just like on the woman seen by the canal. And it's the same color as the red braid in Chris's shoe box. *You* were the lover. It was you he cheated on Adalida with."

"No!" she spat out venomously. "He cheated on *me* with *her*! He loved me!"

"Right. Everybody loves Lilly. Or they should. Because she *so* deserves it."

"I did deserve him! He appreciated me! From the moment we met, building houses for charity, I knew we were meant for each other. He was only a kid then. But when he came back, I made him a man. That bitch, that spoiled daddy's girl, Adalida, she didn't deserve him!"

So, that's the daddy's girl she'd been talking about in the hospital!

Rage roared in my mind. Nothing—not being shot at, bombed, almost drowned, knocked unconscious, or threatened with jail; not Mr. Keeper's death; not Jake's death; not Nestor's betrayal—*nothing* compared to the fury I felt looking at the self-righteous gleam in Lilly's eyes.

I breathed through my nose, fighting to keep my quivering voice calm. "I knew you had an overblown sense of entitlement, but this . . ." I shook my head. "I should have seen it coming, but I was so busy feeling sorry for you. No. You know what? I was feeling sorry for myself: I saw so much in common between us that I made excuses for you. I was such a fool."

"You're going to be a dead fool, soon." Her voice was ice, utterly confident.

Chills raced over my skin like a million spiders. "I'm the one with the gun."

Calmly, she said, "For the moment. But your hands are shaking."

I stared at my fatigued, trembling hands. Adrenaline will keep you moving in a crisis, but it's your worst enemy when you're trying to stand still. "They are not!"

"And the minute you let go, I'm going to take that gun and blow your head off."

Unable to restrain my contempt, I said, "Let me ask you something, Lilly. I mean, my gun, my rules kind of thing. Okay, your gun. But still my rules since I'm holding it, yeah? On behalf of victims of violence throughout history—prey to psychopaths—let me ask you." I paused and looked her dead in the eye. "What is *wrong* with you?"

She merely glared at me.

"I mean, seriously! Did you miss the whole 'thou shall not kill' thing? Because it's been pretty well advertised: books, movies, after-school specials. What, were you out sick that day? Confused by the concept? Because, honestly, what the fuck, bitch?"

She smiled, evenly and coldly.

"Your partner is lying dead," I nodded in the direction of

Nestor's body, cringing at the memory of my heartlessness to him in his final moments. "To think that I blamed him—"

"Oh, don't fool yourself. He was guilty."

"As distraught as he was over the death of an innocent man? That's not the reaction of a stone-cold killer, nor is suicide. That's a good man driven to despair with remorse and shame—"

"Ha! That's a man who couldn't handle getting caught. Look, I'm going to kill you, but you don't get to die blaming me and feeling sorry for him. He meant for Cord to go down."

"Who?"

"The bomber—a two-bit crook named Dennis Cord who'd been in Iraq with Nestor's brother-in-law. They both came back screwed up: drugs, violence, petty crimes. Nestor's pregnant sister lost her baby from the stress of it all."

I shrugged. "Okay. So? Then you arrest them both."

Sneering, she said, "Nestor would never give family up, and we couldn't catch Cord red-handed. Hell, all Nestor would do was whine about the *injustice* of it all—how cops save people, but he couldn't save his own unborn nephew. Fuck. But *I* figured out what to do about it."

I sputtered, unwilling to give ground. "You're not smart enough."

"Don't you play superior to me, you elitist whore! *I* figured out how to use Nestor's problem to solve mine. He wanted Cord caught, I wanted that bitch's father dead."

"For God's sake! Why? What did Jake ever do to you?"

"He let Chris die!"

"No! Goddamn it! That's not how it happened! Hunter told us that Jake said—"

"Fuck Jake *and* what he said. I know in my heart what happened!"

"You stupid bitch, you don't know anything!"

Fury blazing out of her eyes, she pushed forward as if to rise.

I thrust the gun toward her. "I dare you!"

She stared at me, and I stared back. Slowly, very slowly, she sat back down.

I drew a shaky breath. "That's better. Nice and calm. Now you don't want to make me cranky, otherwise—" Aiming high, I squeezed the trigger. The retort scattered squirrels, birds and, almost, my wits. It was a stupid thing to do, but, hey, maybe it would draw Hunter to us.

If he ever fucking *got* here!

Affecting calm, I said, "Oopsie. Now, you will tell me what *really* happened."

She smiled snidely. "You want to know how clever I was? Fine. I'll tell you. Yeah, I persuaded Nestor to catch Cord in the act. That was easy. And I convinced him we needed a go-between, so Cord wouldn't know he was involved: a hooker who didn't want to go back to jail."

"The woman who pretended to be Lathos's wife?"

"Yes, but I hid that connection from Nestor. He thought she was hiring Cord to bomb a warehouse. He didn't know she was pretending to be Lathos's wife, and that I was working directly with Cord. How'd you figure it out?"

"It makes sense in retrospect. You must have kept tabs on Chris's sister, so you knew about Lathos. Then, what, you used their dalliance to base a fake case around, to set Jake up? So, where is the ersatz wife now?"

"Hmm. Given the speed of the current, about the middle of Lake Michigan, I'd say."

I exhaled, trying to process her utter lack of scruples. "It doesn't bother you at all?"

She didn't flinch. "It was her fault! All she had to do was call Jake. Of course, when the bomb didn't go off, I had her follow behind after Tina and Lathos snuck into the back room and put the note on the door. But that whore took up with Cord and stole the pictures I took of Jake and tried to shake me down. She even brought Lathos in, thinking he'd help her."

"That's how Lathos got the pictures of Jake and me. So, you killed him, too?"

She glared resentfully at me. "I *had* to. Why can't you see that? They left me no choice."

"You had choices; you chose evil. I mean, why set a bomb if you were going to shoot Jake anyway? An innocent man died! An innocent woman still might!"

Disgust twisted her face into a sneer. "Shooting Jake in the alley was plan B. If that stupid, idiot Cord hadn't fucked up the timer on the bomb, I wouldn't have had to resort to it."

"And the *wife's* call was timed, so Jake would be in place when the bomb went off?"

"But the stakeouts had to be real or Jake would get suspicious. I thought of everything."

I shook my head. "And you had Nestor buy the ingredients, so that he'd get blamed if it was discovered. But how did you get the resin and soot on you? You helped build the bomb?"

"In the empty building across from the alley. We could only work a little each day, to keep our actions hidden. But at least, I got to gloat over Jake as I helped Cord build his death!"

I had to bite my lip to keep from rising to the bait. "And so that's how, when the bomb failed, you knew where to go to get a clear shot at Jake."

"I'm bored with this," she said disdainfully. "Enough talking."

I grunted, as much because my biceps burned as from frustration. I saw the alert glimmer in her eyes as she watched my hands sway and knew I had to distract her until help arrived.

Okay, she wants superior? I'll give her superior! "Granted, your pedestrian logic is an interesting diversion. But even given your mediocre intelligence, having Cord steal the file and lockbox, and then leave the evidence behind, was *especially* moronic."

"That wasn't my fault! He was only supposed to get the file, in case there was anything incriminating in it. But the dumbshit thought the box was petty cash and couldn't resist a chance to score. He dumped them out the window to retrieve later. But when the bomb didn't go off, he ran. So, I told him to finish Jake, or I'd finish him. I don't think he believed me, but he went to the hospital for Jake anyway. I guess he believes me now."

"Because you killed him, too? Oh, so that's the dead man Nestor said had receipts on him. Then . . . then Nestor *knew* Cord would die?" My heart fell.

"Sure, maybe he told himself we'd catch Cord before anyone got hurt. But, he knew *me* better, knew I wouldn't go halfway. I never let go. Pit Bull Killrain, remember? He *knew.*"

I paused, remembering the hopelessness, shame, and agony in Nestor's eyes. Resolutely, I said, "Maybe. But I saw his hands shaking at the canal and his flushed complexion, the uncharacteristic violence, poor judgment. They're classic signs. He was addicted to pain pills."

Grinning, she said, "The extras I slipped him now and then might have helped."

"You fed his addiction and his paranoia. Ah! And you tried to goad Nestor into killing Cord in the parking lot to tie up loose ends. Surely, he became suspicious seeing Cord there."

"I convinced him Cord was there to kill *him.* Now, Cord never knew Nestor was involved: I hid that until the end. But a man of his description was seen at Jake's office, so . . ."

"Nestor knew there had to be a connection; knew Mr. Keeper's death—"

"Was as much his fault as it was Cord's!"

"He started to lose it, rationality already compromised by the Percocet . . ." I sighed.

"You can make all the excuses you want. He's still guilty. By his own deliberate actions, he was responsible for the death of an innocent man. You don't get to let him off the hook."

I thought a while and then said, "He was content to leave that to God. I guess I am too."

"He deserved what he got!" she yelled. "He was supposed to support me, but all he ever did was criticize. He turned them against me, he must have! Why else didn't I get promoted?"

"Gee, I don't know. Maybe because you didn't *deserve* it?"

"Don't you dare dismiss me! They all disrespected me and now—"

"This isn't about you! It's about the people you killed! Lathos, Cord, the chauffeur—"

She snorted. "That wasn't my fault! He was in the wrong place at the wrong time."

"And Tina? My God, she was Chris's *sister*. Doesn't that mean anything to you?"

"Honey, I was aiming at *you*." Her eyes glittered cruelly.

My finger gave a serious twitch on the trigger just as a car skidded to a stop on the road above. Pebbles scattered down the incline toward us. I groaned in relief.

Lilly glanced over her shoulder then turned quickly back to me. I saw her tense for action. "Don't!" I said, leveling the gun at her.

Hunter appeared over the top of the rise and came toward us, gun in his hand. Laughter burbled in my chest. I was so damn happy to see him.

"What kind of a bullshit message—" He halted when he saw Lilly. "What's going on?"

A broad smile split my face. "It's okay. It's all going to be okay now."

He scowled at me. "What are you talking about? What's she doing here?"

I huffed out a breath, trying to regain control. "She told me she came up with Voltaire."

"Not likely. Voltaire's helicoptering in now."

I looked at Lilly. "That's why you came to get me. You knew you were out of time."

Lilly said nothing. She stared over her shoulder at Hunter.

Worry etched Hunter's brow in long tense lines. "Whatever's going on, this is not a good place for an interrogation. We're too much in the open. Let's get out of here."

I pointed to Lilly. "On your feet." She stood and brushed off her backside.

Hunter looked confused, but pointed his gun at her as she rose.

I walked past her, smiling up at Hunter. "After this, you won't be calling me a naive—"

Hunter's eyes shot wide. "Don't cross between us!"

But it was *way* too late.

CHAPTER SIXTEEN

Lilly grabbed me from behind, one hand around my waist and the other on the gun in my hand. She squeezed off four quick shots and blood exploded from Hunter's leg. Another mist of red erupted from his chest. He hit the ground.

Lilly threw me to the dirt and pointed the gun at my head. I swept her feet out from under her. She plummeted onto her back. I jumped on top of her, grabbing for the gun. She jabbed me in the stomach, and I fell back, all the breath knocked out of me. Somehow I managed to hold onto the gun. It went off again, the retort echoing through the air as a flock of birds took off in a frenzy. We held tight, rolling in the forest debris, battling for the gun.

We slid, faster and faster, down the steep slope. I slammed into a large rock and the spiny limbs of a low bush scratched my face. My hand shot up protectively, and I let go of Lilly. We both tumbled down, out of control.

I flailed, trying to find purchase. Dirt flew up, choking me. I finally found something solid and grabbed the sapling with both hands. It bent, nearly to breaking, but held. Scrambling to my knees, I coughed out dirt. I didn't see Lilly anywhere.

Pulling myself up the treacherous slope by saplings and branches, I raced to find Hunter. I caught sight of his custom leather shoes, soles pointed at me. Huffing, I pushed harder, using all my strength to get up the hill and finally falling on my knees beside him.

He lay on his stomach, his face turned toward me, eyes closed. He didn't seem to be breathing. I gasped, fear choking me so hard I couldn't swallow.

Two puddles of blood, one from his chest and one from his right thigh, swelled away from his body, seeping into the still hungry black earth. I brushed dark strands of hair away from his neck and felt for a pulse. It was there, weak but steady. *Thank you, God.*

Leaning in, I put my ear to his mouth. His breath rasped, shallow and ragged, and his skin felt clammy and cold. Not good. The ground would leach the heat from his body quickly. Something wet flowed onto my hand. I jerked it away and stared at my fingers, now covered in his blood. My body began to hyperventilate, but my mind shut that down. I needed to get him warm and get help. *I can't waste time panicking!*

I needed to stop the bleeding first. Grabbing him by the shoulders, I said softly, "I'm sorry, but this is going to hurt."

Grunting with the effort, I turned him over. His leg was bleeding, but the flow was almost stopped. The blood coming from his chest worried me far more. I flung open his jacket and tore open his shirt, then cringed at a terrifying noise: the sound of air being pulled directly into his lungs. *Shit! An open pneumothorax: survivable with attention, fatal without.*

I pulled his t-shirt up over the wound. Blood seeped out, puffed into carmine-tinted bubbles by the influx of oxygen into the wound. I had to plug that hole. *But how?* My hands shook, sticky with blood, cold. Suddenly, my father's voice sounded in my thoughts. *Think, Madison. You know what to do.*

I took a deep breath. *Right, Dad. I know we studied this. Sucking chest wound. I need to seal the wound. How? Come on, Dad. Help me remember. A seal . . . I need something . . . nonporous! That's it! Something air won't get through. You did this once, Dad, at a car accident. You used . . . oh, yeah! A plastic sandwich bag! I need a plastic sandwich bag.*

Crap! I don't HAVE a plastic sandwich bag! God! I'm such an inept fool!

All right. Calm down. What else? Plastic wrap? Nope, not packin' kitchen supplies. Think! He's going to die if you don't. Something nonporous, like plastic wrap or—or what?

"Come on, Hunter," I whispered. Don't you have any thing I can use to wrap—? I gasped with elation. *Wait! Wrap! Of course! Hunter, wrap, sex, penis: a latex-wrapped penis!*

Condoms! I can use condoms!

God, I love how my mind works!

I grabbed Hunter's face and forced him to look at me, trying to ignore the smears of blood I left on his cheek. "Hunter! Listen to me. Do you have any condoms?"

His breath was ragged. He grimaced then opened his eyes. "Wha . . . ?"

I lowered my voice, looking around. I was reasonably sure Lilly wasn't near, but I wasn't positive. "I need something to seal your wound. Do you have any condoms?"

"Wa . . . wallet."

I leaned over him, rummaging through his pockets. "Jacket," he said into my left breast.

"Oh, sorry."

His coat splayed limply around his body. I reached in and yanked out his wallet. My hands shook as I opened it. I licked my lips and tried to concentrate, but fumbling fingers forced me to dump it on the ground between us. Credit cards and high-value bills fell out, along with six small square red packets, each one trimmed in silver and decorated with black italicized writing: *Custom made for M.J. Hunter. Lubricated. Cinnamon-flavored for her enjoyment.*

My mouth fell open. "You've got to be kidding! You have your condoms custom-made? Oh, you have *way* too much money, mister!" Still, I thought, as I ripped open the package, cinnamon is nice. I like cinnamon. *Jeez, I really need a boyfriend.* I studied the candy-red condom. *Damn, they're too thin!* "God, Hunter. They're supposed to be 'ribbed for her pleasure,' you self-centered jerk. If they were they might be thick enough. Crap, now what do I use . . . ?"

A wave of calm spread over me. My brain put two and two together, that wonderful brain of mine, and came up with four. *Plastic. Thick. Heavy. Heavy, thick plastic. Credit cards!*

I shoved the condoms into my pocket and grabbed Hunter's platinum VISA. The trembling in my hands was almost gone. *Yes! Heavy plastic. Oh, but they're rigid, so they won't bend to the contours of his chest. I need a sealant: something viscous. Something, like, like . . . ah!* I reached into my jeans and pulled out my tube of lip gloss. I could picture my father smile as I smeared the edges of the card and placed it firmly on Hunter's wound.

My lungs deflated, pushing out my relief in one breath. It worked! The suction from his laboring lung pulled the card down, and the sticky gloss formed a firm seal with his chest. Hunter's shaky breaths steadied. His body relaxed.

From a distance, I heard rustling. I ducked and pulled Hunter closer to my chest. About a hundred feet away, I spotted Lilly, climbing hard and fast, struggling against gravity. My mind scurried toward escape plans and then realized she was heading for the car.

Yes! Sure, she'd get away, but let her. Revenge can wait. Hunter was my immediate concern. I let out a long, quavering breath. "Let's tie this down. Then I'll get help."

I looked around for a tie and saw . . . his tie. *Well, that's convenient.* I grabbed it, but it wasn't long enough to get around Hunter's chest. After a scan of the area, I realized that my best bet was my own shirt. Yanking it off, determined to ignore the cheesy feeling of being, yet again, in nothing but a pink lacy bra in public, I tore the shirt at the neck and made a long strip.

Lifting Hunter's shoulders, I rested his head on my lap. Using his tie as an added compress against the credit card, I wrapped my ripped shirt around his chest and tied the end in knots. Then I swept up his money and credit cards and slipped them into his coat pocket. He groaned, and I pulled back. "Sorry," I said. "I just don't want to leave them lying around."

Hunter opened his eyes and glared at me, however weakly.

"I know, I know. That's stuff's not that important right now."

"Never," he said, his words heavy with pain. ". . . cross in front . . . got me . . . shot."

"I know. I'm sorry. But please don't die. Just this once be nice and do what I ask."

"You've . . . got . . . to . . . go."

"I know. I'll get help as soon as I get this bleeding under control."

"She'll . . . come back."

I tugged harder at the knot over his wound and cringed as he moaned in pain. "I saw her climb to her car. She has no reason to come back."

"One . . . one . . . reason," he gasped out.

"What?"

"To . . . finish . . . me . . . off . . . you id—. . . you id—. . . you . . ."

"Idiot?"

He nodded breathlessly.

A car door slammed, over the hill and farther down the road. Hunter and I both cringed. We waited: five seconds, ten, fifteen.

Hunter cocked an ear toward the sound. "She didn't . . . start the car."

Shit! He was right. *She wasn't called "pit bull" for nothing!* She'd kill me, if it killed her. I shifted position to grab Hunter under the arms. "We've got to get to cover," I whispered.

He shook his head. "Just . . . go."

"No. If we can just get you into hiding . . . uh!" I groaned as I tried to lift his massive shoulders. "Jesus, Hunter. You weigh a frigging ton."

"Help me . . . stand . . ."

"You can't! Your chest—"

"Then . . . leave me!"

"Damn it, Hunter!" I swung to face him. His face was deathly pale, his lips bloodless, but his eyes still blazed with arrogant determination. And yet, beneath it all, I saw his fear. Maxwell Hunter might have been the baddest badass this side of the Mississippi, but none of us could stare down death without flinching. He blinked and looked away. My heart pulsed, and I wanted to pull him to me. But I didn't. Sympathy would defeat him. I needed to make him want to fight.

"To hell with you, old man!" I hissed. "If you want to lay your sorry ass down to die, be my guest. But that bitch has killed a lot of people. And I don't give a damn if it's the last thing I do, I'm going to take her out. Are you with me or not?"

He turned back to me, surprise softening his rugged features. He smiled hungrily. "Fuckin' A," he growled.

"That's more like it. Here, I'll help you sit up."

"Gun . . ." he said, nodding toward the weapon he had dropped.

"Oh, right." I grabbed it and stuffed it into the holster on his belt. Working together, we got him into a sitting position. But the moment we did, his eyes closed and he started to sway. I braced him and started to lower him to the ground, but he revived and shook his head.

"No . . . we do this," he said through gritted teeth.

Nodding, I put his arm around my shoulder, eliciting a painful gasp. I studied his chest wound. My repair job was holding; it was a good, tight seal. He hurt, but he could breathe. But

297

what about blood loss? How much longer could anyone, even a man that strong, hold up?

I chewed my lower lip, trying not to give into the worry. "Ready?" I said.

Hunter nodded. He got his good foot under him and, with a muscle-straining heave on my part, we got him to his feet. His weight nearly buckled my knees. He swayed again, and I stumbled under the burden. Gritting my teeth in determination, I tightened my grip on Hunter and braced myself. He recovered and leaned more of his weight on his good leg.

"Great," I said and looked around. The uneven ground was strewn with pebbles, twigs, and loose dirt. How the hell would I get him up this slope?

"Where's . . . your phone?" Hunter gasped, his voice weaker still.

I grabbed for it, but it wasn't there. Damn! I must have dropped it. "Yours?"

He shook his head. "On the dash. Trying . . . to listen to you and . . . drive."

Licking my dry lips, I looked around. "If we can get you to a big tree, at least you'll have cover. Then I can get to your car and call for help. Do you have your keys?"

"Pants pocket . . . left."

Working my hand between our bodies, I found his keys and shoved them into my pocket. "All right. Let's do this." I faltered under his weight as he hopped on his good leg, but we finally made it to a massive pine. We maneuvered him against it and he struggled to lean on his side.

"She'll try to . . . get—" He stopped, laboring to breathe.

"I know. The slope's too steep for her to get behind us. She'll either come from the road or from the side. The best thing is to have the tree between you and the road above."

That got me a genuine, if exhausted, smile. "Hope . . . for

you yet," he gasped out. He leaned against the tree, its sweet clean scent washing over us both. Sweat streaked his skin and he raised a trembling hand to wipe it from his eyes.

"You rest," I said. I couldn't believe he was on his feet. Sure, I'd seen less miraculous feats of strength while helping my father at his practice, and Hunter was an exceptionally strong, healthy man, yet even he couldn't go on much longer. "I'll get to the car—"

The sound of falling pebbles stopped us both. Hunter's hand went to his gun and he pulled it out more smoothly than I would have thought possible. His breath steadied and his eyes focused with fierce determination. Yeah, this guy could be a real dick, but he was tough and insanely brave. And from the look of him now, damned dangerous.

I scanned the area, trying to locate the sound. "Do you see her?"

He shook his head.

"Could you hit her if you did?"

He held the gun out in trembling hands. "Not from . . . a distance."

I ground my teeth. We both looked around. Hunter's eyes narrowed as he studied the trees. "Got a . . . plan," he said.

"I'm glad one of us does."

Blinking against the sweat, he nodded to the tree. "You go . . ."

"I'm not leaving you! Not while we know she's close."

"Listen!" The outburst almost did him in. He swayed. "Get to the tree . . . opposite me."

"I get it. She ends up between us. And then what? I distract her while you shoot her?"

He nodded.

"In the back?" I said, brow furrowing. "Isn't that rather unethical?"

Hunter's eyes shot wide.

"Yeah, you're right. I'm an idiot." I ducked into a crouch and started out but then pulled back. "Hey, what if she shoots me while I'm distracting her?"

"Don't . . ."

"Yeah?"

"Let . . ."

"Yeah?"

"Her."

"Oh, yeah, sure. Don't let her. Good plan. Have I mentioned recently that I hate you?"

He grinned weakly. I launched myself, low and quick. My heart pounded and my hands shook nearly as badly as Hunter's. But I didn't have two bullet holes in me. I set my jaw. *If Hunter could stay on his feet, I'd be damned if I'd wimp out.*

They say time slows down in times of danger. That's crap. It ceases to exist. One minute, you're here, the next you're there. Primitive instinct takes over and you simply fucking *move!*

I reached a tree about thirty feet away from Hunter. Crouching down, I peeked out.

Lilly came into view. She cleared the hill above us, closer to me than Hunter.

I dove to my belly, startling a squirrel as I did. It scampered off and the whole forest echoed with the sound of rustling leaves. I froze.

So did Lilly.

I leaned forward just enough to see her crouch. Underbrush tickled my chin and the earthy scent of dirt coaxed a sneeze. I stifled it and looked up toward Hunter, but he was completely behind the tree, out of Lilly's sight and mine.

I turned my attention back to Lilly just in time to see her ease out her gun.

So that's why she went to the car. She had a spare!

I lay perfectly still. Hunter made no sound. I heard nothing but the somber cooing of a dove in the trees above me. After a moment, Lilly moved forward, cat-like and quiet. Her gaze followed the trail we'd made to Hunter's hiding place. She smiled, a predator's smile, probably assuming he'd crawled away on his own. After all, how stupid would I have to be to come back?

I saw it in her cold, green eyes. He couldn't have gotten far. He'd be easy to finish off. She straightened and walked carefully toward Hunter's hiding place, keeping within easy ducking distance of each tree she passed.

Anger surged hot as lava inside me. She'd kill him without hesitation, like she probably killed Jake. She'd told me that Nestor smothered him, but she probably had done it herself, the bitch! My jaw ratcheted tight. No way in hell! No! She would not get my Hunter too!

Okay, brave words, Madison. But think. You need to distract her when she gets close to him. But how? Probably best not to jump up and yell "shoot me," as she most surely would.

Silently, I rose to my knees and scanned the ground around me. The forest floor was loose and thick with dirt and small pebbles. Discarded branches were too thin to do damage. What I needed was a big, heavy rock to throw—that would distract her long enough for Hunter to get the drop on her. But nothing bigger than a blueberry lay within reach. Like, what, it's so damned hard to have a big, heavy rock in the woods when you need it? *Damn it!*

I rummaged through my pockets. *Aha! Hunter's keys! And condoms! Oh, but what good are they? I need something solid, with heft. The keys will simply tumble in the air. Shit!*

Stumble fingered, I dropped the keys into the dry leaves.

Lilly whirled and fired straight at me. I dove again to the ground. Immediately, a second shot rang out, pinging against the tree by her head. Lilly plunged behind the trunk.

I'd covered my head with my hands, my face buried in the leaves and dirt. After a moment, I slowly raised my head and peered out at Lilly. She stood directly between me and the road, and, as luck would have it, also between Hunter and me. Her body faced me, but she peered over her shoulder in his direction and clutched her gun in both hands, finger on the trigger. Carefully, she leaned out. Another shot rang out and tree bark splintered above her.

"Give it . . . up!" Hunter called.

"I don't think so!" she yelled back. "You sound a couple pints low, Hunter! You can't hold out as long as I can. And it looks like the little preppie deserted you."

My turn. "Wrong again, Lilly!"

She pivoted in my direction.

I stayed plastered to the ground. "You're surrounded! If Hunter doesn't put a hole in you from one side, I'll do it from the other. Why don't you be smart and put the gun down?"

"Why don't you come and get it?"

"Oh, please, may I? Toss another one her way, Hunter. Give her a little incentive."

THUMP!

The sound hit me like a blow to my lungs. *Uh-no! I do not like the sound of that thump. That is definitely a wounded-man-hitting-the-ground-unconscious kind of thump.*

I peered along the ground, past Lilly, toward Hunter's hiding place. From my vantage point, I could see the sole of a very expensive shoe. *Ah, crap!* Could Lilly see it too?

She didn't move from her shelter, but I saw her brows knit in suspicion. She glanced back over her shoulder. *Shit! If she knew Hunter was down, he and I were both dead.*

"Yeah! You're right, Hunter!" I shouted. "No need to waste the bullets. You save yours, and I'll save mine." I rolled my eyes. *Clever, Madison, that'll fool her. Geez!*

Lilly's eyes narrowed. She leaned out farther toward Hunter's location. When no shots rang up, she started to rise.

Damn it! I have to delay her long enough to find a weapon. "Think this through, Lilly!" I yelled, "Voltaire's going to want to minimize the bad press from all this. If you give up now, it'll go easier on you. Drop the gun and lay on the ground, and I promise I won't shoot."

A suspicious smile played at the corner of her mouth. "And where did you get a gun?"

Yikes. "Uh. Hunter. Those macho boys always pack enough heat to start a small war."

"That true, Hunter?" Lilly called over her shoulder. "I can't see you arming the wimp."

Hunter said nothing. I couldn't blame him, though, since he was probably passed out cold and bleeding to death.

Lilly looked back toward my hiding place. She hadn't lunged for me yet, which meant she wasn't quite sure I didn't have a gun. "Your hero's awfully quiet, isn't he? Maybe I got him good enough after all. Now who's going to protect you? You should have stayed in school, little girl. You're in way over your head, and you're going to die for it."

Fear shivered through me. She wasn't bluffing; she'd kill us both. Desperately, I rummaged through my pockets to find only lip balm. Great, just great. Lip balm, condoms, and keys. *What the hell can I do with these?* "You know Lilly, I've been thinking."

She laughed. "That'll make you bulletproof." Ducking low, she worked her way around the other side of the tree, closer and closer to Hunter.

A thought suddenly crystallized, and I knew just what I could do with keys and condoms. But I had to keep her talking, *for a few more moments.*

"I get why you wanted Chris." Lilly edged another tree closer to Hunter. When no shots rang out, she stood fully. My stomach did a free fall. "I mean it! I'll shoot! Drop your gun!"

She smiled. I watched her consider her options: take me out first, or Hunter? If Hunter was faking, she'd be shot in the back going after me. If she went for Hunter, she could keep an eye on me and blow me away if I broke cover. She moved toward him.

Heart pumping at high speed, I tore open one of the condom packets and then hefted the keys in my hand; the condom might be too thin. *Wait. If I put several together, nested one inside the other*—I ripped through more packets and pulled one out. *Oh, lubricated.*

A branch snapped, and I looked up to see Lilly creeping closer to Hunter. "Chris had a knack for making people feel good," I shouted. "But that little man-slut made everyone feel *real* good, didn't he?" I knew I was being unfair to Chris, but I had to distract her.

"Watch your mouth." Her voice sounded startlingly far away.

"And, hey, a good-looking young man, such stunning eyes, would make for great arm candy. He'd be a real asset for someone climbing through the ranks—your own little 'trophy boyfriend.' I mean, after all, why should sexual exploitation be limited to men?"

I shoved my fist into the first condom, unrolled it up my arm, then unrolled two more on top of it. They went halfway to my elbow. *Whew! Hunter was one impressive man.*

"I loved him!"

"You don't have it in you. You're a shallow, selfish bitch with a fetid soul, blaming everyone else for your shortfalls. But the truth is you're just a *failure.*"

"I'll fucking kill you!" She started toward me, and I shrank back. She paused, as if remembering her plan, then started toward Hunter again. *Thank God! I really didn't want to be found dead with my arm shoved up three extra-large, cinnamon-flavored condoms.* Hurriedly, I pulled the nested condoms off of my arm and stuffed the sack with keys and pebbles. Soon both of my hands and half of my right arm shimmered with lubricant. I checked Lilly's progress.

Eyes bright with anger, she trudged closer to his tree. "Chris loved me! He understood me! Everyone else always sold me short!" Her voice sharpened. "But Jake made him suffer. He made his daughter suffer. That hypocrite cheated on his wife and even helped Hunter get away with attempted murder, but he thought he had the right to judge someone as loving and gentle as Chris." The final sound caught in her throat. "And then he sat there and watched Chris die!"

"No! I saw Jake with Chris and the other kids on a video. He cared about them all. You could hear it; feel it. He may have gotten mad at Chris for hurting his daughter, but he would never have hurt him. Come on! Jake gave up everything to take care of him."

"For her! Never for him."

I tied off the end of the condoms like a balloon. "What difference does it make why he did it?" I yelled. "And you stand there whimpering that nobody understands you. Well, welcome to Earth, baby! Because, that's what we do here. We don't understand each other! Deal with it!"

"You have no idea—"

Hatred rose up in me like magma. "How you feel? Here's news for you: I don't care! And let's get this straight, Lilly, *you* killed your beloved Christopher." I peeked around the tree. Lilly was partially turned toward me, gun shaking in front of her. I tossed my homemade blackjack in my hand, getting a sense of its weight. "You poisoned them, didn't you—Chris and Adalida?"

"No! I, I didn't mean to. It was *her* fault. I—" Lilly trembled, her expression practically rabid. "She gave him the poison. She shared it. But she must have known!" Lilly's eyes darted from side to side. "She made him drink it! What happened to him wasn't my fault!"

Disgusted, I whispered to myself, "*It's not my fault!* Jake was right. The best lies are the ones we make ourselves believe. Well, that may be your best, bitch, but I'm going to make it your last." Aloud, I shouted, "Chris left you, all right, and we both know why!"

Lilly had reached Hunter. She raised her gun and leveled it at his prone body, then paused, is if my words worked on a three-second delay. She looked over at me, and I ducked.

I sneaked a peek, maliciously thrilled to see the anguish in her eyes. She shook her head as if to ward off doubt. I plowed on, my tone mocking, brimming with contempt. "Chris left you because you're a joke, Lilly. We all know it: me, Chris, Jake, Nestor, Hunter, Voltaire. We know you for what you are: a pathetic, weak-minded *joke!*"

"Shut up!" she screamed. "*Shut up!*" She fired. I hit the ground. She swung on Hunter. I leapt to my feet and fired the coin-filled condoms at the back of her head with all my might.

The package slammed into the back of her neck. She flinched and the gun went off. The ground near Hunter's head exploded into a shower of dirt.

I ran and threw myself at her back. Lilly fell to her knees beneath me. The gun flew out in front of her, and I lunged at it. She grabbed my feet. I kicked her hands away. With a surge of joy, I spotted Hunter's gun wedged between his body and the tree. I dove for it, but she kicked me in the kidneys. I yelled in agony and rolled onto my back.

Lilly got to her knees and aimed at me. I clenched my jaw and reached out for Hunter's hand. I raised my head, angry and terrified, tears burning my eyes, praying for no pain.

A loud blast sounded. I flinched.

There was no pain.

Lilly fell to my feet, face down in the dirt, blood streaming from a wound in her head. "What the hell?" I murmured.

Footsteps crashed through the underbrush, scattering leaves and fallen branches. A shout echoed in the distance. Then something very heavy moved down the slope, blocking the sky. I struggled to my elbows and looked at it.

For a moment, I couldn't believe what I saw. My mouth fell open and tears of utter joy and disbelief blinded me. "Oh, my God! *Jake!*"

Had she shot me? Was I hallucinating? But he kept coming, leaning heavily on a cane. A Canadian cop came up beside him. Behind them, Voltaire strode over the crest.

"Get an ambulance!" Jake yelled to him.

My eyes went to Lilly's still form. "Oh, you wonderful, lying bitch! He isn't dead. He isn't!" Then I gasped as the next thought hit me. "Hunter!" I struggled to my feet and ran to him.

He lay on his back. My heart plummeted into my stomach as I saw his bloodless lips. I skidded to a stop beside him and lifted his head onto my lap. "Hunter! Oh, please be okay."

He groaned and rolled his head to one side. I caressed his face. "Just a little longer," I said. "The cavalry's here, right over the hill, just like they're supposed to be."

His eyes opened slightly, somber gray slits against his pallid skin. His lips curled into a small smile. I leaned over and kissed them.

When I pulled back, his dark eyes focused on me. "Not bad . . . Angel," he whispered.

Then he stopped breathing.

CHAPTER SEVENTEEN

The funeral was held two days later.

Exhaling in resignation, I took off my black suit jacket and laid it over the back of one of the leather chairs flanking the wall of windows. The Chicago skyline glistened behind Hunter's massive mahogany desk. Towers of steel and stone crowned with the city's signature masonry filled both walls of the cavernous corner office. Beyond them, Lake Michigan reflected the noon sun on a thousand arching wavelets. The sight filled the room with a sense of power and potency, with uncompromising and unapologetic bravado. It was so very *Hunter*.

"Thank you for coming to Mr. Keeper's funeral," I said to Zach.

"Only seemed right," he replied. "Being I was there when, well, you know."

I nodded. Zach swiped at me playfully with his hat before putting it back on his head. He looked good in his black hat, black jeans, and black twill shirt. Far better than the two-sizes-too-small shiny blue suit I'd talked him out of earlier that morning. He cocked his head at me, clearly trying to elicit a smile. When he couldn't, he wrapped an arm around my waist and pulled me close, playfully bumping hips. "Don't look so down, Darlin'. He lived a good long life."

"It's not that. It's, well, it's that I feel like I failed everyone."

"Now why on God's green Earth would you say that?"

I disengaged and walked to the windows. "I should have

308

figured it out earlier! I'm supposed to be so smart, but I'm a total moron when it comes to psychopaths, apparently."

"Not a *total* moron," Zach said, following me.

"Gee, thanks."

He smiled, his white teeth brilliant against his cowboy tan. "Only Jesus walked on water, Darlin'. You can't be faulted for getting your ankles wet. You'll catch on, more's the pity."

"What do you mean?"

"This ain't your quiet and polite world of book learning. You hang around Jake and you're going to meet a whole lot worse than that crazy female. You really want that?"

"I don't *want* to meet people like that, but I do want to see them coming next time."

Zach chuckled and nuzzled up behind me, resting his chin on my head and gently rubbing my arms with his hands. "You put your mind to a thing, I got no doubt you'll get good at it."

"I'd better. Of course, if the Evil Little Dream Pixie had been clearer about the clues she was feeding me, I'd have caught on sooner." I playfully bumped his chin with my head, easing into the comforting dynamic of his presence. "At least Naked Dream Zach tried to help."

Zach straightened, and he spun me around. His eyes were wide. "Whoa! What? Huh? Hang on, what? I was naked? When did—what?"

"Sure. That's how it works, the dreams. Most people think scientists *start* with equations and theories. But in fact, it starts in the *gut,* with an intuition of how the world works."

"Wait, wait, wait. Were you naked too?"

"Um, actually, you were only semi-naked. You see, how it really works is that the puzzle gets into the mind, and we can't stop thinking about it, turning it over and over, a mental Rubik's Cube of possibilities, twisted in every imaginable way. All the time, every minute, thinking about it, dreaming about it.

And then, wham! The pieces fall into place."

"There was whamming? Who was—how naked is semi-naked? Were you semi-naked?"

"In the last one, for example, when Dream Zach pointed out that the gum I saw in the floor of the automobile reminded me of resin. And it's what that whole 'Candygram for Mongo' *Blazing Saddles* vignette thing was all about—you know, which I probably would have caught on to much sooner, if I weren't so preoccupied with *everybody* having sex but me."

"Hold on, you! Who was having sex? Was I having sex?"

I put my finger to my chin, reminiscing. "I know it sounds crazy, but it all fits. The gum reminded me of resin. And the silver snow falling on soot—only it wasn't silver, it was silver-*colored*. Aluminum, actually. That's why I dreamed of a plane disintegrating into dust."

Zach grabbed my head in his hands. He peered intently into my eyes. "Woman, you need to focus on what's important here."

I shook him off, grinning—although, honestly, I was a tad annoyed that he wasn't more excited about my insights into my dreams. "I am! You see, most airplanes are made of lightweight alloys, including, largely, aluminum. The plane became a pile of aluminum dust. And the jail bars reminded me of pencil lead. But 'pencil lead' isn't lead; it's graphite, like Semi-Naked Dream Zach said. And graphite is a form of carbon, like charcoal. And when I hit the bars in my dream, they disintegrated into—any guesses?" I smiled, feeling empowered. There's nothing like putting a puzzle together to bring a thrill to the heart and a chill to the brain.

I went on. "Charcoal powder! And that pile of bull manure? It was fertilizer, containing primarily—yes, you guessed it—ammonium nitrate! And what does all that make: aluminum powder, charcoal powder, resin, and ammonium nitrate? A bomb! In this case, the bomb that blew up Jake's office. You see?"

"There were only women in this dream, right? I don't want to hear there were naked men."

I waved my hand. "Hunter was there, but he was on the other side of the bars."

"Slow down! There were bars!" His eyes twinkled, "Like bad-girls-in-jail bars?"

"Zach! Will you pay attention, please? You see, it wasn't just that my dreams were trying to tell me that I had actually seen all the elements of the bomb. That wasn't enough."

"Darlin', it's never enough, semi-naked or not."

"What are you talking about?"

"What are *you* talking about?"

I blinked several times. But then, dismissing the mental derailment, I went on. "I'm trying to say that it's *the when* that matters. Now, I first saw the charcoal powder on the bottom of Jake's cup. And it had been on his desk. There was resin on the file folder. So the bomb was put there *before* we went to the stakeout. I should have realized that! Later, I saw the aluminum powder on the note from the alley and charcoal powder in the apartment from which Jake was shot. That's where Lilly and Cord made the bomb, taking advantage of the fact that it was under renovation and they only had to watch out for a few painters. The soot on the desk *and* in the apartment links them together, the bomb and the shooting. How could I have missed it? It was so obvious!" I smacked myself on the side of my head. "Oh, and there's more."

"More sex or more people?"

"Both, actually. I figure that when Lilly told Nestor she was working on the day I was kidnapped, she was lying. It was an alibi in case Lathos and I floated to the top too soon. Nestor had said he was watching me and Hunter, but Lilly must have been watching him, saw me ditch Hunter at the alley, and took the opportunity to get rid of me and Lathos at the same time."

He stepped back and put his hands on his hips. "Okay, let me see if I got all this."

"Ask away," I said, proud of how I'd laid it out so neatly.

"Were all the people having sex semi-naked, or were they completely naked?"

"Zach! Were you listening to me at all?"

"Sure I was, Darlin'. I heard all the important parts."

I huffed and put one hand on my hip. "The semi-naked sex parts?"

He looked at me like I was unbelievably dense. "Well, yeah!"

Laughing aloud, I shook my head and punched him on the arm. He reached out to cup my chin in his hand, his own eyes lit with affection. But just as he leaned in, lips barely brushing mine, the door opened. He snarled playfully, and I shrugged in response as we both turned toward the door.

Jake lumbered forward, leaning heavily on his cane, followed by Hunter on his crutches. I shot Jake a look of disapproval. No amount of nagging over the last two days had gotten him back into bed. Even at Hunter's hospital bedside, he'd insisted on sitting up. "I'll sleep enough when I'm dead," he'd grumbled. *Stubborn old man!* I shook my head as he dropped gently onto the calfskin couch before me. *At least he's my stubborn old man.*

He scowled as if annoyed, but the smile in his eyes said otherwise. Grunting, he moved his leg out of the way as Hunter swung by him, settling into a chair to my right and leaning his crutches against the glass table between us. Still pale, Hunter looked a hell of a lot better than he had just before the medic resuscitated him. He pointedly refused to meet my gaze. Whatever had happened between us in Canada had dissipated. Maybe he was embarrassed over having let his guard down. Who knew? For whatever reason, he'd shut me out again.

What puzzled me more was Lilly said that Jake had helped Hunter get away with attempted murder. What did that mean? How do you get away with *attempted* murder? And I still had no idea why Hunter had a grudge against me. When I'd asked Jake, especially when I mentioned Sara, all I got was a soul-piercing stare and cold, stone silence. It was going to take some doing to wear that secret out of him, as well as get to the bottom of what really happened to Hunter in D.C. and what got him kicked off the force. And I still had to figure out what the list and receipt Zach and I had found in Jake's box meant. So many questions still unanswered.

To be sure, pushing my nose into Hunter's business was sure to irritate the hell out of him. The thought brought a grin to my face. Sometimes life just works out in your favor.

Jake kicked my foot. "What're you smiling about, you monkey?"

I shrugged. "Oh, nothing. Did Fancy get the time off? Will we see her soon?"

He nodded. "She'll be up for the weekend." His eyes held a wistful cast, mitigated by a touch of uncharacteristic self-consciousness. Two ex-lovers, meeting on the lee side of trauma, with all the baggage of added weight and wrinkles and all the benefits of having seen each other through worse. I wondered how things would develop.

Hunter drew a deep breath and cast a sidelong look at Jake, showing equal mixtures of annoyance and chagrin. Jake's reaction to finding out about Fancy tricking Hunter into a jail cell had resulted in a clucked tongue at her and merciless ribbing of him, which somehow had actually seemed to relieve Hunter. I chalked it up to yet another bizarre example of men's predilection for affection by proxy: shoulder punches as hugs.

Hunter's hostile glare at me was proxy for nothing. He had

clearly decided that I was as much at fault, if not more so, than Fancy.

I ducked my gaze, letting him catch the hint of smugness in my smile before saying to Jake, "Mrs. Naidenheim will be coming home in a few days. I talked to her last night. She's feeling much better. And she was able to give me more detail on what happened the morning the bomb was set. The stranger that 'Clarisse heard' must have been Cord. Probably Mrs. Naidenheim's wandering around in search of the source of the noise spooked him enough that he messed up the timer on the bomb. I mean, it's as good a guess as any. It's not like we'll ever know."

"That Clarisse is a pistol, all right," Jake said. "She pegged it right when she had Mrs. Naidenheim warn me I was in danger. That's why I left the note for Madison in George's cage. I had my own bad feeling when Chris died. Clarisse being upset just solidified it all."

"Jake! Dolls don't have premonitions. It was all a coincidence."

"Did it work, or did it work?" he said, as if I were the one being absurd.

I stared at him for a few seconds. "I can't tell if you're serious or you're baiting me."

He shrugged and sat back, grinning enigmatically.

"Fine. Whatever. I just wish *Clarisse* had warned Mr. Keeper too."

His eyes taking a more somber cast, he said, "Me too. But don't go there. Nagging on how bad things should've been different only keeps them alive and stinging. Trust me on that."

"All I care about is that you're okay. And Mrs. Naidenheim is going to be okay." I pointed at Hunter. "And even *it's* going to be okay. In total, that's worth smiling about."

Jake's self-satisfied smile returned, and he turned to Hunter. "So, like I was saying in the hall, Vince thinks they've got it all worked out. On the day she shot me, Lilly had Nestor call them in on a break, citing *female issues*. So, he didn't think much of it when she was in the bathroom for so long. Of course, she was really in that building that was close by."

A chill passed over my body. "I wonder if she didn't kill me then because she hadn't planned on it, or just couldn't get to me at the time. With her in a coma and missing a nice chunk of her brain, we'll probably never know. She'll never wake up again."

Zach glanced over at me, his voice solemn. "People have come back from worse."

We all fell silent for a moment, each clearly contemplating the consequences. A foreboding chill raised the hairs on my arms. *No.* I shook my head. What are the chances that a serial-killing, psychopath ex-police officer, trained in hand-to-hand combat and a variety of lethal weapons, with a deeply embedded entitlement complex, whom I helped to defeat and disfigure, would come back, practically from the dead, to take vengeance on me?

I mean, that's just absurd.

I pressed on. "I'm thinking she felt desperate to throw me off track. So she lied—to me, to Nestor, to everyone. I guess she was delusional enough to think she could cover up as many murders as she needed to." I nodded to Hunter. "Then again, she found some legitimately suspicious information about you and Adalida."

He shifted uncomfortably. "Don't start that again."

Jake laughed. "Come on, Max, it's funny, you and my 'pretty little cajun queen'—like she'd settle for a bum like you."

I smiled. Now that I remembered the refrain from the George Strait song, "Adalida," which Jake always played on jukeboxes, I understood the reference the bird made in my dream.

He paused, his expression solemn. "But I'm going to sleep a

hell of a lot better knowing that she didn't die hating me." His voice broke. Hunter and Zach looked at their hands.

Jake coughed and then smiled broadly. "But the thought of you two together, that's just funny as all hell. My Adalida was a pistol, but old Max likes a different kind of challenge, likes 'em too smart for their own good." He cut his eyes to me and then to Hunter. "Although after *the other one,* you think he'd have learned better. Eh, Max?"

Hunter's eyes darkened, but he said nothing. I tried to read their expressions. Men liked to torment each other, just for the fun of it, apparently, but something deeper lingered in the air.

Hunter leaned forward, sneering at me. "You bought every lie Lilly told. Idiot."

I sulked at him. "Not every one." *Well, actually, yes I did.*

"Hah!" Jake said. "You believed her about my being dead, and that was the lamest of the lies. Don't you think someone would've called you if that had happened?"

"I was distraught! Although I can't imagine why, except perhaps because it meant I'd have to look for a new job."

He grinned. "Yeah, but you didn't have to help her along. For an egghead geek, you got a knack for putting two and two together and coming up with six half the time."

My thoughts sobered, and I looked down at my hands. "Like with Nestor?" I swallowed hard. "If I hadn't let myself believe he was a killer, maybe I could have stopped him."

Jake reached out, touching me on the knee. "You don't know that, pichouette. And there ain't no good that'll come from believing it."

My throat ached, as if about to close up on me. "The last thing I did was tell him to rot in hell. He asked me to forgive him and I—" I stopped, choking on the words.

"Ah, petite, he knew he had God's forgiveness. You said you saw it on his face. He was at peace. That's what he took to his grave, and that's what you have to remember. He was a good cop and a better man, who loved his family and who, well, who let his need for justice cloud his judgment." He shot a meaningful glance at Hunter. "It can happen to the best of us."

Hunter averted his eyes, although I caught the glimpse of deep pain there first. He muttered, "And to the worst of us."

Jake's gaze lingered on Hunter another second. Then he leaned back and said, "And I believe with all my soul Nestor would never have gone as far as he did if that *she-witch* of a partner hadn't been feeding him those extra pills. She . . . that murderess bitch, she did it." I saw the unbridled hate for his daughter's killer in his eyes. And it was a terrifying thing to see.

Zach broke in. "How's his family handling his death? Catholics and suicide . . ."

Jake nodded at the implication. "Voltaire put in a call to Cardinal George himself."

My eyes widened. "The Archbishop of Chicago?"

"The very man. His Eminence got Nestor absolution on the grounds he wasn't in his right mind at the time. So," he sighed deeply, "that helps. And I talked to the padre about my little girl." A genuine, if exhausted, smile made it to his eyes. "He's going to clear her name too."

I patted his hand, still on my knee.

Clearing his throat, Hunter leaned forward and took a polished wood box off the table. "I say we celebrate all these good folk with something that makes life worth living." Inside the box lay rows of thick cigars, neatly stacked. I could smell the heavy cherry scent from where I sat.

Jake nodded. "Damn straight! And a little of this to wash it down properly." He leaned his hefty bulk forward and plucked a cut-crystal bottle of amber liquid from a tray. Then he grabbed one of the matching glasses and filled it halfway. He hefted one to his nose and sniffed. "Smoky as a room full of nuns on Fat

Tuesday. This the Ardbeg?"

Hunter shook his head. "Laphroaig, 40 years old."

Jake nodded appreciatively. "Good shit, my friend. Expensive."

"Hang on!" I said, sitting forward. "Neither of you should be doing that."

Hunter cocked an eyebrow at Jake. "You had to bring Miss Priss along."

I narrowed my eyes at him. "Don't start on me. The two of you are still recovering—"

Hunter ignored me and took the glass that Jake proffered to him as Jake poured another. Jake lifted the glass toward Zach. "Son?" he said, by way of offer.

"Thank you, no, sir. I'd sure like to, but I got a match tomorrow night. And I never indulge the night before. But, um," he said, pointing at the box, "I wouldn't mind one for later."

Hunter sniffed his own cigar deeply and nodded. "Absolutely, my boy."

Zach took the cigar and rolled it between his fingers.

Tsking at him, I said, "Zach! Those things are killers."

Jake laughed loudly. "So's a ton of bull flesh, but that doesn't stop him from jumping on its back," he said, cutting off the end of his cigar with a steel clipper and handing the device to Hunter. "God damned idiot thing to do. But you got to admire his balls."

"I'm not so sure." I crossed my arms and flopped back in my chair.

"Hey!" Zach said.

"I didn't mean your, you know, those." I glanced below his belt. "I meant you take enough risks, as is. And don't encourage those two clowns." I gestured toward Jake and Hunter.

Jake lit his cigar and puffed.

Hunter clipped his and reached for the lighter. "She called us clowns. I think she's insulting us." He smiled at Jake.

Jake took in a deep drag and then leaned back into the couch. "Too bad we don't care."

Hunter lit his own cigar and pointed to Zach. "You got it right, boy. You need to keep your focus. You can't afford to jinx yourself, especially now that we're partners."

I gaped at Zach, who sniffed the cigar and put it in his pocket. "What's he talking about?"

Zach smiled uneasily. "You remember how I was planning to sell my bull?"

"Yeah . . ."

"Something happened."

"What happened?"

"I sort of . . . didn't."

I had that old feeling best labeled "this will not end well." "You didn't sell Fido?"

Jake shook his finger. "Oh, no! You are *not* calling a prime bucking bull that."

"No, no!" Zach said. "I've got the perfect name. Are you ready?"

Hunter nodded and took a deep drink from his glass. "Lay it on me."

Zach spread his legs and put his hands out at shoulder height, as if reading off a marquee. "Spinal Snap!"

"What?!" I said, sitting upright.

Jake nodded. "That's not bad. Yeah. That's good."

"Kind of like that band those years ago," Hunter said. "What was it, Spinal Tap?"

I got to my feet. "You can't call him that!"

"Why not?" Zach said.

"Because it's sick. It's perverted. It's like calling him Gut Stomper or Spleen Splitter."

"Now, those aren't bad either." Jake took a sip from his glass.

319

I exhaled and rubbed my eyes with the palms of my hands. It was no good being annoyed with men for being men. "You are all in serious need of help."

"But, Darlin'," Zach said. "You came up with the name."

"I did no such thing!"

"Sure you did. You said we should call him 'Get the Hell Off My Back Before I Snap Your Spine.' I shortened it, more or less. I mean it's not as catchy as Bugger Butt or Chicken on a Chain. But a lot of the good ones are taken."

"It's good! Spinal Snap. I like it," Hunter said. "We'll keep it."

I put my hands on my hips. "Since when do you have a say in it, Hunter?"

"Since I'm his new sponsor, not to mention being half owner of the bull."

"What? Zach? But . . . but why?"

"I've always wanted to raise bulls. And with Mr. Hunter's help, I can afford to. Hell, you can't buck forever. Eventually you get worn out or dead. I'm counting on worn out, so I'd better have something to fall back on when it happens. Plus, it sure helps to have someone's name on your vest, footing some of the bills."

I chewed on my lower lip. What was the big deal? Why be upset? *Maybe because the two men you most want to end up in bed with are partners? Yeah. That's a good reason.*

"Fine," I said. "Whatever. It's your funeral. Um, I mean— that is, let's not talk about funerals right now. Let's talk about Hunter's other offer, the one that actually makes sense." I kicked out at Jake. "It's a good deal, Jake. And it's going to be a while before your insurance comes through. We need work, and you need a place to work out of. The way I figure it—"

Jake huffed like one of Zach's bulls. "I told you, girl. I'm not taking charity."

Hunter put his head down and swirled the liquid in his glass. He had that tight-jawed frown on his face I see in men trying to avoid the emotions around them.

"It's not charity!" I said. "It's a legitimate offer that benefits everyone. Hunter's got more work than he can handle. And he has extra rooms we can use as offices. So, he hires you to take some of his cases, and we have a place to work while we wait for the settlement. It's—"

"I said no!"

"Well, I said *yes!*" I put my hands on my hips and glared at him.

"And where the hell do you get off—" Jake said.

"This is none of your business." Hunter was red-faced.

Zach leaned forward. "Darlin', maybe you ought to let this go."

I turned to Zach. "No! I have something at stake, here too—"

All of the men started talking at once. Hunter and Jake complaining about my sticking my nose in where it "did not goddamn belong" and Zach making half-hearted attempts to defend me. I tried to interrupt repeatedly, but the voices swelled, cutting me out altogether.

In a blaze of impulse, I pulled off my shirt.

I'd donned one of my trademark cotton camisole-type shirts beneath my black funeral suit, under which I'd had the foresight to wear my best white lace bra. The push-up one.

They all shut up and stared, open-mouthed.

"Now that I've got your attention," I said. "You're going to listen to me."

Hunter took in a breath, as if gearing up to say something.

I held up a cautioning finger. "Eh-eh! You say one word, and I put it back on."

Jake kicked at him, staring at me with a mixture of shock and amusement.

Yes, I felt a twinge of embarrassment stripping to my bra in front of Jake; he was quickly becoming a father substitute to me. But rather than reproach, the glint in his eye conveyed a message of "give 'em hell, girl." Feeling empowered, I stood up straight and took in a deep breath. That *really* got their attention. "While, in fact, I show more flesh than this when I go to the beach, it is nonetheless sufficient to get your attention and that's what I need."

They looked at each other and then sat back expectantly. "Okay, look," I said. "I know, I've made a few mistakes along the way—" Hunter immediately scoffed, Jake laughed outright, and Zach tried, rather unsuccessfully, to hide a grin. Then all three began to speak at once, outlining my many failures.

"Hey!" I shouted loud enough to silence them again. "Okay, I get it! Maybe more than a few! But I'm still here, aren't I? I didn't go running back to my *mother,* did I?" I stared pointedly at Jake, who gave a "yeah, I guess not" shrug. I turned to glare at Hunter. "And I came back for you, didn't I?" He grunted dismissively, but there was grudging acceptance in his eyes.

"Okay, then. So, yeah, I'm not perfect. But I'm willing to keep at it. I want to get this right, and I'm willing to learn. Isn't that worth something?"

That was met with a shrug from the hard cases and glowing admiration from Zach.

"So, you," I said, pointing to Jake, "just shut up and listen to me, will you?" I pointed to Hunter. "You, just shut up." He rolled his eyes, but said nothing. Last, I pointed to Zach. "And you, get your hands out of your pockets."

Zach grinned, pulled his hands out, and crossed them over his chest.

"That's better," I said. "Jake, you need to take Hunter up on his offer." He opened his mouth, clearly intending to protest. I jabbed my finger at him. "Don't! I mean it! It's a legitimate offer and an act of friendship, not pity. Besides, how about having a little pity on me, will you? If you don't go back to work, I don't go back to work. I've put a hell of a lot of work into breaking you in, Mister, and I'm not going to start over with someone else."

"Bah," Jake said.

No, really, that's what he said.

Hunter snickered, so I turned my attention to him. "And you damn well do owe him, because he's saved your ass a dozen times. Not the least of which was in D.C."

Hunter darted a look at Jake, like the younger brother trying not to look weak before his older idol. Jake shrugged, still clearly amused at my audacity and as if to say that he had no idea how I knew about D.C. What he truly didn't know was that I'd made a copy of the receipt before I returned the lockbox, and I had every intention of following up.

I put my hands on my hips. "Also, you are not going to take advantage of my friend Zach simply because you've got a truckload of money and a desire to play at raising cows."

"Bulls," Zach said.

"Whatever! And give me that." I grabbed the cigar out of his pocket and then circled the table snatching cigars and drinks from Jake and Hunter. "So, this is how it's going to be, gentlemen. Because my future depends on us all working together in harmony. Oh and one more thing." I turned, staring at each in turn. "You'd better get over the notion that I'm going to be pushed, bullied, or *charmed*," I added, looking at Zach, "out of what I want. From now on, what Madison wants, Madison gets. And, frankly, if a little bit of cleavage gets you to *shut up* and do the right thing, I can live with that. As far as I'm concerned, it's your weakness, not mine. Questions?"

"I have a few," a smoky voice said from behind me.

The men's eyes widened. I turned, already knowing, and

dreading, what I'd see.

A woman stood in the doorway. She had shoulder-length, silken black hair, piercing blue eyes, and a presence few world leaders could pull off. She raised one elegant eyebrow.

My hands flew up to cover my chest. "Uh. Hi, Mom."

After that, things got complicated.

ABOUT THE AUTHOR

Kennedy Quinn has a master's in nuclear science and a doctorate in physics and is a director of research by day. But this scientist-turned-administrator didn't get there the easy way. She enlisted in the US Air Force immediately after high school and served as an aircraft mechanic before achieving an officer's commission and earning her multiple degrees. After a diverse military career, she retired to federal service where she continues to lead research on a wide array of science and technologies. By night, she grows roses in northern Virginia with her family. They're owned by two rescue cats.

F
QUI

Quinn, Kennedy.

The last, best lie.

$25.95

DATE			